A Crimson Warning

Also by Tasha Alexander

And Only to Deceive

A Poisoned Season

Elizabeth: The Golden Age

A Fatal Waltz

Tears of Pearl

Dangerous to Know

A Crimson Warning

Tasha Alexander

Minotaur Books ❧ New York

A CRIMSON WARNING. Copyright © 2011 by Tasha Alexander. All rights reserved. Printed in the United States of America. For information, address St. Martin's Press, 175 Fifth Avenue, New York, N.Y. 10010.

www.minotaurbooks.com

The Library of Congress has cataloged the hardcover edition as follows:

Alexander, Tasha, 1969–
     A crimson warning : a Lady Emily mystery / Tasha Alexander. — 1st ed.
          p.   cm.
     ISBN 978-0-312-66175-5
     1. Upper class—England—Fiction.   2. Mayfair (London, England)—
Fiction.   3. England—Social life and customs—19th century—Fiction.
I. Title.
     PS3601.L3565C75 2011
     813'.6—dc23   2011026218

ISBN 978-1-250-00718-6 (trade paperback)

First Minotaur Books Paperback Edition: August 2012

10 9 8 7 6 5 4 3 2 1

For Christina, Carrie, and Missy,
who have stood by me for more years than I can count

There are only two people who can tell you the truth about yourself—an enemy who has lost his temper and a friend who loves you dearly.

—Antisthenes

A Crimson Warning

I was dancing while he burned, but I had no way of knowing that, not then, while spinning on the tips of my toes, my husband's grip firm around my waist as he led me around the ballroom again and again, glistening beads of sweat forming on his forehead. My heart was light, my head full of joy, my only complaint the temperature of the room. Its warmth was oppressive, humid and thick; the air heavy with the oil of too many perfumes. Looking back, I realize I had not even the beginning of an understanding of real heat, or of the pain of fire with its indiscriminate implacability. How could I? I was in Mayfair at a ball. The man meeting his fiery end might as well have been on the opposite side of the earth.

That evening, my side of the earth was Lady Londonderry's ballroom, one of London's finest, where I stood surrounded by friends and acquaintances, happy and safe, with bubbles of political gossip and society rumors floating around me. The ornately decorated room, with its columns and gilded surfaces, took up nearly the entire first floor, and was rumored to have been modeled after the site of the Congress of Vienna. Lord Londonderry displayed his collection of paintings on the walls. Marble statues, in the Greco-Roman tradition, stood in regularly-spaced nooks. The house seemed to pulse as the orchestra began a waltz, my favorite dance.

"Shall we continue?" Colin asked.

I shook my head, out of breath. "It's too hot, even for a waltz."

Colin Hargreaves, a man always capable of anticipating a lady's every need, whim, and—sometimes more importantly—desire, steered me through the crowds in both the main room and its antechamber until we'd reached the landing of the grand staircase. Here, leaning against the gilded railing, I was considerably less cramped. I could almost breathe.

"Better?" Colin asked, removing two champagne flutes from the tray held by a waiter who disappeared with swift precision before we could thank him.

"Much." I lowered my fan—cerise silk to match my dress—and gulped the cool drink.

Colin touched my cheek. "Easy, my dear, or I'll have to carry you home in disgrace."

"The thought of you throwing me over your shoulder is hardly a disincentive." I tilted the glass again and drained it, marveling at how handsome my husband was. His neat black jacket was perfectly tailored, his crisp shirt and narrow tie both spotless white, his skin tanned from the summer sun and flushed from dancing.

"I should hope not," he said, his dark eyes full of the sort of heat to which, unlike that caused by extremes of weather, I would not object.

"If anything, it encourages me to overindulge. I may need quite a bit more champagne."

"Champagne or not, I've plans for you when we get home," he said. "Dancing with you always has a profound effect on me." In the early days of our acquaintance, after the death of my first husband, Colin had inquired whether the conventions of mourning helped me manage my grief. I'd told him no, and admitted to keenly missing dancing. He'd taken me in his arms at once, there in my drawing room, and the waltz we shared left me breathless, tingling, and more than a little confused.

All these years later, the memory of that evening never failed to make me tremble with desire. My eyes met his and I felt the delicious anticipation that comes with waiting for a kiss.

The kiss did not come. The pleasant sounds that had surrounded us—the Highland schottische, laughter, and the rustle of silk skirts—faded to nothing as a voice boomed below us.

"I'll kill you!" The speaker was standing at the bottom of the stairs, talking so loudly no one in the immediate vicinity need strain to decipher every syllable of the conversation. "She's innocent in all this. I will not stand by and see her ruined."

He looked like every other man at the ball, elegant in his evening kit. But the strain on his face—bulging eyes, cherry red splashed across his cheeks—came from anger, not from the exertion of dancing. The gentleman across from him stepped back, raising his hands as if to push away his companion.

"It's not any business of mine," he said. "I was only trying to warn you. To keep you from making an enormous mistake."

"Speak of this to anyone else and you are a dead man. I'll not have Polly's reputation destroyed."

He was already too late to save it.

"Emily!" Ivy Brandon, my dearest childhood friend and quite possibly the sweetest woman in England, tugged at my arm. "Have you heard? Polly Sanders, who's to marry—"

"Shhh, listen," I said and motioned to the gentlemen below.

"Oh. Oh, I say." Ivy's eyes widened and she lifted her hand to her mouth as she watched Thomas Lacey punch the other man square in the jaw. "It appears he already knows."

Colin broke away from us and rushed down the steps, forcing himself between the fighters, ducking to avoid a blow.

"That's enough," he said. "Whatever it is, you're causing more of a scene than it sounds like you want, Lacey. Walk with me and tell me what's going on." They hadn't taken more than five steps when the

Londonderrys' butler approached and pulled my husband aside. Their heads bent together for only an instant as the servant handed Colin an envelope. He bowed to my husband and retreated but not before shooting a disparaging look at his mistress' recently fighting guests.

"Sort this out amongst yourselves in private if you must," Colin said to the gentlemen, folding the note when he'd finished reading. "I've no more time for your antics." He turned on his heel and took the stairs two at a time, reaching Ivy and me in a matter of seconds.

"Urgent business, I'm afraid. There's been a fire in Southwark. Forgive me? I know I can rely on the Brandons to see you home," he said, giving me a quick kiss on the cheek. "I'll meet you there as soon as I can."

One might have thought the ball would fall to pieces after such a scandalous interruption, but this was not the case. The orchestra continued to play, couples turned around the dance floor, and the guests consumed a steady stream of champagne. But Ivy and I had lost our taste for frivolity and asked her husband to call for the carriage and take us to my house in Park Lane.

At the end of festive evenings, my friends and I often retired to my library, with its tall windows, wide fireplace, and cherry bookcases that went all the way to the ceiling. I displayed my collection of ancient Greek vases here, and felt more sentimental about them than I did any of the other objects in the house. It was a Greek vase owned by my first husband that had sparked my interest in antiquities. As for the room itself, it had been my preferred gathering spot from the moment Colin and I were married. Tonight, however, it felt too hot and close. The night had cooled, but the air inside was still cloying, so we sat in the garden, Ivy and I perched on wrought-iron chairs while her husband, Robert, leaned against a large tree near one of the Japanese lanterns lighting the space around us. Behind him rose a sculpture of Artemis, her graceful arm steady as she pulled back an arrow in her strong bow. An old friend of mine had made the piece, a modern copy of a Roman copy of the long-lost Greek original, fashioned by my favorite ancient sculptor, Praxiteles.

"I still hold out hope for Polly," Ivy said. "Thomas Lacey is a younger son. It's entirely possible his mother will let him go through with the marriage. It's not as if it would make any real difference to the family."

"There is no possibility that Polly Sanders is going to marry any son of Earl Lacey. The countess is far too proud," Robert said. Robert Brandon was a man of principle who had once been a great political hope for the Conservative party. A staunch traditionalist, he had seemed on a fast path to greatness until he was charged with murdering his mentor, a man universally despised throughout Britain. Desperate and abandoned by all his former supporters, he'd summoned me to his cell in Newgate and asked me to help clear his name. I was more than glad to assist. The fact he was with us now was a testament to the success of my subsequent investigation.

I pressed my hands against my temples. "Let me understand. A woman of ill repute steps forward to claim she is Polly Sanders's mother, and that Lord Sanders persuaded his wife to raise the child as her own?"

"It wouldn't be the first time such a thing has happened," Ivy said. "Georgiana, Duchess of Devonshire, raised her husband's illegitimate daughter."

"Ivy." Robert shot her a sharp glare.

"It's true," Ivy said. The beadwork on her gown, made from Nile-green embroidered silk, sparkled as she moved to reach for her husband's hand. "Even if it was a hundred years ago."

"Why are we to believe this woman?" I asked. "What has Lord Sanders to say about the matter?"

"Unfortunately, he's chosen to remain silent on the subject," Robert said. "He left the ball without uttering a word. Which, naturally, leads those around him to assume the veracity of the woman's story."

"She decided to confront him in the Londonderrys' ballroom?" I asked. "She couldn't possibly have thought she'd gain admission."

"She didn't need to. She did a masterful job of causing a scene outside. More effective than if every guest in the house had seen her, I'd say," Robert said. "Far better to let the story make its way through the crowd on its own."

"Our old friend gossip," I said.

"It was hideous," Ivy said. "Half the room knew what had happened before the countess—and they were all breathless, waiting to see what she would do. I was standing not three feet from her when she turned on poor Polly. The girl withered in an instant."

"Lord Thomas seems more concerned with defending his fiancée's honor than in throwing her over," I said.

"That will change as soon as his father's through with him," Robert said. "The family will not allow him to marry the daughter of a housemaid."

"I'd imagine not," I said. "Of course, if her mother had been a mistress of higher class, we'd all turn a blind eye, wouldn't we?"

"We would not!" Ivy said.

"No," I said. "You're correct. Because a mistress of higher class would have raised the child herself and everyone would have pretended to believe it to be her husband's, not her lover's. Society prefers a fine, well-bred deception."

"Emily!" Ivy's smooth brow furrowed. "You know perfectly well that sort of thing hardly ever happens."

"I won't argue with you, Ivy. It's too hot."

The sound of crunching gravel announced the approach of my incomparable butler, Davis, who arrived carrying a tray heavy with a large pitcher of cold lemonade.

"Madam?" he asked.

"Please pour for us, Davis," I said. "I'm exhausted and can hardly move. Too much dancing in the heat."

He did as I asked, then bowed and turned to leave, stopping before he'd taken more than half a step. Looking back at me, he raised his eyebrows and his lips quivered ever so slightly.

"Yes?" I asked.

"I left Mr. Hargreaves's cigars inside, madam, as the combination with lemonade would be rather atrocious."

"You're very bad, Davis," I said. "I'll expect an entirely different outcome the next time I call for port rather than lemonade." With another bow, he left us. "He knows Colin doesn't mind when I smoke, but dear Davis refuses to be an accessory to what he views as my ruin."

"A good man, your butler," Robert said.

"I won't take any nonsense from you, sir." I smiled. Robert had long ago given up on trying to influence me. He had come to tenuous terms with his wife's own small rebellions (drinking port with me, for example), so long as she restricted them to private situations. Decorous behavior, however, he required in public.

It was I who had corrupted Ivy, just as I'd corrupted myself. While locked up in mourning after the death of my first husband, I'd undergone an intellectual awakening and taken up the study of Greek. I'd learned to read the ancient language, reveled in the poetry of Homer, and become a respected collector of classical antiquities. As I became more enlightened, I'd also come to despise the restrictions of society, and in the course of rejecting them, had come to discover the simple pleasure one could afford from a glass of port, a drink ordinarily forbidden to ladies. Now, at the prodding of another dear friend, I'd expanded my studies to include Latin, and had convinced Ivy to learn it as well. She might not have been quite so enthusiastic a student as I, but she had a sharp mind and was learning quickly.

The lemonade cooled us and we sank into more relaxed postures as the blue light of dawn reached for the dark sky. I wondered how much longer Colin would be. His work as one of the most trusted and discreet agents of the Crown took him from me at odd times of the day and night, and I had come, after more than a year of marriage, to trust his competence absolutely. His missions might be dangerous, but no one was better suited than he to handle them. When he at last staggered into our garden that night, his evening clothes were tattered, his face black, and the bitter smell of smoke heavy on him.

"Colin!" I cried, jumping out of my seat. He raised a bandaged hand to my cheek, a crooked smile on his face.

"Don't be alarmed, my dear, I'm perfectly fine." He dropped onto a chair and Robert poured a tall glass of the now lukewarm lemonade for him, emptying the pitcher. "But I'm afraid I do come with terrible news. Mr. Michael Dillman is dead, burned to death in his warehouse south of the river." He swallowed hard and ground his teeth.

I hadn't known Mr. Dillman well, but there was no one in London unfamiliar with his stellar reputation. He ran a successful export business and treated the men who worked in his warehouses more decently than was the current custom. He paid them generously and ensured his personal physician was on hand whenever their family members fell ill. Several charities depended on his generosity, and he was a great supporter of the arts. Yet, despite all this and a not insignificant fortune, he wasn't much of a fixture in society. He could be socially awkward, not because he was unkind or disinterested, but because his personality tended to a quiet shyness rather than the buoyant joviality required during the season. I regretted that I had not taken the time to know him better.

"What happened?" I asked.

"Someone chained him to the bars on the office window and set the building on fire. I'm sorry, Robert, to speak of such horrors in front of your wife, but I see no point in disguising the truth. The newsmen were there almost as soon as I was. There will be no hiding from the story."

"He . . . he was to be married next week," Ivy said, her voice thin. "Cordelia showed me her wedding dress not two days ago."

"Cordelia Dalton?" I asked. Ivy nodded. Cordelia was a quiet, thoughtful girl who'd made her debut the previous season. She'd not made much of a splash amongst the fashionable set, but that was likely due to a failing on their part rather than hers. We'd discussed novels when our paths crossed at parties, and she always seemed more interested in reading and sketching than in dancing. I was quite fond of her.

"I'm more than sorry, Ivy," Colin said. "Your friend will need your comfort now."

I did not listen to the rest of the conversation; the words no longer made sense to me. I could not stop imagining the hideous scene, the terror the poor man must have felt when he realized what was happening, the pain he must have endured before succumbing to death.

I shuddered. And remembered that only a few hours earlier, I'd had the audacity to complain about the heat in a ballroom.

6 June 1893
Belgrave Square, London

*How quickly things change! I was pleased when Colin asked Robert and
me to bring Emily home from the Londonderrys' ball. Not because Colin
had been called away for work, but because I was looking forward to
quiet time with my dearest friend and discussing all the gossip of the
night. Polly Sanders has all my sympathy, and I do wish there was something I could do to secure her happiness. But the moment Colin arrived
with his dreadful news, Polly's plight seemed utterly insignificant.*

*I felt almost paralyzed when he told us Mr. Dillman had been mur-
dered. Emily was equally affected, though she retained her composure
better than I. She's more experienced in such matters. But I know she gets
little crinkles that creep around her eyes when she's upset, and I saw
enough of them tonight to tell me I was not alone in my reaction. I hope I
never see enough of this sort of brutality to control my emotional response. To acquire such strength would swallow who I am.*

*Poor, poor Cordelia. When I think of what she must be feeling I can't
help but cry. Robert says it's unbecoming to take on someone else's misery,
and I'm certain he's right, yet I can't find a way to stop. I remember the
joy that consumed me as I became a wife. Cordelia will never feel that.
Even if, years from now, she finds affection somewhere else, how could she*

ever escape a constant dread that her happiness is about to be ripped away from her?

I suppose it can happen to any of us, at anytime. I feel so fortunate to have escaped a similar fate. My husband languished in prison, but only for a relatively short period of time (although at the time it did not seem so). He wasn't taken from me forever, he was returned to me, and now I've the sweetest daughter on earth. What does one do to deserve such luck?

I'm off to see Emily now. She's persuaded me—much against my will—to accompany her to some dreadful meeting. I never could refuse her anything. I have two hopes: one, that it won't last too long; two, that it is more interesting than Latin. Surely the latter is a certitude.

Violent death was no stranger to me. In the past few years, I'd been intimately involved in apprehending four heinous murderers, one of whom had killed my first husband, Philip, the Viscount Ashton. Only a year ago in Normandy, I'd found the brutalized body of a young girl, and had been kidnapped and cruelly tormented by her killer, whose subsequent trial and execution had enthralled Britain and the Continent. Try though I might to shake the images of these ghastly events from my mind, I found I could not do so, and now the news of Mr. Dillman's death was taking its own gruesome hold on me.

"We were dancing, Colin," I said. "Dancing."

"It's a disturbing contrast, I agree," he said, smearing ginger marmalade on a piece of toast. We were sitting next to each other at the round table in our sunny breakfast room. On the bright yellow walls hung a Roman mosaic, an *emblema*, its tiny pieces of glass carefully laid out to depict an elaborate scene of Apollo driving his golden chariot across the sky, sunbeams streaming from the crown on the god's head. I'd purchased it in a small village near Pompeii, and promised the British Museum I would eventually donate it to them. I couldn't yet bring myself to part with it.

"More than disturbing, I'd say."

"There's nothing to be done about it, Emily," Colin said. "You'll drive yourself mad if you keep tally of such things. Not everything in London is gaiety and balls."

"I'm well aware of that," I said. "I—"

He reached for my hand and interrupted me, his dark eyes fixated on mine. "I know you are, my dear. Forgive me if you thought I was implying otherwise. I know how well suited you are to our work."

"Thank you," I said, squeezing his hand back. "You can't believe Mr. Dillman was killed by one of his employees? He treated them far too well for any of them to want to do him harm."

"We can't rule anything out at this stage of the investigation."

"You wouldn't have been called in if they thought this was some sort of common crime."

"Quite right, Emily." He smiled. "And that's all I can say at the moment. What do you have planned for today?"

I studied his handsome countenance, taking careful note of the intensity in his eyes and decided not to pursue the subject further. Not yet, at any rate. I capitulated and moved to another topic. "Your mother wrangled Ivy and me invitations to this morning's meeting of the Women's Liberal Federation."

"And you're going?"

"Yes. First, because you've made it clear you don't need my help with this investigation. Second, because I'd like your mother to feel pleasantly disposed towards me when she moves back to England. But most important, because I'm being brought round to the idea that I should have the vote." I sat up a little straighter and pushed my plate away from me.

"Heaven help us. Next thing you know, you'll want to stand for Parliament."

"You'd object?"

"They'd be lucky to have you," he said. I questioned his sincerity, but appreciated that he did not outright balk at the suggestion. "But what would *your* mother say?"

"More like what *will* she say," I said. "To her, the mere act of considering the possibility of getting the vote for women is anathema. I'll live out the remainder of my days in disgrace. *He who submits to fate without complaint is wise.*" I swallowed my last drop of tea.

"Epictetus?" Colin asked.

"Euripides," I said.

"Ah. At any rate, disgrace is a powerful motivator, to be sure. Which interests you more: casting a vote or scandalizing your mother?"

I folded my napkin neatly and placed it on the table. "Isn't it marvelous when two noble causes can be addressed in one fell swoop?"

Davis stepped into the room. "Mrs. Brandon is here, madam," he said.

Ivy entered the room in a swish of silk, her skin glowing with the flush of summer heat. "Good morning," she said as she gave her hand to Colin. "You don't mind that we're doing this, do you?"

"Not at all," he said. "I always believed it was only a question of time before Emily became a suffragette. In fact, I've known it longer than she has. I do, however, draw the line at her chaining herself to the gate at Downing Street."

"He keeps insisting it will come to that," I said to Ivy. "But I can't imagine anyone would ever do such a ludicrous thing."

"It would make a powerful statement," Colin said. "Don't, however, take it as a suggestion. Enjoy your meeting." He kissed me and picked up the *Times*.

I adjusted my straw hat, Homburg shape with a large brim, and we set off for Lady Carlisle's house in Kensington. Crossing Park Lane, we entered the sprawling expanse of Hyde Park at the Grosvenor Gate and made our way along crowded paths shaded by towering trees. Sunshine and warm weather had brought most of society outside, and the park was a favorite gathering place on summer mornings. All around us, couples tilted their heads close together as fearsome chaperones walked beside them, ready to poke with well-placed parasols any overeager gentlemen. Friends waved to us, calling out greetings, but we had no time to stop and chat.

Until we saw Winifred Harris.

I would have liked to pretend not to have noticed her, but the figure she cut was too imposing to miss, not only due to her larger-than-average height and girth, but also because of her booming voice. I walked faster, but to no avail.

"Ivy, dear!" she called, then stood, unmoving, as if waiting for us to come pay homage to her.

Ivy smiled and crossed to her friend. "My dear Winifred," she said. "What a delightful surprise to see you."

"It can't be much of a surprise, Ivy," Mrs. Harris said, squinting at us through a fashionable lorgnette that was attached to her too-snugly tailored jacket. "It's the Season. Where else would you expect to find a woman of my standing at this time of day? Hyde Park is the only place to be seen."

"I only meant it was a pleasant surprise for me," Ivy said. "I never meant to suggest you would—"

"Yes, yes," Mrs. Harris said. "How is your husband, Lady Emily? I understand he's embroiled in this unpleasant business that occurred in Southwark last night."

"He's involved in the investigation, yes," I said.

"A very dodgy business," she said. "I do hope his insistence on working doesn't harm your reputation. It's unseemly for a man of his fortune to seek gainful employment."

"He's never shirked from his duties to the Crown," I said. "The queen quite depends upon him."

"He's charming enough—and handsome enough—for us to tolerate nearly anything he does. But you don't quite share his status, my dear. It would behoove you to be very careful when choosing how you occupy yourself. People are prone to talk. You should keep well clear of the investigation. I know you've insisted on doing otherwise in the past."

"Mr. Hargreaves is taking care of everything," Ivy said. "You've no need to worry on Emily's behalf."

"Only intervenes when he gives her permission, does she?" Mrs. Harris asked, as if I weren't standing directly in front of her. "I'm glad to hear someone in the family has a drop of sense."

"Forgive me, Mrs. Harris," I said. "Ivy and I will be late to the Women's Liberal Federation if we don't beg our leave at once. It was as lovely to see you as it always is." The sentiment was strictly true. If she chose to take from my statement that I found it empirically lovely to see her, that was her choice. Pulling Ivy by the arm, I dragged her back to the pavement before she could protest our hasty departure.

We walked along the southern side of the Serpentine, the park's long, curving lake and then continued on towards the Round Pond, where countless children were playing with toy boats. The pavements were slightly less crowded here, and became even emptier as we passed Kensington Palace and moved out of the park and into Kensington Palace Gardens, one of my favorite streets in all of London. Tall plane trees lined both sides and elegant houses stretched the half-mile length of the edge of the park. We turned left to reach Palace Green, the southernmost part of the road, but stopped before we'd taken ten paces. There was Polly Sanders's house. Its noble edifice was gracious and neat, but the front door and the steps, along with the fence in front of the property—all of which had been gleaming white—were covered with a swathe of dark red paint.

"What happened here?" I asked, inquiring of the servant on her hands and knees, scrubbing the bottom of a white square pillar that stood between sections of the fence.

"Madam?" She looked down, seemingly afraid to speak to me.

"I'm Lady Emily Hargreaves, a friend of Polly's," I said. "Who did this?"

"It was a vandal of some sort, madam. We don't know who. I've been at it for more hours than I can count, but it's right near impossible to remove. They've sent someone off to get turpentine."

"When did it happen?" I asked.

"It was like this when we woke up yesterday morning. Terrible thing, 'specially now. The missus doesn't need any more trouble."

"No, she certainly doesn't," I said. "Don't let me distract you from your task."

"Yes, madam." She returned to her work, her face tense with effort.

We continued towards Lady Carlisle's house in the bottom of the street. "This is dreadful," Ivy said. "Poor Polly is all but ruined. And now this? It's grotesquely unfair. Who would have done such a thing to her house?"

"I can't imagine," I said. "Isn't it enough that the family have suffered such pain and humiliation? Why would someone want to draw further attention to their plight?"

We'd reached our destination. I looked up at Number One Palace Green. It was smaller than the other homes on the street and looked as if it had been built more recently, although its red bricks fronted a relatively plain façade. I pulled open the iron gate and felt a twinge of nerves as we walked up concrete steps to the narrow, arched entrance to the house. I felt as if I were on the precipice of something important, as if I were about to enter a world full of other people who shared values similar to my own, a place where I would not be ostracized for my intellectual interests and social radicalism. I took a deep breath and lifted my hand to knock on the door.

In retrospect, I admit *precipice* might not have been quite the right word. The ladies of Women's Liberal Federation, while charming and welcoming, weren't as different from the rest of society as one might have thought. I'd expected—or perhaps hoped for—firebrand politics. Instead, we entered a pleasant drawing room papered in a William Morris design and found ourselves in a crush of violently fashionable ladies. Their sleeves, in every bright color of fabric, were so wide one could hardly squeeze past them. We drank tea and enjoyed genteel conversation that focused as much on needlepoint and which balls everyone planned to attend that evening as it did the issue of we ladies gaining the vote. It was pleasant, but a little anticlimactic.

"I confess I'd worried they would be more radical," Ivy asked, her voice hushed as she scooted her chair closer to mine. The meeting had started in earnest, though many of the ladies weren't paying much attention.

"I thought they would be, too," I said, not voicing my disappointment to find they were not.

"Can you hear me, Lady Emily? I need to know if we can count on you." Lady Carlisle's voice carried over the group, and I felt like a child caught talking out of turn at school. "Will you distribute pamphlets with us?"

I had heard everything she'd said about these pamphlets, which the group planned to hand out to specially selected ladies in the most unobtrusive way possible so as not to put off any possible recruits.

"I should like very much to be in charge of handing them out to the Conservative MPs, if that would be allowed," I said. "I'm not afraid of direct opposition."

"Well, now," Lady Carlisle said. "I do admire your determination." Our hostess was well known for the fervent support she lent to her favorite causes: temperance, Irish Home Rule, and free trade. It was she who had directed the movement for the Women's Liberal Federation to pursue an aggressive agenda to get votes for women, a policy that had caused a schism in the group. Nearly ten thousand members had resigned and started their own organization, the priorities of which did not include supporting such controversial stances.

"As soon as I have the documents in hand, I'll set off for Westminster. I'd like to confront them there," I said. "I want to present myself as if I'm already a constituent and coming to them with a concern. I think they'll respect me for taking a direct approach, even if they don't agree with our position. My goal will be to identify those who show the slightest hints of sympathy and then I'll begin cultivating relationships with their wives."

"What an interesting idea," Lady Carlisle said. Her smile suggested she was pleased, and I wondered if she was glad to have found someone else who shared a more radical vision. "I look forward to hearing about your results. You shall all have pamphlets and distribution lists by the end of the week. And unless anyone has something else to add, I believe that concludes our business for today."

Ivy and I milled around the room for another quarter of an hour, drinking tea and listening to the usual sort of society gossip. No one mentioned Mr. Dillman's brutal death out loud, though I knew it was on everyone's mind. We'd all seen the sensational coverage given to his murder by the morning papers. Instead, most of the chatter focused on Polly Sanders. The words said about her were not kind, and she was not the only person to suffer under the rule of icy tongues.

"That hideous Lady Glover sent out another round of invitations," one of the ladies said to another. "I do hope no one has the bad form to accept."

"I don't understand why she even bothers," the other said. "No one is going to befriend her, no matter what airs she puts on."

"Have you ever met Lady Glover?" I asked Ivy, keeping my voice low. "She drives her phaeton through Hyde Park with zebras pulling it."

"Yes, I've seen them," Ivy said. "She makes it rather hard to miss."

"Zebras, Ivy. Zebras," I said. "Why are we not better acquainted with this woman?"

"Because the matrons of Society have never forgiven her for having got her start as a pantomime girl at the Surrey Music Hall," Ivy said. "Or so I've heard. Apparently there are some crimes even a good marriage can't erase, no matter how much money is involved."

"She lives just down the street from me," I said. "Perhaps we should call on her."

"I'm not sure that's a good idea."

"Don't be silly," I said. "It's an excellent idea."

"What is an excellent idea?" Lady Carlisle asked, coming to my friend's side.

Ivy looked at me questioningly, and I knew she was afraid of what I might say. Undaunted, I took a deep breath and soldiered forward.

"Calling on Lady Glover," I said. "I've been longing to question her on the care and maintenance of zebras in town."

6 June 1893
Belgrave Square, London

I'm home again, thank goodness!

The Women's Liberal Federation are frightfully boring. Worse even than Latin, which does at least have Emily's enthusiasm to recommend it. I nearly fell asleep twice in the meeting. Are there any causes less soporific to be found? I do so want to be useful, but is it too much to want to be entertained as well? I don't want to disappoint Emily, but I may have to focus my own efforts on a charity instead of politics. Robert suggested I support the Church of England Central Society for Providing Homes for Waifs and Strays. I'm certain I'd be better at serving children than convincing gentlemen I should have the right to vote, particularly as I'm not sure I even want it.

Is it so wrong to let our men take care of us? I've enough to do managing a household, dealing with my servants, seeing to the care of my daughter. I like the womanly arts, and want to focus on them. But is that selfish? Not all ladies are looked after so well as I. Would having the vote improve their lives?

Perhaps it would, but I haven't the slightest clue how. It seems a hopeless business.

Colin was in his study when I arrived home from the meeting. He loved this room the way I did the library, and I teased him that this was because he no longer owned any of the books in my favorite room, after having given all of them to me (along with every bottle of port in his cellar) when he asked me to marry him. He'd decorated, as he should have, with an eye to satisfying no one but himself. Old Masters hung against the navy silk walls—Raphael, Botticelli, and a sketch by Da Vinci. He'd bought the marble fireplace mantel while traveling in Italy soon after he'd finished at Cambridge. Shipping it back to England had proved problematic, so he'd hired four local men to transport it for him. They still worked for him, now serving as footmen, and I often practiced my Italian on them.

In one corner, he had a cabinet where he stored his best whiskies. Four bookcases shared the wall with the fireplace, two on each side. He had a large desk placed underneath the windows so he could look across the street to the park when he was working at it, and two leather chairs with a small, low table between them, sat in front of the fire. And then there were the chess sets. On a table along the wall opposite the windows, he had four sets, each continuously in various stages of play. My favorite was the ivory John Company one, from India, with the kings and queens perched in elaborate seats on top of exquisitely carved elephants. He had a French Regence set with large pieces carved out of wood, and an elaborate German one whose figures were based on Charlemagne, but the one Colin preferred was English. Manufactured by Staunton, its simple bone pieces in red and white sat majestically on a matching papier-mâché board. He kept his mind nimble by working problems on an ongoing basis, and we played frequent games. There were two more sets downstairs in the library.

A hidden door at the end of the chess table led to Colin's billiard room, a place he'd occasionally disappear to with his friends. I was bound and determined someday he would teach me how to play. He'd tried several times, but on each occasion when he'd stood behind me, his arms around me, helping me to hold the cue stick properly, I'd become hopelessly distracted. Some things are far more pleasant than billiards could ever hope to be.

Entering the room, I kissed him hello and flopped into a chair, waiting to speak until he'd placed the bishop in his hand on the rosewood board in front of him.

"It's to be Mate in Four," he said. "I have two ideas, both of which can wait until you've told me how your morning was."

He shook with mirth as I recounted for him the details of the meeting. "I don't know which I find more diverting: your planning to call on Conservative members of Parliament to bring them round to radical schools of thought or suggesting to Lady Carlisle you're concerned about the welfare of zebras."

"Are you anti-zebra, then?" I raised an eyebrow.

"Not at all, although I'll never be convinced the beasts could be happy in London. Or anywhere outside of Africa, for that matter. Please tell me you're not longing for a pair?"

"Fear not, dear husband. I'm a confirmed horsewoman, and have no desire to expand my expertise to other species."

"Thank heavens for that," Colin said. "This paint on Lord Sanders's house is troubling. Is there anything more to the story?"

"No," I said. "All I can imagine is someone wanted to cause additional pain to the family. As if the scandal weren't enough on its own. Have you further news about Mr. Dillman?"

"Not as of yet," he said. "Trying to reconstruct his accounts is proving nothing short of a nightmare. Nearly all his records were destroyed in the fire."

"What's to be done?"

"Lots of interviews with those who had contracts with him."

"So you suspect his death had to do with his business?"

"It seems the most likely motivation," Colin said. "His personal life has yielded no clues. I would be hard-pressed to name a more honorable man. All I hear when questioning those who knew him are tales of his kindness. I've yet to uncover one disgruntled employee or disloyal friend."

"I'm not surprised." I slouched deeper into the supple leather chair. My S-posture was made much easier in the Liberty gown that I'd changed into upon arriving home, with its soft, draping fabric and lack of need for a corset. Its lighter boning offered greater flexibility and range of motion than that to which I was used. I liked being able to slouch.

My mother, however, did not share my opinion.

"What on earth are you wearing?" she asked, barging past Davis as he opened the door.

"Mother, don't be so dreadful to poor Davis. You didn't even allow him to announce you. You know I value him above everyone else in the household. I can't have you scaring him off."

"I know, madam, that should I ever leave your service, you would no doubt replace me with a man of lesser character," my butler said. "One who might not keep you from your husband's cigars. You can't possibly think I would stand by and allow such a thing to happen."

With that, he exited the room, leaving my mother sputtering in disbelief. "Emily! You are conversing with your servants. Have you lost all of your breeding?" She lowered herself into the chair across from me, keeping her own posture pointedly erect. "Stop slouching. It's unbecoming."

I straightened my spine, pulled back my shoulders, and sighed. "To what do we owe this unexpected pleasure, Mother?"

"I have heard the most scandalous rumor. Talk in the park is that you attended a meeting of the Women's Liberal Federation this morning. Surely it must be a falsehood."

"Not at all," I said. "I did attend, and enjoyed it greatly."

"I will not have it, Emily. I will not be embarrassed by you. Not after the lengths I've gone to in what will undoubtedly prove to be a vain attempt to preserve the tattered shreds of your reputation, given all your eccentricities."

It would be difficult to discern which of my so-called eccentricities most vexed my mother. She objected to my study of Greek (I adored reading Homer in the original), was appalled when I set to cataloging the works of ancient art housed in England's great estates (it was mortifying for her to see her daughter apply for admission to her friends' houses for such a purpose), and despaired at my involvement in criminal investigations. That I was good at it held no sway with her, and no one could suspect my enjoyment of the work might soften her views on the subject.

Colin cleared his throat. "I'm afraid I owe you an apology, Lady Bromley. It was my own mother who invited Emily to the meeting. I had no idea allowing her to accept the invitation would upset you." He met my eyes and grinned while my mother sputtered for the briefest of moments before pulling herself taller and composing herself.

"Mrs. Hargreaves is involved in such groups?" she asked, her mouth very nearly hanging open.

"Oh, yes. A founding member, in fact," Colin said. "Perfectly respectable, I assure you."

"I don't like it, Mr. Hargreaves, I don't." She shook her head, her expression grim. "I know the difficulties you face in trying to control my daughter, and allowing her to associate with those people—your mother excluded, of course—will not help your cause."

"My cause, Lady Bromley, is to see to it your daughter has the happiest of lives. If she requires the Women's Liberal Federation, she shall have it."

"She's corrupting you," she said. "I feared as much."

"I'm afraid there's nothing more to be said on the subject," Colin said.

They stared at each other, neither wanting to be the first to back down, but no one could best my husband when it came to matters of will. My mother, defeated, rose from her seat. "I shall leave you to your unruly wife, Mr. Hargreaves. Heaven help you both."

I sighed and sank back deeper into my chair before the door had closed behind her. "She's exhausting."

"Always," Colin said. "But in a most entertaining way."

"You say that only because her energy is not focused on you," I said, pleased to find that my mother's interventions no longer sent me spiraling the way they used to. Instead of feeling vaguely ill and something like a disappointment as I used to following similar encounters, I was ready to return to the subject at hand without giving her any further thought. "We were discussing Mr. Dillman. If his friends and employees reveal no clues, where shall you turn next?"

"I'll continue to sift through his business dealings. Dillman's company did a great deal of work for the government, and I want to make sure he wasn't killed as a result of it."

"What sort of work?"

"I'm not at liberty to say."

"So it's his work for the government that led you to be asked to investigate?"

"Yes," he said.

I frowned. "What is he exporting to the rest of the empire that could land him in trouble? Was he engaging in some sort of official subterfuge?"

"Not. At. Liberty." He stared at me, just long enough to let my insides turn to a pleasant, warm mush. Then he bent over and kissed me.

"I shan't be distracted from my purpose," I said, trying not to kiss him back. My effort was halfhearted at best.

"Oh, yes, you shall." He narrowed his eyes and pulled a mockingly stern face. "Upstairs, wife."

I laughed as in one swift movement he picked me up and carried me towards our bedroom. My body tingled with anticipation and I no longer made any attempt to resist his kisses. At this time in the afternoon, there could be no doubt the servants would be scandalized.

Some hours later, Meg, my maid, interrupted our extremely satisfying— and vigorous—interlude. Truly, marriage was full of the most delightful pleasures. Her knock was more tentative than usual, and she would not meet my eyes when we called for her to enter the room.

"There's a lady here for Mr. Hargreaves," she said, curtsying.

"No need to be so formal, Meg," Colin said. "Who is it?"

"Mr. Davis sent me to fetch you. It's a Miss Cordelia Dalton. She's in mourning, sir, and really oughtn't to be calling on anyone. It must be an emergency."

"Thank you, Meg." He adjusted his tie and slipped on his jacket as she skirted back into the corridor. Meg had been with me from before I'd made my debut, and I was confident no one else was capable of so well taming my hair. Our early days together had their share of rough patches—she had been decidedly xenophobic and it was only through careful and insistent indoctrination that I'd persuaded her to take a more open-minded view of all those things in the world that weren't English. I'd got her to the point where she admitted to liking Paris. It was one of my finest accomplishments.

"Cordelia was to marry Mr. Dillman," I said.

"I remember Ivy mentioning that," he said. "Let's not keep Miss Dalton waiting."

We went downstairs and found our visitor huddled in shadows, a black-hemmed handkerchief clutched in her hand. Davis had closed the curtains in deference to the girl's mourning. She started to rise when we entered the room, but Colin bade her to stay seated.

"I'm so very sorry for your loss," I said.

"It's beastly of me to come here, I know," she said, tears welling in her eyes. "Mama will simply—oh, I can't even fathom what she'll do. But I had to see you. Ivy's told me so much about you, Lady Emily, and everyone knows Mr. Hargreaves is the best at . . . well, I can't say I'm precisely sure what it is he does, but I do know the queen quite depends upon him. And if he's adequate for her . . ."

"In what manner can I assist you?" Colin asked, pulling a chair closer to her and sitting down.

"I understand you were there when Michael's body"—she gulped a sob—"when he was found."

"I was," Colin said. "Nothing more could have been done for him. I'm terribly sorry, Miss Dalton."

"I know that. Please don't think I was suggesting otherwise. I want his murderer brought to justice, but my parents won't let me speak to the police."

"Do you know something about the crime?" I asked.

"I'm not entirely certain," she said. "My father insists it's nothing, but I can't believe it's coincidence."

"Please do explain," Colin said, his voice gentle and reassuring.

"Nearly a week ago when Michael called to take me for a walk in the park, he told me his house had been vandalized. Someone had thrown red paint all down the front step and the door. He hadn't particularly thought anything of it beyond it being a nuisance. But now I've heard said someone has given the Sanderses' house the same treatment—and did so right before the rumor broke about Polly. It just seemed to me there must be some connection," Miss Dalton said.

"You're a brave girl to come to us," Colin said. "And you've done the right thing. This is extremely valuable information."

"I want you to find him, Mr. Hargreaves," she said. "I want you to promise me the villain who killed my fiancé will be brought to justice. He took away all my happiness, and left me not even a widow. I've barely a right to grieve."

My heart broke for her. She'd have a relatively short period of mourning, but before long her parents would have her back on the Marriage Market.

"I promise you, Miss Dalton, I will find the man who did this," Colin said. "You have my word. I cannot return your happiness, but you will have justice."

"Thank you, sir. I know there's no one more dependable in the empire," she said. "Please forgive me, I must rush off if I'm to try to get home before my mother notices I've gone."

We bundled her back into her carriage and watched it pull away.

"What do you think of this?" I asked.

"I'm baffled," Colin said.

"Is there a connection between Polly Sanders and Michael Dillman?"

"There must be."

"How can I help you find it?" I asked.

"Do you have any ideas?"

"One," I said.

4

No trace of red paint remained on the Sanderses' door when I reached their house after leaving Colin, who was off to Scotland Yard. Questioning the family seemed to me the most direct, and, hence, best way to begin looking for a connection between the family and Mr. Dillman. Furthermore, the scurrilous gossip about them that was flying through the park disgusted me. Society was delighted to be able to unite against a single family. Perhaps people felt their own shortcomings would be overlooked so long as they had someone else's reputation to tarnish. This was an attitude I abhorred, and I wanted to make an obvious statement in support of the Sanderses. Calling on them would be a good start.

I knocked on the door. A lanky servant, awkward in what should have been elegant green-and-gold livery, did a terrible job disguising his surprise at finding a caller. He assured me his mistress and her daughter were at home, and urged me to follow him. I waited in a wide corridor while he secured permission for me to enter.

When I entered the sitting room, Mrs. Sanders and her daughter shared similar drawn expressions on faces gray with worry. Polly's eyes, swollen and red, lacked all sparkle. Her mother, dignified and old-fashioned, stood to greet me.

"Lady Emily, I am more grateful than I can say to see you. As you must imagine, our plight is such that most of society is unwilling to receive, let alone call on, us."

"I'm so sorry." I ran my hands along the cool, smooth surface of the horsehair sofa upon which I sat. "My heart goes out to you, Polly. Have you heard from Lord Thomas?"

"His father wrote, ending the engagement," Mrs. Sanders said. Polly sniffed behind a handkerchief. "Their family cannot tolerate such a connection."

"Forgive me, Mrs. Sanders, if I speak out of turn. I know not the truth of Polly's birth, but it seems to me irrelevant. You have never questioned her position as your daughter. Why should anyone else?"

"You're very kind," she said. "But we both know discretion is essential in such matters. Society will accept nearly anything so long as it's not spoken aloud. Once such a secret's out, however . . ."

"Have you any idea who might be responsible for the rumor?" I asked.

"It's no rumor, you may as well know. These things happen, and distraught though I may have been at the time, I can't say I was surprised. We sent the maid off, of course, but my husband wanted the baby to enjoy the same benefits and comforts as his other children. How could I object?"

Polly fidgeted in her seat, wrenching her hands.

"It's admirable that you did not," I said.

"I enjoyed having a little girl to spoil," she said. "Sons are what we're told to want, but after seven of them, I was happy for a daughter, and I've loved Polly as much as I would have had she been my own. Now, though, our whole existence is shattered."

"It's dreadfully unfair," I said. "I know it's difficult, but can you think of anyone who might have wanted to harm your family by exposing your secret?"

"Not at all. My husband is to receive a knighthood. We're an honorable and much-respected family."

"Yet someone did this to you," I said. "We must figure out who it was."

"For what purpose?" Mrs. Sanders said. "I can't see how it will do anything but extend the life of the scandal. We're going to take Polly abroad. Summer on the Continent and winter in Egypt. We'll not return to England until this talk has quieted."

The talk might quiet, but Polly's reputation would never recover. No doubt her parents were hoping to find, during their travels, a respectable enough gentleman in need of cash, someone willing to overlook the accident of Polly's birth in favor of her father's wealth, and agree to marry the girl. If they did not succeed, she had a year, possibly two, before she'd be doomed to the lonely life of a spinster.

"Did you know Mr. Michael Dillman?" I asked.

"I've heard the name, but can't say I'm acquainted with the man," Mrs. Sanders said.

"He was murdered this week. And before his death, someone painted his door and stoop with red paint, just as someone has done to yours."

"Murdered?" She gasped, alarm stretching her thin features. Her daughter shuddered. "I had no idea. I've been too consumed by our own troubles to read the papers. Do you think we're in danger?"

"I don't have evidence one way or the other," I said. "Although it appears this villain has already done his damage to you. Were you acquainted with Mr. Dillman, Polly?" I asked.

"I know his fiancée better. We were all occasionally at the same parties, and Cordelia might have introduced us. I can't say I remember."

"Was he friends with Lord Thomas?" I asked.

"Not so far as I know," she said. "They both could have belonged to the Turf Club. Lord Thomas spends loads of time there."

I made note of the information, determining to find out whether Mr. Dillman was also a member, although it seemed unlikely. He hadn't been known for aristocratic connections and I couldn't imagine he would have much enjoyed the company he'd find there. "You and Mr. Dillman both have been singled out by someone with brutal intentions. Can you recall any other connection you or Lord Thomas might have with him?" I asked.

"I don't see any point in thinking further about Lord Thomas," Mrs. Sanders said.

Polly lowered her eyes as they filled with tears. "I'm doomed, aren't I?"

"I don't know," I said, knowing full well the unforgiving nature of society and not wanting to deceive her. "But I promise I will do everything I can to help you."

"I don't feel safe in these circumstances," Mrs. Sanders said. "Not after a murder. I must speak to my husband at once about pushing forward our departure for the continent. Will you excuse me, Lady Emily? Please know how deeply I appreciate the gesture you've made by calling on us. The significance of a woman of your rank and reputation maintaining civil ties with us after this devastating incident will not be lost on society. I thank you for that."

I wished there was more I could do for Polly, but there is little that offers respite from a well and truly broken heart. When, heavy with sadness, I stepped back into shade-filled Kensington Palace Gardens and headed for the park, I saw Ivy standing across the street from me. She waved.

"Emily!" she called, beckoning me to her. "You'll never believe what's happened."

"Have you been waiting for me?" I asked.

"Yes, Colin told me where you'd gone. I thought you'd never come out."

"You could have come in, Ivy," I said. "The Sanderses are in dire need of friends at the moment."

Her pretty face clouded. "You're right, but I'm not so brave as you. I will call on them, I promise, truly. But you wouldn't have wanted me there this afternoon. I never would have been able to refrain from telling you what happened."

"What?"

"You'll agree, I'm sure, it wouldn't have been appropriate to mention this in front of Mrs. Sanders." She twirled the handle of her lacy parasol as we walked.

"I can't agree if you don't tell me," I said, knowing my friend sometimes needed coaxing, especially when she had something important to say.

"Right." She took my arm and guided me along the pavement in the direction of the park. "Red paint has been found on another doorstep." She spoke with a measured but deliberately dramatic flair.

"Whose?" I asked.

"The Mertons'," Ivy said. "Lady Merton's laughing about it. I saw her earlier on Rotten Row. But everyone's already speculating."

Lady Merton, one of the most celebrated hostesses in London, lived, so far as I could tell, a blameless life.

"What are they saying?"

"It must be something her husband's done. She's as harmless as they come. But it's all very strange, don't you think?" She tilted her head closer to me. "And rather a bit exciting, in a terrible way."

"Not exciting for the victims," I said.

"I didn't mean to be cruel."

"Of course you didn't, darling," I said. "You don't have a cruel bone in your body. I understand what you're trying to say. It's unsettling and exciting all at once. But we must not forget it's damaging as well. Lives have been ruined and we don't know what will happen next."

"It makes me half afraid to look at my own doorstep every morning."

"You can't be worried, Ivy. You've nothing to hide."

"Everyone has secrets, Emily."

The Sanders family may have found a measure of relief in the attention given to the Mertons over the following days. Polly's birth was no longer a mystery and the story had grown tiresome. Society was now focused on speculating what secret scandal might have inspired this new splash of red paint. Theories had been circulating for nearly a week when I came down to breakfast and found Colin waiting for me, the London *Daily Post* spread out on the table at my place.

"I thought you'd want to see this right away," he said.

I put aside my copy of *The Aeneid*, to which I'd been glued for weeks. After nearly a year of constant study with my friend, Margaret, who was currently holed up in Oxford with her new husband, I'd become invigorated with my newfound competence in Latin. While Greek would always be my passion, it was a pleasure, sometimes, to be free of the challenges posed by a different alphabet. Virgil's epic was particularly satisfying to me because I liked to see something good happen to a Trojan. Lots of bad happened, too, of course—this was mythology. But if I couldn't have the Trojans victorious over the Greeks, I was happy to see one of them become so culturally significant to the Romans. What would Julius Caesar, who claimed Aeneas as an ancestor, have done without the legitimacy provided by the mythical hero?

I bent over the newspaper. A paid advertisement took up an entire page but it was not there to suggest one should buy a certain type of bonnet or shoes. Nor did it beg the reader to visit an attraction or show. Instead, it contained the text—almost lurid text—of a series of love letters. Bold type highlighted a dozen characters:

TERCNOMLKAER.

"I don't understand," I said.

"The letters are signed only with initials—*M* or *C*," Colin said. "Now study the bold bits."

I stared at the letters again. "Merton."

"You're quick," he said.

"Not really," I said. "It's dead easy given I already knew their house had been splashed with paint. What about the rest? C L K A E R."

"Clarke. Samuel, I imagine."

"Samuel Clarke? The cabinet minister?"

"Precisely," he said. "The devoted family man and much-admired politician."

"But Lady Merton? His lover? I can't believe it. She's as prim and proper as they come."

"On the surface," Colin said. "She'd hardly be the first to seek out love once her duty was done."

"Heir and a spare and change. Doesn't she have eleven children?"

"I stopped counting after four."

I sighed and read aloud. *"My soul has awakened at finding you, my darling love, and there can be no happiness when we are apart. I want a home with you, a life, us together. I know all this to be impossible, so will content myself with our stolen moments—and rejoice in those times when we find ourselves with days rather than hours. Am breathlessly awaiting your husband's trip to France."*

"Damning stuff," Colin said. "Merton will be spitting nails if it's true."

"I bet it is true," I said. "The rumor about Polly Sanders was."

"I'm inclined to agree with you." He scrunched his eyebrows together. "Even a paper as unscrupulous as the *Post* wouldn't print such a thing if they had concerns about claims of libel."

"Mr. Clarke must be the target here, don't you think?" I asked. "The victim of a political rival, perhaps."

"But the Mertons' house was the one painted."

"So, are we to believe our villain was more concerned with tormenting Lady Merton than Mr. Clarke?"

"It would appear so," Colin said. "But why?"

"Lady Merton is by far the less likely object of attention," I said. "But isn't Polly Sanders as well?"

"An excellent point."

A footman entered the room with the morning mail on a silver tray. "This was just hand-delivered, sir," he said, giving my husband a separate letter. Colin sliced it open and read silently before passing it to me.

"Paint on two more houses and I've been summoned to Scotland Yard," he said. "I'll be home as soon as I can."

10 June 1893
Belgrave Square, London

My heart is absolutely broken on Lady Merton's behalf. Her husband swears he'll never speak to her again, and I do believe he has the will to carry it off. It was hardly Lady Merton's intention to be so exposed, but no gentleman can tolerate public humiliation well, deliberate or not. Some say she should have been more careful, but I don't know anyone more discreet. Whoever is behind this revelation is clever and must be connected in some way to her household.

To heap misery upon misery, red paint has marked the edifices of two more houses—those belonging to the Musgraves and the Riddingtons. Both are honorable families, but I know all too well we never can be sure who may be hiding something dark.

All this scandal has made me feel on edge, in ways I haven't for years. I'd hoped this dreadful business of mine was behind me, that I might never again be concerned by it, but it's not so easy to free oneself from sins this ghastly. I was half inclined to confide everything in Emily. She's so sharp and competent. I've no doubt she'd take care of it all in a matter of hours. But I'm ashamed, so very ashamed. I can't bear for her to know what I've done. Instead, I tried to make light of what's happening around me, as if it's making the season more exciting. I hope I was glib enough but not too glib. I don't want to make her suspicious.

Colin could help me, but I could never ask him to hide something from his wife and my dearest friend. He'd understand better than anyone what I've done. I'm sure he's seen far worse. Yet Robert, my darling Robert, the sweetest husband England has ever known—what would he think should he ever learn I turned to another gentleman for assistance? It would do no good to work my way out from under all this by burdening myself with yet another secret.

That would only leave me more vulnerable to exposure. Just like Polly Sanders and Lady Merton. And Mr. Dillman.

The thought of what happened to him terrifies me. I'll do anything to avoid a similar fate. I wonder if the Musgraves and Riddingtons feel the same way.

Hating to sit around and feel useless while Colin was working, I decided to call on Lady Glover. As a society outsider, Lady Glover was bound to have an interesting perspective on this spate of vandalism, and it was entirely possible she'd have an insight that could prove useful to our investigation. Once finished with breakfast, I sent a note to Jeremy Sheffield, the Duke of Bainbridge, begging him to accompany me on my visit that afternoon. He acquiesced at once, which came as no surprise. I knew that long ago, he and Lady Glover had been quite close. So far as I could tell, they had remained friends in the following years.

Jeremy had been one of my closest friends from the time we were children, and it was this fact that had kept me immune to his dashing good looks and occasionally irresistible charms. We'd grown up on neighboring estates, and spent many a fine morning playing together when we were young. More often than not he was chasing me with frogs, or we were climbing trees or pretending to lay siege to castles, always having a grand time. Our friendship had remained close into adulthood, the only bump coming when, after I was engaged to Colin, Jeremy confessed to being in love with me. We bungled our way through the ensuing awkwardness, and eventually returned to our old easiness with each other.

Protest the observation though he might, Jeremy had never really been in love with anyone. Pretending to be enamored of me provided him an excuse for being unable to commit to marrying any among the slew of debutantes desperate to win his affections.

As one would expect on a brilliant summer day, the pavement was a crush of people when Jeremy collected me. Fashions had gone more radical. Some ladies had taken to wearing fuller skirts again, and we all feared a return to the days of the crinoline, although what alarmed me more were the wide sleeves one saw everywhere. They made me feel as if I were walking through an ocean of bright-colored balloons.

"So, have you and your much-esteemed husband learned anything interesting in your quest for answers about our overzealous painter?" my friend asked as we walked along Park Lane the short distance to the Glovers' house.

"Not so far," I said.

"It's a delicious business," Jeremy said. "I can hardly wait to see what madness descends upon me when I awaken to paint on my house. I've so many dark secrets. How could anyone limit himself to exposing only one?"

"You're not half so bad as you like to think. And you're hardly subtle in your wantonness—your goal of being the most useless man in England is far from a well-kept secret. If society were going to be scandalized by you, it would have happened years ago."

"That's beyond disappointing. I'm wholly disheartened."

"You torment the mother of every debutante in London by refusing to marry," I said. "Can't you take comfort in that?"

"I could if I weren't so greedy." We'd reached the Glovers' house, and were admitted without delay to a plush drawing room, full of bright sunlight bouncing off the hefty silver vases, candlesticks, and ornaments that adorned the chamber. Lady Glover did not rise upon our entrance, but gestured for us to sit across from her and poured us tea without asking if we wanted any.

"I prefer China tea. You'll find it's much better without milk," she said, handing us each a cup. "I must say I'm surprised to see you, Lady Emily. I'm not much used to grand ladies of society calling on me."

"Do I get no kudos for my devotion?" Jeremy asked.

"None at all," she said. "You, Jeremy, are here far too often to be interesting, and, anyway, gentlemen are an entirely different matter. They have a tendency to forgiveness while we ladies are more prone to jealousy, don't you think?"

"You're hard on your sex," I said.

"You style yourself something of an outlier," she said. "Yet you've never faced being ostracized on an ongoing basis. That makes little rebellions, like calling on me, much easier."

"I'm fortunate that by accident of birth I'm in a position to pursue my own interests without too much interference," I said. "That does not mean I don't sometimes face the unkind judgments of others. You'd be hard-pressed to find anyone in the *ton* who approves of ladies studying Greek."

"True, true," Lady Glover said. "But the accident of my own birth left me in a much different state. I had to earn my living—and you are, no doubt, aware of the limited options for us women in such circumstances. My good fortune came from having a beautiful face. It won me my husband and the admiration of his friends and colleagues."

"Yet not their wives," I said, knowing how brutally she'd been cut by the ladies of decent society. "You intimidate them."

"They don't pause for a moment before choosing each other's husbands as lovers, yet they worry their husbands might choose me. Simply because I was not born one of them."

A young maid entered the room with a tray of beautifully decorated tea cakes and set them down on the table in front of her mistress. She bobbed a curtsy and silently headed to the door.

"Not so fast," Lady Glover said, calling her back. "Has your young friend proposed to you?"

"No, madam."

"I'll have a word with him tomorrow," Lady Glover said. "This is the right marriage for both of you." The maid nodded, and continued out of the room. "I feel such a responsibility for all of them, you know. My staff suffers from my reputation. It's difficult for them to find other posts should they ever leave my employ. I like to make sure their lives are well organized."

"I suppose I should think that's generous," I said.

"You don't approve?" Lady Glover asked.

"Not entirely," I said. "I admire both your concern for her well-being and the fact that you don't treat your staff as furniture. That's an affectation I find reprehensible. But the girl should decide who to marry."

"Girls, my dear, are not always inclined to act in their own self-interest." Lady Glover fingered the heavy ropes of pearls around her neck. "I help them as much as I'm able. But enough of this. What brings you to me today, other than wanting an excuse to have our divine duke escort you?"

"Merely the desire to form a closer acquaintance," I said. "I'm rather fond of your zebras."

"Should I be suspect of your motives?" she asked.

"I'd hardly try to steal them," I said. "I will, however, admit to being curious about your thoughts on this red-paint business."

"I like it," she said. "Why should people be allowed to hide all their sins? I much prefer to know what they're really made of. You learn far more about character from people's secrets than you do their public acts."

"And more still about the characters of those around them by studying their reactions to the secrets revealed." I sipped my rich, golden tea. "So tell me, who do you think is our culprit? Who is behind all this revelation?"

"I wish I knew," she said. "I'd host a ball in his honor. You can judge me as you like, but I'm taking no small pleasure in seeing high society squirm when they've taken such delight in cutting me. At least my sins were those of necessity. Theirs are nothing more than bad judgment and immorality."

"You think ill of Lady Merton?" I asked.

"Not in the least," Lady Glover said. "She's as human as the rest of us. But I do think ill of a society that refuses to let women find love in marriage."

"It doesn't refuse altogether," I said. "I found a husband I adore."

"I seem to recall your mother once wanted you to marry our friend, the duke," Lady Glover said, nodding her head to Jeremy. "Had you not wealth of your own, you would never have been able to go against her wishes. Once again, the accident of your birth has come to your aid."

"I don't deny the truth of it," I said. "Nor the inherent injustice of it."

"It's a tragedy, I tell you, that's what it is," Jeremy said. "I blame the bloody Married Women's Property Act. If you'd not been left so well settled after your first husband died, your mother would have been my greatest ally."

"It's clear you don't have even a bare understanding of the Married Women's Property Act," I said. "And at any rate, you'd despise being married to me, Jeremy. I'd make you read Latin."

"I'd divorce you," he said.

We stayed another quarter of an hour, during which time I twice tried to bring the conversation back to the red paint, but Lady Glover would discuss it no further, changing the subject before I could gain any traction with it. I left the house wishing she'd said more.

"Lady Glover certainly bears a grudge against society," Jeremy said once we'd stepped back into Park Lane and turned towards my house. "Do you think she could be our villain?"

"I like her for it," I said. "She's got the right sort of spirit, though I can't imagine her murdering Mr. Dillman."

"If it is her, I'll be even more angry if I don't get some red of my own," he said. "I'd never forgive her."

"It's not funny, Jeremy," I said. "My heart breaks for Polly, and Lady Merton—I've heard her husband has refused to speak to her ever again—but aren't these situations to be expected in our kind of society?"

"Indeed they are. We value discretion above all else and—" He stopped. Cordelia Dalton, her hair flowing wildly down her back, was running up my front steps and banging on the door.

I started toward her.

She could hardly catch her breath. Davis opened the door, his countenance not altering in the slightest at the sight he beheld. Tears soaked Cordelia's face and the sleeve of her dress was torn. He looked straight past her to me.

"Welcome home, madam," he said, not missing a beat. "Port in the library?"

"Dear Davis, what would I do without you?" I said, putting my arm around Cordelia and ushering her inside.

Jeremy hung back on the front steps. "I'd best leave you to it, Em," he said. "I don't do well with crying ladies." He tipped his hat, gave me an uncomfortable half smile, and took his leave.

"Tell me what's happened," I said, once I'd installed Cordelia in the library's most comfortable chair.

"They think I have something, and I don't—I swear I don't . . . I don't even know where to look. But I can't convince them. They'll never believe me. I don't know a thing about Michael's work. How could they think I would?"

"Slow now, Cordelia. I need to know more," I said. "Who are 'they'?"

"The ones who sent the letter." With a shaking hand, she pulled a crumpled envelope from her reticule.

My dear Miss Dalton,

We are well aware of the sensitive nature of the information passed to you by your late fiancé. Be a good girl and hand it over to us so that nothing more need happen. Bring it wrapped in a plain paper parcel to the statue of Achilles in Hyde Park tomorrow at half eleven in the evening. You will receive further instructions there.

Or, if you prefer, do nothing and suffer a fate worse than that of Mr. Dillman.

A friend.

I read the missive twice, then inspected the envelope, but found no features on either that might identify the sender. "Have you any idea to what this letter refers?" I asked.

"None at all," Cordelia said.

Davis entered with port and two glasses. "Is my husband home?" I asked.

"He is, madam. Working chess problems in his study."

"Bring him to us, Davis. And his whisky as well."

"Do your parents know you've come to us?" I asked. Cordelia, still too upset to speak coherently, shook her head. I rose and went to my desk, pulled out a sheet of paper, and started to write a note to the girl's parents. "You can't hide this from them," I said, scribbling words across the page before shoving it in an envelope and ringing for Davis to have it delivered. Cordelia sunk lower in her chair and sobbed.

"What's all this?" Colin asked, entering the room. I handed him the letter. He read it and then, his face grave, he sat next to Cordelia.

"You're quite certain you've no idea what these people want, Miss Dalton?" he asked.

"None at all," she said, her voice thin and choking.

"Emily, take her upstairs and get her cleaned up. Have you summoned her parents?"

"I've asked her father to come," I said.

"Well done," Colin said.

"Am I in danger, Mr. Hargreaves?" Cordelia asked.

"I'm afraid so," he said. "But I'll do everything I can to make sure no harm comes your way."

Mr. Dalton listened, his countenance growing darker as Colin briefed him on Cordelia's situation. He balked at my husband's suggestion that they go abroad until the situation was sorted, confident there was nowhere in the world safer than England. Because his daughter was in mourning, he said, it would be easy enough to keep her under close watch at home. I understood the desire to stay on familiar ground, and hoped it was the best choice.

Cordelia insisted again she had received nothing from Mr. Dillman that could be significant to the case, but I persuaded her to let me accompany her home and to examine everything he'd given her. In the meantime, Colin would arrange for the Daltons' house to be kept under watch by Scotland Yard. Mr. Dalton, ready to be as careful as necessary, stationed a footman outside Cordelia's bedroom as she and I made our way to the polished wooden case where she stored her most-treasured possessions.

"I swear, Lady Emily, he always looked after me with the most tender care. He never gave me anything these people would want," she said, her voice choked with tears. "He wouldn't have done that to me. Not if he thought it could have endangered me."

I squeezed her hand. "Of course not. But he may not have realized there would be this sort of danger."

Cordelia clutched the case to her chest and sat on the edge of her bed, tears streaming down her face. "I miss him so very much."

I longed to be able to erase her pain.

She set down the box, ran her hand over its smooth top, the surface of which was inlaid with an elaborate pattern of mother-of-pearl, and then unlocked it with a slim key. It opened with a click and she pushed up the lid. Inside were several small boxes and a bundle of letters. The boxes contained items she'd collected while on walks with her fiancé:

brittle pressed flowers, a dried leaf that hadn't lost its bright autumnal red, and a soft, white feather. She didn't meet my eyes when she reached for the letters.

"Do you need to read them?" Her cheeks flushed red.

"I don't want to," I said, frowning. "It doesn't feel right. But it would be worse if we missed something."

With a sigh, she passed them to me.

"I promise you I shall keep these absolutely private," I said.

"Unless you discover something that matters."

"If we discover something of significance, I shall copy out only the pertinent information. It can't be anything obvious, or you would have already noticed it. No one should have to see the actual letters."

"Just the decoding of a code?" she asked.

"If we're lucky enough to find one."

We were not so lucky. Mr. Dillman's letters revealed him to have a kind heart, an occasional ear for poetry, and a touching affection for his fiancée, but nothing suggested he had embedded mysterious messages in them. One of them I read repeatedly, as its postscript implored his fiancée to keep it always, but I could pull nothing useful from it. I asked Cordelia if anything about it stood out to her, but she only sighed and shook her head. The other item left in the box was a slim guide to objects in the British Museum.

"Did you go there together?" I asked, holding up the volume. The museum was one of my favorite places on earth. As a little girl, wandering through the galleries with my father, I used to wish I could run away and live there. As an adult, I'd become a patron of the institution and spent countless hours studying objects in its collections.

"Innumerable times," she said. "When the weather was not good enough to sit in the park, we'd go there instead. Michael preferred it, in fact. We used to play a game, a scavenger hunt of sorts. He'd give me two clues. One was the beginning of an artifact's museum number, and the other revealed something about it, like what it was made of, or a quote that was pertinent in some way. I'd comb through the galleries until I found the answer."

"That must have been difficult."

"Not always," she said. "Many of the catalog numbers start with the initials of the department. And once I was in the right gallery, I could generally home in on what he'd selected, but that wasn't the end of it. Once I'd found the proper artifact, I'd have to figure out how it was connected to a book in my father's library. So when we'd come home, I'd search until I found the book, and either in it or behind it, there would be a little treat."

"Is there any chance, Cordelia, that Mr. Dillman left a last set of clues for you?" I asked. "Perhaps in a manner more oblique than usual?"

"I honestly don't think he did," she said. "I would have recognized clues at once, no matter how oblique he tried to be."

"Do you think it's possible he might have hidden something in the books without leaving a clue? Would he have thought you'd know to look if something happened to him?"

"He might have done," she said. "I hadn't thought of that."

We went downstairs and spoke to her father. Mr. Dalton immediately ordered his staff to pull down the books from his library shelves.

"We can't risk missing something," he said, joining the servants in their work, as did Cordelia and I. We removed every volume and leafed through each in case something was inside. Once they were empty, we inspected the shelves for anything that might have been hidden on them.

But we turned up nothing. Defeated, I started for home, taking a detour to Mr. Dillman's house in St. James near Green Park. I knocked on the door and was greeted by a tall butler dressed in impeccable mourning livery.

"Madam?" he asked.

"I'm Lady Emily Hargreaves, a friend of Miss Dalton's," I said. "And, as you can imagine, I am deeply concerned about all that's happened. I wonder if you can help me? Miss Dalton is in danger—from the same people who killed Mr. Dillman. They believe, erroneously, that she's in possession of some information he had. If you could assist me in finding it, we could give it to Scotland Yard and Miss Dalton would be safe to grieve in peace."

"What sort of information?"

He seemed an honest, forthright man, and met my eyes with an even stare. "I've not the slightest idea," I said. "But I'd like to think, between the two of us, we'd recognize the sort of thing that could inspire a man to murder."

He nodded. "Mr. Dillman was a good man and an excellent master. I can't do anything much for him now. But if you think this would help bring his killer to justice . . ."

"I can't promise you anything, but we can certainly try."

"Why are you here instead of your husband?" he asked.

This surprised me. "My husband?"

"I've read of his many accomplishments and am honored to meet his wife," he said. "I know you were wounded in the line of duty, and that your investigative skills are to be admired as well."

I blushed. Several of the papers had covered the story of our various exploits, but I'd not before encountered someone who'd read them and considered my role praiseworthy.

"You couldn't possibly have thought I would even consider your request if I didn't know of the reputation of the Hargreaveses," he said.

I was rather pleased to learn I had a reputation. This sort of a reputation, at any rate. But I was also embarrassed. I'd expected to be able to talk my way into the house, because I had assumed a servant could be easily persuaded by a person of my rank. Yet here I stood, speaking to a man who judged me by my accomplishments rather than by my father's title or my husband's fortune.

"Thank you," I said. "It honors me more than you can imagine to have earned your respect."

"Please, come inside." I followed him through a wide marble corridor and then into a dark room. This was another house whose curtains remained closed in deference to mourning. "This was Mr. Dillman's study." He lit a lamp and stepped back.

The room was smaller than I would have expected. Red silk covered the walls in a wide, geometric pattern. Walnut bookshelves rose a third of the way to the ceiling along one side. Across the room from them row after row of portraits hung from brass chains attached to long, matching rails, which stretched the length and height of the wall. Three sets of French doors would have provided a spectacular view of the park if their curtains were pulled back, and an elegant, neoclassical desk filled one corner. I motioned to it.

"Shall we start here?" I crossed the room and pulled open the desk's center drawer.

"You'll want these, too." The butler reached down a neat stack of leather-bound notebooks from the top of a bookshelf. "All his business and personal records."

"Thank you." I sat down and started to pore over the notebooks. Most of them were ledgers, filled with financial transactions, and some Mr. Dillman had filled with sketches of flowers, birds, and other wildlife. Remembering Cordelia's treasures, I wondered if he'd had the habit of sketching while they were sitting in the park. The last in the pile was harder to decipher. The first pages contained lists of bills that had gone before Parliament, with numbers and symbols scrawled next to each of them. Following that were page after page of what appeared to be personal notations—reminders of things Mr. Dillman needed to do. All of them had been crossed out save the final seven. The remainder of the book was blank.

"Did the police examine these?" I asked.

"They did, madam."

"Did they take anything from the house?"

"No. From what I heard them saying, it appears they believe anything pertinent to the crime would have been at the warehouse with Mr.

Dillman. That's not to suggest, madam, they were not thorough when they were here."

Colin had told me as much earlier. "Would it be all right for me to take these?" I asked, holding up the notebooks. "I'd very much like to share them with Mr. Hargreaves."

"I don't see why not, madam," he said. "Mr. Dillman's brother is abroad and won't be able to reach London for at least another fortnight. I can't imagine he'd object."

"Thank you. Would it be too much to see your master's dressing room?"

Three quarters of an hour later I'd left the house, satisfied I'd missed nothing. With me, I carried the notebooks and a scrap of paper I'd located in one of Mr. Dillman's jacket pockets. A scrap of paper I hoped would prove to be our first significant clue.

I was convinced the sequence, M E E A M & M E O A O A M E, written
on the paper I'd found in Mr. Dillman's coat pocket were references to
departments in the British Museum. I told Colin about the game Cordelia had played, and he agreed with my deduction, but was quick to point
out these letters could have been used by Mr. Dillman ages ago. Regardless, without more than just them, we had no way of using the information for any further purpose. Colin set himself to search through the
notebooks and continue his investigation of the dead man's business
dealings while, at his urging, I applied myself in another direction. I had
learned when it was time to leave matters to him, at least temporarily.
Marriage is a delicate balance, particularly when spouses work together.
Colin and I had, after a certain amount of unsuccessful push and pull,
found our way to contentment in this department. I was not about to
disrupt it. Lady Carlisle had left a stack of pamphlets for me, and I was
happy to head to Westminster to deliver them to the unsuspecting Conservative MPs.

Tall plane trees brought welcome shade from the heat of the day as I
made my way through Green Park, then crossed the wide Mall and stepped
into St. James's Park, where bright blossoms lined the paths and ducks

and swans zoomed through the lake. The two parks, with Buckingham Palace between them, made for one of the prettiest parts of London, but today everywhere I walked the mood was tense. No scandal had yet been revealed to explain the red paint left on the Musgrave and Riddington houses, but this had not provided relief for the families. If anything, it had ratcheted up tension even further. Society was rife with speculation as to what secrets would come out, but even as gossip spread, people began to worry they, too, would be subject to similar unwelcome attentions.

The Beau Monde were watching each other in ways they hadn't previously. They were more on guard, more skittish. A couple walking a few paces in front of me broke apart with an almost violent force. "Why would you tell me such a thing?" the young woman cried as she pulled away from her companion. There could be no question of the gentleman's motivation. He thought it preferable to tell her himself before he found himself exposed in an indecorous manner. I wondered how many people were making unwelcome, and possibly unnecessary, confessions and destroying lives.

Or were these confessions unnecessary? If someone had told a lie or deceived their partner, in life or business, did that partner not deserve to make an informed decision about continuing the relationship? Would ignorance be preferable? I frowned, crossed Horse Guards Road, and continued on to Westminster, where I asked for Mr. Reginald Foster. Mr. Foster, a schoolmate of Colin's, was touted as having the brightest political future of any man in the history of the British Empire. He'd been universally adored at Eton—elected to Pop and Library in his first year, the darling of every hostess in Windsor, best oarsman in memory— and had finished Cambridge with double firsts in history and classics.

There seemed to be no limit to what this man could accomplish. He spoke seven languages fluently (although he himself counted only six, as he insisted Latin could not really be spoken in modern Europe), dedicated a great deal of his not insignificant fortune to charitable causes, and had proved himself a more than adequate painter during the two years he spent traveling on the continent after finishing at university. Most significant to me, at the moment, however, was the fact he had promised he could gain me admission to the offices of the Conservative MPs.

"Lady Emily," he said, stretching his arms to me as he approached. "What a delight! You're even lovelier than I remembered. Marriage agrees with you."

"I thank you for the compliment," I said. "But you, sir, are nothing like Aristophanes led me to expect. A popular politician, according to him, has a horrible voice, bad breeding, and a vulgar manner."

"I'm glad, then, to disappoint you," he said. "I was so pleased when Hargreaves got in touch. Excellent man. I remember him from school, though he was, of course, considerably younger than I. Wouldn't have it in me to refuse his request I help you, even if I didn't agree with what you're doing."

"You support suffrage?" I asked.

"I do. Seems foolish to reject the input of so many bright minds," he said, meeting my eyes with an even stare. Mr. Foster spoke with such conviction I could almost believe he'd never engaged in so fascinating a conversation. Truly the man was a consummate politician. "Particularly that of my own wife. But I must warn you, my colleagues in the opposition will be terribly hard to convince. They view the entire movement as an attack on their ability to properly look after their ladies. Why should women need the vote if their men are dedicated to protecting them?"

"A terrifying thought."

"Quite," he said. "Right or not, many gentlemen believe letting ladies into the realm of politics would take away from their beauty and charm."

"Ladies are more than beauty and charm," I said. "And to suggest they're not already firmly embroiled in politics is absurd. I can't count the number of wives I know who are renowned as political hostesses—Liberal and Conservative."

"Entirely true. But a social role, however influential, is not the same as an official one," he said. "Come, now. We've much to do."

As he led me through the wide corridors of the Houses of Parliament, my stomach rolled itself in knots and I began to question the wisdom of my strategy. Would it have been wiser to interact with these men at social functions instead of the workplace? I drew a deep breath, pressed my lips hard together, and stood as erect as I could. This last action made me realize the one ground upon which Mr. Foster might be disappointing. He was not so tall as he undoubtedly hoped.

For nearly two hours he guided me from office to office, providing introductions to countless Honorable Members, whose reactions to Lady Carlisle's pamphlets ranged from outright horror ("Get the bloody woman out of here!") to willful misunderstanding ("What a fascinating story. Are you still reading Greek?"). I hadn't expected to win converts on my first day—only to identify candidates for further indoctrination. Which was why, after handing over the slim document and gauging the recipient's reaction, I smoothly transitioned to other subjects.

Subjects like literature. A gentleman interested in the works of the American transcendentalists couldn't possibly be too closed-minded. Two promising leads there. The Right Honorable Member who cited "The Wife of Bath's Tale" as his favorite not only amongst Chaucer's *Canterbury Tales,* but also amongst all writing—an opinion expressed after explaining how the great author "knows women like no other man"—would never come around to a more enlightened point of view . . . at least not in my lifetime. Given his advanced age, it seemed a hopeless business.

As for the rest, I would continue to work on all who admitted a fondness for romantic poetry, detective stories, and those who preferred Hector to Achilles in *The Iliad.* The latter, I believed with all my heart, could not hold such an opinion without some degree of enlightenment.

"I do hope you're not too disappointed," Mr. Foster said, as he escorted me out of the building. "They are a pack of beasts."

"You should be careful of saying such things," I said, opening my parasol to protect me from the glaring sunlight. "You're our best hope for future prime minister."

"You flatter me," he said, bouncing a bit as he stood. He was on tip-toes, giving himself an extra inch or so of height. "Gladstone's in good form. But I do appreciate your confidence."

"I wouldn't expect you to do anything but support your leader. You're too well bred."

He smiled but said nothing.

"I can't thank you enough for your help," I said.

"I couldn't be happier to provide you with assistance," he said. "It's a difficult path you've chosen, Lady Emily, but a worthy one. I wish you much luck with it."

"I know you agree with our principles, but can we count on your public support?" I asked.

"You can be certain I shall never speak against the goals of the Women's Liberal Federation."

It wasn't the same as real support, but I reminded myself that he was a gentleman with the highest aspirations. Alienating a large part of the voting public would not serve him well. Should he ever become prime minister, then he might be in a position to take a firmer stand.

At least I hoped so.

"What do you think of all this red-paint business?" I asked.

"Stuff and nonsense," he said. "Petty gossip taken to a new level."

"But lives are being destroyed," I said.

"Lives have always been destroyed by such things," he said. "This time, it's being done for a larger audience, that's all."

"Who do you think is responsible?"

"Impossible to say, really. Who hasn't felt tormented by the *ton* at one time or another?"

"True," I said. "But wouldn't most people seek revenge against the individuals whom they felt harmed them rather than striking out at all of society?"

"Most would, I suppose. But some people have a higher purpose than personal retribution."

"And you think that is a good thing?" I asked.

"Heavens, no!" He brushed his sandy hair back from his face. "Although one could argue it's time society had a good shaking up. That it lose some of its hypocrisy."

"I couldn't agree more," I said. "But there must be a better way to do it."

"I'm certain there is," he said. "There are times, though, when the final result merits an unconventional approach. Even one that hurts people."

Days passed before I had occasion to think of Mr. Foster again. I'd spent a relatively tedious afternoon at home receiving callers, when relief came in the form of Ivy and Jeremy. They'd arrived late, as close friends do, and we were all laughing as I described for them my adventures in Westminster.

"But isn't Mr. Foster the most handsome man you've ever seen?" Ivy asked. "Other than Colin, of course."

"Colin is much more handsome," I said. "I grant you Mr. Foster is extremely easy to look at, and quite distinguished, though one does wish he was a little taller. He's also smart, which more than makes up for any physical drawbacks. He quotes Byron with such finesse it's almost unnerving."

"Unnerving?" Jeremy asked. "The only unnerving thing I see here is discussing the repulsively perfect merits of some other bloke. Have you ladies no hearts?"

"You know we adore you, too," I said. "But I do like Mr. Foster very much. He's the closest thing we have to a modern Alexander the Great. Except, of course, that he hasn't conquered anything yet."

"Wait until he's prime minister," Ivy said.

"I don't know how these bloody Etonians do it," Jeremy said. "It's bad enough they'll walk over fire for each other to ensure they run the empire. I've learned to tolerate that with equanimity, because I've no interest in running it myself. But I won't have them winning the hearts of all the ladies as well."

Davis opened the door. "Simon Barnes, madam."

"Thank heavens," Jeremy said as the new arrival entered the library. "I'm in desperate need of reinforcements, Barnes. You've saved me."

Simon Barnes stood taller even than Jeremy. His black hair, oiled and combed back in a rather old-fashioned manner, made him look older than his age, as did the heavy creases on his forehead. It was hard to believe he and Mr. Foster had been at school together.

"What a lovely surprise," I said, raising my hand to him. "We've just been discussing the countless merits of your friend, Mr. Foster."

"There's not a better man in Britain," Mr. Barnes said. "He should be prime minister someday."

"I told him just that a few days ago," I said. "His response was all modesty."

"Bloody bore to be prime minister, I'd think," Jeremy said. "I say, Barnes, enough of this. I want to hear about your days in the West Indies. Surely you've troves of stories of pirates and hidden treasure and I know not what else. Anything, really, that gets us off the topic of Foster."

Simon Barnes had spent his childhood in the West Indies, where his grandfather was governor of one of the islands. Barnes's mother had been her father's favorite, and he indulged her every whim. Strong-minded and determined, she'd insisted on marrying a local boy from a well-to-do family. Going native was not something of which English society was much fond, but her father did not object. He had no taste for being the instrument of his daughter's heartbreak. When she died in childbirth a mere eighteen months later, he took her son, Simon, into his house and gave him his name. The boy's father protested not at all. The islanders accepted mixed marriages as little as the English, and he slunk back to his family to beg forgiveness for his choice of bride. Within a month, he was remarried to someone deemed more acceptable.

Barnes's grandfather doted on him, sparing no expense to give him the best. He sent him to England for his education, where the boy excelled academically. Barnes sailed through Cambridge, and had spent the subsequent years working in politics. He'd made himself indispensable to nearly every prominent liberal in the past twenty-odd years, spending all his time in London save a two-year return to the land of his birth when his grandfather died.

"It's not so romantic as you think," Mr. Barnes said. "Unless you've a fondness for muggy nights and enormous insects."

"I shouldn't think I'd like it," Ivy said.

"It can be hard for a delicate constitution to adjust to the extremes of island weather. England does not well prepare one for heat." Mr. Barnes's smile was wide and bright, his voice soft. He didn't quite look English, but neither did he look like a native West Indian. It was as if the familiar and the foreign lived side by side in him. "I'm sorry to be calling so late, Lady Emily. I've no right to intrude in so intimate a gathering."

"There's no need for apology," I said. "We're delighted to have you join us."

"I confess I was hoping to see your husband," he said. "This red-paint business is causing quite a political stir. I'd like to speak to him about it."

"You don't think Mr. Gladstone will find his house vandalized, do you?" Ivy asked.

"No," Mr. Barnes said. "I think we're all aware of the prime minister's quirks and eccentricities. I don't think there's much left for him to hide. But to see so many families under the threat of whoever is behind this smear campaign is disturbing. The government are taking it quite seriously. They feel no one in London is safe at the moment."

"Safe?" Ivy said.

"From scandal and rumor," he said.

"My husband's not home at the moment, but I shall tell him you called," I said. "Will you be at the Fannings' ball tonight? If so, you're sure to see him there."

"I'll look for him," Mr. Barnes said.

"I worried Mrs. Fanning wouldn't soldier on," Ivy said. "Her house was covered with red paint yesterday. Not just the steps and the door, either. The whole front, including the windows, was splashed. She's a brave woman not to cancel the party."

"If I were going to be exposed for some grim deed I'd rather it be in the comfort of my own home," Jeremy said.

"Would you go on with the party, Mr. Barnes?" I asked. "If you found yourself in Mrs. Fanning's position?"

"A person can't be daunted in the face of adversity. One must go on. And if one is to be taken down, one may as well do so in excellent company."

"I always knew I liked you, Barnes," Jeremy said. "We really must dine together more often. Generally I avoid you Old Etonians. You're such an insular lot. But you're different. Bearable, even."

"I shall take that as a compliment," Mr. Barnes said, his voice low and melodic.

"I like you very much, Mr. Barnes," Ivy said. "Have you promised away all your dances tonight? I can think of several young ladies to whom I'd like to introduce you."

"Don't bother to make me your project, Mrs. Brandon," he said. "Much though I appreciate the gesture, you'd find yourself quickly frustrated. Wealth and political influence are not the only things required by the parents of society brides. I shan't disturb the lot of you any longer, but will look forward to seeing you all this evening."

"He's a good man," Ivy said after he'd left. "And so open about his past. Never apologizing for it, never hiding from it."

"It would be impossible for him to conceal it," Jeremy said. "He might look English enough, but there's too much of the exotic in him to pass as one of us. Even his voice sounds magical."

"We must help him find a wife no matter what he says," Ivy said. "I can't think of anyone more worthy of a good partner."

"Not even me?" Jeremy asked.

"Especially you, Jeremy," Ivy said. "I shudder at the thought of what your wife will suffer."

11 June 1893
Belgrave Square, London

I am so fond of Mr. Barnes! How unfortunate that he's not been able to secure a worthy bride. His heritage, no doubt, has made it difficult, but it should not be impossible. I shall make it my mission to find him a suitable girl. Probably one of many sisters—he's enough money to make the details of a dowry irrelevant—and from a family without political aspirations. I've a few candidates already in mind and shall call on their mothers this week to begin planting the idea with them.

This is a pleasant distraction in the midst of so much upheaval. Mrs. Fanning is a wonder to go on with her plans for the ball despite the paint. I do hope her guests don't let her down, though I suppose there's little chance anyone will cancel on her. They'll all be interested to see what, if anything, happens. On my way home from Emily's, I heard that Lady Althway's house has been painted as well. She's Mrs. Fanning's closest friend. It must be a comfort of sorts to have someone who understands the hardship of being marked by this villainous soul and his paint.

I wonder if they were targeted at the same time for a reason. Could they together have done something grievous? I do know Lady Althway can hold a grudge longer than most. She's a most unforgiving sort of woman. Will she now want others to forgive her?

Must go dress for the ball. I shall wear my golden gown tonight. I want nothing close to red.

For Colin and me, the evening began well enough. We had dawdled pleasantly over our toilettes, as was our habit, spending more time talking over glasses of wine than dressing. When my maid had become stern, insisting we would be late if we didn't finish, I'd submitted to her ministrations. Colin, whose appearance required no improvement from its natural state, was dashing and ready to go long before I. He stepped around Meg, who was slipping jeweled combs into the sides of my coiffure, and presented me with a slim parcel. I pulled open the strings to reveal a beautifully bound blank book, its red cover fashioned from the smoothest leather I'd ever felt.

"I thought you should have a notebook to chronicle your suffragette adventures," he said. "I'm immeasurably proud of what you accomplished in Westminster."

"Thank you," I said and kissed him. "It was a necessarily slow start, but a good one." Colin had received a slew of notes from MPs imploring him to put an end to my suffragette activities. Or at least to limit them in a way that would preclude me from troubling them.

"I appreciate you agreeing to hold off on the investigation until a time it's appropriate for me to involve you." He threw a neat white silk scarf around his neck. "Have you heard about today's paint?"

"Yes, the Althways," I said. "Any idea why?"

"Lord Althway has had more than his share of dodgy business deals. He's more enemies in the British Isles than we have sailors in the navy."

"An obvious choice, then. All that remains, I suppose, is to see which of his dastardly deeds will no longer go unpunished."

Meg motioned for me to stand in front of her, stepped back, and took a long look, evaluating her work. "Perfect, madam," she said. "You're lovely. Will there be anything else?"

"No, thank you," I said.

"I'll make sure the carriage is waiting," she said. "And please do consider what I said to you about Paris. We need to go as soon as possible. Your hats are in danger of being unfashionable."

This was a complete fallacy. My hats were in danger of nothing.

"I should have paid better heed when I read *Frankenstein*," I said. "I know you just want to see Paris again."

"I'm only looking out for your best interest, madam," Meg said. "I have my ways of keeping abreast of the latest fashions."

"I'll keep that in mind," I said. "The carriage?"

"Of course, madam."

As soon as she'd disappeared downstairs, Colin took me in his arms and kissed me. "You're stunning tonight. Is that a new gown?"

"It is." Mr. Worth, the greatest dressmaker in the world, designed it in Paris after I chose the fabric, a gorgeous midnight-blue silk that he'd covered with an intricate pattern of shimmering silver beads. My waist had never looked so tiny. I snapped a heavy sapphire necklace in place and slipped its matching bracelet over my wrist. "Something's troubling you, my dear. What is it?" I asked.

Colin rubbed his forehead. "Forgive me. I've tried in vain to distract myself. It's this paint."

"Have you learned anything new?" I asked.

"The pattern of attacks seems to be changing. Two more victims, the Fannings and Althways, before the secrets of the previous ones—the Musgraves and Riddingtons—have been revealed."

"It's early in the game to be analyzing patterns," I said.

"True." He started to pace, and I followed him into our bedroom. "But if my instincts are right, this man is more calculating and vicious than I'd thought. He's interested not just in exposing these people, but in tormenting them."

"By making them wait?" I asked. "It would be agony wondering what he's uncovered."

"I don't think they wonder about *what* he'll expose, but *when*. People are keenly aware of those things they wish to hide."

"Do you have something you wish to hide?"

"You can't be asking that seriously," he said. "If I have something that must be kept from public knowledge, I keep it private. There's no wishing involved. As for our villain, I think the torture for his victims comes from the waiting, not the wondering. They know exactly what lies in store for them." The clock on our mantel chimed. "Come. Meg's right, we'll not arrive before everyone's called to go down to dinner if we don't get a shift on."

The Fannings' house should have done nothing but sparkle that night—between the diamonds around ladies' necks, the garden lanterns bobbing in a perfect breeze, and the thousands of candles suspended from chandeliers in the ballroom, one wouldn't have thought anything else possible. Social carnage was not welcome. Our hostess, certainly, was doing her best to carry on in what many would have considered a deadly situation. Not only had she brazenly refused to let the paint be cleaned off her doorstep, she'd chosen to wear a crimson dress and had every lady presented with a bright red rose as she entered the house. "Have you seen how unsuccessful other's efforts were to remove the stuff?" she'd asked as she stood at the landing in the center of her stairs greeting us. "Far better to embrace a flash of color."

"She's an impressive woman," Colin said, escorting me the rest of the way up the grand marble staircase, moving us towards the sound of gay music. "I almost wonder if she's proud of her secret."

"I think she's terrified," I said. Her smile had exuded a confidence belied by her eyes. "And much to be admired."

The room could not have been more perfect. Enormous urns overflowed with more red roses, guests devoured delicious lemon ices or drank champagne to cool down after taking vigorous turns on the dance floor. Every eligible bachelor in town was in attendance, which should have sent the mothers of debutantes into excited flutters. Instead, their heads bent together in worried conversation. Would it be wise to allow one's daughter to enter into an engagement in the current climate and risk exposing her to untold scandal should her new fiancé wake up to red paint one morning?

We danced and ate and drank champagne. It was like any other ball until a young man in a German officer's uniform barreled past me, nearly knocking me into the pillar.

"Sir, you—" Colin began to go after him, but the man didn't pause. He stalked on, peeling off his gloves as he approached another gentleman, Harry Croft, and shoved his shoulder. Before Croft could react, the officer lifted a glove and used it to soundly smack his face.

Croft appeared unsteady on his feet only for an instant, then stood tall and stepped closer to his attacker, his cheeks sucked in with rage.

"You call me out?" he asked. The musicians had stopped playing and the room fell silent, all eyes focused on the altercation.

"I do, sir, I do." The reply came in a heavy, German accent.

"For what?"

"Your infamous affairs."

Everyone in the room was aware of Mr. Croft's reputation. He was something of a dandy and would have made Casanova feel ashamed of his comparatively small success with the ladies. But his charm and good nature kept him in society's good graces. After all, at least a third of its members were in love with him.

"There's nothing infamous about my affairs," Croft said. "Step away from me while I'm still willing to let you save face."

"There will be no stepping away. I'd fight you now if I could. No decent person would forgive you for what you've done."

"Enlighten me." Croft folded his arms. "My sins are no greater than any gentleman's, my affairs no better or worse."

"I speak of your lovers, Mr. Croft."

If silence could become louder, it did in that moment.

"You know to what I refer, don't you?"

Croft shook his head. "How dare you address me in such a manner! My personal relationships are no business of yours."

"Your personal relationships are insignificant to other gentlemen, perhaps. But I should think the ladies involved would feel otherwise."

"That's quite enough," Croft said.

"What kind of man turns into rivals two such dear friends?"

Now the eyes of the observers in the room began to dart around, and a soft murmur rippled through the crowd.

"You will stop there." Color drained from Croft's face. "I accept your challenge. There's no more to be said in the current company."

"I don't agree." The officer turned, searching the crowd around him. "Where is our inestimable hostess?"

Mr. Fanning pushed his way to the man. "Remove yourself from my house at once." He stood tall, his stout frame rigid with dignity, not the sort to be daunted by any controversy.

"You should have this one ejected instead." He glared at Croft, then raised his voice louder. "Lady Althway, how do you feel to learn the object of your affection is shared by your dearest friend?"

"Get out now!" Mr. Fanning balled his hands into fists as his wife came to his side, her hands trembling.

"Please, sir, please," Mrs. Fanning said, in a voice so small only those closest to her could hear. "You've already done your worst."

"I have?" The man balked. "Where is Lady Althway? Surely neither of you can think I err in calling out this profligate?"

"There's some misunderstanding," Mrs. Fanning said. "Mr. Croft would never have . . ."

Now Lady Althway appeared, her face redder than the darkest of the roses, and stormed towards Mrs. Fanning. "You knew I loved him."

"My dear, I had no idea it was *he* who had so captured your imagination!" Mrs. Fanning reached for her friend's hand but was rebuffed. Her husband looked on, growing increasingly pale. "And who's to say he hadn't captured mine first?"

"What would you have me do, pull out letters to prove my claim?" Lady Althway thrust herself at Mrs. Fanning.

Colin stepped between the two ladies. "This is hardly a conversation to be had in such a forum. Control yourselves." He spun on his heels to grab the officer, who had turned as if to leave the room. "You, sir, are coming with me." The man did not protest. Colin kept a tight hold on him, but paused and spoke to Mr. Fanning. "Leave this to me."

Our host stood, immobile, his eyes tight with pain. I heard Lord Althway's voice booming from the back of the room, but I could not make out his words.

"Emily," Colin looked back at me. "Bring them."

I put a gentle hand on each lady's arm. "Let's remove you from this spectacle." We followed him through a series of brightly colored sitting rooms into a much smaller salon furnished in the Georgian style. Lady Althway tugged her arm away from me.

"I won't stand for this," she said. "I—"

"Lady Althway, now is not the time." Colin's voice, simultaneously

71

firm and soothing, was impossible to ignore. Quieted, she took a seat on a chair in the corner, as far away from Mrs. Fanning as possible. "At the moment, I want to focus on you, sir."

The officer threw his hands in the air, a lopsided grin on his face. "I thought it was a fantastic performance. I do hope you're as pleased as I am." The German accent had vanished in favor of a thick Northern English one.

"Pardon?" Colin asked.

"I was afraid for a minute I'd come on rather too strong, but the boss insisted I not hold back. Who am I to argue?" He tugged at the jagged dueling scar on his cheek, pulling it right off.

"You're an actor?" I asked, my mouth hanging open.

"As you see," he said. "But good lady, you can't say this surprises you?"

"Indeed I can," I said.

The actor laughed. "My performance must have been even better than I thought. You didn't think the accent was too coarse?"

Colin turned to the ladies. "Were either of you involved in the planning of this?"

"What an outrageous suggestion!" Lady Althway snapped open her huge, painted fan and waved it with vigor in front of her face.

"You can't possibly think we would involve ourselves in such a scheme," Mrs. Fanning said.

"Who are you?" Colin asked, his attention back on the actor. "And who hired you?"

"Timothy Blake," he said with a bow. "Ordinarily I perform with a troupe of players based in York, but work's been scarce of late, so I agreed to a solo performance."

"Who hired—"

He didn't let Colin ask again. "Don't bother," he said. "I have no details that would interest you. I received a letter from a Mr. Hopworth-Smythe, asking me to assist in the entertainments he'd been hired to organize for an upcoming party in London. I'd been told all the guests had been given parts to play, along with a handful of professional actors. That we were to stage a murder mystery of sorts and the assembled crowd would attempt to solve the crime. Rather a diverting concept, don't you think?"

"Who are the other actors?" I asked.

He shrugged. "I'm afraid I haven't the slightest idea. We weren't to be able to identify each other—it was to add to the verisimilitude of the event."

"Have you ever heard of a Mr. Hopworth-Smythe, Mrs. Fanning?" I asked.

"I can assure you I absolutely have not. We hadn't planned any such entertainment, though I confess to finding the concept an excellent idea."

"You shouldn't find it so when it destroys the happiness of your dearest friend." Lady Althway sniffed.

"In other circumstances, obviously." Mrs. Fanning sat up straighter.

"What did Hopworth-Smythe do to convince you he was legitimate?" Colin asked.

"Paid me in advance at three times the rate I usually receive for the entire run of a play," Mr. Blake said.

"And you didn't find that suspicious?" I asked.

"Why should I?" He threw his hands in the air. "You aristocrats are wont to waste more money in a single night than I'm like to see in five lifetimes. Who am I to judge when some of the excess benefits me?"

"How many times did you meet Hopworth-Smythe? Can you give me a description of him?" Colin asked.

"I'm afraid not," Mr. Blake said. "We communicated only by mail."

"You have his address?"

"I was to reach him care of the Camden Town post office."

"Of course," Colin said. "I'll need to know how to get in contact with you—no post offices and don't even consider running off. You're not finished with this incident." He pulled out the papers he always carried that identified him as an agent of the Crown.

Mr. Blake nodded. "Whatever you say." He scribbled down an address and handed it to my husband. "I've nothing to hide and am happy to help."

"That will be all for now," Colin said. "Expect to hear from me again soon."

"Fair enough," Mr. Blake said. "Must say I'm feeling a bit of a genius for having insisted on being paid in advance. Sorry to have bungled things for you ladies." With another bow, he left the room.

Colin put his hands on the back of a chair and leaned forward, facing Mrs. Fanning and Lady Althway. "Forgive me for having to be so direct, and for having to broach such a sensitive subject, but I'm afraid I have no option. These things Blake accused Croft of are true? You are—were—both involved with him?"

"So it seems," Lady Althway said. Mrs. Fanning remained silent, tears pooling in her eyes.

"I'm sorry you've been so badly treated," he said.

There was nothing left for us to do. The ladies would have to face the unpleasant task of dealing with their husbands. Our villain had exacted another round of revenge.

While the Fannings and Althways struggled with the revelations of the previous evening, the rest of London waited, wondering when the Musgraves and Riddingtons would see their secrets exposed. Colin and I, longing for a quiet night at home away from rumor and gossip, planned an elegant dinner for ourselves. Settled into our dining room, which had been modeled on banqueting chambers found in ancient Roman villas, mosaics covering all the walls, we started with asparagus soup. Then salmon, followed by curried eggs and sweetbreads (I despised them, but my husband's opinion was quite the opposite), lobster cutlets, then capon with ham and green peas. We skipped the game course—it seemed too hot for it to me—and prepared to move straight to sweets.

Just as the footmen were clearing to make way for our final course, Davis entered the room, his head bowed, his expression serious. He crossed straight to my husband.

"Sir, your presence is urgently required in the blue drawing room."

Colin folded his napkin and placed it on the table. I moved to follow him.

Davis cleared his throat. Colin raised his eyebrows.

"If I may speak, sir?" Davis asked.

"Of course, Davis," Colin said.

"Madam may prefer to remain where she is."

I needed no further motivation. I sprung from my chair and followed my husband. Davis did not hide his displeasure, walking more stiffly than ever as he took us to the sitting room. I knew him well enough to understand he wasn't prone to overreaction, and that the dear man was only trying to protect me. He hesitated before opening the door to the sitting room. Colin nodded at him, and with a sigh, our butler ushered us inside.

A shaking, liveried servant jumped to his feet, nearly dropping the brandy snifter in his hand. "I'm so sorry," he said. "Mr. Davis said it would be all right—"

"If Davis saw it fit to install you in the sitting room and give you brandy, he must have had an excellent reason for doing so," I said. "We never question his judgment. Do sit back down."

I took a chair across from him; Colin remained standing.

"Please identify yourself," he said.

"I am Lord Musgrave's valet, sir. I've come on his behalf . . . well, not precisely. He's dead, sir, taken his own life."

Air flew into my lungs. The newspapers were all keeping close track of which families in town had suffered vandalism on the fronts of their homes—and equally close track of whether their secrets had yet to be revealed. Weeks had gone by since red paint marked the Musgraves, but so far, no one had discovered why they had been targeted.

"It's a dreadful scene, sir. Blood everywhere."

"Who found him?" Colin asked.

"I did, sir." The man looked longingly at his brandy. "He'd been in the bath rather longer than usual. I went to inquire if he needed more hot water. The door was locked, and I could raise no response from my master."

"How did you open the door?" I asked.

"I've a key to the room," he said.

"Have you summoned the police?" Colin asked.

"No, sir. Not yet. Lady Musgrave wanted you first, and asked me to fetch you. Will you come?"

"Of course," he said. "Emily, I'll need your help with the lady of the house."

We piled into the waiting carriage and made our way to the Musgraves' house in Cadogan Place, not far from Sloane Square. Lights gleamed from every window of the façade, as if they'd been lit in an attempt to deny the grisly event that had just occurred. A dour butler threw open the door before we'd reached it. Lady Musgrave, appearing from behind him, waved her arms frantically.

"Inside, quickly, quickly, please!" she said. "We've no time to lose."

Colin took the lead and bolted to her. "Is Lord Musgrave in need of medical attention? I was under the impression—"

"No, no," she said. "Nothing of the sort. But you must come upstairs at once and tell me who murdered him." She took his arm and wrenched him forward. I followed, nearly tripping as I ran up the two flights of stairs that led to Lord Musgrave's bedchamber.

Lady Musgrave's earnest pace slowed once we'd crossed the threshold of the room. "He's through there," she said, motioning across the room to an open door. Colin strode ahead, stopping me before I could take a single step.

"Let me go first," he said.

"It's all a terrible mistake, you see," Lady Musgrave said to me once he'd disappeared from our sight. "His valet said he'd done a harm to himself, but that can't possibly be true. And even if it were, imagine the scandal! It's simply unacceptable."

How does one reply to such statements? I was saved from finding out by my husband's return. "Emily? Are you up to it?"

I nodded and went to him. We passed through Lord Musgrave's dressing room into a small chamber containing the man's bath. In the tub, submerged to the neck in bright red water, was the man of the house, an ugly gash slicing his jugular. I looked away.

"Oh." It was all I could manage.

"You've seen worse," Colin said, and I appreciated both his confidence in me and his recognition of what I'd done in the past. "I can't identify any signs of a struggle. The instrument of his destruction is in the tub."

I forced my eyes back to the scene and saw the straight razor still in the dead man's hand.

"Is there anything to suggest it wasn't suicide?" I asked.

"No. The door was locked from the inside. None of the windows appears to have been opened."

I circled the room, studying everything. "There's dust on the sills," I said. "No one has touched them in weeks—particularly the maids."

"I'll question the servants just to be sure no one heard anything suspicious," Colin said. "But the conclusion seems obvious."

"He certainly had motivation." I frowned. "He preferred death to facing disgrace when his secret was exposed."

"What a terrible waste," Colin said. "He's only heaped more scandal on his family."

"Lady Musgrave will not be pleased."

She was not. We took her downstairs, pressed a stiff drink into her hands, and told her our conclusions. She ranted, pounding her fists on a table, and stamping her feet. "It can't be! It can't be! You must tell everyone he was murdered and the crime so well committed it can't be solved. That sort of thing happens all the time!"

"I'm afraid it doesn't, Lady Musgrave," Colin said. "I've sent for the coroner. He will examine the body in more detail—"

"So you could be wrong, then?"

"I'm afraid not. You yourself admit you heard nothing suspicious in the house tonight."

"We could be dealing with an extremely clever villain, Mr. Hargreaves," she said. "Perhaps one of my own servants. Do you think I should dismiss them all?"

"I wouldn't," I said. "You'll only provide more fodder for gossip."

"You're right, you're right, I know you're right. How could he do this to me?" Her angry desperation faded as her eyes grew moist. "Leave me alone to face whatever he's done to incite this red-paint maniac?"

"You're sure it was something *he* did?" Colin asked.

"Of course I am." She pursed her lips. "I have made a special point of leading a life free from reproof. It's been tedious in the extreme and, as a result, I shouldn't be left to deal with someone else's mess."

"Have you any idea what he did?" I asked.

"No." She dabbed her eyes with a lacy handkerchief. "He was extremely discreet in his private life. We've been married nearly thirty years and have become somewhat distant. He must have had some sort of mistress. The usual sort of thing. Nothing interesting enough to have drawn such attention."

Colin's eyes clouded for just an instant. "Lady Musgrave, would you object to my sifting through your husband's papers? Just in case there's something significant to be found."

"Evidence that he was murdered?" she asked.

"No, I'm afraid there's no chance of that," he said. "But if I can discover what he was trying to hide, I'll do whatever's possible to minimize the scandal."

"I would appreciate that, Mr. Hargreaves," she said. "And I know I can trust you. My husband spoke so highly of you." She lowered her voice. "He told me what you did during the Anderson business."

"Did he?" His face was all composure, but I noticed a trace of color creeping up his neck. He lowered his eyes and brushed nonexistent lint from his sleeve, not meeting my inquiring stare.

"Like him, I'm all discretion," she said. "Your secret is safe with me."

"Would you object to my starting now?" Colin asked, the words tumbling from his mouth in a rush before I could inquire about the Andersons. "His study would probably be the best place."

"Go right ahead. Through that door, cross three rooms. It will be the second door on your left. Your wife and I can chat while you work," she said. "I wouldn't want her sullied by anything untoward you might find."

Personally, I would have happily observed—and assisted in—the discovery of anything untoward, but I didn't see how I could impose myself given Lady Musgrave's wishes. Colin returned less than a quarter of an hour later.

"Your husband's desk is completely empty aside from a handful of pens and pencils, Lady Musgrave," he said. "The fireplace shows evidence of a large number of papers having been burned."

12 June 1893
Belgrave Square, London

I came dangerously close to confessing all my sins to Emily this morning when we were riding. She asked if I'd heard any rumors about Colin's involvement in some business involving a family called Anderson. I haven't, and know nothing. If only Anderson weren't such a common name; I can think of at least six families called that. I could see Emily is worried, most likely because she's as afraid as I am of facing scandal.

Perhaps that's not quite true. She wouldn't be as afraid as I am. Why would she be? She hasn't done anything wrong herself. It's Colin she's worried about. His work must be fraught with situations the public could find questionable. He's so honorable I can't imagine he's done anything in his personal life he'd want to hide, although my friends would assume the same about me. Maybe there is something it would be better if Emily didn't know.

I guess the truth is we never know every detail about another person.

I asked Robert if he knew anything about the Andersons. He had nothing to say on the subject.

10

Even Colin's best efforts couldn't keep the story of Lord Musgrave's suicide from the greedy hands of every tabloid editor in London. A parlor maid, eager for additional cash, spilled what she knew to the *Daily Post*, and the whole town eagerly digested the gory truth. The report painted the girl in a favorable light, explaining she had betrayed the confidence of her employers only so she might afford desperately necessary medical treatment for her ailing mother. On the streets of Mayfair, her decision was greeted with derision, but the less fortunate residents of our glorious capital felt somewhat different. What kind of society required an honest working-class girl to sink to such levels to acquire something they felt should be a basic right? I found myself firmly on the side of the less fortunate.

"You'll forgive my amusement," Lady Glover said. She'd called on me as soon as she'd read the news. "It's bad of me, I know, but can you blame the poor girl? Musgrave should have better looked after his servants. His wife—widow—won't make the same mistake, poor woman. But I didn't come to discuss any of this, Lady Emily. I want to talk to you about our friend, the singular painter. I believe he's left me a clue to his identity."

"Has he?" I asked, leaning forward. She unfolded a sheet of paper she'd pulled from her reticule and passed it to me. I read aloud. *"My soul is full of discord and dismay."* A red swish of paint underlined the text.

"Hamlet," she said.

"Yes." I examined the page for any additional marks. There were none. "Was it delivered in an envelope?"

"No, just folded and sealed and left on my doorstep."

"When?"

"I found it when I returned from driving my zebras through the park this morning."

"And I take it no one saw who delivered it?"

"Alas, no." Her smile cloyed with insincere sweetness.

"What in it makes you suspect the author's identity?"

"The red paint, of course."

"I don't mean that. I understand it appears to have been written by our villain. But does anything in it give you a clue as to whom you think he might be?"

"Someone who knows his Shakespeare, and who writes in a superior hand," she said. "I thought you'd like to see it."

"You were right," I said, disappointed that she could offer no further insight. "Did you notice any markings on the sealing wax?" Little of it remained to be examined.

"I honestly didn't think to look until it was too late," she said. "I assumed it was a letter of a more romantic nature. That's the sort of thing to which I'm accustomed. I was thinking I'd reply to him."

"You were?" I asked. "How?"

"Well, I'll send back an appropriate quote. Maybe something from *Romeo and Juliet.* Or is that too frivolous?"

"How would you have it delivered to him?"

"I'll leave it on my doorstep just as he did," she said. "It's common practice when dealing with a gentleman who wishes his identity to remain a secret. What do you think? I may be more enlightened than you when it comes to dealing with society, but I admit freely you win the day when it comes to experience with criminal minds."

"I think it's an excellent idea," I said. "Shall I help you choose a passage?"

"I'd prefer to do it on my own. But I promise to share with you any response as soon as I get it." She flashed a feline smile, her eyes lighting up. She'd spotted Colin entering the room.

"Oh, what a good surprise!" she said. "I never suspected I'd find you home at this time of the afternoon, Hargreaves. I am a fortunate one today."

"Lady Glover," he said, dropping her hand almost as soon as she'd raised it to him."

"You're such a beast, Hargreaves," she said. "It's been ages since you've been round to see me. What am I to think? Thank goodness your lovely wife deigned to befriend me or I'd feel completely cut. She's such a gem."

I half expected her to reach over and pat me on the head.

"That she is." Colin pulled a cigar out of his pocket and lit it. "I do hope I'm not interrupting delicate conversation."

"Not at all," I said. "Lady Glover has just been showing me—"

"Now, now, Lady Emily, that's to be our little secret. Gentlemen don't need to know everything. We ladies ought to have some mysteries just for ourselves."

"Far be it for me to presume otherwise," Colin said. "How is your husband?"

"Well enough," Lady Glover said. "His gout's troubling him again, the poor man."

"And are you on tenterhooks wondering if you'll wake up to find red paint splashed across your front door?" he asked.

"Me? Far from it," she said. "I'm the only person in London with nothing to hide."

Somehow, I did not believe her.

My doubts about Lady Glover aside, I did find myself enjoying her company. I knew her comments to Colin were meant to get my hackles up—but I had no cause to doubt my husband's fidelity. That was a subject upon which I had absolute peace of mind. No one was more trustworthy than he, and I had utter faith in him. Most likely because I did not respond to her bait, Lady Glover held me in higher esteem after that meeting, and soon became a regular caller at our house in Park Lane.

Today, I was returning the compliment. I raised the heavy knocker on the Glovers' door and, in short order, was shown into what the mistress of the house called the Egyptian drawing room. Every flat surface in the chamber was covered with objects—scarabs, ushabtis, colored beads, small glass bottles—she'd begun collecting some years back, when she first took a fancy to the ancient civilization. A grouping of stone stelae hung on one of the walls, hieroglyphs carved around images of a placid-looking pharaoh. Lady Glover was stretched out on a low settee that looked more Roman than Egyptian, but I meted no judgment on her combining of cultures. Her gown, fashioned from layers of thin linen and belted with a narrow strip of gold, would have inspired jealousy in the finest Roman wives.

"Come, come, Lady Emily," she said, motioning me towards her. As I approached, she sat halfway up and kissed me on each cheek, then returned to her elegant reclining pose. "Do you approve of my Ptolemaic fashion? Roman, of course, if one is going to be proper, but it's what Cleopatra would have worn."

"It's beautiful," I said.

"But you wouldn't have the courage to wear it."

"Not outside a fancy dress party," I said, taking a seat in a low, gilded chair before I noticed we were not alone in the room. Reginald Foster, resplendent in a perfectly tailored jacket, was standing on his tiptoes to greet me. "Mr. Foster! Forgive me, I didn't see you."

"No apology necessary. Who could focus on anything beyond the beauty in front of us?"

"You appear to be in the wrong room, Mr. Foster," I said. "Lady Glover, do you have a designated space for medieval courtly love?"

"What an idea!" She pushed up one elbow and rested her chin on her hand. "I should redo the entire house, making each room reflect a different historical period."

"Just don't have a Waterloo room," Mr. Foster said, masterfully dividing his glances equally between us two ladies. "Apsley House should have the exclusive rights to that. The Duke of Wellington deserves nothing less."

"Fair enough," she said. "But I am going to have a room whose walls are covered in red paint."

"Do you think that's wise?" Mr. Foster said. "The perpetrator is wreaking havoc on society."

"Which is just what society deserves," she said. "Come now, Reggie, you cannot claim you don't agree with me. We've discussed this too many times."

"I do appreciate how passionately you feel about the subject, Valerie, but there must be limits," he said, his voice softer than it had been. "You know that perfectly well. We can't have the public acting as vigilantes. It would lead to no end of trouble."

"You're lucky you're not my husband, Reggie," she said. "I'd force you to openly support my positions."

Their easy familiarity with each other took me aback. I couldn't decide whether to be impressed or shocked that a man with Mr. Foster's political aspirations could openly associate with a woman of Lady Glover's reputation.

Without pausing or giving the slightest reaction to her comment, Mr. Foster changed the subject. "You told me Lady Emily is aware of the correspondence you received regarding the matter at hand?"

"Lady Emily was the first person in whom I confided. Proximity to her husband is nearly the same as being an agent for the Crown, you know."

"I've been trying—with no success—to convince Lady Glover to tell me what she sent this madman in reply," Mr. Foster said. His voice had lost the intimate tone that had crept in earlier, and he sounded more like a politician again.

"I wouldn't count on getting her to crack," I said. "You'll have to satisfy yourself with the content of the note she received."

"And the yellow sealing wax," Mr. Foster said. "One doesn't see that often."

"You were here when Lady Glover opened the note?" I asked.

"No, no, I only just read it before you arrived," he said.

"Our man was clever to leave no clue to his identity," Lady Glover said.

"Or so it would seem. I wonder his motivation is for sending it at all? What can he hope to gain?" I asked. "May I read it again, Lady Glover?" She handed it to me and I analyzed every inch of the page. There was an oily stain where the wax had once been, but no trace of it remained.

"I think it may be your friend, Mr. Barnes, who is reaching out to me," Lady Glover said, leaning closer to Mr. Foster. "He's an outsider, as am I, and might rightly suspect I'd lend a sympathetic ear to his plight."

"That, my dear, may be the silliest thing you've ever suggested," Mr. Foster said. "Simon isn't an outsider. He's nearly as important to this country as the prime minister."

"He's not English," Lady Glover said.

"A fact that hasn't curtailed his influence on those who run the empire," Mr. Foster said. "You won't find a better respected man in Westminster."

"He'd say the same thing about you," I said.

"He's been splendid to me since school. I was a few years behind him and he took me quite under his wing during my first days. He remembered what it was like to be the new boy. I'd trust him with my life."

"I admit that's something of a relief," Lady Glover said. "He's not my vision of a romantic correspondent."

"I don't see how there's anything romantic about receiving correspondence from a murderer," I said. "You should take this very seriously, Lady Glover."

"I assure you, I do," she said. "I shall set Lord Glover to the task of having the house watched. I want to know who is delivering these messages."

"It was only one message, was it not?" I asked. "What makes you think there will be more?"

"My dear Lady Emily," she said. "More are a certainty. I'm in my element here. You can trust me to know when a man will be back in contact."

For years, Ivy and I had made a habit of meeting for a morning ride in Rotten Row, and it had long ago become one of my favorite daily rituals during the season. The morning light would fall soft on leaves and grass and make a glowing cloud out of the dust kicked up by our horses' hooves. We would start off slowly, then I'd pull ahead, goading her to race. She'd protest, worried we'd shock society and horrify the multitudinous other riders. But soon enough she'd be following me, pulling up close, and egging me on.

Today, I regretted not having had more than a small piece of toast and a single cup of tea to fortify me before I'd set off. I hadn't realized Winifred Harris would be joining us, or just how much fortification dealing with her could require. It took fewer than ten minutes for me to confirm something I'd long suspected: try though I might for Ivy's sake, Winifred and I would never be close. Our conversation was stilted from the outset, and she scolded me fiercely the second my horse started to move a beat faster than a canter, explaining to us in overwrought detail how inappropriate our previous behavior had been.

"Furthermore, it's not good form," she said, just as I'd started to hope she was nearly done. "It's dangerous, too, as there are so many riders present. But most of all, think of the talk to which it has exposed you. Do you want to draw ire upon yourselves? Do you want to be left off guest lists because you're considered wild?"

Personally, I was quite taken with the notion. No one had ever suggested to me before that I might be wild. It seemed something to which one might aspire.

"Thank heavens we're both already married," I said, knowing my irony would be completely lost on Winifred. "We'd be scaring off every potential husband we met."

"I don't mean to be stern with you," Winifred said, puffing up her broad chest. "Please understand that. But it's essential we stay vigilant in the protection of our characters. What does a lady have that matters more than her reputation?"

"I can think of lots of things," I said, but wasn't allowed to continue.

"One need only look at how Lady Merton's circle has shrunk since her house was painted. Consider that, Lady Emily, and then consider your connection with the Women's Liberal Federation. It's very off-putting," she said. "People are beginning to talk."

"Let them," I said. "I believe in what I'm doing."

"You're just trying to get attention. No thinking person can believe women should have the vote. It's a revolting concept. You should know your place better than that."

"You know, Winifred, you begin to make me wonder if *all* women should have the right to vote."

My insult was lost on her as her attention was elsewhere. "Look at that! Her posture is appalling!" She pulled closer to Ivy and motioned with a subtle gesture to indicate a rider not far from us, but made no attempt to modulate her voice. "Did you see her at the opera last week? Her gown was atrocious and her manners even worse."

"She is kind, though," Ivy said. "Her younger sisters adore her."

"Precisely," Winifred said. "She's a good woman, yet she doesn't bother to care what impression she makes. Which means she has nothing in store but ruin and loneliness. If she's fortunate, she'll find a post as a governess."

I kept silent.

"I can tell you're angry at me for speaking so openly, Lady Emily. You think I'm hard on my own sex. But I feel the same about gentlemen. Do you see that man over there?" she asked. "An extremely well-known youngest son—there, standing on the pavement perpendicular to us, speaking to a woman in a garish purple hat? I understand his gambling debts are close to ruining his entire family. What sort of a man allows himself to sink to such a level?"

"Isn't it enough for him to live with what he's done?" I asked.

"I know how high the standard to which you hold yourself is, Winifred dear," Ivy said. "But not everyone is so capable as you."

"We must learn from the mistakes of others, Ivy," Winifred said. "That is the only reason I condone paying attention—close attention—to what is happening in the private lives of others."

"Private lives should be just that," I said, unable to hold my tongue any longer. "No good comes of spreading gossip."

"Emily, you can't possibly mean to accuse me of being a gossip!" Her eyes opened wide. "I make these observations only to help my friends because I care about them so deeply. I see all around me the tragedies that can befall those who are not vigilant, and only want to protect those dear to me from suffering a similar fate."

"What an interesting position," I said, realizing the futility of arguing with someone like Winifred. "What do you think, then, of this person terrorizing society with his red paint?"

"I cannot approve, of course," she said. "But I think we'd all have to admit he's catalyzed a welcome change in people's behavior. Who will embark on a bad course of action when he knows he might face exposure and censure?"

"So you believe secrets should be told?" I asked.

"I make no judgment on that," she said. "But I do think we should look within ourselves during this time. I've heard rumors the situation will escalate soon, and you've not exactly led a blameless life, Emily. A bit more caution on your part might be something you should consider."

Wickedness. Her eyes narrowed and beamed undiluted wickedness.

"Oh, Winifred, don't be hard on Emily," Ivy said. "She's my dearest friend! You won't find a more devoted, smarter, or more passionate lady in all of London."

"Passionate, Ivy, isn't a quality you should be discussing," Winifred said. "Its connotation is not what you think."

That was quite enough for me. "Mrs. Harris," I said. "Ivy is perfectly aware of the connotations of the word *passionate*. She's not some simpering fool in need of social guidance."

"I've never suggested any such thing! This is an outrageous accusation, Lady Emily."

"You might find yourself in happier circumstances if you'd treat those around you with more respect," I said.

"I can't remember when I've been so insulted."

"Most likely because you're not accustomed to it being done to your face," I said. "Forgive me, Ivy. I've had my fill of riding today."

I pulled on the reins and turned my horse back towards home. I did not regret what I'd done, but neither did I look forward to the social discomfort it was sure to bring. As I reflected further on the subject, my mind began to change on this point. I was tired of forced politeness, tired of maintaining the appearance of friendship with people who deserved censure.

This was, I realized, similar to Winifred's position. But we came at it from opposite directions—I from that of being more interested in reveling in the good in people and not wasting time with those who had none to offer, while she preferred slander and mockery. I'd never once heard her compliment anyone. When had a kind word ever escaped her hard lips? Misery was her trade and I wanted no part of it.

I handed my horse over to a waiting groom and headed straight for my husband's study, not bothering to change out of my riding clothes, and flung myself into a chair. Colin, his head bent over his favorite book of chess problems, spoke without looking up.

"Was that an exasperated fling or an exuberant one?"

"Exasperated."

He moved the white rook from his John Company set forward three spaces, closed the book, and sat next to me. "Tell me."

I blew out a long breath before launching into the story. He listened attentively, his face without expression, until I reached the end. He then dropped his head into his hands and shook with mirth.

"Oh, Emily, I do adore you," he said. "I know you'll suffer in some circles for what you've done, but not in circles we care about. It's time someone told off that biddy. Her sanctimoniousness is unbearable."

"I'm through with all of it," I said. "I'm perfectly content if we surround ourselves with wonderful and socially unacceptable eccentric friends instead of accepting boring invitations to boring parties filled with boring people."

"Do we have any socially unacceptable friends?"

"Lady Glover?" I asked.

"She's borderline, I'd say."

"We shall have to try harder to find someone truly offensive," I said. "How is your work progressing?"

"Not so well as I'd like," he said, running a hand through his thick hair. "I've discovered nothing out of sorts in Dillman's business dealings."

"And those things he was doing for the government?"

"They don't appear to have been disrupted. We've reassigned them to another company and shall keep a careful eye on what happens next."

"I could help you better if you gave me some details."

"Not possible," he said. "But you know that I'll call you in as soon as I can. What would you like to do this afternoon? I've a few hours free from work."

"I rather fancy a stroll through the Royal Academy," I said, knowing

I could trust him to include me in the investigation when it was appropriate. "We've not yet seen the Summer Exhibition."

Davis entered the room with a single letter on a small silver tray. I picked it up and noticed immediately bright yellow wax sealed it. I opened it in a swift motion, eager to identify the sender.

"Apparently I've greatly angered Mrs. Harris," I said. "She must have written this the moment she reached home. It's a scathing attack on the many flaws of my character." I passed the note to Colin, my hand shaking slightly. Her vitriol upset me, and I could not help but wonder if she was capable of more than just nasty words.

"I grant you it's an interesting coincidence, but she's hardly the only person in London to use yellow sealing wax," Colin said. He'd bustled me off to the Royal Academy almost as soon as I'd put down Mrs. Harris's note. He didn't like to dwell on petty nastiness.

"I've never seen anyone else use it."

"If you were a crazed murderer, would you not be more careful?" he asked. "I should reserve a separate color wax for my personal correspondence and keep back another for anything related to my crimes."

"I'd use the same because even the Crown's best agent would think it was too obvious and remove me from his list of suspects."

"You're good, Emily." He stopped in front of a large canvas. "What do you think of this?"

I stepped closer to the painting, a stunning portrait of Lady Glover by John Singer Sargent. She wore a red velvet dress, cut dramatically low, three long strands of pearls draped around her neck and hanging down to below her tiny waist. A sheer white shawl dangled from one elbow, and she leaned with the other on an elaborate marble mantelpiece.

"She certainly has motivation," I said. "Society's been cruel to her. She's plenty of motive to lash out against the *ton*."

"I wanted to know your opinion of the painting, not of the lady." He took a step back. "Sargent is bloody good, isn't he?"

"He is." I nodded. "You don't think Lady Glover could be our culprit?"

"As you said, she's plenty of motive. But I'd need to find a connection with Dillman."

"There's something about this correspondence of hers," I said. "It doesn't ring quite true."

"You think she's invented it?"

"No, I suppose that wouldn't make sense," I said. "I can't identify what it is that troubles me, but it doesn't seem right. She tried to suggest Mr. Barnes might be behind it."

Colin laughed. "Barnes wouldn't need so flimsy an excuse to start writing to her. She's not exactly fierce with her suitors."

"Should you call them suitors?" I asked, my eyes wide. "She's a married woman."

"Yes, well, the hypocrisy does make things difficult, doesn't it?" Colin asked. "But what else is one to call the blokes vying for her attention?"

We continued to make our way through the galleries. The skylights in the ceilings, above the elaborate plasterwork on the tops of the walls, bathed the rooms in brightness. The crowds were so thick we nearly had to push our way through the enormous wooden doorways between rooms, and we soon decided to explore some of the less popular sections of Burlington House.

It was a strategy that proved extremely pleasant until we reached a door blocked by two policemen.

"What's going on here?" Colin asked, pulling out his identification.

"Vandalism last night, Mr. Hargreaves," one of the guards said. "Thugs have destroyed a painting."

"Thugs?" Colin asked. "Let me see."

With no hesitation, they opened the door and took us inside.

"Why wasn't I notified of this at once?" Colin said.

Before us hung a canvas bathed almost entirely in all-too-familiar red. Splatters of paint had hit the wall around the work and dribbled down to the floor, where it puddled in a sticky mess. It had been applied in such quantity it was difficult to determine what the original picture had depicted. I moved forward, careful to lift my skirts to keep them clean, and read the card on the wall.

"William Handler, Portrait of Mrs. Samuel Tubney."

"Which one of them is the target?" Colin asked.

"Or is it both?" I turned to the police. "Was anything else damaged in the attack?"

"No, Lady Emily," the taller one said. "Just this. They came in through a window on the ground floor and didn't touch anything else. Scotland Yard were here this morning, Mr. Hargreaves. They can give you a full update, but I'm afraid there won't be much to it."

"We'll look around a bit more, if you don't mind. Can you direct me to the window?" Colin asked.

19 June 1893
Belgrave Square, London

I called on Cordelia this afternoon. She remains most distressed over the loss of her fiancé, so distressed I fear for her very sanity. She's barely coherent and utterly on edge. It's not surprising; what she's suffered is intolerable. But I found, as we spoke, that I was becoming increasingly upset by the villain in all this. Mr. Dillman is dead. His house had been painted. Yet we've no hint as to what merited this treatment. What did he do? The paint has proven to be a precursor to the revelation of a ruinous secret. Or has it?

Lord Musgrave took his own life before anyone breathed a word of what his scandal was. Now that he's gone, we still know nothing. Has the culprit lost interest in smearing Lord Musgrave's name? Was his death enough to satisfy the cruelty of this man? The Riddingtons are still waiting, wondering when some sordid detail of their life will be exposed. Is their nemesis hoping one of them, too, will choose suicide over shame?

But what of Mr. Dillman? Who killed him? Surely not the same person who's responsible for the paint? Why would he have bothered with the paint at all if he were planning to kill the man? My mind reels trying to figure it out. Emily's so quick when it comes to these things. I'm glad no one has to rely on me for finding the answers.

Except this answer. Are some sins so great they merit execution rather than exposure? Is that why Mr. Dillman died? And if so, what makes a sin that heinous? Could mine be considered so?

I fear even to write these words in my happy home, where my daughter, so innocent, plays. I don't want to bring such ugliness to her world. How I wish I could hide forever from what I've done.

12

Once Colin was satisfied we'd gathered everything useful we could from the Royal Academy, he headed for Scotland Yard while I set off on an errand of my own. I was worried about Cordelia Dalton and had made a point of calling on her every few days since her fiancé's death. The Daltons' house was quiet and dark when I arrived—too many closed velvet curtains—and a servant set off to fetch Cordelia from her bedroom. The poor girl was like a prisoner. When she entered the gloomy sitting room, I hardly recognized her. Her dress hung on her—she must have lost a stone in the past weeks—and her face, gaunt and dull, looked ten years older than when I'd seen her last.

"Cordelia!" I could not help leaping up and embracing her. "How are you managing?"

She didn't say anything, but twisted and twisted her black-hemmed handkerchief.

"Has something happened?"

"No. No. Not a thing." She twisted harder. "Would you like tea? Ivy was just here, but she didn't want any. She'd be sorry to have missed you."

"I don't require any tea, thank you," I said. I could see she was biting the inside of her cheek. "Are you quite sure nothing else has happened? Please, Cordelia, my husband and I can't help you if you don't keep us au courant of the situation."

She burst into tears and collapsed onto a settee. I sat next to her and put a hand on her back, rubbing softly.

"Have you received another letter?" I asked.

"Three," she managed to gasp between sobs.

"Three?" I did my best to hide the chagrin I was feeling. Making her feel worse wouldn't help at all.

"I wanted to tell you. I did. Truly," she said, keeping her head buried in her hands. "But he insisted I couldn't. Said if I informed anyone he'd kill my mother."

Now I was angry, but not at Cordelia. How dare this person torment her so?

"What else did he say?"

"In the first, he chastised me for not coming to the meeting he'd demanded. Do you remember?"

"Yes," I said. Colin and I had told her in no uncertain terms not to even consider going to the park in such circumstances.

"In the second, he said how important it was that I do what he tells me and that I not share any of what he wrote with anyone else or the consequences, as I explained, would be dire. The third came yesterday. He's insisting upon meeting me tonight, and says that if I don't succumb to his wishes untold evil will befall me."

"It sounds as if his imagination has failed him," I said. "Where does he want you to go?"

"The same place. Achilles."

"You're not to go," I said.

"But he'll—"

"Stop, Cordelia. Think carefully. This man has already killed once. He believes you to be in possession of something that could harm him, some evidence that he wants you to return to him, correct?"

"Yes."

"You don't know what it is?"

"No." Her voice was small.

"So what would you do if you met him? Give him nothing? What would he do to you then?"

"We could invent something . . . something I could give him to satisfy his wishes."

"We have not even the vaguest notion of what that would be. Unless you're hiding something from me?"

"No, I swear I'm not." She started to cry again. "I've already told you everything and now he'll—"

"He won't do a thing. Mr. Hargreaves wouldn't allow it." We did have to do something, but I wasn't sure what. "So long as this man believes you are in possession of this information, he won't harm you. If he did, he'd have lost his way to recover it."

"But if I do nothing—"

"You cannot go. Don't even consider it. How would you even get out of the house? Your father would never allow it."

"He would if he thought my mother was in danger."

"I'll go in your place," I said. "And I'll take Colin with me. We'll confront whoever is there—I doubt it will be the man himself—and do whatever it takes to stop you from suffering further torment."

"Do you really think it would work?" she asked.

"I'm absolutely confident."

She seemed to believe me.

If only I could convince myself.

Colin was less put off by my scheme than I'd expected. He read the letters—Cordelia had let me take them—and agreed we had few other viable options. The meeting was scheduled for ten o'clock, a time when almost no one would be in the park. Thankfully, it would still be light out, but nonetheless, I felt slightly nervous about the undertaking. With Meg's help, I put on one of the mourning dresses I'd stored away years ago and fixed a black veiled bonnet to my head. It was unlikely anyone who knew Cordelia would mistake me for her, but if our villain had sent someone in his stead, it was possible I could pull off the deceit.

Colin left the house well ahead of me, dining at the Reform Club instead of at home, to confuse anyone who might be watching us. He would make his way to the park early, and set himself up in a hiding place well before I—or our adversary—would arrive. Cordelia would have taken a carriage from her house, so though it was somewhat ridiculous to drive so short a distance, I did it nonetheless, taking two footmen with me. One of them I brought with me to the sculpture while the other waited at the gate to the park. There was no one else in sight.

"That's fine, leave me here and go back to the gate," I said to my loyal servant. "This miscreant can't expect a lady to come out at night completely unescorted."

He did as he was told and I stood, alone, at the base of the hulking statue George III had installed to honor the Duke of Wellington's numerous victories in the Napoleonic Wars. It had caused a furor when first erected earlier in the century, a furor that stopped only when a strategically placed fig leaf was added to the piece, giving the Greek hero—I use the term loosely—a more socially acceptable appearance. Not even Achilles was above the vexation of society.

I kept my back to the sculpture, not wanting to leave myself more exposed than necessary, and waited, wondering where Colin was sequestered. I checked my watch. It was nearly ten o'clock, and there was no sign of anyone coming to meet me. I smoothed my heavy skirts, remembering what it had been like to wear them daily, all those years ago, after the death of my first husband.

I started, thinking I'd heard footsteps, but could see no one approaching. My heart pounded, but I knew I was safe under Colin's watchful eye. Knowing and feeling are two different things, though, and my nerves were not soothed by the confidence my head had in my husband. I looked around, searching for any hint of where he might be hidden. His options seemed limited, unless he'd been willing to climb a tree. I found no evidence of him. Not that I would have expected otherwise.

My vigil continued. Then, in the distance, I saw a woman coming towards me. She was walking up the path from the south, which meant she'd not entered the park through the Achilles Gate as I had done. At first, she was a mere wisp of a figure. I could almost believe I was imagining her. As she came closer, though, she scared me. Her boots fell heavy on the ground, despite the fact she was a small woman, a good six inches shorter than I and painfully thin. She looked to be about my age, but the years were written harder on her face than mine. Her mouth was pinched, her nose ordinary, but her eyes, brown and luminous, shone like unearthly gems. She faltered as she approached, reached a hand into the pocket of her coarse skirt, and pulled out a note, which she shoved towards me.

I reached out and took it from her.

Give the girl what you know I want.

The handwriting matched the notes Cordelia had received.

In turn, I handed the girl the letter we'd had Cordelia write in response to her correspondent's unwanted attentions:

I should like nothing more than to offer you whatever necessary to drive you away from me. But, alas, Mr. Dillman left nothing for me that would satisfy your needs. Furthermore, he never spoke of any involvement with a person such as yourself, and I find myself quite at a loss as to what to do.

Please leave me alone.

The girl pulled the envelope from me roughly and glared at me. She did not open it.

"How does he keep hold on you?" I asked. "Does he threaten you? Is he cruel?"

She did not reply.

"Come with me," I said. "We can help you break free from him."

She gave no response, made not even the slightest change in her expression. It was as if she didn't comprehend my words. I tried again, this time in French.

And then in Italian.

And then in my extremely bad German. Which, to be fair, few people would have been able to understand.

Before I resorted to ancient Greek, my attention was diverted by a loud crash coming from behind me. Without thinking, I spun around, and then turned back. The girl remained expressionless.

"Stay there, Emily!" I heard Colin call from a distance. "Do not move."

I heard the sound of fist against flesh. Grunts and strained breath. Too-heavy steps and sharp kicks.

The girl didn't move or react. It was as if she'd heard none of it. And so I, too, stood still, not wanting to alert her to any trouble lest she decide to run. The hideous sounds sickened me, and I prayed Colin was not too badly hurt. My stomach wrenched as I heard him groan. The girl nodded at me and turned, starting off in the direction from which she'd come.

"Grab her!" Colin shouted.

I ran towards her, at first unsure of what to do. Then, thinking as quickly as I could, I dropped down and flung my whole body weight against the backs of her knees. She crumpled over. I rolled on top of her, forced my arms around her shoulders, and held her as tightly as I could.

And then I shouted for the footmen, who came running at once.

In short order, I'd directed one of them to help me secure my prisoner and the other to assist my husband, whom I suspected, from the dearth of sound now coming from his direction, had subdued his attacker. I forced the girl into the carriage, having tied her wrists together behind her back with the veil I'd ripped from my bonnet. The footman sat next to her, ensuring she would not try to escape. Knowing she was secure, I raced back into the park in search of my husband.

He was already on his way to me, pulling his assailant with him, the footman behind, prodding the man along.

"You're hurt!" I said. He was limping and his lip was split. Blood spilled down his chin.

"Nothing serious. Let's get to the carriage. You can worry about me later." In short order, he'd pushed the squat, sturdy man inside, across from the girl. He left the footman next to her and took the seat adjacent to the man, ordering me to sit outside with the driver. "It will be safer, Emily," he said, helping me up to the seat and then disappearing inside to look after our prisoners.

"Scotland Yard, eh, madam?" Our driver, a jolly sort, grinned as he snapped the reins and we lurched forward. "Can't say that's a place I've ever been before. 'Course, that's due to the master generally driving himself."

I appreciated his attempt at cheerfulness, and wished it could calm my heart, which was pounding so hard I could feel it through my entire body.

"You're all right there, madam?"

"I am."

"Exciting times, these, when you work for Mr. Hargreaves. Or are married to him, I expect."

"Yes," I said. My teeth were chattering.

"Keeps a man on his toes, it does. You're sure you're all right?"

"A bit shaken up, but that's all."

"You're a brave lady, madam," he said. "Mr. Hargreaves is lucky to have you."

"Did you see anything when we were in the park?" I asked.

"Not a thing, madam. Just the usual carriages going along Park Lane. Nobody came in or out of the gate."

We were heading down the Mall, and I could not help notice the irony of our current situation. I, sitting with my driver, parading down such an elegant street; my husband inside our carriage with two criminals. Soon we'd turned into Whitehall and were nearly upon New Scotland Yard. I grew nervous again as the gothic façade rose before us, its red brick taking on an eerie shade of rust in the moonlight. The moment we stopped, an officer stepped forward from the door, spoke to Colin, and ushered the lot of us inside.

13

Scotland Yard was exactly how I'd always imagined it: desks piled with heaps of papers, earnest-looking Detective Inspectors bent over their work. Almost as soon as we arrived, Colin disappeared with our prisoners, and our servants were taken to another room for questioning. I was shown to a small office where, plied with tea and repeated enquires after my health, I felt a world away from what had transpired in the park. Nearly two hours passed before my husband returned.

"Ready to go home?" he asked.

"Tell me what's happening first," I said.

He sat in front of me on the edge of a large desk. "They're both deaf," he said. "We brought in language specialists who are schooled in French sign language, but neither of them showed any knowledge of it. They can't read or write, either."

"Do they communicate with each other?"

"They must," he said. "But they were careful not to in our presence."

"What will be done with them?" I asked.

"We'll detain them for further observation and will follow them when they're released."

"I want to go with you."

"I'd welcome the company," he said. "Particularly now that I know your tackling skills."

"How badly are you hurt?" I asked, gently touching his swollen lip.

"Not at all. He got the worse of it. I'll be fine in the morning." He took my hands in his. "What about you?"

"Shaken up, but unharmed," I said.

"It was brilliant how you tackled her," he said. "I was beaming with pride."

"You shouldn't have been watching . . . that's probably when he split your lip."

"It was, in fact. But I wouldn't have missed it for anything."

I found patience difficult over the following days as we waited for Scotland Yard to finish observing our attackers. As a result, I rejoiced when I received a note from Mr. Barnes, asking that I call on him at his office. The day was fine, and I was eager to go out, so I walked to Westminster, arriving far earlier than necessary. Glad for the extra time, I went halfway across the bridge so that I might look back at the spectacular view of the Thames sparkling in the sun and Parliament rising majestic above it. As Big Ben chimed the hour, I made my way back and found my friend.

Mr. Barnes's office was small, but well furnished, in one of the narrower corridors of the building. He greeted me with warmth, but did not offer me a seat. "Thank you for coming to me, Lady Emily. I realize it's something of an imposition."

"Not at all," I said. "It's a pleasure to see you."

"I was hoping we could take tea somewhere if you've no objection? The subject I wish to discuss is somewhat sensitive. I'd feel more comfortable away from so many offices."

"The Savoy isn't far from here," I said. "And it's a fine day to walk along the river." I took the arm he offered and we dropped onto Victoria

Embankment, making our way along the river past Cleopatra's Needle, where the pharaoh's quixotic sphinxes seemed to follow us with eyes that should have been immovable. The river curved and St. Paul's rose majestically in the distance. We entered Savoy Hill, not taking the fastest route, perhaps, but to my mind the most picturesque, and paused to admire the charming gardens attached to a small chapel, all that remained of a hospital that had thrived hundreds of years ago only to fall in the way of construction, when the land was needed to build the approach to Waterloo Bridge. After continuing up to the Strand and reaching the hotel and securing a fine table in a quiet corner of the restaurant, which was illuminated with twinkling electric lights, we looked over the menu in silence. As we'd discussed nothing beyond the weather and the view while we walked, I started to wonder if my friend had changed his mind about talking to me. But once we'd placed our orders and the waiter had departed, Mr. Barnes began to speak, his voice as soft and melodic as ever.

"Forgive me if I'm blunt, Lady Emily," he said. "I know your reputation well. You're an asset to your husband in his work, and for that, we're all grateful. Not that I'm in a position to officially speak for the government, of course." He smiled.

"Thank you," I said.

"I'm hoping you can put my mind to ease on a subject that's been causing me much grief. I'm concerned about a mutual friend of ours: Mr. Foster."

"Has something happened to him?" I asked. "Not red paint, I hope?"

"No, not as yet," he said. "But I'm gravely worried. I must insist that you keep the details of this conversation private, even from your husband. Mr. Foster is an honorable, upstanding man. But everyone makes mistakes."

"What sort of mistakes?"

"Politics are not always pretty, Lady Emily. A gentleman sometimes is forced to take steps which, when taken out of context, seem unethical. I'm not asking you to embroil yourself in the details," he said. "But I would very much appreciate it if you could keep me abreast of any developments in your investigation that involve Mr. Foster."

"You think he's behind the red paint?"

"Heavens, no! I never meant to give you that idea," he said. "But if he falls victim to this madman, I'd like as much notice as possible."

"Everyone would know the instant paint was spotted on his house," I said.

"You may discover a pattern in what's happening, something that leads you to believe he'll be a target. If you do, would you please let me know at once?"

"Of course," I said. "That's no problem at all. But so far, we've registered no such pattern. There seems to be no method to this madness."

"There must be some method," he said. "We all have things to hide, yet not all of us are being targeted. How is he choosing his victims?"

"I don't know."

"I don't mean to put any undue pressure on you. Mr. Foster is poised to be our next prime minister. I don't want to see his position threatened."

"Despite his slips when it comes to ethics?"

"As I said before, they only appear negative when viewed out of context. I hope you'll trust me on the matter."

"I have no reason not to," I said. "And I shall certainly let you know if I think his reputation is about to be compromised."

"Thank you." His shoulders sagged with relief. "I know it's unlikely I can stop any damage, but one does like to feel one has tried everything possible."

"Mr. Foster is lucky to have such a friend," I said.

"He's as good to me as I am to him. No brothers could be closer." Our waiter appeared with steaming pots of tea, jugs of creamy milk, and a gorgeous assortment of delicate pastries. "Well, that's enough of that, isn't it?" he asked once the man was gone. "Who could stay worried in the face of such delights? Have I told you Mrs. Brandon has evil designs on me? She's bound and determined to put an end to my bachelorhood. She's all the makings of a great lady."

"Indeed she does," I said. "A kinder person none of us will ever meet."

Later that night, Colin and I were sitting in the library, enjoying a peaceful evening at home. We'd decided to forgo all invitations, including one from Lady Glover, who had sent a second note imploring that we come to her. I found our second refusal more liberating than the first, but did send a reply inviting her to dine with us another time.

"Any further word yet on our attackers?" I asked as I sketched a fifth-century Athenian panel we'd hung in the room. It showed the three graces, each more elegant than the last, dancing in front of an olive tree.

"They're still being observed by Scotland Yard," Colin said. "You'll know the instant they're released."

"Cordelia's heard nothing more from their master," I said. "I spoke to her this afternoon. I also had an extremely interesting conversation with Mr. Barnes."

"Do tell."

"He's concerned about Mr. Foster. Apparently your friend has ventured into ethically gray areas on occasion."

"Such as?" Colin asked.

"Mr. Barnes wouldn't say. But he asked that I let him know if we think Mr. Foster is to be targeted by our villain. He claims Mr. Foster's done nothing bad, only that it might look that way if taken out of context."

"Barnes has been looking after Foster since before I arrived at Eton. He's not going to lose the habit anytime soon. He has high moral standards and is meticulous to the extreme. He's just being careful."

"Maybe," I said.

"Aren't we home to enjoy each other, not to discuss work?" Colin asked. "I've much better things planned for you tonight."

"Do you?" I asked, smiling and sliding closer to him. "That's exceedingly good news. When will you set your plan in motion?"

Before he could respond, Davis entered the room. "The Duke of Bainbridge to see you, madam." Jeremy appeared behind him, grinning as he handed our butler his top hat and walking stick.

"Hiding out at home, are you?" he asked, peeling off his gloves. "I was counting on seeing you at Lady Glover's tonight."

"Emily's bent on keeping me all to herself," Colin said.

"Dreadful girl." Jeremy flopped onto a chair and pulled the white silk scarf from around his neck. Davis collected it and the gloves and bowed as he left the room. "She has no heart."

"What brings you to us?" Colin asked.

"Ennui," Jeremy said. "Is not this the most tedious season you can remember?"

"How can you say that?" I asked. "With all this red paint?"

"Stuff and nonsense," he said. "How am I to get excited about something from which I've been entirely excluded? What's a chap got to do to be singled out? Am I not profligate enough?"

"One would have thought so," Colin said.

"You should be glad to have escaped notice," I said.

"People are going to start talking," Jeremy said. "I have a reputation to uphold. I'm half tempted to paint my own steps."

"And expose your own scandal?" Colin asked.

"It's crossed my mind more than once," Jeremy said. "But I get hung up every time when trying to decide which of my myriad secrets I should make public."

"You're ridiculous," I said. "But you do raise an interesting point. Why haven't you been targeted?"

"Em, it warms my heart that at last you've taken notice of my bad behavior."

"You've remained unmolested, Bainbridge, because of the nature of your sins," Colin said. "You have, shall we say, an affection for the ladies, but you never trifle with anyone's heart. You never interfere where you ought not, and you don't fall prey to the temptations that might cause a real downfall."

"Opium dens, yes," Jeremy said. "I did try once, but found the whole experience excruciatingly boring. Perhaps I should have made a more concerted effort. If I became a slave to the dreaded stuff, would you try to rescue me, Em?"

"I'd leave you to rot," I said.

He sighed. "How you wound me."

Colin shifted in his chair. "Don't you have anywhere else to go tonight, Bainbridge?"

"Hargreaves, don't give me a hard time," he said. "You've won the heart of the most devoted girl in England and made her your wife. All I get is the occasional chance to flirt with her. Don't take it away from me, I beg you. It would be an unnecessary cruelty."

"No, I suppose I mustn't stop you," Colin said. "I'd be sending you straight into the arms of vice."

"Quite right," Jeremy said. "And you're too much of a gentleman to relegate me to such horrors, despite being a Cambridge man." He pulled two cigars out of his jacket pocket and passed one to my husband. "The best I've ever found."

Colin took a deep sniff and nodded appreciatively. "I'm impressed, Bainbridge. This is worth a flirtation."

"None for me?" I asked.

"Davis specifically forbade me when I entered the house," Jeremy said. "He's very stern, your butler."

"Heaven forbid a duke would go against the wishes of a butler," I said.

"I wouldn't dream of it," he said. "I know who runs this household. He might refuse me admittance, and I can't risk that. And at any rate,

I've not come entirely to complain about my general boredom and disappointment. I've business as well."

Colin very nearly snorted.

"Scoff if you will, Hargreaves," Jeremy said. "But I've had a very strange run-in with Mrs. Winifred Harris, Ivy Brandon's miserable friend."

My husband sat forward in his seat. "You have my attention. Why didn't you tell us this right away?"

"Lead with business?" Jeremy asked. "Can you think of something more soul-crushing?"

"What happened?" Colin asked.

"I was in the park when she accosted me."

"Accosted you?" I asked. "Winifred Harris?"

"Accosted may, perhaps, be too strong a word," Jeremy said. "But she cornered me at the edge of the Serpentine and left me no way to escape without plunging into the water. She's quite tall, you know. I feared for my safety. We had a very strange conversation in which she told me she's heard that Cordelia Dalton is in danger."

"And she said this apropos nothing?" Colin asked.

"Yes," Jeremy said. "She took me by the arm and spoke in a voice laced with the most tasteless melodrama. Said she'd overheard a gentleman of dubious reputation threatening the girl."

"Threatening her how?" I asked.

"She was vague about the specifics," he said, "but insisted Miss Dalton will find herself well in harm's way."

"Because of this gentleman?" I asked. Jeremy nodded. "Who is he?"

"She wouldn't give up the name. But I must say, I didn't entirely believe her. She did make me fear for Miss Dalton's safety, but not because of some mysterious interloper. It felt like she was making a confession to me."

"You think she's the one threatening Miss Dalton?" Colin asked.

Jeremy threw up his hands. "I've not the slightest idea. I merely pass along what I heard in the hopes it would be of interest to you."

"It is," Colin said. "And I thank you, though Emily may not. I'm afraid I'll have to leave you both so that I might look further into this matter."

"Can I offer you any assistance?" I asked.

"Not right now, Emily," he said. "But count on me requiring it later."

22 June 1893
Belgrave Square, London

My subterfuge is beginning to take a toll on those around me. Robert asked me, in jest, if I was afraid our house would be painted red. I completely overreacted, and now he's convinced something's happened to make me doubt him. It never occurred to him the paint would be left because of something I'd done.

He's being doubly attentive now, spending less time at his club, and taking a more active interest in little Rose. Instead of just coming up to the nursery to tell her good night, he's taken to having Nurse bring her to the drawing room so that he might play with her before tea. It's quite sweet, but I can't enjoy it altogether, knowing that it was prompted by misunderstanding.

How did I let things come to this?

14

"Winifred?" Ivy's light eyes widened so much I worried they might pop out of her head. "You think she would harm Cordelia Dalton?"

We were sitting in her garden, eating vanilla ices and watching her little daughter bat at flowers and take tentative, wobbly steps in unsuccessful efforts to catch the butterflies that darted amongst the blooms. Rose's chestnut curls were a miniature version of her mother's, as were her pink cheeks and slender nose.

"I'm not entirely sure," I said. "But she's judgmental to the point of being vindictive. It wouldn't be a leap for her to want to take matters into her own hands."

"You can't possibly think she'd have murdered Mr. Dillman?"

"Her words are awfully bold," I said. "And hurtful. I could well believe she has more than just them in her arsenal. The conversation she had with Jeremy rattled him. Will you poke around for me and see if she's up to anything? You know I can't call on her after that disastrous ride we had in the park."

"She's still furious with you," Ivy said. "But everyone's on edge at the moment. It's unbearable, all of this. I'm tired of the constant tension. The Riddingtons' house was splashed red weeks ago and they're still waiting for their secret to be revealed. They've been on pins and needles so long it's almost inhuman. How much longer will they be tormented?"

"I don't know how they're bearing it," I said.

"And I can't get poor Lady Musgrave out of my mind. How she's suffered! And for what? The villain never exposed her husband's secret. I've heard rumors that more than one gentleman has threatened to do himself a harm rather than risk seeing his door painted red."

"The scandal would be just as bad."

"Perhaps," Ivy said. "But they wouldn't be around to suffer the consequences."

"What a debacle," I said. "And a definite sign of weak character. Do what you can to learn more about Winifred. At least you can take comfort in the fact that you're taking action rather than being a passive observer."

I was home for less than half an hour before Colin burst into the library and commanded me to follow him. He'd bustled me into the waiting carriage before I'd had time even to secure my hat.

"We'll be dropped at Scotland Yard," he said. "And then proceed on foot. Our attackers are about to be released."

"You came back specially to get me?"

"You said you wanted to come. I promised I wouldn't go without you."

"I adore you," I said. "What's our strategy?"

"It won't be complicated," he said. "We'll follow at a discreet distance. I don't think they'll make it difficult for us."

"They were ready to make it difficult in the park."

"Their time under guard was not pleasant. They'll be focused on nothing but getting home."

I winced, uncomfortable at the thought of their detention. Not that they hadn't deserved it. But a dark cell, not enough food, and harsh treatment combined with the heavy silence in which the couple lived must have been deeply unpleasant.

"One of my colleagues brought them back for a final attempt at questioning. It was to no avail, but worth a try," Colin said, and then called to our driver. "Stop here, please."

We alighted from the vehicle. Colin motioned for me to open my parasol, which I did. He positioned it so our faces could not be seen by anyone exiting Scotland Yard, but still allowed him a sliver of sight between it and the brim of his top hat.

"That's them," he said. We waited twenty beats before following and crossed the street to the other side. This gave us a better view of the couple, who looked even more browbeaten and dingier than they had in the park. I winced, but there was no time for compassion at the moment. We increased our pace to match theirs.

They kept their heads down as they passed the edge of St. James's Park and then turned onto the Strand, their postures looking more relaxed as they moved farther east. By the time St. Paul's loomed well behind us and the Tower was long past, they'd begun to move with easy fluidity. The same could not be said for me.

We'd been walking for an inordinate length of time, nearly an hour, and while we were still in London, it was like no London I'd known before. The streets of the East End were filthy, the houses grim, the pavements filled with pedestrians in shades of gray. Not just their clothes, but their skin and hair, even their eyes seemed to lack color. A small boy ran towards us and grabbed at my skirts, pleading for me to give him money. Colin pressed some coins into his hands, and brightness flooded the child's face, washing away the gray. His eyes were blue; I couldn't see that before. My heart ached as he disappeared into a shadow-filled alley. He wouldn't be going home to high tea and a soft bed.

We let our quarry slip farther ahead of us as the streets narrowed and our clothing set us apart from the others with whom we shared the pavement. Another quarter of a mile later, they pulled open the door of a large building. Colin stepped back and peered up at the letters above the door.

"A match factory," he said. He didn't immediately follow them inside. Instead, he took me by the arm and marched me around the perimeter of the building. Long windows lined the seemingly endless brick walls of the largely nondescript structure. Even though the windows were closed, clouds of a hideous, sulfurous odor oozed from them, the scent so strong I pressed a handkerchief to my nose. We went back to the door, opened it, and stepped in.

The entrance had nothing to recommend it beyond an increasingly strong smell of sulphur and some other odor I didn't recognize. The paint on the walls was peeling, the floors covered with dirt and grit. There was no sign of our miscreants. We walked through a door labeled OFFICE and soon were sitting across from a red-faced, portly man who was clearly suffering from the heat of the day. He'd removed his jacket, and his shirtsleeves were in a disastrous state. He wiped his sweaty brow with the back of his hand, then wiped his hand on his trousers.

"Mr. Majors at your service. What can I do for you, sir?" he asked.

"You've two employees who've just arrived back after some days away," Colin said. "I'd like to know more about them."

"Can't say I know what you're talking about."

My husband pulled out his identification. "They've been with Scotland Yard and weren't forthcoming in the least with our officers."

"Are they under arrest?"

"No," Colin said. "They were released after questioning."

"So why do you need them?"

"That's my business," Colin said.

The man shrugged and bellowed to a wiry-looking colleague in the next room. "Who was it what skived off work?"

"Useless Dodson and useless Florence." The other man didn't look up as he spoke.

"Are they related?" I asked. "Married?"

Our host, such as he was, snorted. "You bloody well ought to have noticed they don't speak. They're dumb, the both of them. You think I'm sitting with them for tea and asking if his affections are honorable?"

"Where do they live?" Colin asked.

"Here," Mr. Majors said. "We're a full-service establishment."

"They live here?" I asked. "In a factory?"

"It's a sight better than the workhouse, madam," he said. "All of them here are afflicted, you see. Families don't want 'em, but don't want 'em in the workhouse, either. So they give us their outdoor relief what the government gives 'em and we see to their needs. In exchange for some work, of course. Fair is as fair does."

"Can you put us in touch with their families?" I asked.

"They ain't got none, those two," Mr. Majors said.

"So how did you arrange to get their relief?" I asked.

"Like I've been telling you, madam, I keep them out of the workhouse. Nobody's going to argue with that."

"Do they have contact with anyone on the outside?" I asked.

"Those two got nobody who gives a toss about them," he said. "I only took them in because I was feeling soft when they turned up at the door on a snowy day last year. Let the Christmas spirit get the better of me, did I."

"You know nothing about their backgrounds?" Colin asked.

"Sir, if Scotland Yard couldn't get them to make sense, you think I can?" he asked. "I helped them apply for the benefit."

"How did you know their names if they couldn't speak?" I asked.

"They had a grubby sheet of paper with their details on it," he said. "From their family, I suppose. I've another deaf one as well, showed up in similar circumstances."

Colin's eyes narrowed. "Take us to their quarters," he said. "And I'm going to need to see the rest of your establishment as well."

Mr. Majors looked as if he'd like to grumble, but must have thought the better of it. He motioned for us to follow him as he picked up a gnarled walking stick that had been leaning against the wall.

"It's good there's somewhere better than the workhouse," I whispered, leaning close to Colin.

"This won't be better," he said. "It will be deeply unpleasant at best."

We entered an enormous room, the factory floor. The air hung so heavy with stink I struggled for breath. The workers were crowded in the space, some of them standing over large vats, stirring with wooden paddles as the contents bubbled over hot fires. Others sat at long benches, dipping the slim tips of wooden sticks into the malodorous mixture, then laying them out to be collected by another crew, who carried them to another room, presumably to dry. Colin and I were a curiosity here, and one of the dippers looked up and smiled, revealing a mouth devoid of all teeth. I did my best not to recoil.

"Phossy jaw," Mr. Majors said. "Still happens sometimes. It's the phosphorus what does it, mixed in with the sulphur. Not much we can do but remove their teeth."

"He's missing an arm as well," I said.

"Can't find work that way, can he? We're the only ones who'll take in people like him."

As I looked around, I saw that all of the workers—men and women, with a handful of children as well—had some sort of infirmity. Missing limbs, deformed facial features, club feet. The heat of the room pressed hard on me as I watched them work.

"How much do you pay them?" I asked.

"We take care of them, madam," Mr. Majors said. "Like I was telling you, their families give us their benefit. It's a service we're providing, you see."

"The government pays relief to families who keep their afflicted members at home," Colin said. "It keeps them from the workhouse and is cheaper in the end, I suppose."

"We give them medical care, too," Mr. Majors said. "Come see."

We followed him again, out of the main workroom, and I nearly retched when we crossed into what he called the infirmary. Rickety cots, their linens worn and dirty, were pushed so close together there was no space for a nurse to walk between them—not that there was a nurse anywhere to be seen. Every makeshift bed was full, and the stench in here were worse than that of the sulphur and phosphorus. This place smelled of death and decay, of blood and urine. Our presence was greeted with barely coherent moans as the patients struggled to sit up and reach for us. I didn't need to understand their words to know they needed help.

"Back down, the lot of you," Mr. Majors said, prodding the man nearest to him with his stick. "Leave your betters alone."

"Don't touch him," Colin said, his voice sharp. "Take us to Dobson and Florence."

Mr. Majors looked unimpressed. "As you will have it. But they won't be of any use to you, any more than they're of any use to me. I should throw them on the street after what they've done."

"You know what they've done?" I asked.

"They had a little holiday, didn't they? Sure enough got tangled up with Scotland Yard at the end, but it was a holiday, too. What makes you so interested? They take some of your fine jewels?"

"Do not speak to my wife in that tone," Colin said. "We're here on Crown business. You'll have enough trouble coming your way without standing in the way of my purpose."

"I wouldn't dream of doing such a thing," Mr. Majors said. "I'm running a fine establishment here. You seen a workhouse lately?"

Colin didn't reply, but glared at the man, who scurried along, leading us to a room directly above the one in which his employees made the matches. It was identical in size and shape, but instead of vats over fires and rows of dipping slabs, here were miserable little piles of bedding, laundry hanging from lines strung from wall to wall, and wobbly tables covered with the remains of what must have been a deeply unsatisfying luncheon.

"This is where they live?" I asked, searching the space for Dobson and Florence.

"They're right there," Mr. Majors said, motioning to two huddled figures in a corner. "Only useless toe rags not working." He crossed over to them and poked Dobson with his stick. "Back to work." His voice was loud although he knew the man couldn't hear him. "Now!"

The pair stood up, shirked when they saw us, and scuttled to the stairs.

"I don't like what you're doing here," Colin said. "You're exploiting these people."

"I keep saying—"

"I don't want to hear about the workhouse," Colin said, taking Mr. Majors firmly by the lapels. "You'll be hearing from me."

He pushed the round little man against the wall, took me firmly by the arm, and steered me back into the street.

"You're never coming here again," he said.

Agitation and despair had consumed me by the time we'd exited the building. We started to walk, both of us filled with rage at what Mr. Majors was doing. What had seemed an endless trek on the way there passed almost too quickly on our return. We'd reached the steps of St. Paul's and I still hadn't calmed down enough to speak. Though the day was warm, my teeth were chattering, so upset was I. How could anyone live in such conditions? How had I lived so long without being aware of how bad life could be? I pulled Colin into the church, needing an infusion of peace and beauty. We sat in silence close to the altar for three quarters of an hour, each of us mired in the darkness of what we'd seen. What could one do in such circumstances other than pray?

Take notes, apparently. Colin was scribbling furiously in his book.

"Ready to go home?" he asked, placing a tender hand on my arm. "I need to find out more about Mr. Majors's factory."

"Of course," I said, but didn't rise to my feet. "We have to do something, Colin. We can't let those poor people stay there. It's ... it's ... I don't care what it entails. I don't care if we have to take them into our home. Now that I've seen them, I cannot go on as if my world is the same as it was yesterday."

"I understand, Emily. But there's only so much we can do. Countless people live in similar conditions."

"How can you live, knowing that and doing nothing?" I asked.

He kept his eyes steady on mine. I remembered how, when we first met, this had unnerved me. Now I found it soothing. "I work to make the world more just. You're doing that now, too."

"But it's not helping those people."

"Change comes slowly," he said. "Especially when it comes to social justice."

"There must be more we can do," I said. "We have so much money."

"What would you like to do?"

"Can't we fund a home for them? Something that delivers on the promises Mr. Majors made to those families?"

"We can," he said. "But it will make a very small dent in the problem."

"It's better than no dent at all," I said. "I want to do something concrete that will make an immediate difference in their lives."

"I'll help you arrange it," he said, squeezing my hand. "I love you, Emily. And I love your compassion."

15

Colin headed straight for Scotland Yard after dropping me home. I retired to the library, pulled down my copy of Mary Elizabeth Braddon's *The Venetians,* and tried to settle in for a good read. Davis had opened the French doors in the back of the room, and the delicious breeze coming through them drew me to a chair with a beautiful view of our garden. It was a relief to have a break from the oppressive heat of the past weeks, but I couldn't escape a pang of guilt for enjoying these pleasant surroundings when I knew how those in the East End were living. I rang for a cup of tea and, after a few false starts, lost myself in our heroine's adventures.

So absorbed was I that I did not hear Davis enter the room. Nor, so he tells me, did I stir when he spoke. Nor when he stood two feet in front of me. It was only when he shook my shoulder that I looked up, still half in the dreamy world of reading, and saw him before me.

"Mr. Dalton has sent an urgent message for Mr. Hargreaves, madam. His man is waiting for your reply, which I told him is all he can have at the moment as the master is not at home."

I tore open the linen envelope and read: *Cordelia is gone. Please come at once.*

I slammed shut the book and rushed to the Daltons' waiting carriage. Their house was in an uproar. A parlor maid answered the door and moaned that she didn't know where Mr. Dalton was. The valet who'd summoned me berated her for her lack of decorum. I left them to argue and began to look for the family in the first-floor drawing rooms. Eventually, the butler found me—or I found him—and directed me to his master's study, where Cordelia's parents had sequestered themselves.

Her mother, wearing black in deference to her daughter's mourning, sat stick-straight on an overstuffed chair, her eyes red and swollen. Mr. Dalton had his back to her as he looked out the window.

"Where is Mr. Hargreaves?" Mrs. Dalton asked, her voice strained to the point of breaking.

"I'm afraid he's away," I said. "But I can help you."

"I don't think so," Mrs. Dalton said. "How would you begin to know what to do?"

"First tell me what's happened," I said. "Then I'll be able to tell you if I do know what to do. And I promise if I don't, I'll tell you that, too."

"She did save Robert Brandon," Mr. Dalton said. "I'm not inclined to dismiss her."

Part of the reason—perhaps the only reason—Robert allowed me to corrupt Ivy was the role I played in freeing him from an erroneous murder charge. He'd been accused of shooting his mentor, a man hated by nearly everyone in the empire. While he'd languished in Newgate, refusing to let his wife visit him, I'd traveled to Vienna in pursuit of clues I thought would lead me to the true killer. The crime proved at once more simple and more complicated than it looked, but in the end, my work led to his exoneration and release from prison.

Mr. Dalton's wife flung her hands into the air. "Who am I to argue? And what would be the point? You'd only do what you want, anyway."

Mr. Dalton did not respond to her outburst. "As you know, we've been keeping a close eye on Cordelia. We were vigilant before, but even more so once we knew about these letters she'd kept hidden from us.

We've read every piece of mail that's come for her, and have monitored all her visitors."

"Not that she's received many callers," her mother said. "It wouldn't be appropriate."

"Of course," I said. Heaven forbid the girl receive the comfort of too many friends after having suffered such a brutal loss. "Did she leave the house today?"

"No," her father said. "We've forced her to stay on the property. It seemed the safest course of action."

"No doubt it was," I said. "When did you notice she was missing?"

"She came down to breakfast—"

Mrs. Dalton interrupted her husband. "She was in better spirits than she'd been in so long."

"Had anything happened that might have explained the change in mood?" I asked.

"Her outlook improved after your husband captured those vagrants in the park. She said it gave her hope she'd see justice for her fiancé," Mr. Dalton said.

"Was there anything else?"

"Not of which I'm aware," he said. "Am I missing anything?" He turned to his wife.

"No," she said. "There's nothing else."

"Did you see her after breakfast?" I asked.

"She retired to her room for the better part of an hour, and then returned downstairs," Mrs. Dalton said. "We were both answering correspondence in my sitting room."

"Do you know to whom she was writing?"

"I'm afraid not," she said.

"Have the letters gone out?" I asked.

"Yes. I had several items that needed urgent sending. One of the footmen saw to it."

"I'll need to talk to him," I said. "What did she do after she finished her notes?"

"I'm afraid I'm not entirely sure," her mother said. "I should have been keeping better track."

"Were any of the servants watching her?" I asked.

"No," Mr. Dalton said. "We have someone outside her door all night, but I didn't think she'd be in such danger in the middle of the day."

"It's possible that she left of her own volition," I said. "And entirely reasonable for you to have been more concerned at night." This worried father didn't need cause to take more blame on himself.

"I saw her on the stairs around one o'clock," he said. "She had a book and a parasol. I assumed she was going into the garden to read. It's walled, though, so I didn't think it would prove problematic."

"One of the gardeners saw her soon thereafter," Mrs. Dalton said. "My husband's assumption was correct. She was sitting under a tree, reading."

"And after that?" I asked.

"I'm afraid we know nothing further." Mr. Dalton's voice choked. "Perhaps Mr. Hargreaves was right. We should have taken her abroad."

"There's no point considering what might have happened," I said, keeping my voice steady. "It's entirely possible the same thing would have occurred somewhere else. All that matters now is trying to find her. Have Scotland Yard been here and left already?"

"No," Mr. Dalton said. "We have not contacted them."

"You must—at once," I said.

"I'm afraid we can't." He handed me a sheet of paper. "This was underneath Cordelia's book."

Should you desire to ever see your daughter again, leave the police out of it. I shall contact you when I'm ready to converse.

"But you did try to contact my husband," I said.

"Mr. Hargreaves is not technically police," he said. "I've not disobeyed this villain."

This was correct, but I was more interested in the fact that the letter-writer had not mentioned us specifically—not due to an overblown sense of ego, but because he must have learned of our interference with his cronies in the park.

"Scotland Yard are already watching the house," I said.

"I shall send them away at once."

"We need their help, Mr. Dalton, and their resources," I said.

"I can't risk any more harm coming to Cordelia."

"What if I were to go to them and seek advice? Quietly. You wouldn't be involved."

"I forbid it." He was becoming angry, and I did not want to alienate him.

"I will of course respect your wishes," I said. "Let us put our heads together and see what else we can learn here. Could you please show me where Cordelia was sitting in the garden?"

"Yes," Mr. Dalton said. "And I shall fetch the gardener as well."

"Thank you. Would you object to my sending a note to Park Lane? I would like Colin to join us as soon as he returns."

"I would appreciate that, Lady Emily. Forgive me if I'm—"

I stepped closer to him and touched his arm. "There's nothing to forgive. You've been through too much already today. I promise you I shall do everything I can to help you."

I followed him, my hand firm on his wife's arm to keep her steady, into the garden. On any other day, it would have been a blissfully idyllic setting. The flower beds overflowed with fragrant blooms and tall trees created pockets of shade from the bright sun. The sounds of the street couldn't penetrate the thick walls—all I could hear were the cheerful songs of birds. We followed the neat gravel path until we reached a gleaming white wrought-iron chair. Next to it stood a small, round matching table on which rested the book Cordelia had been reading, *The Heavenly Twins* by Sarah Grand, one of the so-called New Woman novelists.

My surprise at the title must have registered on my face. I'd not read it, and silently scolded myself for the oversight, but had heard much talk about the story of three ladies and their marriages. While that might sound tame and appropriate, it was anything but. Sarah Grand used her writing to attack the double standards in society, particularly those regarding men's romantic relationships before marriage.

"We have never tried to control what she reads," Mrs. Dalton said. "And Mr. Dillman was a very forward-thinking man, you know. He encouraged her."

I liked the deceased man better and better, and wanted more than ever to see his murderer punished. "May I?" I asked, motioning to the book. She nodded. I picked it up and leafed through the pages. No note, no envelope, no scribblings in the margins or on the end papers.

My heart broke a little at the rest of what was on the table. A half-empty glass of lemonade, once cold, water that had condensed pooled around its base, and a plate covered with the crumbs of what must have been lovely biscuits. One could almost imagine Cordelia would reappear at any moment, that she'd gone for a wander and fallen asleep in a shady corner where no one had thought to look.

But I knew that to be nothing more than a wish. Trying to gather control of the overwhelming emotions bubbling inside me, I asked to speak to the gardener.

He was a pleasant man, eager to be helpful. Unfortunately, however, he'd been working in another section altogether and had seen or heard nothing. He suggested it wouldn't be difficult to scale the walls, pointing out to me the bricks, which had been laid in a manner that made them potential, if not easy, footholds. I thanked him, and wondered silently how a girl in a corset and heavy skirts could have made her way over the top.

I walked the rest of the garden alone, insisting the Daltons go sit inside, wanting to be able to focus on spotting clues. A shred of black cloth clung to the thorns of a tall rosebush, and while it might have been from Cordelia's dress, it wasn't much of a discovery. It could have been her mother's, could have come off a different day, and regardless, was a mere four feet from the table and chair. It offered no suggestion as to what might have happened.

I returned inside, where I carefully examined Cordelia's room and spoke to the rest of the servants in the house. My best hope was the footman who'd dealt with the post, but he'd taken no notice of the addresses on the letters. No one else knew anything. It was as if the girl had vanished by magic. Which suggested to me only one thing: she'd gone willingly. No doubt because her attacker had convinced her he would harm her mother if she didn't.

Rage burned inside me. I despised this person for what he'd made Cordelia suffer, and was infuriated he was still free, pursuing his twisted agenda. I returned to the garden and paced, trying to eliminate my nervous energy so I could adopt an appearance of calm before I went to the sitting room where the Daltons were waiting for me. I had nothing useful to tell them, and hated the feeling of being so helpless. The desire to act in a bold and swift manner consumed me—every hour that passed with Cordelia missing gave her captor gruesome opportunities. She might already be dead.

But that wasn't possible, I told myself. He wouldn't kill her so long as he still believed she had the information he had sought from her. That was her insurance. That was her only hope. Which meant it was mine, as well.

We sat, nerves on edge, for two hours more. I didn't want to leave the Daltons alone, but wasn't quite sure what to do with them, either. I was desperate for Colin to return. When at last the butler opened the door to announce him, I leapt to my feet and embraced him before I could help myself.

"We are in dire need of your services," I said, and briefed him on the situation. He did not take a seat, pacing in front of the windows as he listened.

"We cannot involve the police," Mr. Dalton said when I had finished.

"I understand," Colin said. "Do, however, let me assure you that should you change your mind, we can work with Scotland Yard without the kidnapper ever knowing."

"There's no way to guarantee that," Mr. Dalton said. "What if he has connections inside the force?"

"He's done nothing to indicate he does," I said.

"At this point, I'm not much concerned by your wish to keep the matter private," Colin said. "I have full access to their investigation, and will continue to keep current with what they know. We won't miss any possible leads."

"Is there anything we can do at the moment?" Mrs. Dalton asked. "Would you like to speak to the servants?"

"Emily's already done that, and I have absolute faith in her thoroughness," he said. "What I will need is for you to inform me the instant you hear from the miscreant."

"Rest assured, we shall do so immediately," Mr. Dalton said.

"And if you wouldn't object, I'd like to put a man of my own on the house to replace the one from Scotland Yard you sent away. I noticed he was gone when I arrived."

"I felt it the right thing to do," Mr. Dalton said. "If there is information coming to this rogue from within, he'd learn what I'd done and believe I was complying with his wishes."

"So may I set something up?" Colin asked.

"You would not send a policeman?"

"No," Colin said. "Someone in my private employ."

"I have no objection to that. So long as he is as discreet as you."

We finished up with Mr. Dalton and started back to our house. "In your private employ?" I asked as we walked. "I had no idea you'd such resources at your fingertips."

"Not all of our footmen are simply footmen," he said.

"What other secrets are you keeping from me?"

"They wouldn't be secrets if I told, would they?"

24 June 1893
Belgrave Square, London

I spent a great deal of time with Winifred today. It was altogether ordinary for the most part, except for the fact that I felt so guilty trying to pry into her secrets when guarding my own so carefully. It's funny how one begins to notice things only after one starts to look for them. She's extremely protective of her correspondence—hides it whenever someone comes into the room, even one of her servants. And she keeps a journal locked away in a drawer of her desk, the key hidden round her neck.

She told me she knows what secret of the Riddingtons is going to be exposed, but wouldn't give me any details. It seemed to amuse her to keep them from me. She also admitted to having called on Lady Althway before Mrs. Fanning's ball to confront her about her affair with that rake, Mr. Croft.

Yet she's shown no sign of real malice towards any of the victims. That she's a harsh judge of their sins cannot be doubted, but she holds everyone around her to the same standards. I've nothing to tell Emily that would suggest she's behind this paint business. She's just better at seeking out secrets than most of us. Could that be considered a failing?

Of course it could. But only if she's using the information to hurt others, and so far as I can tell, her only goal is to encourage those she loves to behave with care and decorum.

The summer had been exceptionally warm and dry, and after a short break, the heat had returned with a vengeance. I could hardly remember when it had last rained—a situation beyond unusual in England. All of my clothes felt too heavy for the season, even those of the thinnest muslin. Inside was worse than out, for even with every window in the house flung open, the air hung heavy and stale. It was as if the atmosphere itself was bogged down, worrying about Cordelia. I was sitting on my terrace, overlooking the garden, but even being outside provided little relief. I fanned myself with enormous plumes of ostrich feathers and ignored the copy of *The Aeneid* in my hands. I could think of nothing but Cordelia.

"Virgil does not have the hold on you Homer enjoys," Colin said, stepping out from the house. His tone was light, but I saw a deadly calm in his eyes.

"Is everything all right?" I asked, putting the book down on a table.

"Far from it," he said. "I've just come from the Daltons'." He handed me an envelope that had been closed with yellow sealing wax. I opened it and read:

I've decided there may be no point in negotiating with you, and, therefore, am not quite sure what I'll do with your daughter. Thought I should let you know, so that you don't start making all kinds of plans for her.

Or maybe you should. Everything depends upon my whim now.

"What can we do?" I asked. "This is grotesque and cruel."

"And unfortunately there's little, if anything, to be done at the moment," Colin said. "He's given us nothing new to act upon. It's a very bad situation."

"Should I go see Mrs. Dalton?" I asked.

"No," Colin said. "She's not in a state to receive visitors. And who could blame her?"

"You assume the worst?" I asked.

"Not yet," Colin said. "But the Daltons certainly do, and as we've no firm evidence to persuade them otherwise, there's nothing we can do to offer them hope. I wish they would let us involve the police. This matter is getting out of hand."

"Perhaps it's time to inform Scotland Yard, even if it's not what the family wants," I said.

"I don't want to go against Dalton's express wishes," Colin said. "It's a delicate matter. If I did, and his daughter is harmed . . ."

"What would you do if it were our daughter?" I asked.

"I would have called upon every resource I could."

"Doesn't Cordelia deserve as much?" I asked.

"Unfortunately, that's not our decision," he said.

"I can't bear it," I said. "There must be something we can do."

"Keep checking with Lady Glover," he said. "Make sure you know the instant she receives another note. Beyond that, we can only wait."

A week passed with no further news of Cordelia. Colin spent countless hours skulking about, interviewing contacts he had who he hoped might know something about her disappearance, but turned up nothing. He spoke to every member of every family whose house had been splashed red, and then to all of their servants, desperately trying to identify something that connected them, but it was all to no avail. As for me, I called on Lady Glover every day, hoping she would receive something from her mysterious correspondent, but nothing came. She was more than a little disappointed, I thought, to have lost his attention, and this led me to believe she was either telling the truth about the situation or she was an extremely good actress. Colin was still not convinced she hadn't written to herself.

The Daltons, understandably, were in an absolute state. We pleaded with them to let us take the case to Scotland Yard, who could begin a citywide search for Cordelia, but her parents would have none of it. They were adamant about following her kidnapper's orders, and were certain he would kill her if he thought for a moment they'd contacted the police.

One morning at breakfast, Colin told me paint had been found on another house, and I could do nothing but close my eyes.

"How long will this go on? Mr. Dillman is dead, Cordelia is missing. We've no clues worth anything," I said. "All of town is in knots wondering what's going to happen next. It's becoming unbearable."

"You're not concerned about us falling victim to this man?"

"The rational part of me isn't," I said. "But what's rational about any of this? This person has instilled paranoia and terror in everyone. It's permeated all of London. Tell me you aren't on the edge of reason, just from being surrounded by so much tension?"

"It's deeply unpleasant," he said.

Finished with my toast, I went behind the house to the stables for my horse. The grooms were ready for me, knowing I always rode at the same time. "Good morning, madam." One of them stepped forward, holding Bucephalus's reins. I'd named him after Alexander the Great's famous equine, not only because of my admiration for the ancient hero, but out of respect for my first husband, who'd called his horse the same.

"Thank you," I said. "It's a beautiful morning, isn't it?"

He nodded. "I thought you should know, madam, we found someone sniffing around before sunrise today."

"Here in the stables?"

"Yes, madam," he said. "He was trying to put this in Bucephalus's food." He handed me a small glass bottle.

"Poison?" I nearly dropped the odious object. "Where is he now? Did you catch him?"

"We locked him right up, madam, don't you worry. Knew we could hold him safe till you and the master was finished with breakfast, so didn't see the point in interrupting you."

I reached out and touched his arm. "In the future, please don't worry about interrupting us. I do very much appreciate the consideration, but never hesitate to tell me when something like this happens."

"I'm sorry, madam—"

"No need for apologies, I assure you," I said. "I'm extremely pleased that you have the man. I will return momentarily with Mr. Hargreaves and we will deal with him."

I rushed into the house and collected my husband, who was perhaps a bit less generous than I about the grooms having decided not to disturb us before breakfast. He contained his anger, however, scribbled a note summoning Scotland Yard, and in short order we were back at the stables. The grooms, more sheepish in Colin's presence, led us to the small room in which they'd locked the perpetrator.

Colin took the keys from them and opened the door. Inside, a grubby-looking man sat tied to a chair.

"Who are you?" Colin asked.

"He doesn't speak, sir," one of the grooms said. "We tried everything."
Fresh bruises on the man's face gave weight to the words.

"There's nothing more we can do with him," Colin said. "Scotland
Yard will be along to collect him. They'll see if he can sign, but I don't
expect an outcome any different from that we had with our friends from
the park."

"I'm sure he's in Mr. Majors's employ," I said.

"We can let the police follow up on this," Colin said. "We know what
they'll find. And they've already got the factory under surveillance."

"Thank you for being so vigilant," I said to the groom. "I can't bear to
think what might have happened." My voice cracked and I felt tears hot in
my eyes. I blinked them away, but could not stop my hands from shaking.

"Will you still ride, madam?" the groom asked.

"Yes, she will," Colin said. "And I shall as well." He turned to me. "Give
me a minute to change into something appropriate. It's been too long since
I've gone to Rotten Row."

Ordinarily, the sight of Colin in riding clothes, particularly in his tall,
polished boots, sent delicious shivers through me. But today nothing
could wipe the anxiety from my mind, and I wasn't able to muster
enough enthusiasm to approach anything about our ride with my usual
wild abandon.

"Try to look lighthearted," he said. "Our villain is trying to put you
off the case by upsetting you."

"Do you think so?" I asked.

"There's no question in my mind," he said. "Which suggests that
something you're pursuing is on the right track. Don't show any cracks
now, Emily."

When we returned home, I found it difficult to hand Bucephalus back to the grooms. I felt too out of sorts even to sit in the library, and installed myself in the green drawing room, where we'd hung paintings done by Monet and Renoir, talented artists and dear friends. I read the same fifty lines of *The Aeneid* over and over, unable to make any sense of the Latin. Ivy found me in a state when she called to see what had kept me from meeting her at Rotten Row.

"Horrifying! Absolutely horrifying," Ivy said, after I'd recounted for her the events of the morning. "Poor Bucephalus! You must have been beside yourself."

"I was. It was awful. Thank heavens they caught the man before he did any harm."

"I think it's terribly brave of you to be soldiering on."

"What else is there to do?"

"I'd be tempted to lock myself in my bedroom," Ivy said. "And refuse to come out until it's all over."

"I don't believe you," I said. "You can put on all the ladylike airs you want, but you'll never convince me you don't like adventure."

"You know me too well."

"How is the ineffable Mrs. Harris?"

"Still extremely displeased with you," Ivy said. "I've been spending quite a bit of time with her and while I agree she may not be entirely motivated by kindness, she's not all bad, Emily."

"People rarely are."

"I have noticed that she's not using her yellow sealing wax all the time anymore. She's switched to red for most of her correspondence."

"When does she use the yellow?"

"I don't really know," she said. "She doesn't write that many letters, to tell the truth. I've taken to sitting with her in the afternoon—I'd suggested we could answer notes together, to make the task a more pleasant one. She welcomed the idea, although not with much warmth, and set me up the next day at a small table in her music room. That's where she likes to write."

"And you'd bring letters requiring answers with you?"

"Precisely. I had told her I wanted her guidance. That I knew I was sometimes swayed to accept less-than-desirable invitations and that I needed her to help me cull from my acquaintance those she thought beneath me."

"Ivy! You actually said that?" I asked.

"I did indeed and it worked like a charm. She couldn't wait to exert more influence over me."

"You're very good at this, you know," I said.

"Why thank you, Emily," she said, her face glowing. There was no one in Britain lovelier than Ivy when she was happy. Her pink cheeks and porcelain skin could not have been more beautiful. "I'm sure it won't surprise you to learn you were the first person she suggested culling. But as open as she was to helping me, she was quite the opposite when it came to her own letters."

"Did she discuss any of them with you?"

"No," Ivy said. "As I said, she writes very few. Instead, she spends her time on journal entries. She's got at least five volumes, she told me. Needless to say, I've not the slightest idea what she puts in them."

"Perhaps she deals with her correspondence when you're not there."

"No, she told me she doesn't send or receive much."

"Does she sit near you when she writes?" I asked.

"No. Her desk is on the far side of the room from my little table. She keeps herself all hunched over, too, so that no one walking by could get even a hint of what she's doing."

"This is useful, Ivy," I said. "Thank you so much for undertaking the task."

"It's my pleasure entirely," she said. "I do like being of assistance."

"Excellent," I said. "Then you can come with me to Lady Glover's."

"Lady Glover's?" Ivy asked. "I don't know. I—"

"No discussion." I took her by the arm and led her—dragged her, really—to the Glovers' house, only a short walk from my own. The butler admitted us at once, and we followed him through six jewel-toned drawing rooms before reaching his mistress.

"Emily! What do you think of it?" She spread her arms and looked around the room. "It was inspired by you, of course. Only a quick redecoration as of yet. I'll have it done more thoroughly when we're back in the country shooting grouse, or whatever dreadful bird is on the wing in August."

She'd done a credible job turning the chamber from French contemporary to medieval fantasy. A suit of armor stood in one corner, and in the one opposite was a display of horse armor, complete with rider on top. Lances, swords, and an assortment of shields hung from one wall, while the other three were covered with fine tapestries. All of the furniture was heavy and dark. Candelabras on the large table in the center of the room provided the only light save that coming through the windows, which she'd somehow managed to replace with panels of stained glass.

"How did you do this in so little time?" I asked.

"Money makes all things possible," she said. "What do you think, Mrs. Brandon?"

"I . . . I . . . ," Ivy faltered in search of words. "It's extraordinary. I feel as if I'm in the keep of some Scottish castle."

"Oh dear," Lady Glover said. "I was aiming for fifteenth-century France. But it's a start."

"How does Mr. Foster like it?" I asked.

"He's not yet seen it," she said. "I've been keeping him in the Egyptian room, even if he does fancy himself a courtly knight. It's still my favorite."

"And your husband?" Ivy asked. "Which is his favorite?"

"His dreadful smoking room," she said. "Which has been in dire need of refurbishment since approximately 1817. I think he refuses to update it just to ensure I won't disturb him in his little sanctuary. He knows I can't bear to spend a moment there as it is."

"You must know I've come to you with the same question I have every day," I said.

"And today, at last, I have a positive response for you," she said, pulling a rolled paper from her décolletage. I stifled a laugh and took it from Lady Glover as Ivy did her best to hide her embarrassment.

"*We shall have shortly discord in the spheres.*" Across the bottom of the page, just as before, was an ominous swish of red paint.

"It's *As You Like It,*" Lady Glover said. "I admit to having to undertake quite a search to find the quote. I didn't expect something from the comedies, you see."

"No, why would you have?" I frowned. "I wish he'd given some indication of whether he received the reply you'd sent to his first note."

"Well, of course he received it," Lady Glover said. "I saw him collect it from my stoop."

"And you didn't see fit to share this information with me?" Frustration was replacing my feeling of discomfort.

She fluttered her eyelashes. "A lady must have some secrets."

"What did he look like?"

"Well, I suppose I must admit—but only to you—that he didn't come for it himself. He sent a servant of some sort."

"Was he in livery?" I asked.

"No." She sighed and leaned forward. "Truth be told, he was rather scruffy for a manservant."

"How do you know he wasn't some beggar off the street?" Ivy asked.

"Well, he wasn't that filthy. At least, not quite."

"I don't suppose you had someone follow him?" I asked.

"I followed him myself," she said. "It was quite an adventure. At least I'd thought it would be. But he went nowhere interesting—just into the back door of Claridge's Hotel."

"How is that not interesting?" I asked.

"Because he was summarily ejected not two minutes later," she said. "And then went towards the East End. I stopped following at that point. The neighborhood was appalling and I quite feared for my own safety."

I wondered if he had gone to Mr. Majors's match factory.

"Was there anything that stood out about his appearance?" I asked.

"He must have been in a fight recently," she said. "He was rather banged up, though the injuries did not look fresh."

I would have bet anything it was Dobson.

"And you still think he's the servant to a gentleman?" Ivy asked.

"Dear girl, I never said my correspondent was a gentleman! Do you want tea, either of you?"

"No, thank you," I said. "I do think the man sending these notes is a gentleman. Who else would have such ready knowledge of Shakespeare?"

"An actor, Lady Emily," she said. "He'd have a far better command of the Bard's work than any half-interested gentleman with a perfunctory education."

"I suppose you would know more about actors than us," Ivy said, then turned bright red. "I'm so sorry . . . I wasn't meaning to insult you. I just thought that, in the current circumstances, your background as—"

"Don't upset yourself," Lady Glover said. "I've never received such a bungled apology in all my life. You can't be anything but sincere."

"I assure you, I am," Ivy said.

"My experience on the stage has certainly enhanced my view of this entire situation," Lady Glover said. "The stories I could tell you!"

Ivy leaned forward, her eyes wide. She was no longer embarrassed. The red had faded away and she looked well and truly captivated.

"What was it like?" she asked.

"That, my dear, will have to be a story for another day," Lady Glover said. "For now, I want to focus on this man and his ill-bred servants."

"You think he has more than one such person at his disposal?" I asked, my suspicions growing again.

"Why wouldn't he?" she asked, waving her hands dismissively. "Particularly if he's an actor. He'd have any number of unsavory acquaintances at his disposal."

"Surely you don't think ill of stage people?" Ivy asked.

"Not at all," Lady Glover said. "But there are hangers-on to be considered. People in unfortunate circumstances who seek to advance themselves on the stage, when in fact they have no talent, no beauty, and no chance at success."

"But surely even a person like that wouldn't be so scruffy as the man you followed?" I asked.

"He may have been in costume, Lady Emily," she said. "You must consider every possibility."

"She's not at all what I expected," Ivy said as I walked her home. "Which is not to say she's the sort of woman with whom we should be cavorting. But I do like her—much more than I ought."

"I had no idea you were so interested in the stage," I said, checking my reticule to make sure the note was still in it. I'd asked Lady Glover for it so I might show it to Colin. She acquiesced to my request, but only on the condition that he return it to her himself.

"I've always quite fancied it," Ivy said. "I would love to play Juliet."

"Would you?" I asked. "How is it that you've never shared this with me before?"

"I think I was afraid to admit it out loud."

"Perhaps we should stage an entertainment."

"Don't even think of it," she said. "Robert would be horrified."

"No, he wouldn't, not if we did it at home and only for our friends. It would be perfectly acceptable."

"But what if I really liked it, Emily? And wanted to do it again?"

"Afraid of being consumed by the urge to act, are you?"

"Yes," she said, almost in a whisper, looking around furiously as if she were afraid someone might have heard.

"I shan't harass you about it now, but I think we should consider it for Christmas."

"I'm not listening," she said. "I noticed there was yellow sealing wax on Lady Glover's note."

"Well done for changing the subject," I said. "You're right."

"It's identical to that which Winifred has," she said. "I wonder if in the end, Lady Glover will prove the more acceptable acquaintance?"

"That, Ivy, would be an irony I'd love to see."

2 July 1893
Belgrave Square, London

I'm desperately excited for the ball at Devonshire House tonight. We all need a break from the hideous tension—the Lloyds, the latest to be marked with paint, have refused to show themselves in public since their steps were splashed red and are showing signs of distress. One of their parlor maids has left without giving notice, saying that she couldn't bear to be in the house. Apparently her mistress is on edge to the point of madness. No one has the slightest clue what the family is so desperate to keep hidden, but speculating about it are topics number one through ten at every social gathering these days.

I wonder how I would react if I received a warning in crimson? Would I become a recluse? Or would I have the courage to admit what I've done? I'm already excessively fond of Lady Glover, despite the many misgivings I have regarding her character, and hope I would use her as a model. She wouldn't apologize for her sins. She'd be proud of them.

I don't think I have it in me to be like her, wish though I might for the strength.

Tonight I'm going to do my best to avoid all unpleasant thoughts. A certain young lady will be at the ball tonight, and she's already promised Mr. Barnes her first dance. I'm hoping it will be the first of many. It would be an excellent match for them both.

18

Devonshire House was buzzing with energy. The duchess always had the finest musicians in London, and I'd danced and danced, particularly enjoying the waltzes I shared with Colin, his eyes locked on mine as he spun me around the floor. I'd decided to wear my favorite gown—a frothy creation of the palest blue silk damask. Garlands of pearls and crystals hung from the skirt and the bodice in elegant cascades, and flounces of filmy lace fell from my tightly laced waist into a modest train. Meg had spent nearly an hour on my hair, weaving pearls into the curls she'd formed into a coil on the top of my head. I'd refused to wear the sapphires she suggested, choosing instead a dainty diamond necklace set in platinum, fashioned in an intricate pattern that looked more like flowery lace than jewelry.

I turned the matching wide antique cuff bracelet on my wrist and looked around the crowded room, smiling when I saw Mr. Barnes dancing with the daughter of a minor noble whose family had run through its fortune. As the youngest of six girls, all hope had been abandoned that she might marry. Her dowry was nothing, and rumors had been swirling since Christmas that her mother was searching for an elderly lady in need of a companion. She couldn't stay in her parents' house forever. She was smiling at Mr. Barnes, who also seemed to be enjoying himself. Perhaps this would come to a happy end.

Colin, tired of dancing in the heat, had disappeared with Jeremy to play billiards. The thought of the two of them becoming friends was somewhat alarming. I was about to set off in search of them both when Mrs. Dalton appeared from out of nowhere and grabbed me by the arm.

"Please, Lady Emily, please come with me at once."

Seeing the desperate pain in her eyes, I did what she requested with no delay, and sent a footman to fetch Colin before following her to her waiting carriage.

"It's my husband," she said, as soon as the door was closed behind us. "He went off to try to find Cordelia this morning and still hasn't returned."

"Have you any idea where he planned to go?" I asked.

She shook her head. "None. He wouldn't tell me anything. But he did assure me he was going to keep Mr. Hargreaves abreast of the situation."

Colin joined us, his face full of worry as he listened to Mrs. Dalton's story. "I'm afraid I've heard nothing from him. Not at home, anyway. Tell your driver to take us to the Reform Club at once. We had an agreement. If he needed to contact me confidentially, he was to do so through my club, knowing it would be unlikely someone watching him would suspect anything."

He poked his head out the window and called to the driver. "Quickly, man. You've never driven for so urgent a cause."

We reached Pall Mall in record time, the Daltons' driver proving himself an excellent man to have on hand in an emergency. He dodged omnibuses, hansom cabs, and carts with a skill that took my breath away, partly because I was impressed by him, and partly because I was terrified out of my mind that we would crash. When we reached the club, Colin leapt from the carriage and darted inside. He returned in fewer than five minutes, the grave expression on his face having carved itself deeper into his handsome features.

"To Park Lane," he said to the driver, then closed the door with a loud thud and produced for us a letter. "He's gone to the warehouse where Dillman died. Said he'd received another communication from the wretch who took Cordelia and planned to meet him at noon. The club was supposed to forward any messages from him to me at home, but something went awry."

"What time did he leave the house?" I asked.

"It was much earlier than noon," Mrs. Dalton said. "Nine-thirty at the latest, I'd say."

"I want the two of you to return to our house and stay there," Colin said. "I will do everything I can to locate your husband, Mrs. Dalton."

"Thank you." She was clasping her hands together, gripping them so hard her knuckles were all white.

"Is there anything I can do in the meantime?" I asked.

"Take care of her," he said. "And make sure Davis has someone stationed at every door into the house."

"Of course," I said.

"Keep him with you. In the room," Colin said. "I don't want her alone, even for a minute."

The carriage stopped to let us out, then flew away again as soon as we'd cleared its step. Davis opened the door and took our wraps. I relayed to him Colin's request, and he moved at once with master efficiency. Taking his orders as seriously as always, he brought us to the library and rang the bell. A footman appeared moments later, confused when he found it was the butler, not me, summoning him.

"A man on every entrance to the house," Davis said, his voice low and measured. "And one on the door to whatever room Lady Emily is in. You know who to send?"

"Yes, sir, of course." The man bowed to me and left the room.

"You were ready for this, weren't you, Davis?" I asked.

"Yes, madam. Mr. Hargreaves took me aside before you were married and explained to me the nature of some of those in his employ. Most useful chaps, I'd say."

"I'm glad to have them," I said, resisting the urge to add that I wished I, too, had known about them before my marriage. "I'll need you to stay in the room with us."

"It will be my pleasure, madam," he said. "Do you and Mrs. Dalton require anything?"

"Port," I said, then changed my mind. "No. Tea. Strong tea." I wanted my senses to be as strong and focused as possible. Davis cracked open the door and murmured something to the man who was already stationed outside. Forty-two minutes later (I had been watching the clock like a prisoner waiting for execution) I heard a carriage clatter and then stop in front of the house. I rose to my feet at once. Davis motioned for me to stay where I was. I could see in his eyes he was horrified at having to direct me, but disobeying an order from my husband would have horrified him even more. In another moment, I heard Colin's voice in the corridor, and I stepped towards the door. Davis stopped me.

"No, madam," he said. "Please wait for him to come to you. Just in case there's some sort of trouble."

Colin didn't enter the library. I heard him taking heavy steps up the stairs, barking orders as he went.

"Get Lady Emily," he called.

I could not have moved more quickly had I known how to fly. I flung open the door and raced to him, Mrs. Dalton close behind. We both stopped, however, when we saw what was making his steps so labored. He was carrying Mr. Dalton, whose face was battered almost beyond recognition.

Mrs. Dalton let out a low moan and collapsed onto the floor.

"Davis!" He knew immediately what I needed, and set about moving her to a chair and applying smelling salts. "Bring her to us as soon as you can. And send for a doctor."

Colin took the injured man to a bedroom and lowered him gently onto the bed as soon as I'd pulled back the blankets.

"Tell me everything," I said.

"He's in bad shape," Colin said. "I found him in the burned-out warehouse chained in the same spot Dillman had been. He was conscious, but barely, and told me he'd been set upon by thugs as soon as he arrived. They overpowered him, restrained him, and beat him. Flung this at him." He handed me a letter. "I found it on the floor in front of him."

> *Your daughter is not so helpful as I would have hoped. I'm growing tired of her.*

"Despicable," I said. "How hurt is he?"

"Badly. We need a doctor."

"I've already summoned one."

When the physician arrived, Mrs. Dalton had still not come upstairs, so I left the gentlemen alone and went to check on her.

"We may need the doctor here, too," Davis said. "It took a considerable time to bring her round."

Her eyes were barely open, but I could see she was awake. "Mrs. Dalton," I said. "Your husband needs you. Come with me so you can speak to the doctor."

This motivated her to move. She snapped to attention and followed me up the stairs.

"He is alive, isn't he?" she asked.

"Yes," I said. "But he's very hurt. Brace yourself."

I tapped on the door. Some minutes passed before Colin opened it and the doctor stepped outside with him.

"Mrs. Dalton?" the doctor asked. She nodded. "I'm afraid your husband has had a most unpleasant day. His nose is broken, as are three of his ribs."

"Will he live?" she asked.

"I believe so. I'm concerned there may be some internal bleeding, so we will need to keep a close eye on him."

Mrs. Dalton looked as if she might faint again. Colin helped her to a chair, and the doctor bent over her. A few minutes later he stood up.

"She's suffering from shock. Do you have somewhere she can rest?"

We moved her to the bedroom adjoining that where Colin had put Mr. Dalton and stationed footmen at both of their doors before retiring to our own room. We'd not even started our evening ablutions when we heard a commotion in the corridor. Rushing to investigate, we saw Mr. Dalton staggering out of his room.

"I must go to her . . . I must find her."

Now Mrs. Dalton's door opened. "You know where she is?" She grabbed her husband around the shoulders to help keep him upright.

"I saw her. She was there. She spoke to me," he said.

"Did you see the man who took her, or only his thugs?" Colin asked.

"Let me go," he said, shaking his wife off him. "I must find her."

"Who else did you see?" Colin asked.

Mr. Dalton, unsteady on his feet, leaned against the wall. His voice was rough. "They paraded her in front of me after they'd beat me."

"Was it the same men who attacked you?" I asked.

"The same," he said.

"Did you see anyone else?" Colin asked.

"No. I don't think so. I—" He slumped lower, then, with effort written on his mangled face, pulled himself up again.

This set Colin into action. "Get him back in bed," he said to me. "And contact Scotland Yard—"

"No!" Mrs. Dalton said. "We can't—"

"No more of that," Colin said. "There's no time to be wasted. We need all the resources and help we can get. Send for them, Emily. And when they arrive, have a team meet me at the warehouse."

"I'm going with you," Mr. Dalton said.

His wife stepped forward. "Oh no, you're not," she said. "I'll not lose you, too."

There was no further discussion of the topic.

The men from Scotland Yard arrived quickly and were soon dispatched in three groups: one went to search the Daltons' house, one upstairs to interview Cordelia's parents, and the last set off to rendezvous with Colin. When they'd finished speaking with the Daltons, I returned upstairs, opening the door to Mr. Dalton's room as quietly as possible in case he was trying to sleep. He was sitting bolt upright in bed, his wife on a chair next to him, crying.

"I do wish there was something I could do to ease your worry," I said.

"There's nothing to be done," she said. "My poor girl."

"At least we know she's alive," I said. "Surely that offers some hope."

"A little," Mrs. Dalton said. "But the note they left doesn't inspire confidence."

"They may have just been trying to instill fear. How did Cordelia seem?" I asked Mr. Dalton. "Was she in the room with you for long?"

"Not at all," Mr. Dalton said. "They dragged her past me once and that was it."

"Did she appear to be in good health?" I asked.

"Generally, yes, but she was upset," he said. "Still wearing the same dress she'd had on the day he took her. She kept trying to call out for me, but they had a gag in her mouth. I couldn't do anything for her." He choked on a sob, then sniffed, then composed himself.

"My husband will do everything possible to find her," I said.

"Why would anyone do this?" Mrs. Dalton asked. "What can he possibly think Cordelia has?"

"I wish I knew," I said. "We'll search through all her things again and through all of Mr. Dillman's. If there's anything significant, we will find it."

"But you've already done that," Mrs. Dalton said. "And it amounted to nothing. I cannot bear this feeling of helplessness."

"We shall look again, and harder," I said. "There's nothing else to be done. But don't lose faith. It's entirely possible Colin's already found something of use in the warehouse."

"There's nothing there but charred ruins," Mr. Dalton said.

"Countless things could be lost in them," I said. "Possibly even something Mr. Dillman had hidden before the fire."

"Wouldn't it have burned?" Mrs. Dalton asked.

"That depends upon what it was made of. We're not necessarily looking for paper," I said. "And if it is there, Colin will find it. You can depend upon that."

I woke up the following morning cramped and uncomfortable, having
fallen asleep in the library waiting for Colin, who hadn't returned during the night. I stretched my aching muscles as I rose from the settee
and was about to ring for Davis when I saw him standing against the
wall near the room's front windows.

"Have you been there all night?" I asked.

"Yes, madam," he said. "My instructions were to keep an eye on
you. In the circumstances, I thought keeping two eyes on you would be
preferable. Would you like to change your dress before breakfast?"

"Has Mr. Hargreaves sent any messages?"

"No, madam."

"Are the Daltons awake?"

"Mrs. Dalton has breakfasted," he said. "I sent a tray to her. She's
upstairs with her husband, who is still asleep. I've had the footmen report to me every hour so I would not have to leave you alone."

"I don't know how I'd ever manage without you," I said.

"Thank you, madam."

I went to my room, rang for Meg, and readied myself for the rest of
the day. Once dressed, I checked on our guests—Mr. Dalton hadn't

stirred—and went to the breakfast room. Cook, who always refused to alter her menus because of what she called "Mr. Hargreaves's business obligations," had laden the sideboard with enough dishes to feed half of Park Lane. I took a plate and piled some buttered eggs on it, along with deviled chicken and some strawberries, but the fact was I had little appetite. I moved the eggs around with my fork, then took a slice of toast from the silver rack on the table and reached for the marmalade.

"I do hope you can manage to apply yourself with some enthusiasm," Davis said, coming in with the morning mail. "Cook was in a state this morning when she saw how few of her tea cakes had been consumed last night. I'm certain you don't want to cause her further distress over her eggs."

As I scooped up a bite, Colin joined me. His evening kit was covered with dust and grime, and dark shadows smudged deep under his eyes.

"We searched his house, hers, and the warehouse. Sifted through every inch of ash," he said. "This is all we found." He handed me a golden locket hanging from a thin chain. I snapped it open to reveal a lock of hair and a miniature portrait of Mr. Dillman.

"Have you pulled the portrait out?" I asked.

"Yes, there's nothing behind it. I suspect Cordelia was wearing it yesterday, as it exhibits no signs of having been through the fire."

"Her parents would know, surely. Shall we ask them?"

I abandoned my plate and went upstairs, where we showed the Daltons what Colin had found. Cordelia's mother nearly choked.

"She never took it off," she said.

"So she was wearing it the day she was taken?" Colin asked.

"Yes, I'm certain of it."

"Was it a gift from Mr. Dillman?" I asked.

"No, her father and I gave it to her on her birthday last year," Mrs. Dalton said. Her husband, his face even more swollen this morning, did his best to nod in agreement.

"When did she add the portrait and the lock of hair?" I asked.

"That I don't precisely know," Mrs. Dalton said. "Do you think she dropped it on purpose yesterday?"

"I couldn't say." Colin handed the oval pendant back to me, and I set myself to examining it again. Its front was engraved with flowers, the back smooth and clean. Inside, nothing looked out of the ordinary.

"Will you excuse me?" I asked. "I have a thought and need a magnifying glass."

Colin followed at once. "There's nothing there, Emily. I checked thoroughly. Even magnified the portrait, front and back."

"I'm not interested in the portrait," I said, opening the door to the library and crossing to my desk. I opened the center drawer as I sat down, and pulled out a penknife and a magnifying glass. Using extreme care, I removed the lock of hair with the penknife, tugging gently at the tiny bits of narrow ribbon holding the strands together until the knots became undone. I put the hair in an envelope, not wanting to lose any of it, and smoothed the ribbon flat in front of me.

"I checked," he said. "There's nothing behind the hair, or anything hidden in it, either."

Then I picked up the magnifying glass.

"A long series of numbers," I said. "It's written on the inside of the ribbon."

"Well done, Emily," Colin said. "I dismissed it as being too narrow. A careless mistake."

"You've been up all night. You couldn't have been thinking clearly."

"That's no excuse. Good thing I have you, eh?"

"Exceedingly good," I said. "You're a lucky man."

"What do you think it means?"

"I'll assume you mean the numbers, not your luck," I said, thrilling to the feel of discovery. "They're the rest of the catalog numbers from the British Museum—they go with the letters I found in Mr. Dillman's pocket."

"A reasonable guess," he said, jotting them down in the notebook he'd pulled from his jacket pocket. "But even if we identify the objects, we've no reason to think he was using them for anything other than a game. And remember that there was nothing to be found when Mr. Dalton searched his library."

"Maybe they're in Mr. Dillman's library."

"We've both searched there as have Scotland Yard. There's nothing left to be found, Emily."

"We didn't look behind the books," I said.

"I did," Colin said. "As soon as you told me about the game."

"Then there must be another place where he had hidden something. Something in his personal possessions may give us greater insight into his personality—and that, in turn, may point us in the right direction."

"It's an interesting idea."

"I'd like to pursue it this afternoon," I said.

"It can't hurt," he said. "Davis can oversee the Daltons for a few hours."

"The Daltons are *here*?" My mother burst into the room, our butler two paces behind her.

"Lady Bromley, sir," he called to Colin, before bowing and returning to the corridor.

"What on earth are you two up to?" my mother asked, taking a seat without being asked. "I've just been round their house and was told they'd gone to the country. Which made no sense at this time of year. I knew something had to be wrong."

"I'm afraid Mr. Dalton was attacked yesterday by the man who murdered Mr. Michael Dillman," Colin said. "We're keeping him and his wife here until he's recovered."

"Is that quite safe?" she asked.

"You know my primary job is to look after your daughter."

"Oh, Mr. Hargreaves, you are very good," she said. "Forgive me for worrying, but I know enough about the nature of your activities to be concerned. In fact, it's those activities that have brought me here to-day."

"Mother, I'm afraid we were about to—"

"Do not interrupt, Emily. It's unbecoming. I've just seen the queen and had a lengthy discussion with her about the numerous services you've rendered for the Crown. She agreed with me that you should be made KCMG."

"Lady Bromley, please understand I am flattered, but that is not something I could even begin to consider," Colin said. "What I do is no more significant than any other servant of the empire."

"Your modesty is to be admired, sir, but surely you don't mean to refuse the queen's honor?"

"He's done just that on two previous occasions," I said.

"I'm perfectly well aware of that, Emily," she said. "Was it perhaps because—"

Colin stopped her. "Please don't try to change my mind," he said. "It will only cause tension between myself and Her Majesty. She has accepted my position on similar matters before. I'd prefer not to test her goodwill again."

"Which is why you must accept the honor gracefully," my mother said. "It's an outrage you've not been made a peer."

"I shouldn't want that, either," he said.

"I don't believe you, Mr. Hargreaves. I think, in fact, I've identified the problem. You're more ambitious than I'd thought, and that impresses me." She nodded, slowly, a smile creeping onto her face. "I will see what can be done."

"No, Lady Bromley, I wouldn't want you to do that," he said. "You must believe me, I—"

"Enough," she said, rising from her seat. "I take my leave from you both now, but shall hope to return soon with even better news."

"Please—" She was gone before Colin could get another word out.

I put my elbows on the desktop and rested my chin on them. I could feel my eyes dancing. "I think you're beginning to see just what a force of nature she can be."

"I've already witnessed that," he said.

"Yes, but she's never directed her full power at you. I'm rather pleased to see the focus taken off me," I said. "It's a welcome relief. Notice she didn't make any mention of my involvement with the Women's Liberal Federation."

Colin grunted, but said nothing.

"So, to Mr. Dillman's?" I asked.

"Yes," he said. "Let me sleep for two hours and we'll set off."

"Shall I send Davis up with a tray for you when it's time? You'll need something to eat as well as some rest."

"That would be perfect," he said. "Have you work to do, or would you care to join me upstairs?"

"Alas, I've too much to do at the moment," I said. "But maybe I'll bring your tray up myself."

He gave me a kiss and made sure Davis was installed in the room before leaving me. I studied Cordelia's locket and considered the many possible suspects before us. Part of the trouble was there was almost no one in London who didn't have reason to lash out at society. I set myself to the task of writing a list of everyone who'd given me cause to wonder, but had trouble focusing. Distracted and unsettled, I decided to read, but not even Mary Elizabeth Braddon could get my attention in my current frame of mind. I tossed aside *The Venetians* and began to browse the library's shelves. I started in fiction, having no interest in true stories at the moment, running a finger along the spines of volume after volume, when suddenly something struck me. I went back to my desk.

Maybe Cordelia's game had led me astray. Mr. Dillman's numbers could be library catalog citations.

3 July 1893
Belgrave Square, London

I think my scheme to find Mr. Barnes a bride may be more successful than I'd ever hoped! My two candidates are both interested, their families are delighted, and the prospective groom couldn't be happier. It's so lovely to have something good come during this horrid season. I only wish Emily hadn't left the ball in such a rush last night. I'd hoped to enlist her help.

Winifred told me some things she considers alarming about Cordelia Dalton today. She had nothing to say that's pertinent to Emily's investigation of Mr. Dillman's death, only that Cordelia is prone to reading books some would consider inappropriate for young ladies. I can hardly condemn her for it, given my own proclivity for such works. Winifred believes it's a symptom of deeper problems, and has gone so far as to suggest Cordelia's fortunate to have been saved from marrying Mr. Dillman. He, too, it seems, had a penchant for the inappropriate.

I breathed not a word to her about my taste in novels.

20

Colin did not get his two hours of sleep. He came downstairs after a mere thirty minutes and rushed out of the house, explaining that he needed to go to Scotland Yard. I told him my library theory.

"It's an excellent one, my dear," he said. "And we'll investigate it thoroughly when I return. I shouldn't be too long. I need to check on something."

"You must have a theory as well," I said. "Inspiration kicked you out of bed."

"You know me too well."

"Tell me?"

He shook his head. "Not yet. It's not fully formed. But I promise"—he kissed me quickly—"you will be the first to hear the details."

"Ovid," I said. *"A new idea is delicate. It can be killed by a sneer or a yawn; it can be stabbed to death by a quip and worried to death by a frown on the right man's brow."*

"Precisely," he said. "And at the moment, I'm just the right man to frown. I don't want to say it out loud lest I dissuade myself."

Half an hour later, I wished he hadn't gone. Davis brought me a message, sealed with yellow wax, suggesting I take a stroll through Hyde Park.

You will find, if you do, that which you've been missing, al-
though not in the condition you'd hoped.

Nausea flipped my stomach, and I felt light-headed. I raced
to Scotland Yard in search of Colin, but he was not there. He'd gone
on to Southwark, and I had no idea where to find him, or even where
to start looking. I debated telling the Detective Inspector about the
note, but couldn't bring myself to, knowing how adamantly the Daltons were opposed to involving the police in Cordelia's disappearance. I had to respect their wishes, particularly because choosing
not to might lead to the kidnapper causing more harm to their
daughter.

I was not, however, prepared to embark on a search for her on my
own, even in daylight. My driver took me straight to Bainbridge House,
where Jeremy agreed at once to join me. He tried to sound flip and un-
concerned, but his jaw betrayed him as I told him about Cordelia's abduction. He always clenched it when he was nervous.

"I'm sure we'll find some sign of her," he said. "Something mildly
distressing that will make her parents worry more. But he's not going to
harm her when he hasn't got what he wants."

"I hope you're right," I said.

"Do you know I had a very encouraging conversation with an elderly member of the House of Lords this morning at my club? I lectured
him for a good half hour about the merits of giving women the vote
without him giving a single objection. Unfortunately, he was asleep," he
said.

"I do appreciate you trying to distract me," I said. "But I'm afraid it
won't work."

We'd reached the park and were systematically making our way
along its myriad paths. I knew of no other way to approach the situation. Through trees, I caught a glimpse of the gargantuan Albert Memo-
rial, an exercise in ostentation. Built by Her Majesty after her husband's

death, it rose above the trees of the park, its gilded steeple providing a roof for the golden figure of Albert seated below.

Jeremy saw me frown. "You don't like it?"

"Do you?"

"It's grotesque," he said. "In fact, it's one of the reasons I refuse to marry. What if I had a wife so devoted she insisted on building an equally absurd monument to my many fine qualities? I couldn't live with myself knowing I'd have done London such a harm."

"You wouldn't have to live with yourself," I said. "You'd already be dead. Come, let's go this way. I don't think we'll find anything on Rotten Row. The horses would have already trampled it." We turned into a wide path that would lead us past the stream and waterfall that came off the Serpentine. As we approached the water, there were ravens flying all around, far more than was usual. The sun bounced off the water, making it difficult to look directly at the sparkling glow, but as we got closer, I saw the birds that weren't fluttering about were pecking at a shapeless mass bobbing in the shallow edge near a thick patch of reeds.

Bile filled my throat. It couldn't be.

I took another step towards the iron railing that lined the path. Then another.

The sound of the waterfall closed in around me, when before I'd hardly noticed it.

Black cloth blended with the ravens' wings, but it was unmistakably cloth. One of the birds moved, revealing a shock of chestnut-colored hair.

I screamed, sending the creatures into flight.

And now, with them gone, there could be no question. It was a body, bloated and purple, floating facedown in the pond. A young lady, in mourning dress. I didn't need to see more to know the rest.

Cordelia was dead.

"It would have been perfectly reasonable for you to faint," Jeremy said, his face devoid of all color. "But I did not expect to find myself so unsteady on my feet."

My scream had brought a running crowd and a nearby policeman to the wide pavement on which we stood, and in short order, Scotland Yard and my husband appeared on the scene. I turned away when two men, who had climbed over the railing, stepped into the water and turned over the corpse. I did not want to see her face.

"Would you like me to take you home?" Jeremy asked.

"I'd be grateful if you did, Bainbridge." Colin came up from behind us. "There's no reason either of you need to stay here."

"Who is going to tell her parents?" I asked.

"I was going to ask you," Colin said. "Her father will have to officially identify the body, but there's no question it's her. She was dead before she was put in the water. Strangled. I think the news would come better from you than a stranger."

"You'd be better at it than I," I said.

"But I can't leave here now."

I wanted to cry, wanted to be sick, but I couldn't refuse his request. The Daltons needed to know the fate of their daughter as soon as possible.

"I'll take you," Jeremy said.

"Thank you." My voice was barely a whisper.

Colin kissed my cheek. "It's good of you to do this." Someone standing near the body called out to him. "I have to go now, but I'll be home as soon as possible."

Jeremy took me by the arm and we started to walk back through the park. I could hardly see in front of me. Tears blurred my vision and I could not stop shaking.

"It will be all right, Em," he said.

"How, Jeremy? How will it ever be all right again? We promised to help her . . . promised to keep her safe. And now I'm to tell her parents she's dead?"

He put his arm around me, squeezed my shoulder, and held out a handkerchief. I wiped my eyes.

"Well, if you'd had the good fortune to have been educated at Eton, like your dashing husband, you'd have no trouble facing this deeply unpleasant task. You would have been prepared to march headlong into any difficult situation with grace and strength and a nearly unbearable perseverance. But, as you were not, and as I suffered through my years at Harrow paying no attention to anything anyone told me, we shall have to muddle through the best we can."

I said nothing.

"And when we're done," he said. "I'm going to get you extremely drunk on expensive whisky."

"I don't really like whisky," I said. "Colin's the whisky drinker in the house."

"You'll like this whisky."

"I won't."

We'd reached Park Lane and crossed the street, which meant we'd be home in almost no time. My stomach churned and I swallowed hard.

"I hate breaking news like this," I said. Preferring to soldier on rather than to prolong the agony of worrying about what was to come, I increased my pace. The pavement was extremely crowded, and I all but pushed my way through until we'd reached my house. For an instant, I wished I could run away. But then Davis, efficient as always, opened the door.

I handed him my hat and parasol. Jeremy passed over his top hat and walking stick.

"Are the Daltons upstairs?" I asked.

"Yes, madam. The doctor just left them," Davis said.

I did my best to screw my courage to the sticking point, thinking it might be made easier, if not more pleasant, had I someone as fearsome as Lady Macbeth to spur me on, and started up the stairs.

"Shall I accompany you?" Jeremy asked.

"Please," I said. "Just to the door."

I tapped quietly on the wood and heard Mrs. Dalton call for me to enter. I took a deep breath, looked at Jeremy, and turned the handle.

"I'll be right here when you're done," he said.

Sunlight spilled into the room, which overlooked the park. I resisted the urge to close the curtains. Much as I wanted to block the view of a place that would, for the Daltons, be forevermore hideous, plunging them into darkness didn't seem an act that would offer much comfort.

"You only just missed the doctor," Mrs. Dalton said. "My husband is much improved."

"Entirely out of danger," Mr. Dalton said, his head propped up on a tall pile of pillows. "He's no longer concerned about internal bleeding."

"I can't tell you how refreshing it was to have some good news for a change," Mrs. Dalton said, fairly beaming. "And I do hope you've come with more."

"I'm afraid I haven't," I said. "We found Cordelia. I'm so sorry . . . I hardly know what to say."

"No," Mrs. Dalton said, rising to her feet. "Surely you can't mean . . . ?" Her husband gripped her arm.

"I do. She's dead."

"Are you certain?" Mr. Dalton said. "How can they be sure it's her?"

"Colin did a preliminary identification of the body." I did not think it the appropriate time to tell him he would have to do the same, but officially.

"What . . . what did this monster do to her?" he asked.

"I don't know, Mr. Dalton."

"Did you see her?"

Tears spilled from my eyes. "I did. Not her face, just her back."

"Where?" he asked, as his wife buried her face in her hands and sobbed.

"Hyde Park," I said. "My husband is there still, with Scotland Yard. He'll be along as soon as he can and will give you any other information he's learned."

"I want to go home," Mrs. Dalton said. "I want to go now. We don't need protection any longer. We've nothing left to protect."

"I understand how upset you are," I said. "But please wait until you've spoken with Colin."

"I won't," she said, standing up. "I won't do anything else you tell me to. My daughter is dead, Lady Emily. And you did nothing to save her."

21

The Daltons had exited the premises within half an hour. I didn't try to stop them. If they wanted to face their grief in their own home, who was I to argue? I had Davis send word to Colin to go to them as soon as he was finished in the park, and then collapsed in tears in my library. Jeremy sat on the overstuffed arm of the leather chair onto which I had flung myself.

"I don't know what to do with you, Em," he said, picking up a small stone statue of a cat, the goddess Bastet, which Colin had purchased in Egypt years ago. "I'm not allowed to comfort you in any of the ways I'd ordinarily use in such a situation."

"Do you find yourself often in this sort of situation?" I asked.

"Well, not precisely *this* situation. But, you know, ladies over-wrought with emotion. And you know I've never been much fond of cats." He retuned the statue to the table, stood up, and rang for Davis. "As my normal channels are forbidden, I shall have to treat you like a gentleman instead and prescribe my cure for all male tragedy."

Davis stepped into the room and Jeremy consulted with him in a voice too quiet for me to hear. My butler did not look pleased, but was not about to go against the wishes of a duke, and had soon returned to the room bearing a heavy tray.

"I can't bring you Mr. Hargreaves's favorite, sir," Davis said. "Not without his express consent."

"And what would his favorite be?" Jeremy asked.

"The Glenmorangie," Davis said.

"A very good choice," he said. "Would Lady Emily's permission be enough?"

"It would not," Davis said. "Just as his permission alone wouldn't grant you access to Lady Emily's finest port." He bowed and left the room after having removed seven bottles and fourteen single malt glasses to the table next to Jeremy's chair.

"I don't want this, Jeremy," I said.

"You only think that," he said. "There's no better way to forget what we saw. We'll start with something from the West Coast Highlands." He opened the bottle and poured a splash into each of two glasses. "Oban, because I've always thought it tastes like Christmas. Cheers."

He downed his in one gulp. I sipped mine slowly.

"Thoughts?" he asked.

"It's fine, but I'm always going to prefer port," I said.

"I don't think I like finding dead bodies, Em," he said, refilling his glass. "I'm not suited to it."

"Is anyone?"

"Your husband, apparently. You, possibly." He took a large swig. "Finish that, Em, so we can move on to the next. But do try to pay attention to the taste."

Mindlessly, I obeyed. The whisky burned in my throat and warmed my stomach.

"What you saw in France was worse, wasn't it?" he asked. The previous summer I'd found the brutally savaged body of a young woman. The image still came to me in nightmares.

"Much worse." I held my empty glass out to him. He took it from me and replaced it with another.

"Glenkinchie," he said. "You'll find this quite different. It has an almost grassy sweetness."

I sipped. "Grass?"

"With a bit of straw on the finish," he said. "Gorgeous."

"Mrs. Dalton was very angry with me," I said.

"She wasn't angry with you, Em. She's angry with the wretch who killed her daughter."

"I know you're right," I said. "But I feel so much guilt. I'm consumed with it."

"Is there anything more you could have done?"

"There must have been something, or she'd still be alive."

"I don't agree," he said, filling the third set of glasses.

"I can't keep up with you," I said.

"It won't go bad. You can take your time."

"I didn't believe he'd hurt her," I said, tears welling up again. Jeremy, who was now sitting across from me, leaned forward and wiped them away with his thumb.

"Of course you didn't. What civilized person could believe otherwise?" He passed me the next glass. "This is my favorite of what we have at our disposal. Thought I should give it you sooner rather than later or you might not be in a state to adequately appreciate it."

I took a sip and cringed.

He smiled. "Laphroaig 27 year. The strongest-flavored whisky I've ever had. Smoke and peat."

"Am I supposed to think drinking something that tastes like peat is a good idea?"

"It's an excellent idea," he said. "Take another taste. Slowly."

I did as he instructed. "It's so strong!"

He pulled two cigars out of his pocket. "Do you think Davis would forgive me, just this once?"

"Absolutely not," I said. "But I will not stand for you telling me that matters right now."

I found the whisky much improved by the addition of the cigars. Although the effect might, too, have been caused by the quantity ingested—Jeremy did insist he was pouring very small amounts, but I was unused to this quantity of spirits.

"I want you to taste them each, then decide which is your favorite," he said. "And I'll give you a real pour of that one."

"I'm not quite sure how you consider this small," I said, taking the next glass.

"You'll like this one. It smells like summer fruit. Clynelish, from the North Coast Highlands. Elegant and creamy."

I took a sip. "This is nice. I almost like it."

"I knew you'd come around."

"Thank you, Jeremy," I said. "I don't know how I'd get on right now if I didn't have you to distract me."

"I'm rather indispensable, you know."

I held up a hand when he reached for the next bottle. "No, not yet. I couldn't possibly. This may be your male-tragedy cure, but you must remember I am a lady."

He leaned forward. "I had noticed that, Em, when I was about nine. It was rather alarming."

I giggled.

"Maybe just a little more," I said. "This is an extraordinary cigar."

"Your taste is excellent, darling." Now he was laughing. Which made me laugh more, and soon we were both collapsed in mirth.

"So, is this what gentlemen do at their clubs?" I asked.

"It's not nearly so entertaining at clubs," he said, pouring again. "Lagavulin, from Islay. This has a spectacular finish—dark fruit beneath the peat."

"Not bad," I said. It appeared I was acquiring a taste for whisky. "I wonder if the Daltons will bury Cordelia near Mr. Dillman."

"Must we return to morbid?" Jeremy asked.

"Together in death. I suppose that is morbid."

"Decidedly." He poured more Lagavulin into his glass and gulped it down. "I'd prefer to discuss just about anything. Including the Women's Liberal Federation."

"That's quite a claim," I said. "Can it be true?"

"Have I ever lied to you?" His eyes lingered on mine longer than they ought to have.

"Oh, Jeremy. You know I—"

"Just tell me, Em. Could it have been different? If you'd never met Hargreaves?"

Images of the two of us spun in my head—memories from childhood, the kiss we'd shared in Vienna when he told me he loved me. But I could not wrench my eyes away from his.

"It might have been different," I whispered.

He dropped to his knees in front of me. "Emily—"

"No, Jeremy. No." I stood up and stepped away from him. "It can't be like that now."

Just as I was about to become seriously concerned about the state of our friendship, he shook his head and started to laugh again.

"Oh, I know, Em," he said. "But you're bloody near irresistible to me. We need more whisky." He returned to his chair and reached for the next bottle on the table. "Talisker, from the Isle of Skye."

"It smells salty," I said.

"Good. And the taste?"

"Sweet at first, but then peat."

You're learning," he said.

"I don't know about that."

"Do you think Cordelia's still in the park, or will they have moved her by now?" he asked.

"They've probably moved her."

"To the morgue?"

"I suppose so."

"I don't know how you stomach all this, Em," he said. "You're stronger than I am."

"I don't like this part. But it's worth it if I can find the person who did it to her."

"Me, I'm inclined to crawl into bed and refuse to come out until he's been hung, drawn, and quartered."

"We don't do that anymore," I said.

"Maybe you don't, but I certainly do. There's nothing like the protection that comes from one's bedcovers. My nurse taught me that when I was very small and she never, ever steered me wrong."

"I was referring to hanging, drawing, and quartering," I said.

He pulled open the last bottle. "I think you'll like this. Cragganmore, from Speyside. Fruit, caramel, and toffee in the nose."

"I do like toffee," I said, taking the glass and raising it to my lips. "This is good. It feels so rich on the tongue."

"I knew I'd bring you round to my way of thinking," he said. "And as I've got such finely honed powers of persuasion, perhaps I ought to consider spending more time in the Lords. Get people rethinking the idea of acceptable punishment."

I don't know why, but this made me laugh. Hysterically. "Good heavens, I'd all but forgot you've a seat there. Have you ever even been?"

"Until now I've not had a suitable agenda to pursue," he said, laughing with me.

"It took punishment to inspire your political passion?" I asked.

"Can you think of something better?"

"Hundreds of things," I said. "This cigar, for example."

"You've descended to the ridiculous."

I would have agreed with him if I could have stopped laughing long enough.

"What's going on here?" Colin asked, opening the door and looking at the two of us with more than a hint of irritation on his face.

Jeremy waved a hand at him. "Consolation, my friend. Your wife needed consoling, and whisky was all I could offer her in the circumstances. Would you like some?"

"No, I wouldn't," he said.

"Did you speak to the Daltons?" I asked.

"They're in bad shape," he said.

"I know. Very angry."

"It's entirely justifiable," he said. "I'm sick that we didn't stop this."

"As am I," I said.

"Which is why I plied her with drink," Jeremy said. "Don't be cross with me, Hargreaves."

"Believe me, I'm not," Colin said, taking the chair next to mine. "I'm thankful you were here to distract her. It's the rest of it that's tormenting me. More paint has been found—and the news of Cordelia's death has already reached the far-flung corners of town. If you thought people were on edge before, wait till you step outside again. London feels on the verge of implosion."

Jeremy rang the bell, and Davis appeared. "The Glenmorangie for your master, good man. I'll brook no argument."

Davis looked at Colin, who nodded before turning to Jeremy.

"I don't suppose you have another one of those cigars?"

22

The Glenmorangie may indeed have been the best whisky, but the following morning, I found myself devoid of pleasant memories of any of them. Colin pulled the curtains back in our room and I groaned as the light hit my face. I rolled onto my stomach and dove under my pillow.

"You can't hide from me," he said, sitting on the edge of the bed.

"Why not? *All I know is that I know nothing.*"

"Socrates won't help you now."

"I can't believe Cordelia is dead," I said, feeling hot tears sting my cheeks. "And I've no interest in moving a single muscle today. It all feels too hopeless."

"We have to go to Dillman's to investigate your theory, remember?"

I lifted the pillow enough that I could peek at him with one eye. "I'll be ready in an hour. It's not as if rushing can help her now." I heard the door open.

"I've brought Lady Emily's breakfast, like you asked." Meg's voice was far too cheerful for the time of the morning, but the smell of bacon and egg was beginning to bring me round. I sat up and let her arrange the tray over my legs.

"I didn't think I was hungry," I said, applying myself with unexpected vigor to the plate. "Anything new to report yet today?"

"I thought I should let you sleep. I've been to two houses with freshly painted red fronts."

"And?"

"Nothing yet that will help us there," he said. "The occupants are all in panic, as you can imagine."

I gave him a piece of my toast. "Have you spoken to the Daltons again?"

"That was the worst part of my morning. I took him to identify the body."

"Oh, Colin." I squeezed his hand. "I'm so sorry. Was it awful?"

"He faced it bravely and is doing as well as can be expected. He's summoned his sons home from India."

"It's heartbreaking, all of it," I said.

"It is." He took a bite of the buttered toast, then added some marmalade.

"Whose houses have been painted?" I asked.

"The Stanburys and that chap in Belgrave Square who fancies himself an archaeologist."

"Yes, I remember him," I said. "He's a neighbor of Ivy's."

"Stanbury wouldn't tell me anything, but it's clear he knows why he's been targeted."

"And the archaeologist?"

"He's convinced he's being punished for having criticized the methods of his more professional colleagues."

"The Riddingtons' secret still has not been exposed," I said. "How long have they been waiting?"

"Too long," Colin said. "They must be going mad."

"Have you learned anything further about what happened at the Royal Academy?" I asked.

"Quite a lot, actually." He handed me the *Times.*

"Heavens," I said, as I read. Mrs. Tubney, whose canvas had been destroyed, had taken out a full-page ad, apologizing to a long list of merchants to whom she owed money. Gambling, she confessed, had decimated her fortune, and she promised to stop buying things on credit. "Do you think she paid cash for her portrait?"

"I hope so, for the artist's sake."

"It's an interesting approach, preempting the news," I said. "Not that it is likely to make much of a difference in the long run."

"She may gain a shred of respect for having come forward herself," Colin said. "Finish up now, and get dressed. We've lots to do today."

Our search of Mr. Dillman's home revitalized me. The numbers we'd found on the ribbon convinced me he was guiding us to a library, and in a matter of minutes, I'd laid hands on his reader's ticket to the British Museum Reading Room. "This is just what we needed," I said. "Now we know where to go."

Colin was somewhat skeptical of my position, and insisted on going through everything else in the house, but it was to no avail. "I don't think there's anything left," he said, slamming shut the final drawer in Mr. Dillman's dressing room.

"You're the one who reminded me the house has been searched repeatedly," I said. "And I am convinced what we want is in the reading room."

He blew out a sigh and ran a hand through his hair; he was frustrated. "I don't have a better suggestion, so we may as well try there."

The trek to the British Museum was long enough that Colin insisted on taking a cab. We didn't have the luxury of enough time for a walk. As we turned onto Oxford Street, I tugged at my husband's arm.

"Tell the driver to stop," I said. He did as I requested without asking for further explanation. "Look."

Out the window, on the corner, stood Lady Glover and Winifred Harris, deep in heated conversation, the latter towering over the former. They both looked upset, and I was ready to surmise they'd been arguing when Mrs. Harris took Lady Glover's hand, her face full of sympathy. Lady Glover took a step closer and now they looked more like conspirators than enemies.

"If only there were some way to hear what they're saying." Colin stretched as if having his head closer to the window could enable just that.

"When we're finished at the library," I said, "let's call on Lady Glover and find out."

We'd reached Great Russell Street, and stood in front of the imposing entrance of the British Museum, one of my favorite places in the world. But there would be no browsing antiquities today. We stepped into the courtyard and made our way straight to the reading room, where, beneath the enormous blue-and-gold plaster dome, I accosted the first available clerk. Upon seeing Colin's credentials, he was quick to offer his assistance.

I opened my notebook and showed the numbers to him. "Does this sequence mean anything to you? Could it be a list of catalog numbers?"

The clerk shifted on his feet and bobbed his head back and forth. "It doesn't look quite right for that."

"It's possible the numbers aren't in precisely the right order," I said.

"That's unusual," he said. "And will make finding them extremely difficult."

"What should the format be?" Colin asked.

"Five digits followed by a letter and another number. There could also be another number in parentheses."

"The letters could be from the paper in Mr. Dillman's pocket," I said, and flipped to the page in my notebook where I'd written them down. "We have five three-digit numbers: 118, 104, 152, 187, and 930. What remains is 28, which would combine with any of them to give us the five digits. That, along with one of the letters could be a catalog listing."

"It's conceivable," the clerk said. "If you write out each possible combination, I can try to sort you out."

"That would be most appreciated," I said.

"If I do find matches for any of them, would you like to request the books from the stacks?" he asked.

"Please," I said.

"Do you have a reader's ticket?" he asked. "I can't get the books if you're not registered."

Colin waved his credentials again. "This is Crown business," he said. "As quickly as you can, please."

The man hesitated, as if the library gods would strike him down for committing such an offense. "I'll have to check with the deputy superintendant." He conferred with a distinguished-looking man behind the centermost of the round reference desks, and returned to inform us he'd been granted permission to continue. Once he'd gone, we went to the nearest empty reader's desk. Colin hung his hat on a peg beneath it while I sat in the mahogany chair and rested my hands on the black leather surface of the work space. It was more than an hour later when the clerk returned to us, carrying a small stack of books.

"Do you require any further assistance?" he asked.

"Not at the moment, no," Colin said. "Thank you."

I gave my husband half of the books.

"What are we looking for?" Colin asked.

"I'm not sure." I held up the spine of the first volume in the stack. "Use Mr. Dillman's numbers. If one doesn't appear in the catalog listing, take it to be a page number."

The task took longer than I would have expected. We both took copious notes on what we found on each of the pages in question, but neither of us was struck by anything we read.

"Could the pages be the key to a code?" I asked.

"Perhaps, if we had anything that had been written in code," Colin said.

"Maybe we just haven't found it yet." I sat down at the desk. "I'm convinced there's something here we're missing." I looked around the domed room. General reference books stretched around three levels of its circumference. "What about the stacks themselves? Maybe it's not a specific book that's important, but its location."

We hunted down our clerk, and asked him if we could be admitted to the famous Iron Library, the labyrinthine stacks that held the entire collection save the volumes of general reference that lined the walls of the reading room. He did not look entirely pleased, but agreed to again consult the deputy superintendant, who looked even less pleased than his employee. Nonetheless, he came over to us, inspected Colin's credentials, and nodded.

"It's highly unusual, sir," he said. "But I wouldn't stand in the way of Crown business." He took the books from us, and led us himself through a door into what seemed to be an endless expanse of bookcases. The floor and the shelves were all fashioned from iron, hence the name. I had to walk carefully so the heels of my shoes wouldn't slip through the metal grating of the floor.

"The first came from right there," he said, climbing up and showing us the empty space on the shelf.

"May I?" Colin asked.

"Yes, but please be careful," the deputy superintendant said.

Colin reached up and pulled the books to either side of the space from the shelf, cradling them in his arms.

"Nothing behind," he said, replacing them.

"I'm happy to return them for you," the deputy superintendant said.

"Don't worry. I wouldn't dream of disrupting your order. I understand completely the chaos that would ensue," Colin said. Once they'd all been returned, he removed the books from the neighboring shelves. "And still nothing." He put them back and asked to be taken to the next location. We repeated this at the remaining spots.

"What are we missing?" I asked. "There must be something."

"What, exactly, are you looking for?" the deputy superintendant asked.

"Are you familiar with the murder of Mr. Michael Dillman?" I asked.

"Yes, indeed. The papers were full of the story."

"We have reason to believe Mr. Dillman hid something here," I said. "Something that may help catch the man who killed him. We're not sure precisely what, but it seemed that the numbers we showed you were a clue to the location."

"Are you quite certain you want the library?" he asked. "Those numbers could also correspond to items in the museum catalog."

"That was another theory we had," I said. "But we thought we'd try the library first."

"Is there anything else I can do for you?" he asked.

"No, thank you," I said. "You've been most helpful."

"Do not hesitate to ask for me should you require anything further. It will be my pleasure to assist you."

Colin and I discussed our options, and quickly reached the conclusion that it would make sense to try the museum. As soon as we entered its hallowed halls, we were greeted with considerable enthusiasm. My first husband had donated many objects to the noble institution, and I'd continued to support it in every way I could. In short order, a gentleman came to assist us. I explained the situation and showed him the numbers and their corresponding letters.

"Yes, I see," he said. "It's difficult to say, Lady Emily. These don't look as if they could be complete catalog numbers. There would be more digits."

"Is it possible they're meant to be combined?" I asked.

"Of course, but again, there's really not enough to go by. Have you tried the library?"

"We've just come from there," Colin said.

"If you'd like, I'll see what I can come up with, but I can't promise anything," he said. "I may not be able to tell you anything but which departments the letters represent."

"Even that would help," I said.

"Very good. May I send you a note with the results?"

"Thank you," I said. "I'd very much appreciate it."

"And if you could, please go as quickly as possible," Colin said. "Lives may depend upon it."

"Of course, sir. I'll do my best."

4 July 1893
Belgrave Square, London

Cordelia is dead. I can hardly bear to write the words. And all this time I didn't even know she'd gone missing! I understand why Emily couldn't tell me, but I'm disturbed nonetheless. Mostly, though, I'm consumed with sadness to have lost a friend to so heinous a crime.

And I'm scared, as well. Is this paint business more sinister than it appears? Will there be more death? Or are we to take comfort in the fact that, beside Mr. Dillman and Lord Musgrave, none of our villain's victims has suffered anything but humiliation? Poor Lord Musgrave. His death silenced all the rumors about him.

I had a most disturbing experience today while walking home from calling on the Duchess of Devonshire. Perhaps my nerves are getting the better of me, but I could have sworn someone was following me. I looked behind me, half convinced I'd see no one out of the ordinary, but that was not the case. There was a boy, most likely thirteen years old, who stopped walking just as I turned around. When he saw my gaze fall upon him, he ran.

He stood out amongst the fashionable people filling the pavement. His clothes weren't tattered, but neither were they smart. He had that wan look of one suffering from consumption.

And I'm convinced he must be his son. The man who, through no fault of his own, stands between ruin and me. I've tried and tried to distract myself, but I cannot do it. I must find some way out of this mess.

In the meantime, I want to speak to Emily. I must find out everything she knows about what happened to Cordelia.

23

Ivy had been sitting, silent, in my library for nearly an hour when I told her we had to leave. She'd asked question after question about Cordelia, about the abduction, about what had been done to try to find her, about everything except the state of her body when Jeremy and I found it. After that, she'd gone quiet, very calm, and very still. I did not disturb her until the last possible moment.

Then, telling her that I was to meet Lady Glover to discuss what could be correspondence from the murderer himself, I asked her to accompany me, explaining that taking action to seek justice for Cordelia's killer was the most important thing either of us could do. This snapped her to attention, and we made our way to Piccadilly, then cut down St. James's Street to Pall Mall. I sighed as we passed Berry Bros. & Rudd, wishing we had time to pop in to see if they had any port I ought to be laying down. Trafalgar Square was full of people and pigeons—one of the feathery creatures had perched on top of Lord Nelson's tricorn hat, lending an air of absurdity to the otherwise elegant admiral and his column.

We stepped into the museum, crossing through the portico's graceful arches and to the stairs that led to the galleries. Halfway up I stepped carefully across the mosaic floor of the landing, not wanting to ~~trod~~ *tread* on Calliope or Apollo. From above, light filtered through the opaque glass of the dome, illuminating the elaborate plasterwork and its gilt decoration.

Lady Glover was waiting for us inside the room containing the gallery's Botticellis. Specifically, in front of Botticelli's painting of Venus and Mars.

"She is lovely, don't you think?" she asked, kissing me on both cheeks as a greeting. "I've been told she looks rather like me."

I studied both the lady and the painting, and sighed. "A reasonable claim, I suppose. But then, I have seen you in Roman attire, which makes the comparison easier, doesn't it?"

"The other Venus is pedestrian," Lady Glover said, motioning to another painting in the gallery. "I've heard rumors it's not a real Botticelli. Apparently there was quite a scandal, but I think it's all been covered up."

"I didn't come here to talk about art, Lady Glover," I said. "Cordelia Dalton is dead. We need to focus. You have received another note?"

"I have." She glanced around the room, an elegant space papered in a rich dark-green silk. "Do you think it's safe to show it to you here?"

"I can't imagine anyone knows what you're doing," I said.

"I could have been followed," she said.

"This person is writing to you," I said. "He's not instructed you to keep his messages secret, has he? And he's never threatened you."

"True, true," she said. "But I like to think that if he killed that poor Cordelia Dalton he could do the same to me."

"I'm not sure *like* is the word you want," Ivy said, her voice sharp.

"It is, Mrs. Brandon," she said with a wide smile. "I do enjoy a little excitement."

Her cavalier attitude did not sit well with me.

"I find your enthusiasm distasteful," Ivy said. "You might find you'd feel differently if you were actually under threat."

"But I am!" she said. "He's singled me out, hasn't he? Chosen me as the one to whom he sends his words. We can't do anything for Cordelia now. You should be concerned about me."

"Show me the letter," I said.

After another show of reluctance, she gave it to me.

> *Confer with me of murder and of death.*
> *There's not a hollow cave or lurking-place,*
> *No vast obscurity or misty vale,*
> *Where bloody murder or detested rape*
> *Can couch for fear, but I will find them out;*
> *And in their ears tell them my dreadful name,*
> *Revenge, which makes the foul offender quake.*

For a moment I wondered if I had judged her too harshly. This quote—Shakespeare again—was more frightening than those she'd received before. But she was nodding her head and smiling as I reread the words. She was enjoying this too much.

"*Titus Andronicus* is not my favorite of the plays," I said, folding the paper and sliding it back in its envelope. "Revenge describes well what he seems to be after, but this passage makes it feel more personal than it did before, doesn't it? It's not just paint flung to expose the hypocrisy of society. It's more pointed than that."

"Are you going to reply?" Ivy asked.

"Well, of course," Lady Glover said. "No one else in London has the man in the palm of her hands."

"I don't think you'd want him there," I said. "Have you shown these letters to Scotland Yard?"

"Absolutely not. I won't have them taken from me."

"They could study the handwriting," I said.

"What good could possibly come of that?" she asked. "It's not as if they have some book filled with handwriting samples from every murderous wretch in Britain."

"May I at least share it with my husband?" I asked.

"Yes, but only if you communicate to him in no uncertain terms that he is to be much, much kinder to me when he calls to return it. He disappointed me terribly last time."

"I'll be sure to deliver the request," I said, tapping my foot on the marble floor, impatient.

"I'll count on you."

I wasn't quite sure why she thought fluttering her eyelashes at me would help. "I need something from you, though. Tell me what you were doing on Oxford Street with Winifred Harris?"

"I've no idea what you mean," she said, tugging at her long, black gloves to straighten them.

"Since when are you and Mrs. Harris friendly?" I asked.

"I despise the woman," she said. "She's never been anything but terrible to me."

"I was under the same impression until I saw the two of you in rather cozier circumstances this morning. And now you're summoning me with a letter, one that seems to raise the stakes, and you are refusing to give me any of the information I need. What are you and Mrs. Harris up to?"

"Nothing at all," she said. "I was courteous to her this morning as I have no interest in creating public scenes."

"I suppose that's why zebras pull your carriage," I said.

"One has nothing to do with the other," she said.

"Tell me what she is to you."

"I can assure you it's nothing to do with the paint," Lady Glover said. "And our meeting was anything but cozy."

"Then tell me what it was," I said.

"I think we should go outside," Ivy said. "People are beginning to stare."

We brushed past a group of overly interested ladies and wound our way back through sumptuous gallery after sumptuous gallery until we had stepped outside into Trafalgar Square. Clouds had begun to form in the sky, and a cold gust whipped summer out of London's air. I held tight to my hat as I leaned against the square's empty fourth plinth.

"What is going on between you and Winifred Harris?" I asked.

"She's a wretched cow," Lady Glover said. "The worst sort of lady, and I use the term loosely. I'm surprised her entire house hasn't been covered with red paint. Perhaps I should do it myself."

"I share your lack of enthusiasm for her," I said. "What, specifically, has spurred your ire?"

"You are well aware that I had a career before I met Lord Glover." The wind strained the ribs of her parasol, so she shut it.

"Yes," I said. "You were an actress. We've discussed this."

"But not in detail," she said. "When a girl in such circumstances is first looking for work, she's not always in a position to find herself being offered the best roles."

"And?"

"I was desperate for money, you see . . . starving," she said. "And I didn't want to find myself on the streets. So no, don't think I did that."

"What *did* you do?" I asked.

"I posed for a series of artistic photographs that were later sold on postcards," she said. "It was years ago—in another lifetime. It never occurred to me someone like Mrs. Harris would find them."

"Are artistic photographs so terrible a thing?" Ivy asked.

Lady Glover lowered her voice. "I was nude."

I knew there was no possibility I could keep the shock I felt from showing on my face. My cheeks must have been crimson, and my eyes widened to the point of straining. Nonetheless my change of expression could not have begun to touch the look of horror on Ivy's delicate features.

Lady Glover shrugged. "It could have been much worse."

"How?" I asked, then pressed my hand against my forehead and shook my head. "No, don't answer. Is Mrs. Harris threatening to expose you?"

"She's blackmailing me. Says that if I don't pay her an outrageous sum every month, she'll expose me."

"Her own version of red paint?" I asked.

"She told me it wouldn't matter whether there was paint," Lady Glover said. "The end result would be the same."

"What is the end result, Lady Glover?" I asked. "Please know I don't mean to offend you—you know I'm fond of you. But it's not as if the ladies of society have drawn you to their collective bosom. Wouldn't these pictures only confirm what they're already convinced they know?"

"Yes, yes," she said. "But if I don't appease her, what will my friends think? Gentlemen aren't forgiving of everything. I've made a decent life for myself, and I'm not going to see it ruined."

"You're not going to pay her, are you?" Ivy asked.

"What else is there to do?"

"Colin may be able to help you," I said. "What she's doing is illegal, and she must be stopped."

"She'll get her due," Lady Glover said. "Of that I'm sure. I've half a mind to write to our Shakespearean friend and tell him all about her. Request some paint if I can."

"Then you'd be no better than she," I said.

"Lady Emily, I'm only interested in being as good as myself."

Colin was extremely troubled by the letter sent to Lady Glover.

"*Titus Andronicus* is a bloody, violent play," he said. He started pacing again, never a good sign. "And this passage, in the current context, is disturbing. Do you still have the note Lady Glover sent you asking you to meet her at the National Gallery?"

"I do," I said.

"I want to take it with this one to Scotland Yard."

"Why both?" I asked. "Do you suspect Lady Glover penned both of them?"

"I do," he said. "Particularly because of what she said to you—that she was going to suggest Mrs. Harris for paint."

"She was awfully glib when she first showed us the note. I would have thought she'd be upset."

"Something's rotten here," he said.

"I agree, but I'm not convinced Lady Glover is the person we're after," I said. "And what of Mrs. Harris? Where would she have come across those postcards? Surely that's not a coincidence."

"No, but it's possible they were"—he coughed—"in the possession of her husband."

I raised an eyebrow. "An interesting possibility, to be sure, but wouldn't that still be something of a coincidence?"

"That would depend on how popular that particular batch of cards was. My understanding is that they were quite the rage amongst a certain set."

"How would you know such a thing?"

"I've heard it discussed," Colin said. "Lady Glover needn't worry about her 'gentlemen friends.' They're all perfectly aware of her sins and forgave them long ago."

"That doesn't surprise me," I said. "But if the pictures were to become public, she'd find herself in a difficult position. What gentlemen accept in quiet club gossip is quite different from what they'll publically condone."

"True," Colin said. "She has a sticky enough time with society now. If the old dragons had solid proof of her indiscretions, every husband in town would be forbidden from speaking to her."

"And what of her own husband? We've no idea if he's aware of the full breadth of her past activities."

Davis entered the room. "Sorry to disturb, sir. A gentleman from the War Office is here to see you on what he insists is urgent business."

24

Our caller was not just any gentleman from the War Office, but the head of the whole department. His mustache reminded me very much of the Prince of Wales, and his erect bearing suggested a man who had spent many of his younger years serving the empire on the front lines rather than from behind a desk. He and Colin exchanged pleasantries and he bent over my hand with perfect politeness, but his eyes twitched when my husband told me to stay in the room while they spoke.

"Er, right," he said. "I've come, Hargreaves, on a rather sensitive matter." He looked at me.

"Lady Emily has served the queen in sensitive matters," Colin said. "She's instrumental to my work. No doubt you heard of what she did in Constantinople."

The man cleared his throat. "Quite. Yes. Well. No time to fuss about, is there? This business of the red paint—we've received some rather disturbing information about one of the gentlemen involved. A Captain Riddington."

"Yes," Colin said. "We've been wondering when his secret would be exposed. The poor family have been beside themselves waiting."

"Well, I don't think it's likely they'll be feeling anything akin to relief soon. A package arrived at my office yesterday detailing a battle that took place during the Zulu War."

"Captain Riddington was serving at that time, if I recall correctly," Colin said.

"He was. He was one of the most decorated soldiers in the combat—due in no small part to his deeds at Kambula. But now, it seems, the information upon which the honors were based were incorrect. His commanding officer, who was also a friend of his from school, invented much of the report. We've already spoken to several members of the unit, and they all corroborated the new version of events. Far from being a hero, Riddington hid instead of fought."

"That's outrageous," Colin said. "Was Riddington aware of what the officer was doing?"

"Hard to say, but he certainly knew he didn't deserve any of his medals."

"What will happen to him?" I asked.

"He'll be immediately stripped of the honors," the man said. "We'll see what shall be done beyond that."

"What about his commanding officer?" I asked.

"He died some years back," the man said.

"Riddington's offense is grievous," Colin said. "To lie about such a thing when so many others gave their lives is the sort of thing that merits its own circle of hell."

"Quite," the man nodded. "I've half a mind to support this campaign of red paint. Riddington deserves censure."

"He does," Colin said. "But we can't allow an unknown madman to mete out justice as he sees fit. May I see the letter he sent?"

"It's not a letter, actually, but a printed pamphlet." He pulled it out of a small, leather case he'd brought with him and handed it to my husband.

"I was hoping for handwriting," Colin said, flipping the pages and then holding the paper up to the window. "No watermark."

"A man who wishes to remain safely anonymous," our visitor said. "Can't say as I blame him. Although if he'd stuck to exposing this sort of infraction, he'd have more supporters than he could count."

"I'm afraid you're correct," Colin said. "This sort of vigilance would be welcomed."

"We wanted to keep you informed, as we've been told you're the one running this show," he said. "You may keep the pamphlet."

"Thank you," Colin said. "Does Riddington know yet?"

"Riddington's always known. But I'm setting off to see him next and will have him relinquish the medals." He rose from his seat.

"Thank you again," Colin said. "And I'm sorry you've such an unpleasant task ahead of you."

"Not unpleasant in the least. Just glad the coward is finally getting what he deserves."

Captain Riddington's public humiliation started almost at once. When I went riding the next morning, Hyde Park was full of copies of the pamphlet we'd received from the War Office. Stacks were heaped on every bench, at the foot of every statue, and in all the boats waiting to be rowed on the Serpentine. While other people's secrets had garnered at least some measure of quiet sympathy from the public, Captain Riddington's did not. By the evening, a pile of white feathers, the symbol of cowardice, had been deposited on his doorstep.

The red paint had long been stripped from his house, but now new graffiti appeared. Someone had written *Coward* and *Liar* in bold, black letters on the walls and pavement, and the shattered remains of broken eggs dripped down his door. Had he dared show his face in society, he would have been cut dead, but he refused to see anyone. He must have known there was nothing he could say to defend his actions. Proving the truth of his character, within days, he'd packed up his family and fled to the United States. No one ever saw him in London again.

His exposure changed the tenor in town. In general, people were no longer so tense as they'd been before. It was as if this latest incident changed the collective view of what had been happening. Some even spoke openly of supporting what was now being called The Campaign of Red Paint, viewing it as a necessary evil if we were to rid the empire of the unworthy. A scary sentiment at best.

Not everyone took this view, but those with painted houses and secrets not yet revealed faced increasingly obnoxious treatment. Someone had spit on Mr. Stanbury when he was going into the opera, and his wife admitted to me she'd had four invitations rescinded before she'd finished breakfast one morning. Our would-be-archaeologist in Belgrave Square had fled to Egypt, despite it being the wrong season in which to dig. Ivy had seen him leave his house, his face a mask of panic.

Colin had continued to methodically make his way through Mr. Dillman's business associates, but had found nothing that linked him either to a scandal or to any of the other parties who'd fallen victim to red paint. "It's incredibly frustrating," he said. "Have you had any word back from the British Museum yet?"

"Yes," I said. "Unfortunately, they don't have anything for us but the names of the departments. There wasn't enough of the numbers for them to provide anything else. I was thinking perhaps I should speak to the Daltons and see if I could take another look at the letters Mr. Dillman sent Cordelia. I hate to disturb them, but it may be necessary."

Just then, something banged against our front window. We both rose to our feet at once and moved to investigate. Another sound, this one more like a cascade of pebbles.

"What the—" Colin pulled the curtain aside to reveal a boy, dressed in Lady Glover's livery, pulling his arm back to throw more pebbles at us. He stopped when he saw my husband, dropped the handful of rocks, and looked in the direction of his employer's house. Colin opened the window. "What do you mean by this?"

"I . . . I . . . my . . . Lady Glover sent me, sir!" His voice was young and reedy.

"Go to the front door at once," Colin said.

We met him on the front steps, where Davis, having opened the door, gave him a stare so withering I nearly felt myself shrink before him.

"You will not throw rocks at this house again," he said.

"No, sir. I wouldn't, sir."

Davis did not take his eyes off the boy. "Will that be all, sir?" he asked Colin.

"Yes, thank you, Davis. You, boy, come inside."

"Oh, I couldn't, sir, there's no time," the boy said.

"What do you mean?" I asked. "Why are you here?"

"It's my mistress, madam, they've come for her," he said. "And the last thing she did as they was driving . . . were driving . . . her away was to shout for me to get you. Said I shouldn't speak to anyone but you. That's why I threw the rocks, madam. I didn't think I should talk to your butler."

"Where were they taking her?" Colin asked.

"I don't know, sir, but she's gone, sir. Taken in a black carriage."

Given that one would be hard-pressed to find a carriage in London that wasn't black, this was not a particularly helpful detail. Colin looked at me quizzically and I nodded, ready to follow him down the street.

We were at the Glovers' in a matter of minutes, and found the house had descended into a chaos that fell only just short of madness. Lord Glover was not at home. We sent word to his club and began to interview the staff while we waited for his return. The servants were more than ready to talk to us—eager, in fact—and it took no considerable effort to get them all to quiet down and speak in turn. In the end, Colin directed them, one at a time, into a sitting room decorated in rather more restrained taste than I would have expected to find in Lady Glover's house.

"It's the only place in this house I can tolerate with equanimity," he said.

"I've never been in it," I said.

"That's because you don't often call on Lord Glover, I imagine. His wife doesn't use it. Insists it doesn't suit her style."

Within the better part of half an hour, we put together a picture of Lady Glover's last minutes at the house. She'd changed into a riding habit, but then decided to drive her phaeton—pulled by her zebras—instead of taking to her horse. As a result, she had been waiting in the stable yard behind the house while her grooms readied the vehicle for her. All at once, two wild-looking men appeared and dragged their mistress away. They chased after her, but she was thrown into a waiting carriage before any of them could reach her.

Her maid, who witnessed the scene from an upstairs window, reported that Lady Glover's elegance was unmitigated even as she was being abducted. Her screams when she was first grabbed, the girl insisted, were as beautiful as a song. It was all apparently rather operatic.

The boy, who ran quicker than the grooms, got close enough to see Lady Glover trying to yell to him out the window. The rest of the story we knew.

"Did anyone else hear what she said to you?" I asked the boy.

"No, madam, only me."

"And you work in the stables?"

"I do, madam."

"You're a stable boy yet you wear livery?" I asked.

"Lady Glover prefers it, madam. Insists upon it," he said, bouncing back and forth between his feet. "And if I may say, madam, I don't object at all. Makes me feel quite fine, it does. Splendid, almost."

I smiled. "I can understand that."

"You will get my mistress back, won't you, sir?" he asked Colin. "I don't know what we'd do without her. She's like no other, you know—no ordinary fine lady. Even made sure I learned how to read."

"We'll do everything possible," Colin said, patting the boy's shoulder and giving him a reassuring smile.

Lord Glover's arrival needed no announcement. We could hear him coming all the way through the house. He was shouting at servants, giving directions and reprimands all at once, and stepped with the grace of a wildebeest, opening and slamming doors as he went before his staff could take care of them for him.

"What is being done?" he asked, waving a piece of paper in his hand. "Where do we go from here?"

"Glover, take a seat," Colin said. "You're remarkably quick. Thank you for responding to my summons so quickly."

"Summons? I got no summons. I came as soon as these miscreants sent their bloody note."

"Note?" Colin took the paper Lord Glover was waving at him.

If you do not pay us £1000 pounds by the end of the week, your much-cherished wife will be the next corpse to beautify Hyde Park. We will contact you with instructions.

The words had been formed from letters cut out from a newspaper. Below the message was a swish of red paint.

"There's no identifying feature to the paper itself," Colin said. "But the letters are from the *Daily Post*. I recognize the typeface."

"A thousand quid's an awfully hefty sum," Lord Glover said. "Do you think they'd be open to negotiation?"

"I wouldn't want your wife to hear you'd suggested such a thing," Colin said. "Have you any idea who might have taken her?"

"It's obvious, isn't it? That bloody fool with his red paint. He signed the note with it."

"But why would he want to kidnap your wife?" I asked.

"Why did he want to kidnap that unfortunate Dalton girl?"

"Because he believed her to be in possession of some sort of evidence that would incriminate him," Colin said. "Did your wife have any such thing? Documents, perhaps?"

"Hargreaves, you know as well as I that my wife has nothing of the sort," Lord Glover said. "She's an affable one, isn't she? Wouldn't think of blackmailing anyone for anything."

"I didn't mean to suggest she was blackmailing someone," Colin said.

"She did have a keen interest in this case," I said. "Were you aware she was corresponding with a gentleman who claimed to be responsible for the paint?"

"I remember her mentioning something about it," he said. "Can't say I paid it too much attention, though. Who can keep track of such things? She's always got some sort of intrigue to attend to."

"Weren't you concerned about what she was doing?" I asked. "Writing to a known criminal?"

"Truth be told, Lady Emily, I never believed the letters were from the genuine article. She did—well, she liked the excitement, you see. I wouldn't be half surprised if they were written by some young bloke who fancies himself in love with her and wants attention."

"I can understand your position," Colin said. "But it does appear now that there was something more nefarious afoot. And knowing that, is there anyone you suspect of wishing her ill?"

"Doesn't sound to me like this bloke has the vaguest interest in her," Lord Glover said. "It's my money he wants."

"All right, let's start there," I said. "Do you have any enemies?"

"I wouldn't be a successful businessman if I didn't."

Lord Glover had received his peerage after a distinguished run as the head of a brewery. He'd built his fortune—an enormous fortune—with the modest sum he inherited at twenty when his father died. His mother, whose family was old, titled, and distinguished, but impoverished, was ashamed he'd decided to earn a living when the family money ran out. But in the end, she accepted what he'd done. Not, however, until he'd been made a baron.

"So who would be the most likely suspects?" Colin asked.

"I really don't know, Hargreaves," he said. "Can't Scotland Yard figure it out? I'm a busy man."

"Aren't you worried about your wife?" I asked. "Cordelia Dalton is dead, most likely at the hands of the same person who has taken Lady Glover."

"Heaven help whoever he is," he said. "They'll have their hands full."

5 July 1893
Belgrave Square, London

*It's all over the papers this morning that Lady Glover has been kidnapped.
I feel terrible, particularly as I was so angry at her at the National Gallery. She was so glib, though, so pleased with this vandal. But now I see
she was only naïve, and in need of more help than I knew. I can hardly
sleep for worrying that she'll suffer the same fate as Cordelia.*

*Regarding my own troubles, I've sent three letters that have gone un-
answered. The accounts are all still in order. Nothing has happened that
should have alarmed him. But why isn't he replying? I can't very well go
all the way to Newcastle and investigate. This is turning into an absolute
nightmare.*

*Yet I can't say I regret entirely what I've done. How could any wife
have acted differently? I must remain calm—become calm—and have
confidence in the discretion with which I handled the matter. I was extremely careful. No one could find out what I did.*

Except him. And the solicitor. And the bank.

I must try not to think about it.

25

"I do hope," I said the following morning over breakfast, "that should I ever be kidnapped you'd show a bit more concern than Lord Glover." I'd slept later than Colin, and went to him in his study once I'd got dressed.

"He's more upset than you think," Colin said. "Just doesn't want anyone to see." I found this unlikely, but Colin did know both husband and wife better than I did, so I was willing to concede the point without argument. I was not, however, convinced. Regardless, every measure was being taken to find Lady Glover.

We'd stayed at the Glovers' until well after midnight, conferring with Scotland Yard on the matter of the kidnapping. At present, there were no leads to follow. All we could do was wait, just as the Daltons had, for further word from the madman.

If, indeed, that was who had taken Lady Glover.

"Why do you think he switched from handwritten notes to one pieced together from newspaper letters?" I asked. "That doesn't seem logical to me. Unless he's not the same person who sent the Shakespeare quotes."

"An excellent observation, my dear," Colin said. "It's quite strange."

"I know you rejected the idea last night, but I think we have to look at Mrs. Harris," I said. "She was blackmailing Lady Glover."

"If she wanted to raise more money, all she would have had to do was demand it of Lady Glover. Why kidnap her?"

"Her husband has more than she does," I said.

"And if Lady Glover had needed more than she could afford to keep Mrs. Harris at bay, she would have persuaded her husband to increase her allowance."

"I still don't trust Winifred," I said.

"As you shouldn't," he said. "But I don't like her for this—really, for any of it. She's judgmental enough, but not so clever as to be able to carry it off."

"I wouldn't underestimate her," I said. "When someone's judgmental enough, she can generally do whatever necessary to accomplish her bitter agenda."

"I won't deny the possibility," he said. "But I still don't like it."

"Poor Lady Glover. She has the attention of every gentleman in London except her own husband," I said. "That was obvious after speaking to him for two minutes, no matter what you say."

"I admit they may have an unconventional marriage," Colin said. "But I'm sure he is fond of her. Let's hope he gets the opportunity to treat her better. At any rate, Scotland Yard are taking the matter extremely seriously. How could they do otherwise after what happened to Cordelia?"

"Of course," I said. "They can't risk a repeat of that tragedy. What I don't understand is how Lady Glover fits in. It's clear Cordelia was murdered because of some sort of evidence her killer believed Mr. Dillman had given her. But what's Lady Glover's connection? Did Cordelia say something that led him to consider Lady Glover a threat to him as well?"

"That, my dear, is what I'm working to find out," he said. "I've got my whole day mapped out, starting with another search of the Glovers' house."

Davis brought the mail to us, first handing Colin a note that had arrived via messenger. I sorted through the rest, setting Colin's in front of him before starting to divide mine into three piles: invitations that needed only a yes or a no, correspondence requiring detailed responses, and everything that could be ignored. The third stack was not so high as I would have liked.

Colin passed me the hand-delivered note before I'd opened any of mine.

Colin, darling, this vagabond is watching me write—is directing me to write—to you and my husband and anyone else he's decided might care about my fate. I'm to tell you I'm being well looked after, but to remind you that if the ransom isn't paid as directed, he'll start hurting me.

He's very scary, Colin, and very fierce. And is looking rather too pleased to see me write such words about him. Please take his threats seriously so that we can play cards again.

—Valerie Glover

"There's nothing on the envelope to indicate from where it was sent. Scotland Yard may be able to tell something from the paper," he said.

"We should find out if Lord Glover has had a letter," I said.

"Excellent idea." He gulped his coffee and shoved the paper back into its envelope. "I'll head there at once."

Davis stepped into the room again. "Mrs. Brandon, madam. She asked to see you at once. May I bring her here?"

"Yes, please do," I said. Ivy appeared a moment later, looking nothing like her usual spirited self. Her eyes were puffy from lack of sleep, and her forehead bore the marks of tension.

"Are you quite well?" I asked.

"No," she said. "Did you get one of these, too?" She held up an envelope and thrust it at me.

Dearest Ivy, I'm absolutely beside myself with fear and angst. My captor is standing over me, watching me write to you. He wants my friends to understand just how perilous my situation is, and I chose you to write to as I know you've a kind heart and will do everything you can to ensure my husband follows his directions as quickly as possible. I'm terrified of what will happen if he doesn't.

"Lady Glover," I said.

Ivy nodded. "What am I to do?"

"When did this arrive?" Colin asked.

"This morning," she said. "Not half an hour ago."

"And it came regular post?" I asked.

She nodded again.

"This is quite disturbing," Colin said. "And is making me believe all the more firmly she's been taken by the same man who took Cordelia. Having her write letters is just in his vein. He wants her family and friends to worry while they wait. I'm off to Glover at once."

Once again relegated to waiting, Ivy and I sat, reading aloud from *The Iliad*. It was our version of seeking comfort, a vain attempt to distract us from what we imagined Lady Glover must be suffering.

"*The other chiefs and princes slept soundly all the night long: but not Agamemnon. No sleeps visited his eyes; the lord and commander of that great host had too much to make him anxious.*"

"I'm not sure this is making me feel better," Ivy said. "Perhaps we should try something else. Can't you read a bit about Hector and Andromache?"

I started to flip through the volume, but was interrupted by Davis.

"Madam," he said. "A colleague of mine is here to see you. I've put him in the blue drawing room."

I nearly gasped when I saw Mr. Dillman's butler standing nervously in the center of the carpet.

"I apologize for coming to you like this," he said. "But I thought you would know best what to do with this. You've handled this matter with such thoroughness and discretion. I know I can trust you." He handed me a folded sheet of paper.

My lovely, sweet girl—

The memory of your ivory skin radiant in the candlelight burns in my heart. To see you tonight was, as always, like a dream, and no one could argue that shade of jade green doesn't suit you, no matter what that dreadful neighbor of yours says about your new ball gown. I do wish you wouldn't take criticism to heart, but you are a dear, sensitive thing, aren't you? It's part of the reason you're more valuable to me than gold.

So greet that old dragon with stone silence next time you see her—and worry about her no further. She is not worth any more of your time.

To finish on a lighter note, if, when we're married, you still insist on having that dreadful bronze statue in the garden, I won't argue. I want nothing more than for you to be the happiest girl in the world. Which is why, as I hope you've noticed, I've written this letter on the finest paper I could find. I know how you like that.

I am your most devoted,

Michael

"Where did you find this?" I asked, fighting to keep tears from filling my eyes. I wished Cordelia had been able to read it. I passed it to Ivy.

"I feel quite stupid, really," he said. "It was in my own ledger book, between the endpapers in the back. I've no idea how it got there."

"Mr. Dillman put it there," I said, my mind springing to life and vanquishing my sadness. "He hid it in plain sight, figuring that you would give it to Cordelia when you found it."

"I would have, were she not—" he started.

"And if she'd read it, she'd have known exactly what to do with it," I said. "Luckily, I do, too."

"You do?" he asked.

"Ivory, jade, gold, stone, bronze, and paper," I said. "Clues to what we need to be looking for in the British Museum."

26

I thanked the butler, and Ivy and I headed straight for the British Museum. In the carriage on the way over I organized my notes. First, I considered the departments: Ancient Egypt and Sudan, Ancient Near East, Oriental Antiquities, and Medieval and Modern Europe. There were two references to both Ancient Near East and Oriental Antiquities, so I expected to need two objects from each. We had six numbers to go with them, and the six materials.

"Pity there's nothing Greco-Roman," Ivy said. "You'd have anything identified along those lines in approximately three minutes. But I suppose these things are never easy, are they?"

We piled out of the cab in Great Russell Street and headed for the entrance of the museum. We went straight for the desk, where I asked if my friend, Mr. May, was available. He was an assistant keeper in the department of Greek and Roman Antiquities, but had a vast knowledge outside of his field and a sharp intellect whose match I'd never met. We'd become congenial on my many trips to the museum, and he helped me on occasion with my work on Homer. I explained the situation, and he grasped it at once.

"Let's start with Egypt and Sudan," he said. "That will probably be the most difficult as the galleries will be so crowded. I always prefer to get the hardest out of the way first." I'd copied out the numbers—118, 104, 152, 187, 28, and 930—along with the list I'd generated from Mr. Dillman's letter, for each of us.

The first room we entered contained mummies and artifacts that had been buried with them. I knew the mummies were not what we sought, but there was plenty else to investigate. We combed through canopic jars and amulets and sarcophagi, but turned up nothing. Our luck proved no better in the next room, either. When we were halfway through the third, Mr. May pulled me aside.

"I think we're making a mistake," he said. "How much did Mr. Dillman know about the Egyptians?"

"I can't say I know," I said. "He loved the museum, but I'm not sure he would have considered himself an expert in anything regarding it."

"That's exactly what I thought. Come."

Ivy and I followed him back into the second Egyptian room, where he led us to a case holding several examples of *The Book of the Dead*.

"A layman may have mistaken papyrus for paper," he said. At once, we all began checking the numbers.

"Here!" Ivy said, beckoning to us. "I've found a 104 and think it may be what we need. It's from the papyrus of Ani."

The scene on the papyrus was an image of scales—on one side of them sat a human heart, on the other, a tall white feather.

"The Egyptians believed when a person died, his heart would be weighed against the feather of Ma'at—justice," Mr. May said. "If his heart was too heavy and didn't balance, he was thrown to the monster you see there." He pointed to a figure that was part lion, part hippopotamus, and part crocodile. "The devourer, as he was called, would eat him, and he'd be denied the afterlife."

"Who officiates the weighing?" I asked.

"Anubis—the jackal-headed god standing in front of the scales. If the heart did balance, the deceased was declared justified, and would be presented to Osiris, god of the underworld."

"Judgment certainly feels appropriate in the current circumstances," I said. I copied down the full catalog listing, EA 10470/3, and crossed *104* and *paper* off my lists. "Where shall we try next?"

"Let's continue in the Ancient Near East galleries. We've two things to search for there, do we not?" We marched through several galleries to a room containing objects from ancient Turkey.

"I never spend enough time up here," I said, astonished at the array of objects before me. As always, the sense of history overwhelmed me. "Perhaps I'm too focused on Greece."

"It's impossible to be too focused on Greece," Mr. May said. In theory, I could not have agreed more, but I was beginning to think perhaps I should consider broadening my horizons.

We split up and began our quest. This time it was easy—in a matter of minutes, I was calling to my friends.

"Here," I said. "An ivory griffin-headed demon from Anatolia."

"It's beautiful," Ivy said, bending over for a closer look.

"It probably was part of a throne and meant to provide protection," Mr. May said. "Eighth to seventh century BC."

There were two griffins in the case—one black, one white—displayed next to each other. Ours, the white was, in my estimation, the finer, if smaller, of the two. It was more delicate, and the intricate detail was breathtaking. Every feather on the creature's wings was exquisitely carved, as were the rippling muscles visible on its legs. The darker material of the other seemed to hide more of its detail despite its larger size.

"Protection and judgment. Perhaps Mr. Dillman trying to make a point to Cordelia," I said.

"It's so sad," Ivy said. "But I suppose we must not lose focus. Where to next, Mr. May?"

"I think we should remain here," Mr. May said. "We've got a second reference for this department, do we not?"

He was correct. Unfortunately, however, our quarry was not so easily found this time. Over the expanse of the Ancient Near East galleries, I looked at what felt like hundreds of objects: gold jewelry, stone statues and reliefs, bronze weapons. But nothing had the right numbers. I circled back to where we'd started, deciding to take each substance in turn. I would begin by focusing on stone.

Nearly an hour later, I still hadn't met with success. I rubbed my eyes and closed them, wanting to make them focus better. Mr. May came up beside me.

"I've found it," he said, leading me to a case on the far side of the room. He pointed to a row of small heads that looked like they might belong to deranged dogs. "Pazuzu. He can be good or bad. He either spreads evil or stops disease. So he provides a bit of protection, when he's not busy being an underworld demon. Obviously we want the bronze one."

"He's frightful," Ivy said. "I have a hard time believing he's ever good. Where is he from?"

"The Assyrians worshipped him as did the Babylonians," Mr. May said.

"It's hideous," I said, staring at the menacing face, its eyes set too far apart and its wide mouth partly open to reveal long fanglike front teeth. "But gloriously hideous." Again, I copied down all the information from the display card, not knowing what might be important.

"We have two objects from the Department of Oriental Arts," Mr. May said. "Shall we proceed?"

Oriental Antiquities took up three galleries on a level slightly above the ground floor. We descended the slick marble stairs, pausing to gape at a magnificent Chinese sculpture from the landing halfway down.

"Jade's obvious for this section," Ivy said. "Let me set myself to finding it. I shouldn't have any trouble doing that on my own."

"Very good," I said. "That leaves stone and gold. The only other department is Medieval and Modern Europe. What do you think, Mr. May? It seems to me our gold is likely to be there."

"Entirely likely," he said. "Let's look for stone in here."

I knew very little about Oriental art, and was taken aback by its exotic beauty. Within seconds, the Hindu gods and the elaborate carved scenes depicting their trials and triumphs that filled the gallery space had thoroughly captivated me. I wanted to make sketches of them, to find books that recounted their mythology. I shook my head, forcing myself to regain my focus, and concentrated on my work.

I'd worked through two-thirds of the main gallery and was almost at the end of the Indian section when I saw it. It was the number that first caught my notice, as I'd made myself read the cards before looking at the objects, lest I found myself distracted by their beauty. The number 187 popped out at me and as soon as I'd confirmed the object was indeed what we were looking for, I waved to Mr. May, who had moved into the Chinese portion of the exhibit.

"Mrs. Brandon is up to her ears in jade," he said. "She wants us to meet her when we're done."

"Durga," I said. "OA 1872.7-1.89. Isn't she spectacular?"

"Indeed," he said. "She's attacking Mahisha, a demon who's trying to plunge the world into cosmic disorder. It's a wonderful story. She's got Shiva's trident and Vishnu's discus—they've lent them to her because they're afraid they'll be destroyed if they go after the beast themselves—see how Durga's stabbing him with the trident?"

"He looks like a buffalo," I said.

"Precisely," Mr. May said. "A terrible buffalo demon. Durga means *invincible,* you know."

"Fitting," I said, gazing upon the magnificent piece. The goddess's arms—I was trying to make out if she had six or eight—were clad with wide cuff bracelets. She held a sword above her head in one hand and the trident in another. Unfortunately, some of her other hands had been broken off. I wondered if originally she'd been even better armed than she appeared now. Some sort of fearsome creature—a lion, perhaps, crouched below the demon, his jaws clamping down on its leg. I loved the tall, elaborate headdress on Durga's head, and her heavy earrings. But most of all, I loved her strength, loved that it was she whom the other gods summoned when doom seemed inevitable.

"Are you still with me?" Mr. May asked.

"Of course," I said. "You do know how I love this place. It's hard not to get a little distracted. But I promise, I am on task. We should see what Ivy's got up to. Once we're done with jade, all that's left for us is the Middle Ages."

We went off in search of my friend, who stopped us the moment we approached. "Don't even think about interfering," she said. "I am determined to find this one on my own."

The cases in front of her were full to the bursting, many of the items in them tiny. There were amulets, combs, beads, and countless discs with holes in the center. One case held blades made from jade, which surprised me, as I would not have expected something essentially translucent to be strong enough to be an effective weapon. There were brush pots carved with stunning landscape scenes and images of farmers hard at work, pendants shaped like curvy dragons, and strange, square objects called *cong,* with tubular holes in the center. I particularly liked a small statue of an animal—some sort of leopard, I thought, crouched and ready to pounce on its prey.

It took only a few more minutes for Ivy to throw up her hands, victorious. "I see it: 28," she said, a smile on her face. "And look at him." The piece was a jade mask, barely human, with horrible veins in his forehead, horns on his head, and fangs shooting out of his open mouth.

"Jade was considered extremely potent by the ancient Chinese. It could offer one protection, even in the afterlife," Mr. May said. "But this isn't the sort of thing I'd want in my house, no matter how powerful it was."

"It's scary," Ivy said. "I'd have nightmares."

"Do you think?" I asked, tilting my head. "There's a beauty to him. And such a lovely contrast—the frightening demon fashioned out of such a beautiful, smooth stone."

"I'd be happy to never lay eyes on it again," Ivy said. "But that may be due to nothing more than it having taken me so long to find it."

"This last one shouldn't be too difficult," Mr. May said. "Come back upstairs. The Medieval and Modern Europe galleries aren't excessively large, and we know we're looking for gold."

He was right; it wasn't difficult. We each started at a different spot and quickly read the catalog numbers of each pertinent object. For all the breathtaking gold in the museum, Mr. Dillman had chosen something understated but deeply moving to represent the category. I found the piece, and felt my limbs go heavy and my blood seem to stop moving when I saw what went with the number. A slim, gold and enameled ring.

"Seventeenth century," I said as my friends gathered around. "A mourning ring. The inscription reads, *Memento mori*—'In remembrance of death.'"

Around the outside of the ring was a series of bleak images. First, a skeleton holding an hourglass, which I took to be a reminder of our own mortality. Then came tools for digging a grave, and a sheath in which a body could be wrapped before burial.

"It reminds me of Cordelia's locket," I said. "That didn't start as mourning jewelry, but it certainly became just that."

The room felt colder, and I was happy to turn away from the ring. In the case behind me, there was another display. More mourning rings, a great heap of them, all from the seventeenth century. I thought of all the people who died during the great plagues of the Middle Ages, and wondered what had become of those who had worn these rings. How long did they survive after the loss of their loved one? Did they succumb to the disease as well? Next to the rings was a small, gold cup, which had been made out of melted-down bands. After their owners had died, there must have been no one left to want even their most precious jewelry.

It was frightening how temporary the significance of any person was in the end.

We thanked Mr. May profusely, and promised to return for tea and scones another day, as we couldn't pause even for a short break at the moment. I was terrified that every moment squandered put Lady Glover in more dire peril. We left the museum and went straight to the reading room, where the clerk who had previously assisted Colin and me recognized me at once.

"Ah, Lady Emily, back so soon, are you?" he asked. "Let me get the deputy superintendant for you."

The gentleman came quickly, and greeted us with an easy affability. He became more tense, however, when I told him what I wanted to do and why. "That will be no small undertaking, Lady Emily," he said. "And we can't possibly go through the entire library."

"We won't need to," I said. "Mr. Dillman would take his fiancée to her father's library after she'd found the object he'd wanted her to in the museum. The object was a clue of its own—she'd use it to find a book, and he'd hide something for her either in or behind it."

"I'm afraid I don't know what to look for," the deputy superintendant said.

"Let's take each of the six subjects in turn. Perhaps we can look through the stacks and see if anything's out of place. Because I know your books are not misshelved."

"No, madam, they are not. But we have three miles of bookcases, and twenty-five miles of shelves. This is an impossible task."

"We don't have to search the entire library," I said. "But if there were enough of us working, we could cover each subject in a relatively short period of time."

"I'll let you try," he said. "And will offer as much assistance as I can. I feel I must warn you of possible disappointment, however." He summoned four clerks and took us back into the Iron Library. Light streamed into the stacks from its glass roof, traveling through slats in the iron floor designed to keep even the lowest levels bright. Bright was perhaps too strong a word. The librarians told me they carried lanterns with them nearly all the time.

We made our way through the maze of iron and set ourselves in front of the section where all the volumes to do with ancient Egyptian papyri were shelved. Ivy and I focused on bottom shelves, while the librarians climbed tall ladders and inspected everything above us. Together we checked that each title belonged to the subject.

They all did.

So we followed with Medieval mourning jewelry. And then Assyria and Babylon. Halfway through the books on ancient Chinese jade, I shouted *Huzzah!*, which brought the clerks and Ivy to my side in a flash. I apologized for having been so loud, but could not squash my delight. There, tucked between two innocuous books about the Ming Dynasty was *The Seven Great Monarchies of the Ancient Eastern World; Or, The History and Geography, and Antiquities of Chaldaea, Assyria, Babylon, Media, Persia, Parthia, and Sassanian, Or New Persian Empire*, written by a Mr. George Rawlinson.

"It's exactly what I wanted," I said. "He left it in the wrong place to tell us where to look."

Ivy peered over my shoulder. "I don't doubt for a moment these great ancient monarchies are devastatingly fascinating, but I still don't quite understand what you're on to."

I pulled the surrounding books off the shelf and reached my hand to feel where I wasn't quite tall enough to see. Straining, I stretched farther, and felt something distinctly unbooklike. I inadvertently pushed it, rough and prickly, out of grasp when I tried to pick it up. One of the taller clerks stepped forward and brought it down for me.

"Well done, Emily," Ivy said, looking at the parcel. "I admit I had very little faith in the enterprise."

Before we turned to analysis of what we'd found, we carefully returned all the books to their proper places. Then, thanking the deputy superintendant and his clerks profusely, we started to leave.

"Aren't you going to open it?" the deputy superintendant asked.

"I'll leave that for my husband," I said. "It's Crown business, after all." I didn't mean it, of course, but I didn't want to open it in public. Not without having any idea what it contained. All I knew was there was a screaming good chance the information therein was important enough to have cost two people their lives.

Within a few moments, we'd secured a cab and were speeding back to Park Lane. We did not, however, stop at my house. Instead, we continued on to the Glovers', where from out the cab's window we could see a group of police officers had gathered on the front pavement, my husband standing in the middle of them.

"What's going on?" I asked, standing on my tiptoes in a vain effort at being seen.

"Emily?" Colin spun around and pushed his way to me. "Go inside at once, and don't come out until I get you. You, too, Ivy. I hope you both enjoyed the museum."

I knew from his tone not to ask questions, or to tell him yet what we'd found. A dour servant opened the door for us and put us in the Egyptian room, where we sat and waited.

"Do you think it's safe to look?" I asked Ivy, pulling the mysterious package out from the folds of my skirts, where I'd hidden it when we alighted from the cab.

"I don't see why not," she said. "There's no one else here."

Which was when the door opened. We both jumped, but it was only a maid who entered the salon, not someone who might have a nefarious interest in what we were hiding.

"Would you ladies care for some tea or perhaps cognac? Cognac's what madam preferred in the afternoon."

"Have you had news of her?" I asked. The girl's use of the past tense worried me.

"Have you not heard?" she asked. "I thought that's why you were here."

"No," I said. "Please tell us."

She was a little skittish. She went to the door, opened it, peered into the corridor, then shut it again and returned to us. "I don't know all the details, madam, but it seems they've found one of the sleeves from the dress Lady Glover was wearing when they took her."

"Where did they find it?" I asked.

"In Hyde Park, madam," she said. "I don't think I'd be going there anymore if I was you. Isn't safe there, is it?"

"I'm inclined to agree with you," Ivy said. "Did they find anything else?"

"Not that we've heard below stairs, but that's not saying there couldn't be more."

"Thank you," I said. "And I think we will have some cognac."

"Feeling the need for fortification?" Ivy asked after the girl had gone.

"I'm worried sick about Lady Glover, but I know I can't let that distract me," I said. I'd buried the parcel in my skirts again when the maid had opened the door, and hadn't pulled it out yet. "We should wait until we know we won't be interrupted."

It took nearly a quarter of an hour for our drinks to arrive. I asked the maid to ensure we would not be disturbed except by my husband,

and then took a sip of the golden liquid. Its warmth was soothing. Confident we were alone, I set the parcel on the table between us.

It was wrapped in coarse fabric, a sturdy burlap. I tugged at the twine that bound it—it was much narrower at one end than the other and round, like a cylinder. Or a bottle.

Which is exactly what it was. Wrapped tightly around it was a stack of papers. I removed them and examined the bottle first. It was about half full with a muddy-looking liquid. Long, rusty nails stuck out above the muck, and as I turned it in my hands, I saw the sad remains of a little toad in it. And then a large, black spider floated to the top.

"I don't like this," Ivy said. "I don't like spiders. Not at all."

"This one can't do you any harm," I said, placing the bottle carefully on the table. I wasn't any happier than Ivy with what we'd found. Not because I disliked spiders—they didn't bother me in the least—but because there was something deeply disturbing about the contents of the bottle. Everything about it seemed evil.

I shuddered.

And then I unrolled the papers and started to read.

"Mr. Foster is going to have a great deal of explaining to do," I said.

Colin sorted things out with Scotland Yard as quickly as he could, but it was nearly another hour before he joined us in the Egyptian room. I offered him cognac, but he wanted to go home, and he did not want to discuss what we'd found until we were there. Three police remained in front of the Glovers' house, and I could see them watching us as we walked along the street. They gave a brisk wave when they saw we'd arrived with no incident.

"Is there some reason to think we, specifically, aren't safe?" I asked, pouring my husband two fingers of Glenmorangie the instant we were settled in the library.

"No," he said, taking the glass and thanking me. "They're just on edge, that's all."

"Has Lord Glover received anything more from the kidnapper?" Ivy asked. "He must be absolutely torn up over this."

"Someone found the sleeve, along with a note pinned to it—I assume the servants would have told you that—in the park this morning. It didn't take long for the police to figure out it belonged to Lady Glover. Her maid confirmed it was what she'd been wearing when she was last seen."

"What did the note say?" I asked.

"Would you like to see more of your wife than just her sleeve?" he said. "They've made a thorough search of the park, but found nothing else."

"Poor Lord Glover," I said.

"He's seeking consolation in his club," Colin said. "Insists he doesn't want to stay in the house. His man will bring him any messages sent for him—but not until after he's shown them to me."

"So there's no news beyond that?" I asked. "No instructions for the delivery of the ransom?"

"Nothing," he said.

"If it's any consolation, we have a new direction for you to follow," I said. "Our day has been shatteringly productive."

I passed him the papers we'd found wrapped around the bottle.

"Foster?" Colin asked, rising to his feet and starting to pace. "Foster owns the match factory? He's an advocate for the working class. He wouldn't stand for the conditions in that place."

"Perhaps he's never taken the time to visit," I said.

"I've looked into the details of the business," he said. "And saw no mention of Foster's name. Furthermore, what they're doing may not be strictly illegal. There's a way in which, technically, they are providing a service to families who don't want to see their infirm loved ones in a workhouse."

"But Foster does own it," I said. "We've proof of that now. And we know Dobson and Florence are working for whoever killed Mr. Dillman. Surely this implicates Mr. Foster?"

"It may indeed," Colin said.

"He's certainly got motive for wanting Mr. Dillman dead—"

"*If* he knew about these papers," Colin said. "We don't know that he did."

"Mr. Foster knows perfectly well what he's done," I said. "And he must be worried his role in the enterprise will be exposed. I'm certain this is what Mr. Barnes was worried about."

"That's entirely possible," Colin said. "But do remember that Barnes said his friend's action, whatever it is, would only appear unethical if taken out of context." Colin put the documents aside and turned his attention to the bottle.

"Watch out for the spider," Ivy said. "It's horrendous."

"What on earth is this?" he asked.

"I've not the slightest idea," I said.

"Did you ask anyone at the museum?"

"I didn't want to show it to anyone without speaking to you first."

He nodded. "I appreciate your discretion. Take it there tomorrow morning as soon as they open and see if the keepers have any clue as to what it could be. I'll go see Foster at once."

"What about Lady Glover?" Ivy asked. "She asked me to help her. What can I do? I can't let her down. She's in danger."

"Nothing," Colin said. "We need something more before we can act. But don't worry, I'm sure Lord Glover will receive instructions for delivering the money before long."

"Has he decided to pay it?" I asked.

"He's not happy about it, but I have managed to persuade him against negotiation."

"You're a miracle worker," I said.

"We'll find out the truth of that soon enough."

5 July 1893
Belgrave Square

*For all that I'm deathly worried about Lady Glover, I admit to having got
rather caught up in all the excitement at the museum today. Seeing Emily
like that, in her element, so sharp and insightful, quick-witted and capable,
working for justice, made me wish more than ever that I could confide in
her and beg her help.*

But I just can't bring myself to do it.

*Still no reply from him. What we've learned about Mr. Foster has
me deeply concerned. I understand that business records are more likely
to become public than a person's carefully concealed indiscretions, but
knowing how smart Mr. Foster is, I can't help but worry. If a gentleman
of his intellect can be caught unawares—for surely he did everything
in his not insignificant power to hide his involvement in this odious
organization—how likely is it that my attempt at discretion will fare
better?*

Ivy had gone home to Robert. I had Davis bring me a cold supper in the library, so I could read *The Aeneid* while I ate, as had become my habit that summer when Colin went out for the evening. Ordinarily I loved a measure of solitude, but I was feeling little peace tonight. I knew Colin would be careful, but Mr. Foster was quickly beginning to loom ominous and frightening in my mind, and I was worried about Lady Glover. I did not like sitting idle when someone was in danger. I nibbled on some cold ham and tried to distract myself with Virgil's poetry. *Sed famam extendere factis, hoc virtutis opus*: To extend one's fame by deeds, this is the work of courage.

Darkness had fallen by the time I'd finished eating and had poured a glass of port. I wasn't quite sure where the evening had gone, but was well aware of how easily hours could slip away when I was absorbed in a book. I was pondering the late hour when my butler announced Jeremy, who nearly tripped over himself coming into the room.

"Em, where's Hargreaves?" he asked. "I need his help."

"What's happened?"

He pulled a letter out of the pocket of his frock coat. The paper was crumpled. He smoothed it as best he could and handed it to me.

*My darling Bainbridge, I fear the end is nearing for me. Can
you please help? I'm so close to home—I could be there in a
matter of moments if only someone would unlock this door. I see
trees out all the windows of my room, but can hear the sounds of
the city. Today I stood on a table to get a better look and am
certain I am in a building in Hyde Park. Can you not come and
fetch me? You mustn't bring the police—he's convinced Cordelia's
parents contacted them and says that's why he killed her. I don't
know that I'll be able to write again. Come to me. I'm desperate.
I used my wedding ring to bribe the woman who brings my food
to deliver this. I pray she does as she promised.*

"She must be in the park," he said. "There are all kinds of buildings
there: gardeners' and caretakers' lodges. They could be holding her in
one of them. I wanted to get Hargreaves's advice."

"The park seems reasonable," I said. "It's where they found her sleeve.
But Scotland Yard searched everywhere."

"They could have missed something. Please, Em, where's your husband?"

The fact that he referred to Colin without making any dig at him
brought home to me the seriousness of the situation. "He's at Mr. Foster's.
I'll go with you."

Davis called for the carriage and within minutes we'd reached Mr.
Foster's house in Belgravia. I banged on the door. After what seemed an
interminable delay, it opened to reveal an ancient butler.

"The Duke of Bainbridge and Lady Emily Hargreaves to see Mr.
Foster, please," Jeremy said.

"I'm afraid he isn't available, sir," the butler said.

"Is my husband here?" I asked.

"Mr. Hargreaves is inside, yes."

"Will you please admit me?"

"I cannot do that, madam. I'm under strict orders."

"It's urgent. There's an emergency."

He was unmoved. "Strict orders."

"Could you check with Mr. Foster, please?" I asked.

"I'm not to disturb him."

"Would you deliver a message to my husband?"

"The moment he leaves Mr. Foster's company."

My frustration had reached from my toes to midway up my torso. Much more of this and I might do something I'd regret. I decided, in the circumstances, it was best to waste no further time and cut directly to potentially regrettable action. We didn't have time to squander. I thanked the butler and told him I wouldn't leave a message. Then, once he'd closed the door, I pulled Jeremy around the house to the mews.

"We're going in through the servants' entrance," I said. "We'll find where they are and interrupt their meeting."

We didn't knock. Instead, we marched in with purpose and conviction. Two maids pressed themselves up against the narrow corridor's wall to keep out of our way, but neither of them questioned us. We oozed authority. We went up the back stairs to the first floor, but kept to the servants' hallways rather than risk being seen in the main part of the house. Even these passages, though spare in terms of furniture and finishing, were not without a dash of luxury—paintings hung from the walls. Not so fine, perhaps, as those in the family's rooms, but better than I'd seen in many country estates.

"Mr. Foster must be an avid collector of art," I said.

"Either that or he has more money than sense," Jeremy said.

There were no carpets in the hallway, and the heels of my shoes clacked loudly enough on the stone floor to draw unwanted attention, so I removed mine; Jeremy followed suit. We crept along in our stockings, listening for any signs of conversation, and wound our way halfway around the house before hearing any. I came to a stop when I recognized Colin's voice and pressed my ear against the door from whence it came.

"We can't do that now, don't you see?" he was saying. "It's gone too far."

"We're not going back," Mr. Foster said. "That would be untenable."

"And what am I to tell everyone? Scotland Yard? My wife?"

"That can't be my problem right now, Hargreaves. You know that."

I did not like what I was hearing.

"What's your devoted husband hiding from you?" Jeremy asked.

"Quiet," I said. "Someone's coming."

Footsteps echoed down the hall. We couldn't stay where we were. I grabbed Jeremy's arm and we tiptoed to the next turn in the passage. There was no obvious place to hide. Voices came from the other direction, and I did the only thing I could think of—duck into the next door we saw. My heart was pounding, not because I was afraid of being caught, but because of the words we'd overheard. I wanted to know what was going on.

We'd stepped into a sitting room, furnished in an impersonal yet fashionable style, the sort of uninspired décor with which one could neither find fault nor much to admire.

"What is your plan now?" Jeremy asked. "I thought we were going to burst in on their conversation."

"So did I," I said. "But it didn't seem the thing to do in the moment, did it?"

"Then let's go listen to the rest."

We waited, ears pricked, while the voices that had sent us scurrying faded in the distance. Then, with caution, we returned to the corridor and crept back to our illicit *écoute*.

"And thereafter?" Mr. Foster said.

"It's impossible to predict. Things are so volatile right now." Colin's voice was calm. "We need to wait to see what sort of situation we're in after things have settled."

"Sit back down. We need to run through it all again. I'll call for some food. We never did get around to eating."

Jeremy tugged at my sleeve. "We can't stay here all night," he said. "Lady Glover could be in terrible danger. If we're not going to interrupt them, there's no point hanging on when we could be trying to help her."

"You're right." We retraced our steps, pausing to put on our shoes at the top of the stairs that led down to the kitchen. Once we'd made our way halfway down, the butler appeared at the bottom. When he did, he nearly lost his balance.

"Sir! Madam!" To say he was aghast would have been something of an understatement. "I . . . I—"

"Delightful to see you again," I said, neatly stepping around him. "I'm sure we'll meet again before too long. Do enjoy the rest of your evening."

Jeremy and I tumbled out of the house, nearly doubled over with laughter by the time we'd emerged back in the mews.

"I'm beginning to have a vague notion why you like all this intrigue," Jeremy said.

"It's exciting, isn't it? Terrifying, but exciting." I was breathless with mirth. "Come, though, we've no time to waste. Lady Glover is in danger."

We leapt back into the carriage and fairly flew to Hyde Park, crossing through Apsley Gate at Hyde Park Corner. I directed the driver to the first lodge I could remember. We couldn't have him take us all the way—the clatter of wheels might alert our friend's captors. Jeremy and I skulked towards the building.

"You should let me take over from here," Jeremy said. "It would be safer."

"I'll stay back," I said. "But I'm keeping you in sight."

"I suppose I can't just knock on the door?" he asked.

"No." Moving as quietly as he could, he methodically made his way to each set of windows on the building and then returned to me.

"Nothing to see there but a gardener and his contented-looking wife," he said. "Or his dissatisfied mistress. I consider the two interchangeable."

"What would be the wifely equivalent of an extremely pleased mistress?" I asked.

"A widow."

We repeated our pattern at three more buildings.

"I must say I had no idea how pleasant some of these lodges are," Jeremy said. "How exactly does one go about arranging to live in them? I'm ready to give up my house."

As we approached the fourth lodge, a small building in the northern section of the park, I followed Jeremy to the windows. I bunched up my skirts to step over the iron fence—it wasn't particularly high—and then ducked down when I got close to the windows. Inside, two men were sitting, fierce looks on their faces, their attention fixed on the other side of the room. The upholstery on the chairs, which looked velvet, was worn and threadbare. A bookshelf at the far end was empty save for a pile of neatly stacked newspapers. But it was the object in the center of a rough-hewn table that sent the strongest message to me. The side we couldn't see. Stepping with care, we moved farther along the outside wall of the house, hoping for a better view. We still couldn't make out much, but I did manage to catch a glimpse of turquoise satin fabric encrusted with golden-colored crystal beads. Then, one of the men moved, revealing a revolver under his jacket.

Excitement and fear coursed through me. Wanting to operate with extreme caution, we made our way back to the pavement to discuss our options.

"We need a plan," I said. "I think she's in there."

"I agree," he said. "I think I can—" He stopped talking and lunged towards me. Before he reached me, I felt a sharp blow, and everything went black.

29

I tasted dirt when I woke up. Taking a deep gulp of damp, mossy air, I struggled to my feet. My head ached, and I leaned against a tree for a moment, trying to get my bearings. It appeared I was still in the park, but I could no longer see the lodge in which I suspected Lady Glover was being held. There was enough moonlight that I could make out vague shapes around me, and in the not-too-far-off distance I saw the flicker of what had to be gaslight. I walked towards it and found myself only a few paces from the Round Pond in Kensington Gardens. Not finding much to recommend spending any more time in the park than absolutely necessary, I moved quickly in the direction of Kensington Palace.

Jeremy was nowhere to be found. I worried he'd suffered a fate similar to mine, but knew there was little I could do to locate him on my own in the dark. As soon as the lights of the palace came into view, I started shouting, hoping someone inside would hear me.

Unfortunately, as the structure had fallen far from its days of splendor, and was now used primarily as a place the royal family could stick inconvenient and distant relatives, there were no guards on hand to assist me. The gates were locked. I shook them and yelled for help to no avail. Not wanting to stop moving until I felt safe, I ran out of the park and into Palace Green, almost tripping up the steps of Lady Carlisle's house.

I don't know when I've ever better appreciated the comforting warmth of a family home.

Lady Carlisle fussed over me unmercifully, and I welcomed her ministrations. She plied me with tea, then sherry, and wiped the dirt from my face and hands herself with a soft linen cloth. Her husband notified the police and sent a message to Park Lane at once. Colin must be beside himself with worry. It was nearly two o'clock in the morning.

I reclined on the chaise longue and closed my eyes to ward off the throbbing in my head. The sound of Lord Carlisle conversing with someone brought me alert again. Jeremy was standing next to me, along with two inspectors from Scotland Yard.

"Thank heavens you're all right," he said.

"What about you?" I asked.

"I started for the thug who was coming for you. Didn't make it two steps before someone whacked me on the back of the head, too."

"Lady Glover?"

"We've been back to the lodge, madam," one of the inspectors said. "She's not there. We'll conduct a more thorough search in the morning."

"I'm sure she was there," I said. "You must believe me."

"Did you see her?" he asked.

"No, just a glimpse of fabric. But I'm certain—"

"Don't try to exert yourself, Lady Emily," Lord Carlisle said. "Your butler sent a message saying your husband is not at home. Would you like to stay here tonight?"

"He's not?" I asked, confused and wondering where he could be at this time of night.

"No. I'm afraid we don't have any further information."

"I see," I said. "Thank you for your hospitality, but I think it best I go home. He'll be worried if he returns and finds me gone."

"I do wish you'd let me send for a doctor," Lady Carlisle said.

"You're very kind," I said. "But I'm perfectly all right. No permanent damage done, just a little bump. I've had much worse. I would, however, be eternally grateful if you'd lend me your carriage."

They were reluctant to let me go, but in the end were persuaded to agree that Jeremy could see me home.

"I'm no longer so convinced about the merits of excitement," he said. "When I woke up and couldn't find you I thought bringing the police was the best thing to do."

"You were right," I said.

"I do wish they'd been able to find Lady Glover," he said. "It looks like what we saw were some vagrants who had thought they'd find a good place to seek temporary shelter."

"Vagrants don't wear turquoise silk with gold beads," I said.

"Well." He paused. "Vagrants may not, but there are certain women of ill repute who could have access to such garments."

"Hmpf." I wasn't convinced. "They should be taking what we saw much more seriously after what happened to Cordelia. If this man has moved Lady Glover to another location, he's more likely to have decided to kill her. This is the time to follow up on every lead as thoroughly as possible." We'd reached my house. Jeremy offered to come in and sit with me, but I declined. Instead, I went inside alone, then sank down, sitting on the steps in the entrance hall as Davis closed the door behind him.

"Where is Mr. Hargreaves, Davis?" I asked.

"He hasn't returned to the house tonight since he left with Mrs. Brandon, madam," he said.

"And he's sent no word?"

"No, madam. I'm sorry."

With a sigh, I retired to bed.

I hardly slept that night. Colin slipped into the room as the sun was beginning to rise. He was quiet, assuming, I'm sure, that I was asleep, but I sat up the instant he opened the door.

"Sorry to disturb," he said. "Are you all right? Davis said—"

"Davis shouldn't even be awake," I said. "Where have you been?"

"With Foster. Tell me what happened."

"I want to hear from you first," I said.

"I'll humor you, but only because Davis has already assured me your health is fine," he said. "Foster doesn't have any idea of what's going on in that factory."

"You can't believe that," I said.

"I do. I approached him from every considerable angle, and he didn't squirm at all. He's got no clue there's anything untoward that could come out about him."

"Did you tell him what we saw there?"

He hesitated, only for a single breath. "No. I thought it best not to yet."

"Why?" I asked. My head was spinning, and not because I'd been whacked on it. I couldn't believe for a second they hadn't talked about it. "He owns the place from whence our attackers came. How can you trust him?"

"We'll discuss it later," he said. "I'm worried about you. Tell me everything."

I did, but with little enthusiasm. I wanted to know what he was hiding from me.

"You're confident it was Lady Glover in the lodge?" he asked.

"I can't prove it," I said. "But the place must be searched as soon as possible."

"I've no doubt Scotland Yard have the matter well in hand. I'll check in with them as soon as I've changed my clothes."

He rang for his valet and stepped into the dressing room. I followed him.

"You should stay in bed," he said.

"There's no need. I feel perfectly fine. My head doesn't even hurt anymore." This was true. Doubt in one's spouse apparently had miraculous healing powers. "I want to hear more about what Mr. Foster had to say."

"There's nothing else to tell, Emily. It was a thoroughly underwhelming conversation."

"Then why did you stay so long?" I asked.

"He pulled out an exceptional whisky and we got to trading stories about school."

I looked at him through narrowed eyes. "How foolish do you think I am?"

"Not foolish in the least."

"You're on notice, Colin Hargreaves," I said. "I know you're hiding something from me, and I don't like it one bit."

"You know perfectly well I can't tell you everything," he said. "Don't be cross. I will give you one thing. Mr. Stanbury, whose house was splashed with red paint some time ago, owns a significant interest in the match factory."

"Have you spoken to him about it?"

"I will today."

I rang for Meg and asked her to bring me breakfast. I wanted to be at the British Museum the moment it opened, and didn't have time to dillydally. With Colin remaining adamant about keeping the details of his chat with Mr. Foster private, I half wished I had something to bash him on the head with. I had a strong suspicion what he was hiding from me had nothing to do with Crown secrets. From what I had overheard, it had everything to do with two men planning something underhanded.

"You're going to let Mr. Foster hide his role in this, aren't you?" I asked as I prepared to leave for the museum. "Because you agree with his political views? Maybe let Mr. Stanbury take the fall?"

"I told you, Emily, I'm not discussing it."

"Fine," I said. "I will respect that, though I don't like it at all. But you need to tell me how all this fits into the case we are currently investigating. Is he involved?"

"It's highly unlikely."

"Really?" I asked. "So did he murder Mr. Dillman—or have someone murder Mr. Dillman—to keep the evidence out of the public eye? And the red paint was just a coincidence?"

"You're following a very dangerous line of speculation," he said. "This situation is more complicated than it appears at first glance. I'm not convinced Mr. Foster knows anything about the factory. For now, we'll have to leave it at that."

"He owns it," I said. "How can you believe he knows nothing about it? I don't, not for a minute. And until you tell me something that points me definitively in another direction, I'm going to pursue every possibility. Including this one."

When I reached the museum, Mr. May, to whom I'd sent a note almost as soon as I'd woke up, was already waiting for me. We went to his office, where I unwrapped the bottle for him. He took it from me, handling it gingerly. "I've not seen anything quite like it," he said. "It's primitive and contemporary at the same time."

"But you think it's modern?" I asked.

"The bottle dates from before 1850, I'd say. See this?" He turned it up so I could look at a rough round scar on the base. "That's a pontil mark, made by the rod the glassblower would use to hold the piece when it was finished. They're not made that way any longer. The bottoms are more smooth now."

"And what of the objects inside?"

"A toad, a spider, nails—that may or may not have been rusty when placed inside—and muddy water." He rolled the bottle in his hands as he itemized everything he saw.

"Was the water muddy to start, or did it get dirty from the nails and the toad?"

"It was muddy to start," he said. "There's too much muck on the bottom and sides to have come from even an extremely dirty toad."

"What does it mean?"

"I'm not certain, but it appears to be some sort of primitive religious charm. African, perhaps. It could be meant to offer protection."

"Would anyone else in the museum have a better idea of what religion, specifically?"

"We could speak to the keeper who handles ethnography in his collections. He may know more."

Mr. May fetched the man from his office, who then studied the bottle for a good ten minutes before speaking.

"I certainly don't recognize it," he said. "Sorry not to be more helpful. The only thing it brings to mind is voodoo, the sort practiced by some people in the West Indies. I agree with you, May, about the age. It's not new."

"What would such a thing be used for?" I asked. "Mr. May suspects it's meant to provide protection?"

"Again, I'm not an expert. But I could well imagine that a person who hid it with sensitive papers—as you said it was when you found it— would have wanted something he believed would offer protection. If, that is, he dabbled in such things."

"Thank you, both of you," I said. "This has been immensely useful."

"I'm so pleased, Lady Emily," Mr. May said. "And if you learn anything else about the bottle, would you let me know? I'd be fascinated to hear more details."

6 July 1893
Belgrave Square, London

Nothing further on Lady Glover.

I spent a more or less pleasant day at home—pleasant, that is, when I managed to ignore the fact that my friend has been kidnapped. Rose is enchanted by butterflies and chases them around the garden. I don't know when I've encountered a lovelier scene. Yet even when watching my daughter play, I'm consumed with anxiety and fear of exposure. I feel as if my stomach is eating at itself.

Still no word has come from Newcastle.

The tension continues here in London. Lady Glover's kidnapping has made everyone's nerves more raw. They're all looking for red paint and accusing each other of sins more nefarious than their own. How much longer can this go on?

The sun was high and bright when I left the museum, but dark clouds had started to take over patches of the sky and the air had a chill reminiscent of autumn. It felt more like England than it had in weeks. I hailed a cab and went straight to Mr. Barnes's office, feeling my best hope was to appeal to someone who'd lived in the West Indies.

"I have a strange question for you," I said as soon as I was seated in a comfortable leather-backed chair. "Do you know anything about voodoo?"

"Voodoo?" he asked, straightening a pile of papers on his desk.

"I found something I have reason to believe may be related to it," I said, pulling it out of the bag in which I'd been carrying the bottle and handed it to him.

He removed it from the bag and touched the glass. "This isn't voodoo," he said, his voice soft and soothing. "It's Obeah, a religion common amongst the natives in the West Indies. The Europeans were often terrified by it."

"Why?" I asked.

"They didn't understand it," he said. "It's all spells and shamans and things unfamiliar to them." He turned the bottle over in his hands and half smiled, his lips closed. "I never expected to see this again."

"You recognize it?"

"I made it," he said. His voice, rich and smooth, was softer than usual. "Not the bottle itself, but I put the contents together. Are you horrified?"

"Should I be?" I asked.

"It's not as if I practice black magic," he said. "But I do remember the spells my nanny swore worked. Mr. Dillman came to me one night—I assume you found this with his possessions?"

"Yes," I said.

"We didn't start off as terribly close friends," he said. "But I saw him on a fairly regular basis at political functions and we realized we shared very similar values. He had progressive ideas about business, and I thought he could offer excellent advice to those making pertinent policy decisions. We came to trust each other very much."

He sat back down, holding the bottle. "One night, he came to see me unexpectedly. He was agitated and desperate. He wouldn't tell me what was going on, but was obviously in need of some friendly comfort. All I could get out of him was that he was terrified someone was trying to destroy him. Without knowing additional details, there was not much I could do for him that would be of real help."

"What a terrible situation to be in," I said.

"It was, but I managed to console him with rather too much claret. Before long, he was saying that he wished there was some way he could strike back at someone—I don't know whom—who had crossed him in a business deal. He became angry and frustrated and fixated on bringing this man, or these men, down. At that point, I thought it best to find some way to distract him from his troubles, and island superstition seemed as good a way as any."

"So you put this together for him?" I asked.

"As I said, there had been rather too much claret consumed," he said. "I found an old empty bottle and we set off to fill it in an appropriate manner. By the end of the evening, his spirits had been restored. He took the bottle, telling me he was going to give it to the man causing his grief."

"He didn't tell you anything at all about what specifically was troubling him?" I asked.

"No," he said. "And I didn't see a need to press him on the subject at the time. You can imagine how this has haunted me since his death. I should have pushed him harder."

"So what, exactly, does one do with something like this?" I asked, reaching for the bottle.

"You put it near your enemy's door and it will bring to him just a touch of trouble," he said.

"Who was he going to use it on?" I asked.

"He wouldn't tell me," he said. "When I heard what had happened to Dillman, I felt ill. I went to Scotland Yard at once and told them everything. They were decent to me, but I could tell they thought I was a little crazy. Still, it seemed the right thing to have informed them, even if it came to naught."

I thanked him for his candor, but was not quite trusting enough to take him at his word. After I left his office, I stopped at Scotland Yard to corroborate Mr. Barnes's story. The detectives were less than pleased to see me, but showed signs of amusement when I asked them my question.

"Right," one of them said, thumbing through a file. "I do remember something like that. Yes, here it is." He held up a paper to show me. "All documented, black magic and everything. Mr. Barnes was half mortified telling us, the poor man. Did the right thing, though, coming forward, even if it didn't prove significant to the case. Wish more people were as concerned with justice as he is."

Satisfied, I continued home, where I found Ivy and Jeremy waiting for me in my Impressionist-filled drawing room.

"We asked Davis if we could wait for you," Ivy said. "Jeremy said the two of you have quite a story for me. He refused to breathe a word of it until you got back."

"Indeed we do," I said. "But first, I have some information about our bottle."

"It makes perfect sense, doesn't it?" Ivy said, after I'd filled them in on everything I'd learned. "Instead of leaving the bottle for his nemesis, Mr. Dillman used it to protect the papers."

"Would the charm bring to harm whoever found it?" Jeremy asked.

"I hope not," Ivy said. "Do you think we should be worried?"

"No, I don't," I said. "I don't believe in magic and evil spells. But this does make me want to take a much closer look at the papers we found with it."

"Let's do that," Jeremy said.

"We can't," I said. "Colin has them. So I suppose we should tell Ivy what happened to us last night." We recounted for her all that had happened in the park.

"I've never heard anything so terrible!" Ivy said, leaning so far forward in her chair I feared she would fall over. "Are you all right?"

"Perfectly," I said. "My head is fine today."

"And you?" she asked Jeremy.

"I'm only thankful the ingrate hit the back of my head," he said. "It would have been much worse if he'd mangled my face."

"Vanity will be the end of you," Ivy said.

"I think we should go back to Hyde Park," I said. "Scotland Yard insist they found nothing significant in the lodge, but I don't think they looked hard enough. Are you two game? We cannot let Lady Glover suffer the same fate as Cordelia."

"I certainly wouldn't let you go alone, not even in broad daylight," Jeremy said. "I never would have dragged you there last night if I had thought I'd be putting you in danger."

"I don't believe we were in much danger," I said. "And now I feel even more secure. If they'd wanted to kill or abduct us, they could have easily done so last night. The fact that they didn't suggests to me that we're not causing them much worry."

"They just needed us out of commission long enough to move Lady Glover," he said.

"There's something strange about it, isn't there?" I asked. "You'd think they'd be more concerned about us tracking them down."

"Maybe they're about to collect the ransom and let their prisoner go," Ivy said.

"Perhaps," I said. "Regardless, I want to take another look at that lodge, and I'm going to need both your help."

The afternoon had turned still chillier, and heavy rain clouds were on the verge of expunging the last blots of blue left in the sky. Armed with umbrellas and coats, we rushed to the park, which was relatively crowded given the weather, and made our way to the lodge I'd visited the previous night. There were too many people around for us to gawk in the front windows, so we adopted a different strategy. Ivy and Jeremy walked boldly up to the door and knocked.

"Why aren't they answering?" Ivy asked, far too loudly.

"I've no idea." Jeremy was using his best reading voice. It was not what could be called natural, but it was certainly audible to everyone nearby. "They're expecting us."

A main pavement ran only a few feet in front of the lodge. My friends' subterfuge was providing a necessary distraction.

"Hello there!" Ivy called to a gentleman passing by. "Could you please tell me what time it is?" She stepped towards him and he met her near the gate in the fence. Everyone else's eyes were on her.

I was stunned. Ivy commanded the attention of all the people in the immediate vicinity. She had the presence of a skilled stage actress.

"I despise it when people don't keep an appointment, don't you?" she continued. While everyone was focused on her, I moved from my position behind a shrub on the side of the lodge to its back garden. No one had noticed me, and now, safely installed behind the house, no one could see me. I pressed my face against the windows, but could see very little. There was no light coming from the interior as there'd been at night. I would need to get inside to investigate. Having tested all the windows and the back door only to find them firmly fastened, I did the only thing I could think of.

I removed my shoe and struck its heel against a pane of glass, right above the window's lock. Then, gathering my skirt around my hand, I pushed it inside, released the cloth, and flipped the lock. Now the window opened with relative ease. I looked around, just to reassure myself there was no one watching, and climbed into the lodge. The room into which I descended was a pokey bedroom, small, with no furniture in it. I walked towards the front of the building, to the chamber into which I'd peered yesterday.

The chairs were gone, as were the newspapers. The bookcase remained, empty, as did the table. But the table had a dark stain in its center. I touched it. It was damp. I bent over and sniffed.

Cognac.

They must have spilled some in their hurry to clean out the room.

It was decent evidence, but not enough to convince Scotland Yard Lady Glover—or any woman of rank—had been in the room. I covered the room in measured steps, studying every detail that I passed. The wide, deep windowsills were clear and entirely dust-free, which did not suggest long-term vacancy. The floor itself left something to be desired— there was dried mud and scattered leaves on it . . . mud that must have been old, for it had been so long since it had rained.

As I turned direction, continuing my study of the floor, something caught my eye: a golden crystal bead. One that had clearly fallen off the dress of the lady who'd been here last night. I picked it up. There was nothing else of interest on the floor. The fireplace showed signs of recent use—I wondered if Scotland Yard had noticed—but rather than the faded embers one would expect to find from burning coal, the hearth was filled with ash like that from burnt paper. I pulled a sheet from my notebook and scooped some onto it, folding the page to form a sort of pocket around the ash.

Finally, I crouched in front of the bookshelf. Not even a crumble of newsprint remained in it, but on its top, stuck to the wood, was the slightest bit of wax.

Yellow sealing wax.

I left part of it in situ. The rest I scraped off with a fingernail and wrapped in another sheet of paper. Ivy and Jeremy had started knocking on the door again, our prearranged signal to alert me it was time to go. I crawled back through the window and to the path on the side of the house. I peeked around the edge, making sure it was a good time to make my entrance, then stepped onto the pavement and waved at my friends.

"Whatever can you two be up to?" I asked, trying to modulate my voice to sound like Ivy's had during her earlier stellar performance. I would never be the actress she was.

"We were trying to pay a call, but they're not home," Ivy said. "What a bother. Shall we go for tea?"

It had started to drizzle, but not quite hard enough to justify opening our umbrellas. She and Jeremy met me on the pavement.

"Success?" he asked.

"Yes," I said. "I'll show you everything when we're home."

31

We walked back to Park Lane as the rain began to fall more steadily. Cold and damp, we shuffled into the library and called for tea. Fortification was in order. On a long table, we laid out everything we'd gathered over the course of the investigation: the bottle, the ash, the wax, the bead, and a letter from our villain that Colin hadn't returned to Lady Glover. The only thing missing were the papers pertaining to Mr. Foster's ownership of the match factory.

I picked up the wax I'd collected from the park lodge and compared it to that on Lady Glover's letter. They were identical. I searched through my desk, then Colin's, but could not find the scathing missive Winifred Harris had sent to me, sealed with yellow wax.

"We have no time to waste," I said. "Ivy, can you call on Winifred and try to get a sample of her sealing wax? I'm going to meet with Mr. Foster. Given that he has the most to lose, it seems likely to me he knows something about the papers Mr. Dillman was hiding."

"What about me?" Jeremy asked. "Am I to be left with no occupation?"

"I never thought the most useless man in England would desire such a thing," I said, grinning.

"I'd love it if you came with me," Ivy said. "You can distract Winifred while I get the wax."

"It would be my pleasure to offer you any assistance I can, Ivy," he said. "Anything in the service of Crown and country. Just don't make me flirt with her."

As soon as they left, I went to Colin's desk, pulled out a sheet of his stationery, and, using his pen, wrote a note to Mr. Foster in what I hoped was a reasonable approximation of my husband's handwriting. I chose my words carefully and did not doubt for a moment he would arrive on my doorstep as soon as he could.

I explained my plan to Davis and then paced, waiting for Mr. Foster to arrive. It took him less than half an hour. Davis showed him into the library, brought him a whisky (I tried to insist on the Glenmorangie, but my butler would have none of it, not even in the cause of justice), and we let him sit there for a little while before I descended upon him.

"I realize you were expecting my husband," I said. Davis had stayed in the room, standing tall and motionless next to the door, but Mr. Foster was too much of a gentleman to comment. "But I'm the one who needs to talk to you."

"I'm terribly sorry I wasn't able to see you when you called earlier," he said, all politeness. "I was locked in a meeting it seemed might never end. I'm sure you understand."

"Of course." Part of me wanted to confront him about the papers I'd found wrapped around the bottle, but I knew I couldn't do that. Instead, I pulled out the bottle. "Does this mean anything to you?"

"A dirty old bottle?" He leaned back in his seat. "I can't say it does."

"You've never seen anything like it?"

"Never. But surely you haven't summoned me here under false pretence to discuss some old piece of rubbish?"

"No, I was hoping you could explain some of the finer points of politics for me. I'm coming up against some interesting bumps in my work for the Women's Liberal Federation."

"I hadn't realized you were still pursuing it," he said. "I thought Mr. Dillman's death had changed your direction."

"It has to a large degree, but I'm not privy to everything my husband is. There are frequent occasions on which all I can do is wait. I'm told patience is not a quality I possess in abundance."

He smiled. "No, I imagine it wouldn't be. What are your political woes? I'm happy to help you pass the time until more exciting work comes your way."

"If women do get the vote, I can't imagine anything could be more exciting," I said. "So let's see if we can help make that happen, shall we? Several gentlemen I've spoken to have offered various levels of support for our cause."

"Excellent news."

"Yes, except it's come to my attention that some of them, in their personal lives, have attached themselves to projects, shall we say, that are less than desirable."

"Projects? Do you mean affairs?"

"No, no," I said. "Nothing of the kind. Business, I mean. They're engaged in business practices that fall short ethically."

"And what is your concern?"

"Do we want our movement to include them, given their moral shortcomings?"

"The unfortunate truth is that gentlemen do fall short sometimes, particularly when it comes to business. They let their desire for wealth trump their desire to conduct themselves ethically."

"I can't condone that," I said.

"Nor can I," he said. "It's an issue that's troubled me greatly for years. I've done much work trying to ensure better conditions for the working class, but try to convince their employers to help when it requires cutting back even slightly on their profits."

He smiled again, his composure utterly intact. This was not a gentleman concerned his own role in such scandalous dealings was in danger of being revealed. Or rather, this was not a gentleman concerned I was a person likely to cause him any problems, despite my role in the investigation.

"It's outrageous," I said. "I recently had occasion to become better informed about the way the working class live. Something must be done. Given that I feel so strongly on the subject, how can I overlook the failings of those persons supporting the vote for women?"

"That, Lady Emily, is the problem of politics. You should speak to Mr. Barnes. He's an expert on refusing to compromise when it comes to morality. Because he works to shape policy from a distance, he insists on higher standards. He can distance himself from anyone who doesn't measure up. As a result, people on both sides of the divide listen to him— they know his opinions and analyses aren't tainted by overwhelming desire to win the next election."

"Like you."

"Yes," he said. "Like any of us whose fortunes rise and fall with the whims of the people."

"I don't know how you can bear the pressure," I said. "I couldn't."

"One doesn't enter politics unless one is thrilled by every aspect of it. Elections are titillating times during which anything can happen."

"But what if the outcome is all wrong?" I asked. "That must be infuriating."

"The loser always thinks the outcome is wrong," he said, pulling his brows in close together. He tugged the sleeves of his jacket. "Which is why it's best to never find oneself in the position of losing."

"I've heard stories of unscrupulous politicians going to great lengths to ensure victory. Surely that's no way to secure the right outcome? A man willing to cheat has proven he's a bad choice to hold office."

"What made you think of that?"

"Nothing in particular," I said. The truth was, it had seemed to me a fairly obvious jab at political scandal.

"It's not something that happens," he said. "Not really. Not these days. People can't just go about stealing elections, no matter what anyone tries to claim." His voice had an edge to it I'd not heard before.

"I imagine it happens more than anyone cares to admit," I said. "Unscrupulous men who care about winning above all? I can easily picture their sort arranging to have ballot boxes stuffed."

He balled his right hand into a fist and released it, again and again in rapid succession. "No, Lady Emily, you're off the mark on this one. It doesn't happen except in fiction."

Unethical business practices didn't cause him any unease, but his entire demeanor had changed when he spoke about elections. That gave me enough for the moment. I would figure out what to do with it later. "What do you think of this business with Lady Glover? It's terrifying, isn't it?"

"I imagine she's undaunted, even in the face of abduction," he said. "She's a brave girl and will come out of this with stories to dine on for years."

"You're not worried about her?"

He sighed and flushed just a little. "I am. But I'm trying not to give up hope altogether. Too easy to fall into despair if one thinks on it too much."

"After what happened to Cordelia Dalton, we're all on edge."

"Of course," he said. "Try not to trouble yourself with it. It will be sorted out. Forgive me, but I must be off. I've a meeting with the prime minister. It's been a pleasure speaking with you."

"It's always a delight to spend time with you," I said.

He got up to leave, but turned back as he was about to leave the room. "Emily, next time you want me to come to you, there's no need to pretend it's your husband who's in need of company. I assure you I'll always give you my utmost discretion."

Four hours after Mr. Foster left me, the *Post* ran a special evening edition. A boy from the East End who rented his affections by the hour had sold them his story, and all the lurid details of his encounters with Mr. Stanbury had been exposed for public consumption.

Colin came home at nearly seven o'clock. "You've seen the paper?" he asked, tossing a copy of the *Post* on my desk.

I nodded. "We need to talk about Mr. Foster. I saw him this afternoon."

"You didn't speak to him about the papers you found, I hope?"

"No. I knew you'd want me to leave that to you," I said. "But I've learned quite a bit today, and your friend, Mr. Foster, may not have quite the character you'd like to think." I told him everything that transpired.

"Well done, Emily," Colin said.

"Don't you think it's odd that Mr. Stanbury's secret was exposed so soon after I'd unnerved Mr. Foster? Mr. Stanbury, who's also connected to that dreadful match factory?"

"Foster got agitated when you mentioned election fraud, not the mistreatment of working class," he said. "Why would that push him to do anything to Stanbury? And Stanbury's secret didn't have to do with the factory. I'm telling you, Emily, the factory isn't what you think."

"I despise the place," I said.

"I know," he said, placing his hand softly on my cheek. "I've spoken to our solicitors and set up an account for you to use. We will look for a building in a suitable location and you can design a better plan for Mr. Majors's charges."

"Thank you," I said. "I still don't trust Mr. Foster, though I am sorry

I seem to have made him think I was sending for him on false pretenses."

"You did send for him on false pretenses."

"Yes, but not *those* false pretenses. You must make a point of letting him know we're blissfully happy so he doesn't get the wrong idea."

"Gentlemen don't speak to each other in such ways," he said.

"Could you not make an exception, just this once?"

"Absolutely not," he said. "It's a good lesson for you."

"You're a savage," I said.

"Good work with the bottle, though. And I'm pleased you got Scotland Yard to assist you without me."

"I was rather happy about that myself. But we need to return to the subject of your good friend, Mr. Foster. You're going to have to tell me what happened with him last night."

"I've already shared all I can," he said.

"So would you prefer that I draw my own conclusions from the bits of conversation I overheard? *'We're not going back. That would be untenable.'* Or do you prefer, *'What am I to tell everyone? Scotland Yard? My wife?'*"

"How did you hear that?" he asked.

"I called at the house to fetch you when Jeremy and I decided to look for Lady Glover. The butler wouldn't admit me, so I went in through the servants' entrance and skulked through hallways until I heard your voice. I was planning to announce myself to you, but then I heard what you were saying."

"Emily!"

I looked away from him, knowing he must be furious.

"Did no one see you?" he asked.

"Two maids and the butler. It's amazing what walking with an air of authority can accomplish."

He dropped his head into his hands. I stood up, bracing myself for the inevitable reprimand. I crossed my arms and waited.

"You are bloody good at this, aren't you?"

This took me by surprise. "I thought you'd be angry."

"I probably should be. But we're working together on this, Emily, and if I'm to accept you as a partner in life as well as in work, I can hardly balk when you show this sort of initiative, even if I'd like to."

"Marrying you was an extremely good decision," I said.

"Yes, well, I do feel I ought to remind you of that periodically," he said.

"Do so as often as you feel necessary," I said. "You won't find me objecting."

He kissed me. "Tell me what else you learned today."

I went through everything, omitting no details, and showed him everything we'd collected.

"Poor Foster!" he said. "He must have been dead worried when you started questioning him."

"He was—but only when it came to talk of elections. That seems to be the one thing that can cause a crack in his composure. He should, perhaps, be more concerned about the possible exposure of the papers Mr. Dillman hid."

"He'd be embarrassed by that, but not ruined. He's a good man, Emily, and I'll do everything I can to protect him from political trouble."

"You and Mr. Barnes," I said. "Maybe Mr. Foster isn't so good as you both think. I assume the match factory is what Mr. Barnes was worried about. And now you're ready to dismiss it. Why?"

"Reginald Foster is the man who ought to lead this country when Gladstone's done."

"Even if he's embroiled in business practices that are destroying lives?"

"Would you rather see the country run into the ground by some incompetent lout?" he asked. "I'm as upset by the factory as you are, Emily, and I'm convinced we can find a way to improve the lives of those people.

But when it comes to politics, I'm inclined to take a long-term view and support the man best able to lead the empire."

"What if he killed Mr. Dillman to keep his secrets private? And what if those secrets aren't limited to the factory, but also to election fraud?"

"Prove it, Emily, and we'll find ourselves having a very different conversation."

7 July 1893
Belgrave Square, London

I am no good at subterfuge. I'm afraid everyone around me is beginning to suspect something's wrong. The only time I can forget what I've done and act normal is when I'm helping Emily. Partly, I suppose, because I'm working to stop the person who could destroy me, and partly because active employment gives the mind less time to worry.

Perhaps it's hideous of me, but I truly enjoyed our adventure in the park. I loved playing a role, pretending to be in another life. A life in which I was doing something that might help save Lady Glover. A life in which my secrets didn't exist.

I'd never realized how debilitating secrets can be. Am inclined to confess everything, but only once all this is over. If it ends, and the villain is caught before I'm exposed, I'll own up to what I've done. There's no getting away with things like this, only periods of time where one forgets to be frightened of what would happen if everyone knew. I don't want to face that ever again.

I'm not quite so good at liberating objects from people's houses. Thank goodness Jeremy was with me at Winifred's. Still, I can't feel good about what we've done or what we learned.

32

I'd invited Ivy and Jeremy to come for breakfast and a council of war; I wanted to discuss all that we'd learned after we'd split up in the afternoon. Jeremy was much put out, insisting he couldn't be anywhere before two o'clock in the afternoon, but managed to drag himself out of bed, and at nine o'clock, the four of us were seated comfortably around the table. The breakfast room looked over the garden, but there was no view today. The rain, which had started while we were in the park the day before, had grown heavier overnight, and now showed no signs of stopping. Fog and clouds socked in the town, and all we could see out the rain-streaked windows was a heavy gray mist.

Ivy poured milk in her tea and stirred it. "We spent a very strange afternoon with Winifred. I'm afraid, Colin, that we may need to intervene soon."

"Why is that?"

"She told us about Mr. Stanbury's scandal," Ivy said. "Before the paper came out."

"I don't like the woman at all," Jeremy said. "She gives me the willies. If you could have heard the glee in her tone as she told us."

"It was disturbing," Ivy said. "Jeremy did an admirable job of keeping her distracted, though. I've brought a sample of her wax." She stood up and went to the sideboard, where we'd spread out our other clues. I followed her.

"An exact match," I said.

"I can't say I'm surprised," Ivy said, her voice a bare whisper. "Winifred's growing more and more fixated on people and their secrets. She . . ."

"What?" Colin asked.

". . . she told us she's keeping a list. A list of people and their secrets. She said she's going to make sure they're all exposed." Ivy's hands trembled as she sat back down and picked up her teacup.

"Ivy, did she confess anything to you?" Colin asked.

"No," Ivy said. "But I wouldn't be more alarmed if she had than I am now. I was surprised she spoke so freely in front of Jeremy."

"I'm not," he said. "She took it as an opportunity to warn me off bad behavior."

"I can't believe I've been so naïve, thinking she ever had my best interests at heart," Ivy said. "This is an obsession for her, not a kindness."

I reached for her hand and held it. "You always see the best in people, Ivy, and that's a wonderful quality."

"I was stupid," she said.

"I don't think so," Jeremy said. "If anything, your charming habit of adoring everyone around you is endearing. I may throw Emily over for you."

"You've done excellent work, Ivy," Colin said. "And if you hadn't accepted Mrs. Harris—and her faults—as a friend, we wouldn't know to suspect her now. Emily, share with us what you learned from Mr. Foster yesterday."

I relayed to them the details of our conversation.

"I don't trust him at all," Ivy said. "He's such an appearance of goodness, yet he's got better motive than anyone else."

"It's never wise to trust someone who looks good," Jeremy said.

"I can't say I'm sure what I think about him," I said.

"What about Mr. Barnes?" Colin asked. "He admits he put together the bottle."

"For Mr. Dillman," I said.

"What if he learned that Mr. Dillman was trying to destroy Mr. Foster?" Ivy asked. "He could have left the bottle on Mr. Dillman's step in an attempt to make him stop."

"It's possible," Colin said. "Barnes wouldn't have had such an easy time getting the respect he has if he didn't have Foster's backing."

"So they both have motive for wanting to keep those papers hidden," I said. "But Winifred Harris would have no such compunction. If anything, she'd want to expose them."

"Could she have killed Dillman in an attempt to get them?" Jeremy asked.

Ivy cringed. "I cannot believe her capable of that."

"I've gone through all the files in painful detail," Colin said. "We don't seem to be missing anything. None of our three has a credible alibi for the murders—they were all in London at the time and not indisposed. They each have motive, and they each have the ability to move around with enough freedom to have given them opportunity."

"Our villain, whomever he or she may be, is exceedingly clever," Ivy said. "Look at all he's done without leaving any real clues to his identity."

"It's true," Colin said. "You'd think he would slip up eventually and reveal something."

"He's like you," I said. "Maddeningly calm in the face of adversity."

"Perhaps *I'm* your villain," he said.

"No, I don't like you for it," I said. "You're too fond of architecture to go around vandalizing people's houses."

"That's quite a vote of confidence," he said.

Jeremy sighed. "I don't suppose it ever crossed your mind to suspect me?"

"No," we all said in unison.

"Another crushing disappointment."

"I'm sure you'll recover unscathed," I said. "And if you don't, we'll have to soothe you later. There's no time now. What we need at the moment is to incite in our villain an emotion strong enough to cause him to make a mistake, preferably one that will lead us to Lady Glover."

"How do we do that?" Ivy asked.

"I'm not sure yet," I said. "But take Mr. Foster, for example. Whatever we did would need to have something to do with elections—they're the one thing that made him lose his composure. I'm inclined to see what his thoughts are on fraud in such circumstances."

"Mr. Barnes?"

"He's knowledgeable about Obeah," Colin said, "and wouldn't have remembered how to cast an appropriate spell after all these years away from the culture unless he believed in it at least a little bit. What, in a similar vein, might frighten him into thinking someone is after him? If he's guilty, he couldn't help but react."

"Mrs. Harris deserves a measure of her own medicine," Jeremy said. "Perhaps we need her to think she's been beaten at her own game."

"Find out her secret and expose it?" I asked.

"Precisely," he said.

"There may be something there," Ivy said. "But we should focus on Winifred's attempt to blackmail Lady Glover. Nothing she's hiding could be worse than facing imprisonment for extortion, and we wouldn't have to dig around in search of some unknown fact about her."

"That's good thinking, Ivy. Do you think Lord Glover would let us search the house?" I asked Colin. "I can't imagine his wife didn't keep some sort of evidence against Mrs. Harris."

"She's far too smart to have neglected that," he said. "I can speak to Glover, but I think it would be preferable if you did the actual searching. I don't want to rifle through her belongings."

"Why not?"

"It would be more seemly for a lady to do that, don't you think? Or, if you're ever under suspicion, should I send a burly policeman to go through your bedroom?"

"Fair enough," I said. "So that leaves Mr. Foster and Mr. Barnes. I'd like to take Foster as I suspect you, Colin, have an inclination to protect him?"

"I'm not ashamed to admit it," he said. "And will be desperately disappointed if I have to acknowledge murder as one of his sins."

"At least you're admitting he sins," I said. "I'll consider that a step in the right direction."

"You're awfully hard on him," Ivy said. "He's the one who helped you in Westminster."

"If he were prime minister, you'd have a much better chance at making real progress towards winning the vote for women," Colin said.

"I wouldn't want his help if he's as bad as those papers suggest."

"I don't want to get distracted arguing politics right now," he said. "But would you really rather hold back equal rights for women than let slide some accusations that can't be sufficiently proven?"

"I'd wager that they could be sufficiently proven if you were willing to thoroughly investigate them," I said.

"I don't agree."

"I see your point," I said. "But I still can't concur. I don't want to support a crooked politician just because he supports my cause."

"No one has proven him crooked."

"As I said, no one has bothered to try. Except perhaps Mr. Dillman. And we all know how that turned out."

33

The next morning, even before I'd finished with my toilette, Ivy called for me. I had Davis send her to my dressing room, where Meg was struggling with my hair while I tried to read *The Aeneid*. The persistent rain had made it even more disobedient than usual and I was half convinced my maid was using my body weight in pins in her attempt to tame it.

"You're soaked," I said when Ivy pulled up a chair to sit next to me.

"It's apocalyptic out there," she said. "And only seems to be getting worse."

"Do you need tea?" I asked.

"No, thank you. I've been thinking," she said, picking up the silver-backed hairbrush from my dressing table and pressing her fingertips against the bristles. "I need you to help me with Winifred. I've lost my nerve."

"You know Winifred despises me," I said.

"I know. But there must be some way."

She looked every kind of distraught. Her face was crinkled and pale, her pupils tiny and hard. I took the hairbrush away from her before she made permanent dents in her fingers.

"You're very good at this, Ivy," I said. "Just think how well you did in the park."

"That was different," she said. "It was in front of strangers, not someone so well acquainted with me."

"We'll come up with something. Don't be upset."

"What if she flies into a rage?" Ivy asked.

"She will, but not against us," I said. "In fact, you've given me an idea of how I can help. We'll call on her as soon as we're done at the Glovers'."

It did not break Meg's heart to have to give up on my hair. With a sigh of relief, she handed me a bonnet that would hide at least some of its unruliness.

"Truly, madam, in weather like this there's no hope for you."

I threw a waterproof over my shoulders, Burberry gabardine lined with a fine wool.

"Really?" Ivy asked. "You look like you should be in the country. Possibly shooting something."

"You said it was apocalyptic outside. I've no interest in getting as soaked as you."

"I won't try to stop you," she said. "But it does pain me."

We went downstairs and she collected from Davis an elegant mantle, with enormous sleeves and wider-than-could-be-sensible shoulders. He held an umbrella over our heads as he led us into Ivy's carriage, and we arrived at Lord Glover's house as dry as possible in the downpour.

The man himself was not at home, but his butler said we were expected, and led us upstairs to Lady Glover's bedroom. He invited us to ring should we need any further assistance, and disappeared, closing the door behind him.

Her boudoir reminded me very much of Constantinople. The walls were tiled, rather than papered, and her bed was draped with richly colored silks hanging from tall posts. Instead of a settee or chaise longue, she had a collection of large pillows—also silk—piled in a corner. A book sitting in the middle of them suggested she liked to curl up there to read.

"I can't imagine that would be comfortable," Ivy said.

"Try it. I think you'll change your mind."

Ivy looked skeptical, but did as I suggested. "She's on to something here, Emily. This is decadent."

Getting up from the pillows proved somewhat more difficult with tight stays. I clasped her hand and pulled her to her feet so we could begin our work. We searched through every drawer in the chamber before moving on to the dressing room, where we met with equally little success. I rang for the butler.

"Is there anywhere else that Lady Glover tended to her work? Or answered correspondence? Does she have a study?"

"Follow me."

He led us up another flight of steps to an elegant room, furnished in the neoclassical style. It contained a desk and three tall bookcases with glass fronts. The desk drawers had been fastened shut, but it took me fewer than sixty seconds to open them with my lock picks.

Each drawer was stuffed full of letters, most of them from amorous gentlemen eager to express their admiration for Lady Glover. It horrified me to see the names signed on the bottoms of some of them. Was there a man in London immune to her charms?

"I'm almost afraid to keep looking," I said, "lest we find a name we don't want to see. Let's sift through the correspondence, but not read it. It's unlikely she would have hidden her evidence in a love letter. Unless . . ."

"What?" Ivy asked.

I passed her the contents of the next drawer. "Search for anything from Mr. Harris."

"Mr. Harris!" Ivy's eyes nearly popped out of her head. "You can't possibly think—"

"Oh, yes, I can," I said. I didn't add that if I were married to Mrs. Harris, I, too, might seek affection elsewhere.

A quarter of an hour had gone by before either of us spoke again. Then Ivy threw back her head. "I stand corrected," she said, and handed me a bundle of letters. Lady Glover kept each of her lovers' notes separate. Mr. Harris's missives were tied with a wide, red ribbon. Ivy had identified him from the first in the pile.

"We don't need to read them," I said. "Just check to see if there's anything hidden amongst them or in the envelopes." I gave half the stack back to her. Halfway to the bottom of those I'd kept, I found a bank receipt for £200, with the words *For Mrs. Harris and her evil purposes* written across the top. Attached to the receipt were two rather shocking photographs of a young Lady Glover in an extreme state of undress and a scrap of paper that read, *I have more.*

Ivy nearly fell over when I showed her. "I didn't know things like that . . . I . . . I . . . What is one to think when confronted with such an image?"

"I don't believe it's meant to inspire thinking," I said. "Come now, we've got what we need."

We put everything else back in its place, thanked the butler for his assistance, and continued on our way, reaching the Harrises' house just as the rain started to slow. Winifred received us in her private sitting room, near her bedroom. "It's so early!" she said, embracing Ivy and cringing when she saw me. "Whatever can you be thinking?"

"Forgive me, Mrs. Harris," I said. "I begged Ivy to bring me to you. I realize that we haven't got off to a good start, and I wanted to try to remedy that."

"You'd better serve your cause by trying at a reasonable time of day," she said. "Morning is reserved for the calls of only the closest friends."

"I'm well aware of it," I said. "But I chose the time deliberately because I couldn't risk coming to you when anyone else was here. Not given what I plan to show you."

"You know I wouldn't have agreed to bring her at this hour if it weren't urgent, Winifred," Ivy said. Any nervousness that she'd felt before we'd set off seemed to have evaporated. She was poised and composed, but I could tell she wasn't enjoying herself the way she had in the park.

"I admit I've been opposed to your judgmental views. Offended by them, even. And I don't agree with many of your actions," I said. "But there are some things so extreme that decent people must rise up against them. When I realized what you'd done—and that you were about to be named as the villain in the story—well, I couldn't stay quiet any longer."

"You have my attention, Lady Emily," Winifred said. "What is going on?"

"You've seen these atrocious pictures?" I held up one of them for her. She shielded her eyes and looked away.

"More than I want to," she said. "Where did you find them?"

"It doesn't matter," I said. "What does matter is that Lady Glover is bent on destroying you over it."

"Lady Glover?" She laughed. "She's the one who'll be destroyed."

"I'm afraid not," I said. "She's filed charges against you—accusing you of extortion. I only know this because my husband is privy to certain information at Scotland Yard. They're nearly finished with their preliminary investigations and are likely to put you under arrest by the end of the day tomorrow."

Winifred turned bright red and stood up, slamming her fist down hard on the table next to her. "This is outrageous!" she said. "All I was trying to do was keep that woman from further corrupting those around her. Our husbands are at risk, Lady Emily."

I felt just the slightest twinge of sympathy for her. "I know they are, Mrs. Harris."

"Thank you for alerting me to the problem," she said. "But I don't understand one thing. Hasn't Lady Glover been kidnapped?"

"She'd already spoken to the police when she disappeared," I said. "Because of the rest of what they're having to deal with, it took a little while before they were able to look into her claims."

"I see."

"I just hope . . ." I let my voice fade.

"What?" Mrs. Harris asked.

"If anything were to happen to Lady Glover now—like what happened to Cordelia Dalton—the police would suspect you at once. We have to pray that whoever has her doesn't lay a hand on her."

"I hadn't thought of that," Mrs. Harris said, her face going pale.

"Is there anything I can do to help you, Winifred?" Ivy asked. "I hope you know you'll always have my support."

"I shall count on it, Ivy," she said. "But for the moment, I have things well in hand. Lady Glover will live to regret this action. She should have left well enough alone."

Ivy was trembling when we climbed back into her carriage, proving once again her skills as an actress. I'd truly believed she wasn't struggling during her scene with Winifred. The rain had come back in earnest, and there was no sign of it slowing again soon. She pulled her mantle tight around her as she sat down.

"I don't feel good about this at all," Ivy said. "I'm betraying a friend. Even if she is a bad one."

"You've done the right thing," I said. "We need to find out just how far her vindictive judgment has gone."

"I want to believe you," she said. "I do, in fact. But why do I feel so awful?"

I leaned forward and squeezed her knee. "Because you're such a decent person, Ivy. Try not to think about it. Even if she's not guilty of murder, she is guilty of extortion, and we can't let that go unpunished."

"Do you mean she'll really be arrested?"

"Not at the moment, no," I said. "But we'll be in a position to persuade her to return Lady Glover's money and stop her from behaving like this ever again. We must continue to be careful, though, in case she has kidnapped Lady Glover. We don't want to incite her to violence."

"But we wouldn't have to involve the police?"

"No, we wouldn't have to right now." I thought about this, and wondered if I was treating Winifred the same way Colin was Mr. Foster, protecting her from public censure. The situations were different, of course, but if I was going to argue that justice was black and white, I could hardly keep Scotland Yard in the dark about what she'd done.

Now was not the time to worry about such things. I would get Ivy home and settled and then finish with my plans for Mr. Foster. The rest could be dealt with later.

34

Mr. Foster's butler opened the door the moment I knocked. His master, however, was not at home. He'd gone to Westminster first thing in the morning, and wasn't expected back until late. I returned to the carriage (Ivy had insisted I keep hers rather than going home for mine) and directed the driver to take me to Parliament. The bottom six inches of my skirt were drenched just from walking the distance to the building's entrance.

Mr. Foster's assistant greeted me warmly—he remembered me from my previous visit—and brought me a cup of tea to ward off the dampness that had started to permeate my bones. It was hard to believe that so recently we'd all been complaining about the relentless heat. "I'm not sure how long it will be," he said. "Mr. Foster went in to the prime minister about twenty minutes ago."

"That's quite all right," I said. "I'm in no rush to go back into the rain." I pulled *The Aeneid* out of my reticule and read until Mr. Foster stepped into his office's antechamber nearly an hour later, apologizing for making me wait. He ushered me to a chair near his desk, then sat down, folded his hands, and placed them on top of his blotter.

"What a pleasant surprise," he said. "I hadn't expected any respite from work today."

"I'm not sure you'll feel so pleased after you hear what I have to say."

"Has something happened?"

"I'm afraid so," I said. "Perhaps it's wrong of me to come to you like this, but after our conversation yesterday, I felt like I had to."

"Go ahead, Lady Emily. You know I'll keep anything you say in confidence."

"Please, you must," I said. "I've been tormented all morning deciding if I should stay silent. But I could tell, last time we spoke, that elections are a matter of great importance to you."

"That's true of every politician."

I bit my lip and hoped I looked anxious. "We've come across something in the course of our investigation into Mr. Dillman's death that's extremely disconcerting. It concerns election fraud. I can't say more than that, but I thought you should know."

"Fraud? What sort?" Hunched shoulders and shaking hands replaced his calm demeanor.

"I haven't seen the papers," I said. "Not in detail. But something in Colin's reaction made me think I should tell you. I'm sorry I don't know more. You won't tell anyone I mentioned it, will you?"

"You have my word," he said. Rain beat against the window. "I shouldn't keep you, Lady Emily. I'm afraid if you stay much longer you'll regret not having come in a boat."

"Thank you," I said. As I walked through the corridor leading to the street, I ran though our conversation, wondering what he'd done that made him so concerned about election fraud. Lost in contemplation, I slammed into a gentleman who was walking towards me, a tall stack of papers in his hands.

"I am so sorry," he said, bending over to collect the sheets that had scattered over the floor.

"Mr. Barnes!" My heart pounded. "It was my fault entirely. I'm afraid

I wasn't looking where I was going. I hope I'm not making you late to some pressing appointment." He was wearing his overcoat and had an umbrella at the ready.

"Not at all, Lady Emily. I'm making an early day of it and heading home."

Home? Colin would never have expected him to return so early. What if he and Jeremy hadn't completed their task? I had to delay him.

"I'm doing the same. This weather is so terrible it's become frightening." As if on cue, a loud clap of thunder sounded above us. "I don't know how I shall ever hail a cab on my own."

"Allow me to assist you," he said.

"Would it—" I opened my eyes wide, then looked at the floor. "No, it would be too much to ask."

"Ask," he said.

"Would you be willing to escort me home? This weather is positively frightening."

"It would be my pleasure," he said.

Relieved, I waited in the building's entrance while he secured a cab for us. As soon as I arrived, I'd have Davis send word to Ivy's driver to return home. It was a stroke of luck that I hadn't come in my own carriage.

My umbrella did little to keep me dry as I ran to the cab. The rain was hard as knives, and the wind was blowing it almost parallel to the street. Mr. Barnes helped me inside, then slammed the door behind us. When we reached Park Lane, I turned to him.

"Will you come inside for some tea?" I asked. "I hate to send you off in this weather unfortified."

"That would be most appreciated, thank you."

I felt completely on edge, desperate to keep him away from his house until late enough so that Colin and Jeremy were sure to be done. I realized this might be difficult, but felt I could use the storm as a means to persuade him to stay with me. My worrying reached its apex when, after he'd finished a single cup of tea, he excused himself.

"I must be on my way, Lady Emily."

"Surely you'd like another cup?"

"No, I really mustn't," he said. "I'm having a small dinner party tonight and must get home to make sure it's all properly organized. A bachelor's household does not always run so well as it ought."

"I understand," I said, wishing I could feel relieved, but knowing his excuse was a lie. When I'd been waiting in Mr. Foster's office, a gentleman I did not recognize had come in and asked the assistant if Mr. Foster would like to join him and Mr. Barnes for dinner that night at the Athenæum Club. My blood wouldn't stop racing through my body. "Is there anything I can do to help?"

"Not necessary, I assure you. The tea has improved the afternoon immeasurably."

"Let me order my carriage," I said. "It won't be easy to get a cab here at this time." I leapt up before he could answer and went to my desk. "And you must let me give you my recipe for raspberry water ices—they're incomparable and you simply must serve them tonight."

He looked bewildered, but was not about to deny me my request. My request to give him the recipe, that is. I had no illusions about them being given to his nonexistent guests that evening. I wrote quickly, something that I hoped could be taken for a reasonable recipe—in fact I had no firm idea of how to make ices of any sort—and then pulled out a second piece of paper, and scratched another note. Making sure Mr. Barnes was not watching me, I folded it into small squares before returning to him with the recipe just as Davis entered the room.

"Madam?"

"Davis, Mr. Barnes will require the carriage," I said. "And could you remove my teacup? There's a smudge of something unsavory on it and I shall need another." He crossed to me at once, and as I handed him the cup—which was perfectly fine—I slipped the note discreetly onto the saucer. He nodded acknowledgment.

"Will there be anything else, madam?"

"No, Davis, that is all," I said. "Let us know when the carriage is ready."

A few minutes later, Mr. Barnes had bade me good-bye. I watched the horses pull away.

"We're all set now, madam," Davis said. Helping me into my gabardine cloak and holding an umbrella above my head, he led me out of the house and around to the entrance to our mews, where a hansom cab waited for me. I ducked into it. The driver, who'd already had his orders from Davis, raced after my carriage with Mr. Barnes in it. I wanted to see where he was going.

Although he'd lied about his evening meal, he'd been truthful about his destination. When we rounded the corner that led to his house in Chelsea, near the river, I wondered if I'd overreacted. I peered out the window, trying to look around the coaches in front of us. I could just barely see him getting out of my carriage and starting up the steps to his town house as it pulled away. My cab inched forward, closer to the house, and my view improved. As he reached the top of the steps, he looked down and wavered on his feet.

The staggering lasted only for a moment, and he opened the door and went inside.

I was about to tell the driver to take me home when I noticed another cab sitting across the street. Its door opened, and Mr. Foster stepped out. The vehicle pulled away as he crossed to the house and bounded up the steps. Just as he lifted his hand to knock, he looked down and must have seen whatever had caused Mr. Barnes's unsteadiness. He recoiled, then turned around too fast and fell partway back to the street. On the pavement, he regained his balance, but lost his umbrella. Not stopping to pick it up, he started to run. I shouted to the driver to follow him, then changed my mind. I could still see him at the end of the block, and changed tack. Making sure the driver would keep a close eye on him, I raced to the top of the steps to see what had caused his reaction.

The severed heads of three white roosters were sitting on the top step, blood mixing with the rain puddling around them. This must have been Colin's doing.

Swallowing hard, I returned—now thoroughly soaked myself—to the cab. The driver set off at once in pursuit of Mr. Foster, who had raced out of Upper Cheyne Row and was heading for Chelsea Embankment. Once there, he hailed another cab, and proceeded west, following the Thames until we were almost upon the Houses of Parliament. There, the road moved slightly away from the riverbank. He turned into Broad Sanctuary, and alighted in front of Westminster Abbey.

Pursuing him had been particularly easy once he'd entered the cab. But now that he was back on foot, and heading into a church, it would be harder for me to remain undiscovered. I was confident in my abilities, though, as Colin had trained me in the art of following someone.

I kept my distance, counting to fifty in Greek before following him into the abbey. At first, I stayed close to the doors, letting my eyes adjust to the dim light. He was walking quickly, with purpose, through the nave towards the north transept. I started after him, watching carefully to ensure I was keeping perfect pace with him—our footsteps fell at exactly the same time. I paused, ducking behind an Elizabethan tomb as he approached Statesmen's Aisle. The church was not crowded that afternoon, the weather having kept most people at home, and the corresponding solitude was not conducive to my current purpose. Poking my head around the stone monument, I watched as he veered back towards the center, passing the high altar.

Moving silently, I resumed my chase, but this time did not choose a course of direct pursuit. I could see he was nearing the steps that led to Henry VII's Lady Chapel. Identifying a better vantage point for my purposes, I climbed up the short flight of stairs to the shrine of Edward the Confessor. From there, peeking around the tomb of Henry V, I could watch Mr. Foster below.

He walked along the rows of wooden seats for the members of the Order of Bath, stopping in front of the steps that led to the stalls in which the knights would sit while in chapel. He bounded up the stairs, turned to look around, no doubt confirming he was the only person within sight, then climbed onto one of the seats. Stretching, he reached to the canopy above, shoving his hand between spaces carved in the wood. He pulled something down, but I could not see what. Then, turning at the sound of voices coming from the chamber where Elizabeth I was buried, he climbed back down, straightened his jacket, and retraced his steps to the west door.

I followed, leaping into my waiting cab moments after his had pulled away. It was almost a disappointment when he reached his house and went inside.

I returned to the abbey, where I went straight to the Lady Chapel and climbed onto the same seat in the stalls Mr. Foster had. I could not, however, quite reach all the way to the opening in the carved canopy. Gripping the slender wooden post that divided the seats, I stepped onto the armrest. From here, though, the angle was difficult, but the additional height did prove helpful. I felt around as best I could, but there was nothing there.

"May I help you with something, madam?" a stern-looking priest said, bounding towards me.

"No, thank you," I said, not moving from my perch. "Just enjoying the view."

"Madam, would you please step down? You cannot climb in the chapels."

"Right," I said. "Of course. But how else is one to get a close look at these exquisite knights' crests? I don't suppose you have a ladder? I'm passionate about heraldic symbols."

"Are you?" he asked, his mouth hanging open.

"Do you know much about them?"

"I don't."

"What a pity," I said. "No ladder, then?"

"No, madam."

I shook my head. "What a grave disappointment. I'd always preferred this place to St. Paul's. Perhaps I should reevaluate."

35

I was the last one to arrive back in Park Lane, and I had to change my dress before I could join Colin, Jeremy, and Ivy, all of whom, Davis informed me, had arrived more than an hour ago. Meg helped me dry off and pull on a Liberty gown. I drained three cups of tea in rapid succession and, beginning at last to feel warm again, I descended to the library.

"Ivy's told us about the triumphant morning the two of you had," Colin said.

I pulled my favorite chair close to the fire, which hadn't been lit in weeks because of the heat. How quickly rain can change things. "She was brilliant."

"You were," Ivy said. "You thought of everything to say."

"But there would have been no veracity to anything I'd said if you hadn't supported me," I said. "She wouldn't have even admitted me to her house."

"Did you collect the evidence from the Glovers'?" Colin asked.

"We did, and don't think for a minute I'm showing it to you," I said. "It's obscene."

"Do you really believe I—" He stopped, rubbed his chin. "No, there's nothing I can say here, is there?"

"We both know—" Jeremy stopped. "We both know nothing about, well, nothing."

Colin scowled at him.

"Right," Jeremy said. "And even if we did know anything about those sorts of . . . evidence, did you call it? Even if we knew, we wouldn't be interested in seeing it."

"Don't consider a career on the stage, Jeremy," I said. "Have we heard anything more from Winifred?"

"Not that we know of," Colin said.

"How about Mr. Foster?" Ivy asked.

"I've planted the necessary seeds," I said. "I also saw Mr. Barnes and the grisly souvenir you left on his doorstep. What was it?"

"I did some research on Obeah," Colin said. "And with Cook's help, Jeremy and I acquired the heads of three white roosters. Leaving them at someone's door is, apparently, a foolproof way of heaping evil upon him. We'll see how much of a believer Mr. Barnes is."

"They definitely had an effect on him," I said. "But an even more striking one on Mr. Foster." I told them of my rainy adventures.

"I can't believe you climbed on the armrest," Ivy said. "And claimed an interest in heraldic symbols."

"Are you certain there was nothing more to be found?" Colin asked.

"I can't be absolutely certain," I said. "I felt around as best I could, but I couldn't see what I was doing. And he may have things hidden in more than one place."

"I'll send some men to look into it tomorrow," Colin said.

"Did you see Mr. Barnes at all today?" I asked him.

"No," he said. "I had my poor roosters' heads ready to go and in a small bag underneath my coat. Bainbridge and I called at Upper Cheyne Row only after confirming he was in his office at Westminster. The butler told me his master wasn't at home, I thanked him, and dropped the birds on my way down the steps."

"It was quite gruesome, Colin," I said. "Horrible, really."

"As it needed to be," he said.

"I'm not sure I'll allow myself to be embroiled in another of your plans," Jeremy said. "I could do without the gore."

Davis poked his head in the door. "An urgent message from Scotland Yard, sir." He handed Colin a note that my husband opened and read in the space of a breath.

"Mrs. Harris has attacked her husband," Colin said. "She's been subdued and is in her house under police observation."

Ivy went white. "Do you think she's the murderer?"

"It certainly doesn't look good for her."

"Is Mr. Harris all right?" I asked.

"Apparently, she knocked him over the head with a fire poker," he said. "He's at home with a doctor."

"This is horrible," Ivy said. "And I feel like it's my fault."

"It's not your fault in the least," I said. "She should have restrained herself, and her husband should have had the sense to keep away from Lady Glover."

"We knew she might be violent," Ivy said.

"I think he'll recover fully," Colin said. "They haven't even had to take him to the hospital."

"It sounds like the old boy deserved a good whack," Jeremy said. "He should never have left such incriminating things sitting around the house."

"Quite," Colin said, then frowned and looked at his watch. "I want to get over there right away and don't know how long I'll be gone. Let's hope that by the time I return, this is all settled."

"What about Lady Glover?" Ivy asked after Colin had gone. "What if Winifred's hurt her, too?"

"I don't think she would have," I said. "Not after what we told her today."

Seeing how upset Ivy was, Jeremy excused himself briefly from the room, imploring us to alert him as soon as we learned anything new.

Not a quarter of an hour after he'd gone, we heard someone banging on the front door of the house. Banging on the door and screaming.

"Lady Glover!" I'd rushed into the corridor, Ivy and Jeremy right behind me. Lady Glover was soaked. Her turquoise dress, with its golden crystal beads, which had once been elegant and stylish, was covered with dirt and missing one sleeve—the one that had been found in the park. Her hair was coming down around her shoulders, twigs and leaves sticking out from it. Mud streaked her face. Despite all this, she looked almost like a much-put-upon romantic heroine.

"Emily . . . I didn't know where else—" She started to step forward, but collapsed on the floor in a delicate heap.

Davis, always the master of efficiency, had her upstairs in no time. A maid drew a bath and assisted her in getting cleaned up and into one of my cotton nightgowns. I tried to persuade Lady Glover to lie down, but she refused. Instead, she wanted a wrap to throw over her shoulders and insisted on coming down to the library.

"I've heard too much about your port not to have some," she said. "You must indulge me, Lady Emily. I've been through so much."

I knew enough of her to understand arguing would be fruitless, so I ceded to her demands. She draped herself across a settee, accepted a glass, and asked for a cigarette.

"I don't have one," I said. "Tell us what happened."

"You haven't summoned the police yet, have you?" she asked.

"Only my husband," I said. "He's in the midst of investigating another matter."

"What?" she asked.

"Don't worry about that right now," Ivy said.

"It's not to do with my kidnapper, vicious man, that he is?" she asked.

"No, it's not," I said. "But do you think you could identify him?"

"I will never forget that face," she said. "Beady eyes and thin little mouth. But I don't know his name, if that's what you're wondering."

"Where was he holding you?" I asked.

"In the lodge where you saw me. I cannot tell you how it bolstered my spirits to see you coming to save me!"

"I didn't realize you could see us," I said. "I'm only sorry it didn't work."

"I didn't mean to suggest I'd actually *seen* you," she said. "But he mentioned you and the duke by name when he told me we had to move."

"Did he hurt you?" Ivy asked.

"He was terrible," Lady Glover said, lowering her voice. "You can't imagine."

"We must contact your husband at once," Ivy said.

"No." Lady Glover sat up. "I'm angry at him. He took so long paying the ransom."

"So far as I know, the kidnapper hadn't sent instructions," I said. "Did he say anything about the money when he released you?"

"No. You misunderstand. I assumed the ransom had been paid," she said. "I took a little nap this afternoon—being held prisoner is frightfully tedious—and when I woke up, there was no sign of either of my usual guards. On a whim, I tried the door and found it open."

"So you just walked out, unscathed?" Ivy asked.

"Oh, no! It wasn't so easy," she said. "At first I thought that's how it would be. I crept down the stairs—"

"Where were you?" I asked again.

"In another lodge in Hyde Park. A much nicer one this time. That's due to you, Emily. If you hadn't forced him to move me, I would have been stuck in that awful place the whole time."

"But you did have trouble escaping?" I asked.

"Yes," she said. "Only one of the guards was there, and he'd gone outside. I don't know why. So I ran out the other door and didn't look back until I was out of the park. Actually, I didn't look back then, either."

"Was he following you?" Ivy asked. "Could you hear him?"

"Not that I noticed," she said. "But one does have to make reasonable assumptions in these situations."

"So when did the actual trouble occur?" I asked.

"I suppose it was more theoretical than actual," Lady Glover said. "But I was terrified."

It was clear she didn't need a doctor; she'd risen from her faint with indecent speed. And nothing about her story rang true.

"I don't believe you, Lady Glover," I said.

"What can you possibly mean? How could I have been anything but terrified?" she asked.

"None of this makes sense—it hasn't from the beginning. And look at you now: you're not even upset."

"I'm in shock. Once I've had a chance to react thoroughly I'm likely to be hysterical. How can you accuse me of—"

"Don't," I said, raising my hand. "I don't believe any of this."

She sat, silent, for some minutes, then let out a long sigh. "Was it that obvious?"

"No," Ivy said. "I bought it entirely and it is I who is in a state of shock. Did you really make it up?"

"I am a master of intrigue, you know," Lady Glover said.

"I feel a complete fool," Ivy said. "I never doubted you. You are quite an actress." There was a twinge of admiration in her voice.

"How did you arrange it?" I asked.

"I hired actors. We staged the kidnapping—it was rather exciting, I must say—and holed up in a lodge I knew to be vacant. A few days of that, though, and I started to get bored. My husband wasn't responding to any of the ransom instructions—"

"I don't think he received any," I said.

"He did. My spies saw him read them. He just didn't want to deal with me." Tears flashed in her eyes. Part of me felt sorry for her, but the rest knew she was probably acting. "I tried to increase the stakes by having my men drop my sleeve in the park, but that didn't light a fire under him, either. The whole experience was thoroughly depressing. In the end, I got tired of it and decided to go home. After making a stop here, first."

"Why would you do such a thing?" Ivy asked. "I, for one, have been worried sick about you."

"I guess I can't get the stage fully out of my blood," she said.

"That's not a valid reason," I said.

"My husband used to dote on me," she said. "But lately I'd come to realize he didn't care anymore. I wanted to know if that was the truth. And I found out, didn't I?"

"What about the letters?" I asked. "Did you invent those as well?"

"No, I swear to you I didn't," she said. "And I got one more before my abduction." She pulled it out of her décolletage and handed it to me:

> I am whipp'd and scourg'd with rods,
> Nettled, and stung with pismires, when I hear
> Of this vile politician

"*Henry IV, Part I*," Ivy said. "It's one of Robert's favorites."

"That's it," I said. "I'm going to fetch Colin. And we must send for your husband. Ivy will look after you.

I took the carriage to the Harrises' house, but before I'd reached my destination, I saw Colin walking away from it. I called for the driver to stop and waved for my husband's attention.

"What are you doing here?" he asked.

I told him about Lady Glover. "She wasn't kidnapped any more than I was," I said. "It looked liked she'd rolled around in the mud to lend herself an air of authenticity. I'll tell you the rest later. But when I read the last letter she said she'd received from our painter, I wanted to find you at once."

"What is it?"

"We need to revisit those notebooks I found in Mr. Dillman's house. As quickly as possible. The letter made reference to a vile politician, and the notebooks had all those records of bills before Parliament. I want to study them again."

"They're at Scotland Yard," he said.

"You can tell me about Mrs. Harris on the way," I said.

"That's a mess of phenomenal proportion," he said. "Mr. Harris will be fine, although he'll have a headache for the foreseeable future. His wife has ledgers full of the most horrific gossip. And she'd made large red *X*s by the people whose houses were painted. It's impossible to tell whether that's to indicate that she'd already finished with them or whether she was just keeping track of what someone else was doing."

"Was every single victim of the paint on her list?" I asked.

"All but Mr. Dillman," he said. "But he was the first, and it's entirely possible she didn't start her book until after she was finished with him. And now she's proven herself capable of violence. There's one other thing you might find interesting. She kept a record of her correspondence in one of her journals, and was writing to Foster on a regular basis for the past year. The frequency of her letters to him increased, however, about two weeks before Dillman's death."

"Do you think there's a connection between them?" I asked.

"It's possible," he said. "We'll have to question Foster before we can reach any firm conclusions. Regardless, she looks to be the guilty party."

"I don't think so," I said. "Please, take me to Scotland Yard."

"We'll go, first thing in the morning," he said. "Right now, we need to deal with Lady Glover, who may be facing some very serious charges."

"Can we at least pick up the notebooks and bring them home?"

"You're relentless, my dear."

"Implacable."

"I might as well give in?" he asked, leaning in for a kiss.

"It would be futile to do otherwise." He kissed me again, this time more thoroughly.

And then he did as I asked, insisting that I remain in the carriage while he ran inside to fetch the notebooks. I did not object, having found the ride to Scotland Yard some of the most pleasant time I'd spent all season.

Back at Park Lane, it was difficult to reconcile the wrathful, seething man giving Lady Glover a most severe dressing down with the passionate and attentive gentleman who had escorted me home from Scotland Yard. A shiver of excitement charged through me as I watched him. It was bad of me, no doubt, to admire this side of him, but how could I not? He was a master of his work, and within a quarter of an hour he'd got Lady Glover to confess every detail of what she'd done, down to the names of the men she'd hired to "guard" her.

"They were actors?" Colin asked.

"I needed them to be convincing," she said. "Darling, I'm terribly sorry, you must forgive me."

"You will not tell me what I must do," he said. "Sit up. I'll not speak to you while you're making such a terrible attempt to mimic Cabanel's portrait of Ophelia."

I expected a witty reply from her, but she said nothing. She sat up, pulling my dressing gown close around her shoulders.

"Your husband will be here momentarily," Colin said. "I suggest you go upstairs and put your own clothes back on. It's reprehensible that you're in public rooms in such a state."

"My clothes are all wet," she said.

"Because you chose to make them that way."

"Colin, I could lend her a dress so that she doesn't—"

He interrupted me. "She doesn't need comfort right now, Emily. Lord Glover will take her home in short order and she can wear what she likes once she's there." He rang for a maid and directed her to take Lady Glover back upstairs. "I've no tolerance for what you've done. Not only have we wasted time and resources searching for you, you put my wife and the Duke of Bainbridge in danger when you set your thugs on them."

"I told them not to hit either of them too hard," she said. "You must see I couldn't let them rescue me all the way. I just wanted them to be able to make a good-sounding report."

"What you've done is outrageous and despicable," he said. "Your antics have made it more difficult to find the savage who killed Cordelia Dalton."

She nodded, chastened, and followed the maid from the room.

"I don't ever want you mad at me," Ivy said to him. "You're very fierce."

"She's behaved most appallingly," Colin said. "Two people are dead, and she's staged this farce to get attention? It's outrageous. She's fortunate I wasn't harder on her."

"Fortunate indeed," I said. "Now tell Ivy what you learned at the Harrises'."

"Mr. Harris is going to be all right. She was rough with him, and he's banged up, but the doctor felt there's no need for serious concern."

"I imagine he'll approach marital fidelity with a different view moving forward," I said.

"Will Winifred be arrested?" Ivy asked.

"I don't know yet," Colin said. "Scotland Yard are searching the house right now. We already know she's guilty of extortion, and now this. I'm afraid it doesn't look good for her."

"But you can't think she killed Mr. Dillman," Ivy said.

"Why not?" he asked.

"I just can't believe it, despite what we've seen." Ivy's shoulders were pulled back, stiff and straight.

"She may have had an accomplice," I said. "Which is why we need to look at those notebooks right away, Colin."

I took them to the table, spread them out, and opened the one in which I was the most interested—the one that listed parliamentary bills amongst other things. "We know more about Mr. Dillman's way of thinking since having come to a full understanding of the game he played with Cordelia. Let's see if he was doing something similar to that with the information in these books."

We looked at the numbers and symbols listed next to each bill. I copied out twice each set—numbers and symbols—and gave one to Ivy. Colin and I would use the other.

"Take a notebook and go through, page by page. We need to find all of these."

The meaning of the numbers proved elusive, so elusive that Colin turned to a thick volume of parliamentary records. "They are just votes, Emily. Votes on bills that passed in the last five years."

"So why did he pick these in particular?" I asked. "Can you find out more about the bills?"

"I will," he said, turning back to the book.

Ivy let out a little squeal. "I've found one of the symbols!" She turned the notebook she'd been studying so that I could see it right side up. A quite competent watercolor of a laurel was on the page, its small, white flowers executed with great precision. Incorporated into the bottom of the image was the symbol, an upside-down triangle, so small one would only notice it buried amongst the green leaves if one was specifically looking for it. Beneath the picture were the words *Daphne Alpina* and a date, 18 June 1891. The "a" was underlined.

This spurred us on. Soon we had pictures to go with each of the symbols—and on each of them, something in the accompanying text had been underlined. From the flowers, there were two letters and two numbers. From his drawings of birds, we got thirty letters.

"The first is easy," I said. "Between the daphne and the hellebores we have *A* and *E*. Given what we already know about Mr. Dillman's game, it's reasonable to surmise this should be combined to *EA*, which is how the catalog numbers for all the items in the Department of Ancient Egypt and Sudan begin."

"So the numbers—5 and 9—are the second bit," Ivy said. "We need EA 59 or EA 95."

"And the rest?" Colin asked. "This long string of letters?"

"It's the hint," I said. "He's put an additional layer of disguise this time. And, given the number of letters, it's undoubtedly more than just telling us what the object is made of. Cordelia said he sometimes gave her quotes as clues."

"So we need to untangle the letters," Ivy said.

Colin continued to study the parliamentary record while Ivy and I set to it.

W D T E D M O B R E N A T M O E I A R R D L H U I D Y F H R

"Let's make a list of every word we can find in it," I said. "And then see if we can string them together in some sort of sensible fashion."

"Toady rat in tree," Ivy said.

"Sensible, darling," I said.

"Hide now or die," she said. We fell silent.

Over the course of the next two hours, we'd come up with what seemed an unending list of possible words, almost too many to count.

"This sounded like a good idea," I said, after having strung together another phrase that was almost promising.

Colin came and stood over my shoulder. "I think you're trying too hard to make it fit the museum," he said.

"How goes it with Parliament?" I asked.

"I've found absolutely nothing," he said. "I think we need to take that list of Dillman's at face value."

"That's disappointing," Ivy said.

"Let's focus on the words you lot have found instead," Colin said. *"Dream of water?"*

"Yearn for more?" I tapped my pencil on the table. "This is incredibly frustrating. We have lots of nonsense, but nothing that uses all of the letters."

"Let me see everything you have," he said. I passed him our pages of words. He went to his desk and sat down. "The only thing I prefer to word puzzles is chess."

"Maybe we should just take the whole list to the museum," Ivy said. "We've narrowed down which galleries to search. Perhaps the clue will become evident once we've narrowed down the options with the numbers."

"That's an excellent idea," I said. "We should be there the minute it opens tomorrow."

"I've got it," Colin said, rising from his chair and walking towards us. "It's obvious, really. *Murder thy breath in middle of a word.* It's from *Richard III.*"

"I was really hoping for the *toady rat*," Ivy said.

"You're sure?" I asked.

"Yes," she said. "It's quite an unusual animal, don't you think?"

"Not you, Ivy."

"I couldn't be more certain," Colin said. "There are plenty of phrases we could string together with these words, many of which sound like they are appropriate. But no one will convince me that a line of Shakespeare is going to coincidentally appear within this list. *Toady rat* notwithstanding."

"But our villain," Ivy said. "He quotes Shakespeare."

"My dear girl," he said. "Everyone quotes Shakespeare."

As Colin sketched out his plan for the next morning, Ivy bowed out of coming to the museum. "I've tried Robert's patience enough," she said. "I think he'd draw the line at my being present when you arrest someone."

We promised to give her an update as soon as we were finished at the museum. Once she'd gone home, we retired to our bedroom, where I collapsed, exhausted, on the bed.

"Don't fall asleep just yet," Colin said. "You're still in your clothes."

"I'll ring for Meg," I said.

He sat on the edge of the bed and grabbed my wrist as I reached for the bell. "Don't," he said, his lips so close to my face I could feel his breath on my cheek. "I'll provide any assistance you need." I felt his fingers feel for the buttons on the back of my dress. He undid the top two or three, then pulled me up to sitting. Kneeling in front of me, he started to remove the pins from my hair, one at a time until my curls had tumbled down around my waist.

Blue light had started to force its way around the edges of the curtains before we finally went to sleep. Yet somehow, when Meg brought breakfast to us only a few hours later, I found myself so refreshed, so vividly alive, I felt almost embarrassed.

After eating and getting dressed it was still early enough that we had time to walk to the museum. I pulled on my gloves and made my way to the door. The rain had stopped, though the pavements were damp in spots, and the sun was struggling to make its way through patchy holes in the clouds.

"Sir, I—"

"Not now, Davis," Colin said. "We must hurry."

"Very good, sir. Enjoy your walk, sir." He opened the door. We stepped outside, but he didn't close it. "It's dry, so no need to worry where you step. Shall I have it taken care of at once?"

I looked down and saw that our whole front entrance was bathed in red. The steps, the columns of the porch, the front door. All red.

Colin hardly paused. "Very good, Davis. Carry on." He adjusted his hat and offered me his arm.

"Well?" I asked.

"What?"

"The paint? What's your secret?"

"I assumed it was yours," he said. "I've lived an entirely blameless life." He walked a little bit faster, but other than that, showed no further response.

"I know it's not something I've done," I said.

"I'm not discussing it," he said. "We have work to do and don't need to waste our time taking the bait of some disgruntled miscreant."

I could feel my temples pulsing. "How can you be so calm?"

"Because while there are things in my past others may judge, I've neither done anything of which I'm ashamed, nor anything I feel the need to defend," he said. "So unless you've some delicious deceit to share with me, I am not concerned in the least."

"Don't you care how I feel about what you've done?"

"To an extent," he said. "But the past is the past, Emily. Why would anything I did before I met you cause a rift between us?"

"So it's nothing you've done since we met?"

"Certainly not since I fell in love with you. Unless, of course it pertains to my work. But if that's the case, we have a bigger problem on our hands than we know; that would mean our villain has connections in the highest levels of the government."

"I can't tell if you're teasing me or serious," I said.

"I like to keep you on your toes." He patted my arm.

"But I—"

"No more, Emily. I'm not going to let us fall prey to this person's vindictiveness."

And that was all he would say on the subject. I was still agitated when we got to the museum. Colin stopped and stood in front of me.

"Stop worrying," he said, taking me by both arms. "You are in your element here, and I couldn't be doing this without you. I would not have been able to get Cordelia to open up like you did, and I admit freely I probably wouldn't have taken any note of this game of hers and Dillman's. So stand tall, and show me where we need to go."

This bolstered me. If I had his support, what did I care if everyone else was taunting us about red paint? Well, I did care, and probably too much. But I forced it out of my mind, took him by the hand, and led him straight to the first of the Egyptian galleries.

"EA 59," he said, trailing a bit behind me.

"The numbers will be here." I showed him on a display card. "Keep our Shakespeare in mind—it will provide something essential. To begin, I think we should look for anything with a museum number that begins with EA and includes 59. If a connection between the object and the quote is obvious, we'll know our work is done. If not, we'll keep going."

"I'll take this side," he said. *"Murder thy breath in middle of a word."*

Having two rather than three letters, as we had before, was somewhat more difficult. Particularly as our hint, the quote, was more oblique than when we'd known what the piece we were looking for was made out of. In our first two galleries, I'd located four different things that fit the bill when it came to EA 59, but the Shakespeare didn't mesh with any of them.

"You did a spectacular job figuring this all out," Colin said. "We'd be lost if you hadn't recognized the importance of what Cordelia told you. Or if you'd been unable to put her enough at ease to confide in you."

"Thank you," I said. "We make an excellent team. You can kick people around in ways I'd never be able to. Although you could teach me."

"I'll take a pass on that," he said. "I don't want to render myself useless. Where's the next room?" He'd had as little luck with our search as I so far.

"Turn left here," I said. We split directions as soon as we entered. I worked my way through the gallery clockwise, Colin anti-clockwise. I was looking at row after row of ushabtis, figurines designed to stand in for the occupant of a tomb should he be called to do any work in the afterlife. One set, made from blue faience, charmed me more than the rest. Their faces, though formed in the traditional Egyptian manner, had an endearing eagerness to them. I should very much have liked to have them in my own tomb as working in the afterlife didn't have much appeal to me.

"Emily," Colin called from across the room. "Here's something, but it's a series. EA 59197 through 59200." He stood in front of a display of canopic jars, the vessels used to hold the vital organs that had been removed from the deceased during the process of mummification. These had belonged to Neskhons, the wife of a high priest of Amun. "It could be any of them."

"No," I said, excitement growing. "It couldn't. It has to be this one. The baboon."

"The baboon?"

"Yes. Each of the lids represents a god, and each god is responsible for protecting a different organ. *Murder thy breath in middle of a word.* Hapy, the baboon-headed deity, looks after the lungs."

"Breath," he said. "Of course. Well done, dear girl. What next? A trip to the library?"

"I don't think so," I said. "Partly because I've only just been through the stacks in thorough detail and partly because we're staring at a jar. If I were Mr. Dillman, I would have used that to store whatever I had that needed protection. We should fetch Mr. May."

"No," Colin said. "We've no time for that." He looked around the crowded room. "There are so many people here, we'd be hard-pressed to draw attention to ourselves."

With great care, he touched the ancient object, gently pulling the lid from its base. It moved without too much effort. He held the lid gingerly in both hands. "I don't want to risk dropping it," he said. "You look inside."

I did as he asked and saw a slim burlap package. I pulled it out, hoping I wasn't disturbing the remains of Neskhons's lungs. Colin returned the lid and let out a long breath.

"Glad not to have broken anything."

"Were you holding your breath?" I asked.

"It seemed appropriate under the circumstances."

"This is bad," Colin said. "Very, very bad." We'd taken our find home to examine it, ignoring both the red paint and the curious onlookers outside the house. The parcel was full of papers similar to those I'd found wrapped around the bottle—these giving much more detailed accounts of similar corruption.

"There's more?" I asked, leaning over his shoulder.

"Dillman tracked each of the instances of election fraud. Look at this." He passed a paper back to me. "But it's more than that. Bribery. Extortion. Every good thing—every initiative, every bill, every project—that Foster's been involved with was tainted from the beginning."

"It doesn't make any sense," I said.

"Not given his popularity."

"No, it's more than just that. I understand politicians are prone to corruption. And you know how I feel about what we've already seen regarding his role at the match factory. But who has so little faith in his own success that he tampers with literally everything?"

"It's staggering," Colin said, frowning. "I can't imagine what he was thinking. He's the last person I would have suspected of such under-handed behavior."

"Suspect no more," I said, handing him the last sheet of paper in the stack I'd been reading. "If this is to be believed, Mr. Foster is no more guilty than you."

He read the page slowly, then read it again. "We know where to go from here."

Mr. Barnes looked genuinely pleased to see us. He ushered us into his office in Westminster, offered us tea, and fluffed the cushion on my chair before he would let me sit down.

"Do you know, Lady Emily, I think you've begun to have a real impact on private discourse about women's rights?" He gave me tea even though I'd refused the offer. "Not public discourse, yet, but one must start somewhere. I had a very prominent Conservative in here yesterday who brought up the subject to me. He's not willing to support your agenda, of course, but just the fact that's he's talking is a real step forward."

"Thank you, Mr. Barnes," I said. "It's important work."

"It is," he said. "And I'm rather impressed with the strategy you employed. I know Lady Carlisle well, and I know what the Women's Liberal Federation has done in the past. Your idea of working on the men with the most open minds was a stroke of genius."

"How did you know that's what I'd done?"

"It was obvious to anyone paying attention. A brilliant move. They're hardly aware of what you're up to." His desk was a model of organization, everything arranged in perfect right angles. Except his pen, which he straightened. "But you didn't come here to discuss this, I don't think? Has something happened?"

"You know the answer to that," Colin said.

"You, too?" he asked, shaking his head. "This paint is like a curse. When will the monster stop?"

"I don't know," Colin said. "Why don't you tell us?"

"Forgive me," he said. "I don't quite—"

Colin rose to his feet. "There will be no forgiveness, Barnes. What you've done is despicable." He tossed the papers we'd brought from the museum onto the desk. Barnes's face froze.

"Dillman." He sat up very straight in his chair.

"Foster is your friend," Colin said. "Why did you want to destroy him?"

Mr. Barnes remained very still. "No, you misunderstand completely. I would never destroy him. I've made him what he is."

Colin picked up the papers and waved them in his face. "You have ruined him with corruption and rot. How did you think he would survive this?"

"He'll never have to."

"He'll have to now," I said. "I, for one, am not going to see this buried."

"Foster doesn't know anything about it," Mr. Barnes said. "You can't condemn him for it."

"What do you think will happen when it's all public?" I asked. "People aren't going to believe he's so naïve as you suggest."

"Everything I have done is to ensure this stays quiet and unknown," Mr. Barnes said.

"That's a lie," Colin said. "You're the one who orchestrated it. All of it. It's right here." He flung the papers back onto the desk.

"If I hadn't done all this, he wouldn't have even a third of the power he does now."

"So, I'm to believe you're a public servant, is that it?" Colin was leaning forward, across the desk now. "What is your game, Barnes?"

Mr. Barnes clasped his hands, laid them on his lap, and said nothing.

"All this destruction. All this hatred. Where does it come from?" Colin was almost shouting. Then he lowered his voice. "You're done now, you know that."

"Stop," I said. "The hatred. I know where it comes from. You're more refined than most gentlemen, Mr. Barnes, and far more intelligent. Your manners are impeccable. You're witty and considerate. Your fortune is nothing to sniff at. And yet, they're not going to accept you, are they? Not all the way?"

He looked down.

"They invite you to their houses and let you dance with their daughters, but they don't want you to marry them. Not really, even if Ivy can manage to find the youngest daughter of six with parents desperate to see her married. They're happy to listen to your ideas—and probably to present them as their own. But they won't let you in Parliament, won't give you credit for any of the myriad initiatives you've set in motion."

Now I stood up. "You're not the sort of man who's content to sit in the background, yet you've no choice but to accept it as your lot. Because your father wasn't English. And half-English isn't enough, not when it comes from your mother's side."

"Stop it," he said. "I don't want to hear any more."

"They must have brutalized you at school, punished you for the accident of your birth—it was something for which they could never forgive you. But the further you went—to university and then here—the more you learned about their own shortcomings. They were dishonest and in debt and stupid and cruel. They didn't value loyalty. But most of all, they didn't care in private about the values they held so dear in public."

"Stop!"

"And it didn't matter for them, did it?" I asked. "Because while the accident of your birth can't be forgiven, the accident of theirs guarantees them protection from all their hypocrisy. How could you be anything but angry?"

Now he started to wilt. His shoulders slumped, but he was still look-ing at the floor.

"So what happened?" Colin asked, pushing his head up and forcing him to meet his stare. "How did Dillman find you out?"

He didn't answer. Colin shook him.

"How did he find you out?"

"I don't know exactly," he said. "He'd done some work for me—in one of the elections. I was very careful, I thought, to make sure no single person had a large-enough portion of the entire task to be able to iden-tify what I was doing. But Dillman was curious. Started putting pieces together. I've been much more careful when picking associates since then."

"I've met some of your associates," I said, thinking of Dobson and Florence. "You're exploiting them and laying the blame at Mr. Foster's feet."

"Dobson and Florence are being looked after."

"By sending them to that heinous factory?" I asked. "They can't even communicate with anyone else who lives there."

"I use my associates once or twice, and have to be sure they're indi-viduals who cannot expose me. In this case, it made sense to turn to people already in my employ."

"So you are behind the factory?" I asked.

"It's Foster's in name only," he said. "When the deaf couple came to Majors, I told him to give them a place. They, and another worker who can't hear, helped me with the paint and some other matters, and I planned that in a year or so, when enough time had passed to draw no suspicion, I would send them somewhere safe and comfortable. I had a nanny whose son was deaf and saw how she was able to communicate with him. The experience made it easy for me to do the same with them. There's a school in France that could teach them sign language that would be understood more widely than the crude method I use with them. By getting them to France and providing them with some sort of education, I'm helping them survive in a world extremely cruel to their sort."

"So you're helping them, are you?" Colin asked. "Is that what you call it? So why did Dillman choose to go after you? Is he opposed to the fair treatment of the infirm?"

"Because—and I had no way of knowing this—one of the elections I helped push through destroyed his uncle's career. Which in turn broke his mother's heart. She died the following year, and he set off on a course to find out what had happened. The uncle had been a favorite to win, you see. But I'm very persuasive. It was early on in my role in the game, and I knew the right sort of unflattering information about a gent can compromise his political chances in an instant."

"I remember that election," Colin said. "Please refrain from speaking in front of my wife about the scandal you caused."

"These little things can poison a person against you forever," he said. "Dillman made it his private mission to destroy me. I didn't even know he was trying. Not until he came to me."

"This doesn't explain why you were preparing to destroy the man you claim as your dearest friend," Colin said.

"I would never do that," Mr. Barnes said. "Can't you see?"

"I see, Mr. Barnes," I said. "It was your only way to real power. You get Mr. Foster made prime minister, and then you show him what you've done. He has two choices: let you be the power behind the throne, so to speak, or resign in disgrace after you expose your evidence."

"I'd always wanted to be prime minister," he said, his voice soft. "It was a crushing blow when I was eleven and my grandfather told me it could never happen. I was brought up to love this country, to serve it. But when I got here, I wasn't allowed to do that."

"So instead, you plot to betray your friend and tell yourself it's all right because you have the country's best interest at heart?" Colin spoke in a low tone, his words measured. He was angry. "And when you're in danger of being exposed, you kill the man who dares try to stop you?"

"I didn't want to kill him."

"Irrelevant." Colin did not take his eyes from the man's face. "When you started to worry that wasn't enough, that you might still be exposed, you kidnapped his fiancée and murdered her, too." He picked the papers back up off the desk, rolled them up, and handed them to me.

Mr. Barnes dropped his head into his hands. "I never meant to hurt Miss Dalton," he said. "I only wanted to get hold of the evidence Dillman had against me. She refused to help me find it. And when it became clear to me that no one else was going to find it, either, what choice did I have? There was no other way to secure her silence."

"We found the evidence," I said. "So you murdered her for nothing."

"I'm all too well aware of that," he said. "It was a misstep."

"What about the paint?" I asked. "Didn't it further increase your risk of exposure?"

"It was diversionary," he said, meeting my eyes for the first time since we'd accused him. "It took the attention off Dillman altogether. No one at Scotland Yard spent much time looking into his connections, not once my campaign got under way."

"You have destroyed so many lives," I said.

"I only exposed sins these people decided to commit," he said. "Now they have to live like I do—trapped by their pasts. At least they chose theirs."

"That doesn't make it right," Colin said. "I'd always liked you, Barnes. I thought you were better than most of the louts in society. I never would have guessed someone like you—whom I held in such high esteem—could improve my opinion of them. I'm disappointed."

"I'm sorry," Mr. Barnes said. "It was my only chance. I had to try."

"No, you didn't." Colin crossed his arms. "I'll take you to Scotland Yard and we'll get the rest of this settled."

"Please, I can't face it," Mr. Barnes said. "All the laughing, the mocking. I know what they'll say—that this is what they expected from someone like me." He looked Colin straight in the face. "Could you not give me a moment?"

"Absolutely not. You will stand like a gentleman and face what you have done."

Mr. Barnes nodded. Sweat glistened on his forehead. "May I at least write my confession at my desk instead of in a cell?"

"That I can allow," Colin said.

And then it was like a flash. Mr. Barnes opened a drawer, presumably to pull out paper. But instead of paper, he lifted out a small pistol and raised it to his head. Colin moved so quickly I could hardly see what was happening. He wrenched the gun out of Mr. Barnes's hand, knocked him onto the ground facedown, and pinned his arms behind his back.

"Don't be in such a hurry, Barnes," he said. "You will die, but not like this. I'm not about to let you take the coward's way out."

I could hardly keep my knees from banging together, I was shaking so hard. Colin had sent me to summon help, and I felt lost in the halls of Westminster. Almost without thinking, I went to Mr. Foster's office.

"Something terrible has happened," I said. "Mr. Barnes has been behind this red-paint business. We need Scotland Yard at once."

"No," he said. "No. It can't be Barnes."

"Please, Mr. Foster, we must hurry."

He scrawled a note and handed it to his assistant, then turned back to me. "Now let's go," Mr. Foster said. "I must speak to him."

I filled in the details for him on the way to the office. Mr. Foster looked ill by the time we entered the room. Colin was still holding the gun. Mr. Barnes was back in a chair, but not behind his desk.

"Simon—" Mr. Foster stepped towards his friend. "I don't know what to say. Why?"

"It was the only way forward," Mr. Barnes said. "The only way to bring this country into a new age of enlightenment."

"Not like this, Simon, not like this. You wouldn't have had to blackmail me."

"That was just insurance," Mr. Barnes said.

"You should have trusted me. Trusted me to reach these heights on my own," Mr. Foster said. "And trusted me to keep you as my closest adviser."

Mr. Foster sank into a chair, and they both sat, silent, until Scotland Yard arrived. After the usual sorts of administrative detail, they formally arrested Mr. Barnes and took him away. As I watched him go, I almost wished I'd asked what secret about Colin he'd meant to expose. But I wasn't entirely sure I wanted to know.

"Excellent work, Hargreaves," Mr. Foster said, slapping my husband on the back. "Capital job." There was no enthusiasm in his voice.

"Sorry the result wasn't happier for you," Colin said.

"Nothing to be done," Mr. Foster said. "Difficult to see one's friend stoop to such levels."

"Yes." Colin put the gun on top of Mr. Barnes's desk. "But there is something we need to discuss. This match factory."

"Let me assure you I knew nothing about it."

"I never suspected otherwise," Colin said. "But you are the registered owner of it."

"Would be deeply grateful if you could make it all go away," Mr. Foster said.

"Shouldn't pose a problem," Colin said. "I'll personally see to fixing the records. The rest the government will have no objection to burying. Emily has already begun organizing a better situation for the people working in the factory."

"Do let me know if you require anything from me. I've money, whatever you need. I can't tell you how distressed I am to have had my name associated with something like that."

"Barnes knew you'd feel that way," Colin said. "Which is why he thought it would give him power over you."

"There's something else," I said. "All the rest of the fraud. You claim you knew nothing about it. Yet you were so jumpy when I broached the subject in my library."

Mr. Foster sighed. "Barnes came to me some weeks ago. He told me he'd learned that there had been tampering in my first election and was worried I might be exposed for it, even though there was no proof of any involvement on my part. I swear to you I knew nothing about it at the time."

"That was the beginning of his setting into motion the final part of his plan," Colin said. "He was getting ready to exert his control over you."

Mr. Foster bounced on his toes. "Is this likely to haunt me in the future?"

"I'll make sure it doesn't," Colin said.

"I appreciate it more than you could ever know, Hargreaves," he said. "Pity to have one's career ruined for reasons beyond one's control."

"No one wants to see that happen," Colin said.

"Thank you," Mr. Foster said. "And Lady Emily, don't be a stranger. I'll soon be in a better position than ever to help forward your political agenda."

Another smile, and he left us.

"Are you absolutely certain he knew nothing about what Barnes was doing?" I asked.

"As certain as I need to be," Colin said.

"Shouldn't his possible role in all of it be examined?"

"It would ruin him, even if in the end he was found innocent."

"Don't you want to know the truth?" I asked. "To be sure? This doesn't seem right."

"I understand how you feel, Emily, I do," he said. "But there's nothing more to be done. Take comfort in the fact he's a decent man and will do good work for the empire. In the end, that's all that matters."

"I don't agree, Colin." I crossed my arms. "The means matter just as much."

"In this case, we can't have both," Colin said. "And I'm willing to accept what's best for England. You should be, too."

38

"That's all fine for the lot of you," Jeremy said. "But I'm never showing my face in public again." We'd gathered in the library, each of us still reeling from the events of the previous week. "It's all over and I've got not a single drop of paint to show for it. Not a drop! Meanwhile, our darling Em—*my* darling Em—is the only one of us to have made the cut. She gets paint."

"The paint was for Colin," I said, centering on the table my favorite Greek vase, its black figures depicting the siege of Troy.

"Right," Jeremy said. "Hargreaves, the model of everything good in England, has something to hide? You'll never convince me it wasn't meant for you."

"This isn't funny, you know," Ivy said. "People are dead. And think of all those whose lives have been decimated."

"I hate to agree with old Barnes, but you can't say they didn't deserve it," Jeremy said. "It never pays to live badly unless you're happy for others to know." He puffed on his cigar and looked contemplative for a moment. "I say, that was a bloody good phrase. You think Oscar Wilde would want it?"

"You think too highly of yourself, Jeremy," I said.

"We shouldn't be joking about this." Ivy pressed her pink lips together. Her face was drawn and pale.

"It's all over now," I said. "There's no more need to worry."

Her whole body trembling, she started to cry.

"Ivy, darling, what is it?" I asked.

"I can't live with myself any longer," she said. "I've done something so wretched. Every day has been agony, waiting to see if my secret was the next to be exposed."

"You?" Jeremy doubled over, laughing. "Ivy, there's no one in England—no, the world—less likely to have done something dreadful than you. I've seen you remove ants from picnic blankets in lieu of smashing them."

"Appearances can be deceiving," she said, her voice raw.

"Well, it doesn't matter now," I said. "Barnes has been stopped, and you've nothing more to fear."

"Nothing but your censure and my husband's," she said. "After all these weeks of worrying, I've decided I must confess everything. I couldn't live with myself otherwise. And I certainly couldn't live through another period terrified of exposure."

"There's no need, Ivy," Colin said, moving to sit next to her.

"I must." She took a deep breath. "I did something terrible when you were all in Vienna and Robert was in Newgate, awaiting trial for murder."

"That was a dreadful time, Ivy," I said. "Anyone might have strayed into morally ambiguous territory. You were afraid your husband was going to be executed."

"Very afraid," she said. "And although I had faith in your skills as an investigator, Emily, I still worried that you might not be able to clear his name. I was frantic. And I couldn't think of any other way to save him."

"We were all frantic," I said.

"But I did something immoral," she said. "I found a man, a poor man.

A man with no income, an invalid wife, and more children than he could ever hope to feed. He'd lost his job in some dreadful factory and couldn't find another that paid enough. So I made an offer to him."

We all sat, our stillness almost inhuman. Ivy wiped her eyes with the back of her hand. Colin handed her a handkerchief.

"I told him that if he would agree to confess to the murder, I would see to it that his wife received the best medical care money could buy and that I would support his family in a style better than any in which they'd ever lived."

"But if he confessed—" I started, but she interrupted.

"Yes, he would be hanged for the crime," she said. "But he would die knowing his loved ones would be looked after in a way they couldn't be if he were alive and trying to care for them."

"Oh, Ivy," I said.

Tears poured down her face. "I know how awful it was to do," she said. "I'm ashamed of myself. But I'm not like you, Emily. I'm not strong enough to live without my husband."

"Ivy Brandon!" Jeremy rescued us from the heavy silence engulfing the room. "That you, of all people, would make me look a paragon of English goodness."

"It's no joking matter, Jeremy," she said.

"No?" he asked. "I seem to remember Emily clearing Robert's name and your husband being released from jail. Correct?"

"Yes," she said.

"So, your working-class bloke? Did he ever make his confession?"

"No."

"Which suggests—now, do correct me if I'm wrong for I've not Emily's investigative mind—it suggests he was not, in fact, hanged?"

"No," Ivy said.

"And do tell us, Mrs. Brandon, about the plight of his family today." Jeremy had never performed with such bravado. "Did you, upon finding you didn't need them, cut them off from all support?"

"Heavens, no!" she said. "I've looked after them the whole time. They're happily settled in Newcastle. The children have a governess. Their father has no need for a job."

"And the health of the man's dear wife?" Jeremy asked.

"She suffers from consumption, but receives the best care possible."

Jeremy threw his hands in the air. "Only you, Ivy, could turn a very nearly terrible sin into a great act of charity."

"I was going to let the man hang for a crime he didn't commit," she said.

"I don't believe for one second you would have ever gone through with it," I said. "Look how tormented you are over just having thought about it. In the end, you wouldn't have stood by and let it happen."

"And furthermore," Colin said, "the police would require more than a vague confession. This man would never have been able to give them the necessary details to convince them he was responsible for the murder."

"Are you sure?" she asked.

"I am," he said. "And I agree with Emily. You would never have gone through with it."

"You don't all despise me?" she asked, wiping away more tears.

"Not in the slightest," I said.

"You may depend upon our undying friendship forever," Jeremy said.

"I don't deserve you," she said. "And can only hope Robert takes my confession as well as you all have. But I'm being so selfish and thinking only of myself. What will happen to Winifred?"

"There won't be any charges filed against her. Her husband didn't want the additional embarrassment. Nor did Lady Glover," Colin said. "Mrs. Harris returned the extortion money, and Lady Glover was given the option to forgive or to face charges of her own for staging the kidnapping."

"She made the right choice," I said.

"But why did Winifred do it?" Ivy asked.

"She has secrets of her own that haunt her," I said. "Her mother eloped with a cad of a man who turned out to be a complete profligate. He abandoned her eighteen months later, after which she took up with someone equally as bad and wound up infected with syphilis. She died trying to give birth to her second child, and lost the baby as well. Winifred, only two years old, was sent to live with relatives. She didn't find out the truth about her background until she was an adult. At that point, she became obsessed with protecting her secret. She was convinced her husband would leave her if he knew what her mother had been."

"I don't understand how that led to extortion," Ivy said.

"She was petrified when the paint started, convinced she'd be next, and as a result, starting keeping careful records about every secret she heard. And she heard quite a lot. She tried to analyze the facts and find anything that might enable her to identify who was spreading the gossip, and the paint. In the end, she found connections of one sort or another between each of the victims and Lady Glover. She came to the conclusion Lady Glover was behind the attacks."

"No doubt there were connections because she's trifled with nearly every husband in London," Jeremy said.

"It wasn't all affairs," I said. "There were overlapping charities, servants who had worked for both Lady Glover and the victims, all sorts of things. As soon as she found the pictures and then realized that her own husband had become embroiled with Lady Glover, she was terrified she'd be the next whose life would be ruined."

"She thought blackmail would keep Lady Glover quiet," Colin said. "She'd also started writing to Mr. Foster. I thought this might be evidence of them working together, but it turns out she was campaigning to get him to introduce morality bills into Parliament."

"Morality bills?" Jeremy asked. "Are such things even possible? If they are, I'm denouncing my citizenship and moving to France."

"I wouldn't be too worried," Colin said.

"What about Bucephalus?" Ivy asked. "Who was behind the attempted poisoning?"

"Barnes," Colin said. "He thought he'd make a bid to get us off the case, hoping I'd bow out if Emily was upset enough. When she stood firm after that scare, he sent her the note leading her to the body, thinking that might prove distressing enough to put her off."

"He did have a flair for drama, didn't he?" Jeremy asked. "Which I suppose explains his choice of red paint."

"Barnes told us he'd made the bottle to help Dillman," Colin said. "But in fact he left it for Dillman as a warning. He invented the whole story of Dillman coming to him for help. He waited until after he knew Dillman would have found the bottle, but heard nothing about it. No gossip, no rumors. He then realized his technique wasn't dramatic enough. No one in England knew what it meant. So he switched to paint, which could neither be ignored nor hidden."

"He used the deaf factory workers to splash the paint," I said. "He was confident no one else would be able to decipher their primitive sign language."

"And rightly so," Colin said. "Scotland Yard weren't able to understand them at all."

"Barnes was lucky no one had guards in front of their house waiting to catch the painters," Jeremy said.

"Some people tried that," Colin said. "The vandalism was always done before the first light of dawn. Apparently, at least twice the ill-treated wretches in his employ didn't leave paint as instructed because they saw signs of being watched."

"Which lucky families dodged the attention?" Jeremy asked.

"Barnes wouldn't tell," I said.

"What about Foster and his mysterious visit to Westminster Abbey?" Jeremy asked.

"He's come forward and confessed everything," Colin said. "He was the one sending the notes to Lady Glover that we all believed came from our villain. They've had a relationship for some time—that is information not to leave this room—and he was sorry she felt so unappreciated by her husband."

"And receiving letters from a criminal was supposed to make her feel better about herself?" Ivy asked.

"You saw for yourself it did," Colin said. "He knows her well. He'd hidden the sealing wax and seal, along with a stash of paper in the Abbey, on the off chance someone found it in his possession and thought he was behind the whole nasty business, not just some false letters."

"He picked the spot because he'd formed a habit of ending his days—which were often more like late nights—with a stop in the Abbey for quiet contemplation and prayer. The caretakers were used to this and took no notice of him. He realized he could easily hide and remove his things so long as he did it when the tourists were all gone. He hadn't counted on having to fetch it all in a hurry during the day when he could be seen."

"So why did he do it then?" Ivy asked.

"He was afraid I'd learned about the purported election fraud," I said.

"Fraud he had nothing to do with," Colin said.

"Yes, well, we have somewhat disparate views on that subject," I said. "He thought he should gather up any evidence that could make him seem connected to the crimes and then he rushed to Mr. Barnes's house to seek his advice on what he should do. When he saw the rooster heads, which he recognized as the sort of thing Barnes had told him was used by islanders, he misunderstood. He thought it was his friend's way of warning him not to come inside. So he raced to the Abbey instead to remove the evidence he'd left there."

"You did an excellent job keeping Barnes distracted for so long," Jeremy said. "I don't know what would have happened if he'd stumbled upon us with the unfortunate roosters. But what of the business of him lying about his dinner party?"

"Mr. Barnes saw Mr. Foster in the corridor after I'd left his office," I said. "Mr. Foster told him what had happened and asked to meet him at Barnes's house. Mr. Barnes wanted a handy excuse to head home."

"So Foster was running about like a fool," Jeremy said. "I know, Hargreaves, you're fond of the man's politics. I won't bother to argue with you on that count. But you must admit he'd make a terrible criminal. He has so little foresight. Do you think such a man could really be a decent prime minister? I'd prefer someone who could be devious if the situation required it."

"I wouldn't be so sure Mr. Foster wouldn't fit the bill," I said.

"What about the servant Lady Glover saw collecting the letter she left on her doorstep?" Ivy asked.

"She invented that," I said. "I think she'd be much happier if she chose to return to the stage."

"So, in the end, of all our suspects, only Mr. Foster turned out to be really good," she said.

"I'm not entirely convinced of his much-lauded character," I said. "But shall do as instructed and speak no further on the subject."

Colin pulled a face, then laughed. "I do wish you all could have seen Emily in Scotland Yard. She made quite an excellent report—thorough and well organized."

"They were more than a little shocked that you let me make it," I said, smiling.

"It's time they learn they're going to have to accept you as a force that won't be ignored," he said. "I have a suspicion, though, that is something they'll find easier before long."

"Poor Mr. Foster," Ivy said. "He must be terribly upset to have lost his closest friend in such an infamous manner. Mr. Barnes has proved a master of psychological torment."

"Can you blame him?" I said. "Look at how he was treated. Should we expect different, if we lay such cruel judgment on a person simply because of the identity of his father?"

"It doesn't mean he should go about murdering people," Jeremy said. "It isn't civilized. And I, for one, want to go on the record to say that I never gave a fig who his father was. All things considered, I couldn't be happier with the outcome of this."

"I could be," I said.

"How so?" Colin asked.

"I can't decide which I'm more interested in knowing: Why our steps have been painted red or what your involvement was in the ever mysterious Anderson matter. Perhaps the two are related."

"Anderson? That old thing?" Jeremy asked. "Nobody cares about that anymore."

"Even *he* knows?" I glared at my husband, half serious, half in jest.

"Only because I was there," Jeremy said.

"You were there?" I asked. "What happened?"

Colin buried his face in his hands.

"It was your lofty husband's first foray into service for the Crown," Jeremy said. "A group of us were at Balmoral, part of the royal party, and some useless lady-in-waiting, Miss Anderson, let one of the queen's favorite collies escape. She was beside herself . . . convinced she'd lose her position and be ruined. Hargreaves, here, took it upon himself to save the girl's neck. She was rather a pretty thing, wasn't she, Hargreaves?"

"The dog or the girl?" Colin asked.

"I won't torment you," Jeremy said. "He spent two solid days searching for the wretched creature. By the time he returned to the castle, Her Majesty had been asking for the dog repeatedly and we'd all run out of excuses to explain where it might be. Enter the divine Hargreaves, covered with mud, but with the collie well in hand. The queen has been devoted to him ever since. I believe you found the whole incident slightly mortifying, didn't you, Hargreaves?"

"Why?" Ivy said. "I think it's a lovely story! What became of Miss Anderson?"

"Sophie Anderson married my brother two months later," Colin said. "In the end, she preferred her gentlemen to stay out of the mud."

"Right," Jeremy said. "I quite forgot myself when I called her useless. I should show your sister-in-law more respect."

"No offense taken, Bainbridge."

I watched my husband closely. "Mr. Barnes wouldn't have found that story worthy of red paint. And, knowing my own past as well as I do, I'm confident there's nothing interesting enough in it for him."

"So you're saying the paint was for me?" Colin asked.

"I am."

"No doubt you're correct."

I saw Ivy and Jeremy exchange worried glances, and I considered the situation before me. "Thinking about it, I don't care what you've done. I trust you implicitly. Your work has, no doubt, required morally dubious action from time to time, but far be it for me to question your judgment. You're welcome to your dark secrets. I know everything I need to about what kind of a man you are."

"What an enlightened girl I've married," he said, kissing my hand. "Thank you, Emily. Your faith means everything to me."

So lost was I in the warmth of his eyes, I didn't notice Davis standing in the doorway. He cleared his throat loudly. "Lady Bromley to see you, madam."

"Heavens, she waited to be introduced," I said, noticing that at the sound of her name I'd already sat up straighter.

My mother was beaming as she walked into the room. "My dear Mr. Hargreaves, I come with the best of news. How wonderful that you're surrounded by friends to hear it with you."

Colin stood up. "Lady Bromley, I think it's probably best—"

"No, no," she said. "This is to be my treat. Her Majesty is allowing me specially. You, dear sir, for the many services you've rendered for queen and country, are being offered an earldom."

"An earldom?" Jeremy all but jumped to his feet. "Thank heavens it's not more. I couldn't have him with precedence over me. That would be unbearable."

"You need not worry, Bainbridge," Colin said. "I couldn't possibly accept such an honor."

"Don't be silly," my mother said. "Of course you'll accept. Isn't it delightful, Emily? You'll be a countess! I couldn't be more pleased."

"I won't accept," Colin said.

My mother ignored him.

"What an honor," Ivy said. "It is a wonderful thing, you must admit, and very well deserved."

"I shan't even discuss it," Colin said. "Although you may inform Her Majesty I would be quite pleased to see my wife's name on the New Year's Honors list. Can you see to that?"

"Emily?" My mother balked. "Whatever for?"

"Until you can answer that question for me, with sincerity and no hesitation, I shall never consider accepting an honor of my own," Colin said.

My mother so forgot herself she let her mouth hang open. "I don't even know how to begin to respond to that."

"Hence our problem," he said. "Do think on it, though. I'm of the opinion the Royal Order of Victoria and Albert, Fourth Class, would be just right. In the meantime, we've port and cigars waiting for us. I don't suppose you'd care to join?"

"I most certainly would not!"

"Then I suppose we've nothing further to discuss," he said. My mother sputtered incoherently for a moment and then stalked out of the room, not bidding farewell to any of us. Jeremy collapsed in laughter, Ivy at his side.

"Forgive me," Colin said. "It was crass, I know. But I don't care who I offend or what ire I draw, be it your mother's or the queen's. I will see you appreciated in your own right, my dear, no matter what it takes. And until you are, I shall never, ever, accept an honor of my own. Not even should you decide you fancy having a noble husband."

"No husband could be more noble," I said.

"That's quite enough of this romantic nonsense," Jeremy said. "I've been promised port and cigars. Hargreaves?"

"Some things, Bainbridge, are more important than port and cigars," Colin said, taking me into his arms and pressing his lips hard against mine, right in front of our friends. "Having just taken care of my favorite of those things—thank you for the kiss, dear wife—I'm going to tend to the rest of them straight away. Do you think I'll have any trouble persuading the queen to see me on such short notice?"

Author's Note

Research is one of the best parts of writing historical fiction, particularly as truth is often more fantastic than fiction. My character, Lady Glover, is based on London's infamous Lady Meux. After being a pantomime girl at Surrey Music Hall and a barmaid at Horseshoe Tavern, she won herself a £20,000-a-year allowance from her wealthy husband, a brewer, after her marriage. She collected Egyptian antiquities and had a menagerie of exotic animals at her country house, along with a Turkish bath, and a roller skating rink. Like Lady Glover, she drove a carriage pulled by zebras in London. No fortune in the world could gain her the good will of society, however. She described herself as "a woman not received."

Mrs. Fanning and Lady Althway sharing a lover was inspired by an incident in the life of Lady Londonderry, the leading Tory hostess of the time. A sharp, well-read woman, she had the respect of nearly everyone but her husband, who refused to speak to her in private after he learned of her affair with a gentleman called Harry Cust. How was the affair exposed? Gladys, Marchioness of Ripon, another of Mr. Cust's mistresses, found in her lover's house a stash of letters written to him by Lady Londonderry. The marchioness read them aloud to guests in her home, causing a scandal and a lifetime feud. Lady Londonderry begged her husband's forgiveness years later as he lay dying, but he refused to give it. Later, the marchioness begged the same from Lady Londonderry, who was as unforgiving as her husband. I would hope Mrs. Fanning and Lady Althway come to better ends.

The New Poor Law of 1834 included a provision called "outdoor relief," given to the elderly and disabled who chose to stay in their own homes instead of taking up residence in a state-run facility. It is this relief our villain seeks to exploit in his match factory.

Catherine, one of William Gladstone's daughters, was instrumental in founding the Women's Liberal Federation in the late 1880s. By 1892, ten thousand members left in a schism caused by a disagreement over women's right to vote. Rosalind, Countess of Carlisle, was an influential member of the federation, eventually serving as its president.

Obeah is an Afro-Caribbean form of witchcraft full of violent rituals and often tied to slave rebellions in the islands. The British outlawed it, giving punishments as severe as death to those caught practicing what many colonists viewed as devil worship. For the slaves, however, Obeah offered not only religion, but also a sort of justice, something they could not assume they would get from their owners. Islanders and colonists alike feared obeah practitioners as their spells, dances, and secret rites fueled imaginations and nightmares.

Acknowledgments

Myriad thanks to . . .

Charles Spicer, a dream of an editor. An author couldn't ask for better.

Allison Strobel, Andy Martin, Matthew Shear, and Sarah Melnyk, my wonderful team at Minotaur.

David Rotstein and Elsie Lyons, for designing a drop-dead gorgeous cover.

Anne Hawkins, my wonderful agent and dear friend.

Kate Kelland and Daniel Pett, for giving me a magnificent insiders' tour of the British Museum.

Stephanie Clarke, archivist, and Charles Hoare, librarian, for assisting my research at the British Museum's library.

Aimee Grabowski Frey, for putting me in touch with the ultimate whisky expert.

Robert Strickler, who made sure Jeremy and Emily thought the right things about the right whiskies.

Stu Gruber, whose generosity and kindness are much valued and appreciated, as is his infinite knowledge of British medals, decorations, and awards. Someday we'll have to let Emily learn to shoot.

Rob Browne, for one particularly spectacular plot suggestion. Sometimes the little things make an enormous difference.

Brett Battles, Bill Cameron, Kristy Kiernan, Elizabeth Letts, and Lauren Willig, whose friendship and advice make writing even more fun.

Nick Hawkins, for hot dogs, cookies, postcards, and friendship. Not to mention taking Andrew to football.

My parents, for making books a part of my DNA.

Xander, whose quick mind and knowledge of history never cease to amaze me. Katie and Jessie, the most excellent stepdaughters ever.

Andrew Grant, for always knowing what I need before I do. Like two-in-the-morning champagne and pineapple.

1. How do you feel about keeping secrets? Are some things better never revealed?

2. What would you do if you knew someone was about to expose something you wanted to keep hidden?

3. Emily has become increasingly enlightened through the series. How do you feel about her work for the Women's Liberal Federation?

4. Why does Colin refuse knighthood and ennoblement? Would you consider doing something similar?

5. Is the villain in the novel responsible for Lord Musgrave's suicide? Did Lord Musgrave have any other options?

6. Does Ivy's secret make you more or less sympathetic to her?

7. Why is Jeremy so upset that he is not a target of the villain? Do you think his displeasure is sincere?

8. How do Lady Glover's insecurities belie her external appearance and attitude?

9. Is there any justice in the villain revealing society's secrets?

10. Was Emily right not to pursue Colin's secret? Why or why not?

For more reading group suggestions, visit www.readinggroupgold.com

*A
Reading
Group
Guide*

Turn the page for a sneak peek at
Tasha Alexander's new novel

Death in the Floating City

Available October 2012

1

"I'd expected jewel encrusted, not encased in a layer of dried blood." Almost cringing, I fingered the slim medieval dagger that felt heavier in my hands than its size suggested.

Tourists come to Venice, the city Petrarch called *mundus alter,* "another world," to take in the opulent beauty of the floating city's palaces, the soft colors and vibrant gold of St. Mark's Basilica, and the rich elegance of Titian's paintings. My trip, however, came without the prospect of such pleasant things. I was standing in a dark, musty palazzo with my childhood nemesis glowering over my shoulder as I inspected the knife an intruder had used to kill her father-in-law. An unpleasant sensation prickled up my neck as I stared down. Instruments of murder are not something with which a lady contends on a daily basis. Particularly not one still bearing evidence of its evil use.

"The police returned it to me in just that condition," Emma Callum said, wrinkling her nose. "I wasn't about to touch it. And the servants point-blank refused to clean it. I'd fire the lot of them if my Italian were better."

I liked to believe the majority of my fellow countrymen were excellent travelers abroad. Credits to the empire. An Englishman ought to conduct himself in a manner more likely to draw admiration than scorn, and should use his explorations of the world as an opportunity to expand his mind and improve his character. Emma showed no sign of such aspirations, a condition unusual in someone who has chosen to go beyond simple tourist and embrace the life of an expat. Then again, Emma had lived in Italy for three years without bothering even to learn the language.

My husband took the knife from my hand and studied it before laying it on a table. We'd been married just over two years, and Colin Hargreaves still took my breath away every time I looked at his preternaturally handsome face. Early on in our acquaintance (even before I'd abandoned my erroneous suspicion that he'd murdered my first husband—but that's another story altogether), I'd decided his perfectly chiseled features looked as if Praxiteles, my favorite ancient Greek artist, had sculpted them. His dark eyes and darker wavy hair lent him a romantic air that would set Mr. Darcy to permanent brooding and send Heathcliff stalking across the moors, never to return. No man, fictional or real, could compare.

Our hostess, however, was an entirely different matter. One might, perhaps, compare Emma to Miss Bingley or Mrs. Dashwood, but she did not quite reach the level of a great villain of literature. Still, nothing short of murder could have induced me to renew my acquaintance with Emma. We had never been close, and it was unlikely this would ever change. Put simply, she despised me, and I'm ashamed to admit I returned the feeling. When we were six years old, she destroyed my favorite doll, smashing its porcelain face with her boot. She scooped up the pitiful remains of the toy my father had specially brought for me from Paris and ran downstairs from the nursery to the conservatory where our mothers were having tea.

I will never forget the way the conservatory looked that day, the way the sunlight filtered through the leaves of my mother's precious lemon trees, and the scent of the bright lilies, which forever after would seem to me heavy and cloying. Emma held out her bounty, her eyes wide with horror, and spoke, her voice trembling.

"Look at the terrible thing Emily has done," she said. From where she conjured her tears, I know not, but her voice grew even more pathetic as she continued. "I told her the dolly was pretty, but she insisted she wanted one with better curls. So she stepped on her. Crushed her head in with her foot and said now she knew she'd get a new one."

"Did she?" My mother's face was inscrutable, but I knew the trouble I was in for.

"It doesn't seem right," Emma said. "To destroy something only to be rewarded."

"I can assure you, Emma, that will not happen."

When I woke up the next morning, all my remaining dolls had disappeared from the nursery, and there was never another one seen in the house.

I knew better than to tattle and didn't even try to defend myself. Any attempt to do so would have been met with even more trouble. Emma and I continued to be thrown together throughout childhood due to our mothers' friendship, but I refused to engage in any but the most basic interaction with her. She did not improve with age. As a debutante, she barraged with attention any gentleman who showed even the slightest interest in me, culminating with a clumsy attempt to wrangle Philip, the Viscount Ashton, and at the time my soon-to-be-fiancé, away from me.

It was unlikely our acquaintance would ever grow into a real friendship.

Now Emma needed me, and I was not about to walk away from her, despite our past. Her father-in-law had been murdered, and her husband had disappeared shortly thereafter, an act that, so far as the authorities were concerned, proved his guilt. She sent for me, begging for help. This, in itself, was proof of how desperate she was feeling.

Seeking our assistance was no rash act on Emma's part. My husband, an agent of the Crown, had a reputation for his ability to crack any investigation with his trademark discretion. And I, if I may be so bold as to give myself such a compliment, had proven my own mettle after successfully apprehending six notorious murderers. As a result, the day after reading her panicked wire, my husband and I traveled to Venice and, almost immediately upon our arrival, climbed into a boat and glided out of the slim canal that skimmed the side of the Hotel Danieli. The gondolier rowed us under a single bridge and into the lagoon before turning into the Grand Canal. Sunlight poured around us, its reflection dancing over the ornate facades of the buildings that rose, majestic, straight from the water. We passed the domed church of Santa Maria della Salute, built in the seventeenth century to give thanks for the end of the plague that had killed upwards of a hundred thousand people in the city, and we crossed under the Ponte della Carita, to my mind the ugliest bridge in the city. It was made from iron, did not have a graceful arching form like the famous stone bridges prevalent throughout Venice, and had been placed too low over the water, making it difficult for gondoliers during high tide. Around us, the canal was crowded with boats, the only method of transport in a place with no streets. I'd already decided I didn't miss them. I much preferred the sleek gondolas, with their singing boatmen, to the clatter of horse and carriage.

On both sides of us, glorious palazzi lined the water. Although built with precision, they had succumbed to centuries of shifting waters that left their facades with a pervasive asymmetry. This did not detract from their beauty. It only enhanced the feeling that one was gliding through something out of a dream.

As the elegant stone arches of the Rialto Bridge came into view, the gondolier steered us to the side of the canal and slowed to a stop in front of an imposing fourteenth-century palazzo, seat of the Barozzi family and Emma's marital home. I nearly lost my balance as I stepped out of the gondola onto the slippery marble pavement at the water entrance. My shaky legs told me I was nervous to meet my old rival.

A sinewy man opened a low wooden door and ushered us inside. "Signor Hargreaves?"

Colin nodded.

"*Buongiorno.* Signora Barozzi is expecting you."

Although Emma's husband bore the title *conte* even before his father's death (it was given as a courtesy to all of a count's sons), no one in Italy used the term in direct address. Emma, who had made much out of becoming a contessa—always using her title when signing letters and insisting that her parents' servants address her as such when she visited England—must be disappointed to be referred to as *signora.*

We walked along a dark corridor and up a flight of marble stairs into a dim room, the *portego,* which ran the entire length of the house. At one end was the Barozzi family *restelliera,* a display of swords, scimitars, spears, shields, and banners hanging on the wall, below which stood two suits of fifteenth-century armor. At the other, large trefoil windows looked onto the canal, the light pouring through them providing the only illumination in the room. Neither of the large lanterns hanging above us was lit. Portraits of the Barozzi ancestors, in dire need of restoration and cleaning, lined the remaining walls, staring down as if to assert the family's noble roots. The fresco covering the tall ceiling was showing signs of decay—the paint had started to peel—and the bits of terrazzo floor that peeked beyond the edges of a threadbare Oriental carpet had lost their shine. Eloping might not have served Emma quite so well as she had hoped.

Some years back, at the insistence of her parents, Emma had accepted the proposal of the younger son of a minor English nobleman. It had appeared, after several unsuccessful seasons, to be her only hope for marriage. She had resisted the gentleman's affection for months, and we'd all believed she'd done so because she harbored higher aspirations. Who could have guessed that all along the dashing Conte Barozzi had been wooing her from afar and that they had plotted their elopement almost from the time they'd met in a London ballroom?

After their secret marriage, Emma and her new husband fled to the conte's home in Venice, scandalizing the *ton*, everyone fashionable in society. Her family stood by her, and I'd heard rumors that her father, ever devoted to his difficult daughter, continued to offer her financial support. This gossip led in turn to stories about the conte's lack of fortune. But, as is often the case, trading cash for a title was not considered a bad bargain. Most people agreed the new contessa had done well for herself.

Emma rose from a seat near the windows and crossed the room to greet us. The bright yellow satin of her gown suggested time in Italy hadn't altered her taste in fashion. Garish had always been her signature. She was as skinny and angular as ever, all hard bones and frown lines. I pushed unkind thoughts out of my head, displeased that old habits had got the better of me. I was prepared to let go the troubles of the past. Emma and I were no longer sparring schoolgirls or rival debutantes. I was here to help her.

She did not meet my eyes but focused on Colin instead. My heartbeat quickened as I wondered if she would launch straight into her usual flirtatious ways or if marriage had tempered her.

"Darling Hargreaves," she said, holding a hand out to him. "It's so good of you to come. Both of you." She made a point of looking away from me. "I know I do not deserve your kindness."

"Think nothing of it," I said, feeling an unfamiliar warmth toward her. "It's time we move beyond our differences. We're not children anymore."

"Thank you, Emily," she said. "I simply had no one else to turn to. I suppose that ought not surprise me. After all, what lady of my rank would associate with persons who investigate crimes? That I know even one is astonishing. Two, if we count your charming husband."

She winked at him.

I pressed my lips together hard. "Emma, we need to know exactly what happened the night of your father-in-law's death." Exchanging social niceties with Emma was far less pleasant than thinking about murder.

"I had no idea anything out of the ordinary had occurred until the following morning," she said. "I'd seen Signor Barozzi before I retired to my room and he was in perfect health. The next morning, our steward informed us that he was dead. I know you'd much prefer it if I could give you some sort of juicy clue as to what happened, but I can't. I do hope having the murder weapon helps."

I took the slim dagger back into my hands. Its blade was eight inches long, and precious stones—diamonds, emeralds, rubies, and sapphires—encrusted its hilt.

"It belonged to Paolo's mother," Emma said. "She kept it next to her bed."

"For protection, or just because she liked the way it looked?" I asked.

"Protection. It's an old family habit," Emma said. "You know how these Italians can be. Very passionate and very dramatic. Not at all like we English. It's quite alarming."

"Was anything else in her room disturbed?" I asked.

"I can't really say." Emma clasped her hands and looked down. "My father-in-law hasn't let anyone into her room since she died more than a dozen years ago."

"No one was allowed in the room?" Colin asked. "Not even servants to keep it clean?"

"No," Emma said. "He couldn't bear to have anyone touch her things. He dusted them himself and even went so far as to wash the floors."

"Have you gone into her room since the night he died?" I asked.

"I did, just to see it," Emma said. "Perhaps it sounds callous after having lost a family member, but I admit I was curious."

"If no one has been in the room for so many years, how can you be certain the knife came from there?" Colin asked.

"Paolo—my husband—recognized it."

"May we see the room?" I asked.

"If you wish," Emma said, "but you won't find anything of interest."

We followed her into an ornately decorated room where the frescoes on the ceiling were in slightly better condition than those I'd seen in the rest of the house. The furniture, some of which could have been original to the palazzo, was fashioned from heavy, dark wood. The bed was enormous, with a canopy high above it and long velvet drapes pulled to enclose it on three sides. Through the fourth side, where the curtain had been drawn, we could see the bedclothes of fine linen, still rumpled as if the bed's occupant were in the next room taking breakfast. There was still a slight depression on the pillow where Signora

Barozzi's head had rested on the night of her death. My skin prickled at the sight.

A quick search of the room yielded nothing of interest to our current case. Colin checked each of the windows and then asked Emma to show us where her father-in-law's body had been found.

"It was here." She had taken us back to the *portego* and pointed to a spot on the floor. "We believe his assailant entered the room through the window just above."

"Is it generally kept open at night?" I asked.

"No, but it was open when the servants found him. It had been shut the night before."

"It's possible the conte opened it himself," I said, pulling a notebook out of my reticule and starting to scribble in it. "Of course, that doesn't preclude the possibility someone else did."

Colin peered out the window. "It's a long way down," he said. "Someone climbing up from canal level surely would have been noticed, either by neighbors or boaters."

"The police looked into that," Emma said. "No one came forward to say they'd seen anything unusual, and it would be impossible to know who had been passing by at just the right moment. A hopeless business, really."

"You said in your wire there was a ring found with the body," I said.

"Yes." She pointed to a table on which sat a heavy gold band with a deep red corundum ruby set high in its center. "He was clutching it in his hand."

I took it from her. "It's medieval," I said. "Probably fourteenth or fifteenth century." I moved closer to the window, where the light was brighter, to read the inscription on the band.

Amor vincit omnia

"Love conquers all," I said. "A common phrase on poesy rings of the period. Is it a family piece?"

"No," Emma said. "I'm afraid there's not much family jewelry left. The house is expensive to run, and old fortunes . . . well, they don't often last. We don't know where it came from. Paolo didn't recognize it."

"Was anything tampered with in the rest of the house?" Colin asked.

"Nothing was taken," Emma said. "Nothing was disturbed. We all slept through without so much as noticing." Blotchy red streaks colored her face, and I felt a surge of compassion for her.

"Don't blame yourself," I said. "Whoever did this was careful not to wake any of you. We will do everything we can to identify the guilty party and bring him to justice."

"And Paolo?" she asked, her voice small. "He'll come back to me once he's exonerated. I know he will. He's innocent, Emily. He would never have raised a hand to harm his father."

"I believe you." I smiled in as reassuring a manner as possible. I hoped she was right. Her husband had disappeared mere hours after a maid had found his father's body. Why had he fled, without so much as a word to his much-adored wife? Would an innocent man have assumed he'd be implicated in the murder? I surveyed the room and shuddered, feeling suddenly cold, as if an oppressive evil were closing in around me. What secrets did this once-beautiful house hold?

Lady Emily is "Victorian London's most colorful and delightfully eccentric sleuth."—Jacqueline Winspear

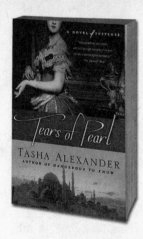

Don't miss
DEATH IN THE FLOATING CITY
available October 2012